Gallatin Warfield earned his law degree from the University of Maryland Law School. He is a former Assistant Attorney General in the criminal division of the Maryland Attorney General's office and a former chief felony prosecutor in the Howard County, Maryland, State Attorney's office.

His previous novels, *State v. Justice* and *Silent Witness*, were also published by Headline.

STATE v. JUSTICE

'Legal know-how and polished narrative skills ... a credible, absorbing narrative' – *Publishers Weekly*
'A tense and original thriller' – *Sunday Independent*
'Mixes murder, mystery and international tension ... some very interesting twists' – *Sunday Sun*
'If you are hooked on legal eagle thrillers by the likes of Scott Turow and John Grisham, then don't miss STATE V. JUSTICE ... it's a real cracker' – *Peterborough Evening Telegraph*

SILENT WITNESS

'Warfield is an expert at keeping up the pace... The mystery is satisfyingly hard to solve' – *Sunday Telegraph*

'An enthralling courtroom drama' – *Worcester Evening News*

Raising Cain

Gallatin Warfield

First published in Great Britain in 1995
by HEADLINE BOOK PUBLISHING

First published in paperback in 1995
by HEADLINE BOOK PUBLISHING

A HEADLINE FEATURE paperback

10 9 8 7 6 5 4 3

ISBN 0 7472 4507 X

Typeset by Keyboard Services, Luton, Beds

Printed and bound in Great Britain by
BPC Paperbacks Ltd

HEADLINE BOOK PUBLISHING
A division of Hodder Headline PLC
338 Euston Road
London NW1 3BH

Many thanks to my agent, Artie Pine, President and CEO of Warner Books Larry Kirshbaum, and Warner Senior Editor Susan Suffes, for their patience, perseverance, and expert guidance in the production of this book. I am forever grateful.

G.W.

PROLOGUE

The country road had no name. Originally cut by loggers to access the Appalachian forest, it was now just a dirt path through the trees. Cracks and ruts scarred the surface, and sticker bushes clawed the sides. And it was two lonely miles long.

The old man's feet hurt. He had walked halfway and was beginning to tire. Maybe he had made a mistake. Maybe he should not have come this way tonight, attempting the shortcut in the September twilight.

The air was still, the birds silent. The only sound was the man's laboured breathing and the scrape of his shoes against the gravel.

This was Tuesday, 'checkers' day at the senior centre. He'd spent the afternoon as usual, working the boards with the guys, and enthralling them with stories, tales from his thirty years at the service of Eastern Atlantic Railroad. He'd whooped it up, and won some games. But the last one was over at four-thirty, and he'd slipped up the road for a few minutes. And now, it was almost dark.

His steps quickened, despite his fatigue. Althea was

waiting at home with a plate of greens and boiled ham. She was probably worried and a little angry.

Joseph checked his gold watch and tried to keep up the pace, but the lumpy ground made it difficult. Suddenly there was a loud crack in the underbrush. He stopped and peered into the thicket, looking for movement. Maybe it was a deer. They often ran these woods.

But he saw nothing, no gentle brown eyes gazing back. The silence returned. He started walking again.

After a few more steps there was another snapping sound in the brush. This time Joseph did not stop. Dinner was waiting. He had to get home.

Suddenly, a dark form moved from the woods and blocked his path. 'Dear God,' Joseph whispered.

The light had almost yielded to night, but there was still enough of an afterglow for the old man to discern what confronted him. It was a crimson ghost in a satin robe and hood. His face was covered, but his eyes glared through holes in the cloth.

'What do you want?' Joseph asked shakily. This was not supposed to happen anymore, not today. The Klan had died out around here. Black folks could come and go in peace.

The ghost moved closer but said nothing.

'What you want?' Joseph took a shaky step backwards.

The hooded figure moved forward slowly, silently.

'We don't need any of this...' Joseph stuttered, 'this foolishness ... Leave me alone!' He considered running but decided against it. He wouldn't get far, not in these woods.

The ghost lifted a canvas bag in a latex-gloved hand, and

seized Joseph's wrist with his other. That too was gloved, and it felt cold against his dark skin.

'Stop this now!' Joseph begged. 'Please!' The hand gripped tightly and led Joseph to a tree off the pathway.

'Don't,' Joseph said, trying to squirm out of the grasp. He was beginning to sweat, and his heart was pounding.

His arms were forced around the tree, and his wrists were wrapped in a thick piece of cloth. Then the wrists were bound together with a cord.

'Awww...' Joseph moaned. 'Why you doin' this to me?' He thought of Althea and his greens steaming on the table. He should have gone right home after checkers, the way he was supposed to.

The ghost silently hefted the canvas bag.

Joseph twisted his neck, trying to see. 'Don't!' he yelled, straining to look. What was happening?

The ghost stood behind him, and Joseph pulled and yanked against the cord, but it was too tight. He couldn't turn, and he couldn't see. 'Please!' he begged. 'Stop this... Please!'

The ghost rustled the bag close behind, and Joseph stopped struggling and held his breath. What was happening now?

Suddenly he felt something move against his neck. It was scaly and muscular, encircling his throat like a writhing rope.

'Nooooo!' Joseph screamed in panic. It was a snake! The one unreasoning terror in Joseph's life had a forked tongue. It was an absolute, incurable phobia. He *hated* snakes.

'Uhhhh!' Joseph twisted his head wildly, trying to throw

it off, but the ghost had looped the snake so it would stay in place.

'Get it off!' Joseph hollered, 'Get it off! Please!!!...' The belly muscles contracted.

The ghost was impassive as the struggle continued.

Joseph was gasping now, and his chest was tightening. 'Uhhhh...' He'd only touched one snake in his life, and it had almost killed him. A buddy had put it in his car as a joke. It had brushed his leg while he was driving, and he'd panicked and almost crashed. He'd abandoned the car on the side of the road, and never returned.

'Get it...' Joseph moaned. He could hardly breathe now, and his chest was burning. Grandma had warned that a snake would take him if he didn't behave. And so he was a good boy, very, very good. But that didn't stop the nightmares, the sweaty dreams of slithering hell.

The snake finally slipped to the ground, and Joseph let out a gurgling gasp. But the ghost picked it up, and put it back in place.

Joseph tried to struggle again, but his strength was gone. He had been bad and Grandma had put him in the shed. And now the snake was here to take him away.

Finally, Joseph groaned and slumped against the tree. The ghost moved forward, cut the cord and removed the material from his wrists, lowering his body to the dry earth. The snake was still entwined around his neck. He snatched it below the head and flung it into the underbrush.

Joseph's eyes were rolled back, and he was breathing in trembling gasps. The ghost raised his hood and bent down to check for a pulse. The old heart was barely beating.

He dragged the body back to the road and obliterated the

drag marks with a tree limb. Then he kneeled and examined his victim again. Joseph was struggling for life, his chest shaking with each breath. Suddenly, consciousness flickered. Joseph blinked and tried to focus. His chest ached and his voice was gone, but he was awake. He moaned.

The ghost froze. Maybe he was reviving.

Joseph moaned again and arched his back.

The ghost looked into his face.

'Rrrrrrr...' Joseph cried out, his eyes wide. He was trying to speak, but the word wouldn't form.

The ghost pulled away and jerked his hood down.

Soon Joseph's lips went slack, and he closed his eyes. His chest stopped heaving, and he let out a long slow breath.

The ghost peered at him through the eye-holes, waiting for something to happen.

The body lay quiet now. The ghost checked his pulse. The old heart was finally still.

The ghost scanned the area a last time, and smoothed the dust. Then he dashed into the forest and lost himself in the night.

PART ONE

SHADOWS

CHAPTER 1

State's Attorney Gardner Lawson stared at the handgun on the table. He was alone in a cubicle at police headquarters. It was 6.00 p.m., and the detective bureau was deserted. He picked up the pistol and rotated its cylinder, listening to the click-click-click as the feeder port passed the barrel. It was empty now, but last night there had been five .357 magnum rounds in those holes, and a young farmer named Tom Payson had fired two into his wife, two into his son, and one into his own brain. Three people dead, just like that, all because the August drought had wiped out the corn crop, or some other silent demon had seized Tom and thrown him over the edge.

Gardner laid down the weapon and lifted the cover of a police report. 'MURDER–SUICIDE. CASE CLOSED', the bottom line read. It had been signed by the investigating officer and the chief. There was a space below that for the endorsement of the State's Attorney. Gardner removed a pen from his jacket and slowly wrote his name. Then he snapped the cover shut and shoved the folder under the gun.

This was Gardner Lawson's world: a daily diet of mayhem and sorrow. As the chief prosecutor in a remote Western

Maryland county, Gardner had seen a lot of Tom Payson cases. Too many to count. At forty-five years of age, he was beginning to tire. He'd been prosecuting crime for two decades. He was tall and imposing, a courtroom wizard. But he was running out of steam.

Gardner lay back in his chair and closed his eyes. He saw Tom Payson in the hallway of his farmhouse. He saw Mary Payson and Tommie junior asleep in their beds. Tom was getting closer, the magnum raised in his sweaty hand. Wake up! Gardner warned. Tom was at the door. Wake up! Mary stirred. Tom yanked open the door. Wake up! Get out! Mary opened her eyes. But it was too late.

'Buzzzz...' The pager on Gardner's belt vibrated against his abdomen. Gardner sat forward, rubbed his dark eyes, and brushed a wisp of greying hair behind his ear.

'Buzzz...'

He removed the pager and squinted at the number display, adjusting the distance so he could read it. '777-3454.' Carole. His ex-wife. There was a second read-out after the number: '911'. Emergency.

Gardner grabbed for the phone. A '911' from Carole could be about one thing: Granville. His son was in trouble.

He fumbled with the buttons, misdialled, and redialled. The phone rang.

'Hello?' It was the voice of an eleven-year-old.

'Gran?' Gardner's heart was racing.

'Dad!'

'You OK?' He sounded OK.

'Yeah. I just paged you.'

'I *know*. What's wrong?'

'Nothing.'

'*Nothing*? You paged me with a 911. That means emergency.'

'It *is* an emergency.'

Gardner sighed. He'd delivered the 'never cry wolf' sermon a hundred times. 'What's the matter?'

'I have a spelling test tomorrow.'

Gardner fought a smile. For a spunky blond sixth-grader, that *was* an emergency. 'Did you ask Mom for help?'

'She's not here. She's over at Aunt Vera's.'

Gardner felt a rush of heat under his collar. Granville should not be left alone. He was still too young. 'When's she coming back?'

'Hour or so.'

'What about your dinner?'

'She's gonna bring a pizza.'

Gardner firmed his jaw. There were a million ways Carole irritated him, but he was not supposed to let it show, not in front of his son.

'Can you help me, Dad?'

Gardner checked his watch. They were well on the downside of six o'clock, and Jennifer was expecting him back at the State's Attorney's office soon.

'Can you, Dad?'

'Of course,' Gardner finally said. 'Read me the list, and we'll go through it.'

Granville ticked off twenty words, and Gardner copied them down.

'OK, ready?'

'Yup.'

11

'Turn your book face down.'

'It's closed.'

'OK. Here we go...'

For the next half-hour, Gardner quizzed Granville on the spelling of 'PASSAGE', and 'PARROT', and 'POTATO', and the other words on the list. Suddenly there was a voice in the background.

'Mom's here,' Granville whispered, 'got to hang up.'

'OK,' Gardner whispered back. 'Good luck on the test. And Gran...'

'Yeah, Dad?'

'Go easy on the "911". Remember the wolf boy.'

Granville laughed.

'Love you son, love you very much. See you soon, I hope.'

'Love you too, Dad.' And he hung up.

Gardner stared at the phone for a moment. Then he stood and stretched. His leg was cramped, and his lower back ached. He was getting *old*. He massaged his calf, but the pain didn't go away. The muscles were sore from too much jogging on the old wheels.

Gardner walked to the Lieutenant's office and placed Tom Payson's gun and report on his desk. Then he half-timed it down the hall, past the security post, and out of the station. The work day was finally done. And Jennifer was waiting.

Assistant State's Attorney Jennifer Munday looked at the woman sitting across the conference room table. Her left eye was puffed up with a bruise, her lip was cracked, and a grimy tear streamed down her cheek. She was gripping her hands so tightly her knuckles were white.

'It's all right,' Jennifer said softly. 'He's never going to hurt you again.'

The woman stared blankly.

'We're going to nail him,' Jennifer said firmly. She was a terminator in court. A lithe, brown-haired dynamo in round-lensed glasses. 'If you testify, he'll be locked up for a long time.'

The woman released her grip slightly.

Oh, no, Jennifer thought, don't waffle on me.

The woman shook her head. 'Can't,' she moaned.

Jennifer touched her arm. 'You *must*, Cathy. Without your testimony we have no case. I explained that. You have to tell the judge what happened.'

'Can't,' Cathy repeated.

'I know you're afraid...'

'That ain't it.'

'What *is* it?'

'I still *love* him.'

Jennifer tried to stay cool. She'd played this scene fifty times before. 'Love' was an abuser's best defence. 'You *have* to do this,' Jennifer said. 'You *have* to. For yourself. I know it's hard, but there's no choice. He could kill you next time.'

'He'd never do that.'

'He almost *did*.'

A tear ran down Cathy's other cheek, but she didn't say anything.

Jennifer knew it was over. Under state law, a wife could not be forced to testify against her husband. She could do so voluntarily, but she couldn't be coerced, no matter how serious her injury.

'Please,' Jennifer urged. 'Think about your future...'

But Cathy's body was rigid. She was going back to Billy.

'I'm sorry, Miss Munday, I *love* him and he *loves* me. I can't do this to him.'

'But look what he did to you!'

'Sorry,' Cathy repeated. She stood up. 'He's gonna change.'

Jennifer grabbed her arm. 'No he's *not*! He's going to do it again!'

Cathy wrenched her arm free. 'I gotta go. Thanks for trying to help.' She started for the door.

Jennifer handed her a business card. 'If he does *anything* to you, *anything*, call me. Day or night, it doesn't matter. My home number is on the card. Call me, Cathy. And think about what I said. *You* have to take a stand.'

Cathy mumbled another thanks and left the room. Jennifer followed and let her out the front door of the office, then listened as her footsteps faded down the marble courthouse corridor.

Jennifer leaned against the receptionist's desk and crossed her arms. It was late, and she was tired. Tired of pushing people who didn't want to be pushed, tired of carrying the burden of righteousness, tired of a lot of things. She was senior assistant prosecutor in the county and Gardner Lawson's live-in girlfriend. They shared an office and a bed. They were together around the clock.

But, somehow, it wasn't enough.

'Mama is going to her room,' the woman told her seven-year-old daughter. 'You and Molly play quietly.' They lived in a big house on a shady Arlington, Virginia street. It had a wide porch, a grassy back yard, and a narrow wooden staircase

leading to a long hall on the second floor. The lightbulb at the top of the stairs was always burned out. Mama's room was at the end of the corridor.

Daddy worked for the Government. He was gone all day, and didn't come home until late at night. Jenny and her sister watched TV in the den: cartoons, and puppets, and racing robots. And Mama stayed in her room.

'I'm hungry,' Molly said.

Jenny looked at the clock. It was six-thirty, dark outside.

'I'm hungry,' Molly repeated, twisting an auburn curl with her tiny finger.

Jenny tiptoed up the stairs and felt her way along the oriental runner with the tip of her sneaker. She knocked on Mama's door.

'What?' Mama called.

'Molly's hungry. Can we have dinner?'

'In the freezer.'

'Are you coming down?'

'No.'

Jenny went to the kitchen and removed two TV dinners from the refrigerator. She heated the oven and put them in. Then she set the table, poured milk, and helped Molly up into her chair.

'Hungry,' Molly groused.

'Dinner coming right up,' Jenny laughed, pulling the foil off the top of the tins.

'I hate chicken!' Molly complained.

'Eat!' Jenny said.

Molly picked up a drumstick and gnawed it with her baby teeth. And the two girls dined in the twilight of their silent home.

* * *

'Jen!' Gardner called as he came through the office door. She was sitting on the desk in the alcove, looking dazed. 'What's wrong?'

Jennifer stood up. 'You're late.'

'Sorry.' He kissed her cheek. 'I had to review the Payson file. Hell of a mess ... And Granville called...'

'What about?'

'Big spelling test tomorrow. I had to quiz him.'

'Couldn't his *mother* do that?'

'She, uh, she ...'

'Don't make excuses for her, Gardner. *She* couldn't help him?'

'No. *She* couldn't.'

They looked at each other for a moment. Jennifer had been with Gardner long enough to know the priorities in his life. Granville came first, above everything. If Carole dropped the ball, Gardner was right there to pick it up.

'Uh, how did that domestic case go?' Gardner finally asked.

'It didn't.'

'Spousal immunity?'

'She *loves* him.'

'Shit.'

'She might change her mind, but I doubt it.'

Gardner held up Jennifer's coat. 'You can't force these things, Jen. They have to come around voluntarily.'

'If they're still alive.' Jennifer slipped her arms into the sleeves.

'What say we stop by Paul's Place on the way home? Grab a meal?'

Jennifer hesitated by the door. 'No.'

'No? You must be starved.'

'No,' Jennifer repeated. 'I'm really not hungry.'

Sallie Allen adjusted the volume on the miniature tape recorder in her pocket as the preacher's voice rattled the tin roof of the open shed and echoed out into the night.

'Praise God, and be healed of all your mortal sins!' the preacher cried, as he gesticulated from his makeshift pulpit.

'Praise God!' fifty believers answered.

Sallie joined in the refrain. She had to make it look authentic, like she was part of the programme. A petite woman in her late twenties with an angular face and straight blonde hair, she'd arrived at the isolated compound three days earlier and applied for admission to the 'CHURCH OF THE ARK, INCORPORATED', acronym: 'CAIN'. After interrogation about her financial assets and beliefs, forfeiture of her cash and a pledge of faith, she was welcomed into the group. No one knew that she was really an investigative reporter for *Interview Magazine*.

'You must give yourselves to the Lord, body and soul,' the preacher continued, '*Body* and *soul* . . .'

Sallie studied the man as he held forth on the platform, testing phrases for her article on 'Inside Cults, USA'. He was 'tall, handsome, intelligent, and charismatic', a man with refined Germanic features and a 'piercing' stare. No. Too trite. 'Deceptive eyes'. That was better. It had more punch. And his name was a killer: Thomas Ruth. Biblical as hell.

'Others may not understand our beliefs,' Ruth continued,

'but *we* stand firm in what we *know* to be the truth!' He raised his arms in the air. '*We* see the light! *We* hear the call! *We* feel the touch of the Almighty on our skin!'

Sallie cautiously glanced around. The crowd was mesmerized. This was hot stuff.

'We take our instruction from no one but God,' Ruth went on, 'and we follow his word to the letter.' His blue eyes narrowed. 'To the letter.' There was a warning in that line. 'God's punishment for nonbelievers is swift.' His eyes narrowed again. 'And it is *deadly*.'

Sallie felt a shiver race up her spine. This was what she had hoped for: the newest cult flavour. 'CAIN'. A fire and brimstone church in an abandoned granite quarry deep in the Appalachian mountains. A stunning preacher, a docile following. Secrecy, intrigue, danger. It was going to make dynamite copy.

'Do you believe?' Ruth suddenly called out.

'Yes!' came the reply.

'Do you believe?'

'Yes!!!'

Sallie felt a tingle in her pelvis. Ruth's voice was tender, seductive.

'Can you prove your belief to God?'

The crowd suddenly hushed.

Sallie had heard one other sermon since she'd come to the compound, and it wasn't like this. She wondered where he was heading.

'Are you ready to walk the valley of *death*?'

'Yes,' someone murmured.

'*Who* will take the walk?' Ruth looked at the first row.

A hand went up.

18

Sallie suddenly felt uneasy. What was going on?

'Will *you* take the walk with me?' Ruth pointed at a young man in the third row whose hand was down. The man nodded.

'Raise your hand, son!'

The hand came up slowly.

Ruth smiled, his teeth gleaming white in the light of the naked bulbs strung down the centre of the shed.

Sallie adjusted her recorder again. This was getting interesting. Too bad she didn't understand it.

'Who *else* will walk?' That wasn't a question. It was a demand.

Others began to raise their hands, and Sallie became nervous. What did it mean to walk the valley? She raised her hand too.

The room fell silent, and Ruth gazed at the congregation from his perch. Every hand was up. 'Each of you agrees to walk the valley of *death*?'

'Yes!' they replied.

'*You*?' Ruth moved his finger from person to person.

'Yes!'

'And *you*?'

'Yes!'

Every person singled out said yes. Just then Sallie noticed that the finger was nearing her position.

'And *you*?'

That was one row away.

'And *you*?'

Sallie heard no response.

'Will *you* take the walk?' Ruth repeated loudly.

Sallie gulped. He was pointing directly at her.

'Yes,' she said tentatively.

'Come.' Ruth beckoned her up to the stage. 'Come to me.'

Sallie made her way forward, and as she did, the crowd began to chant, 'Fear no evil! Fear no evil! Fear no evil!'

Ruth took Sallie's hand and helped her onto the platform. Up close, he was even more handsome. His blond hair was thick, his skin unblemished. He could play himself in the movie, Sallie thought. He was wearing a gold medallion around his neck, but she couldn't make out the raised image. 'Be not afraid,' Ruth said gently.

Sallie nodded OK, but she was too nervous to speak. Ruth motioned to two men at the side of the shed, and they left the lighted area. In a moment, they returned with a large wooden barrel.

'Fear no evil! Fear no evil!' the crowd refrained.

The men set the barrel in front of the stage. It was sealed with a metal cover.

Ruth detached the lid. 'Tonight you and I will walk the valley of *death*.'

Sallie's knees shook, and she tried to hide it. She looked into the barrel and saw something move.

'Be not afraid,' Ruth repeated, tipping the barrel over.

A cluster of rattlesnakes slithered out. And Sallie felt like she was going to faint.

'Trust the Lord,' Ruth said. Snakes were still gushing out of the barrel.

Sallie's eyes almost crossed. This scene wasn't in her publishing contract.

'Take my hand.' Ruth slipped his slender fingers into hers as the assistants arranged the snakes in two writhing columns on the dirt floor. Sallie squeezed his hand and leaned against him, inhaling a sweet male aroma from the sleeve of his silk shirt. She felt dizzy.

'Walk with me,' Ruth said. 'Fear *no* evil...'

Sallie balked. She couldn't do it.

The earlier chanting of the crowd had given way to an expectant hush. 'Walk,' Ruth said calmly, holding her hand in a powerful grip.

Sallie took a deep breath and looked at the floor. The snakes were coiling and uncoiling across one another. She'd worked hard for this assignment, jockeying ahead of other reporters, pulling strings. It was showtime, and she had to perform. If she didn't, they'd bounce her out of the compound.

'Walk,' Ruth repeated, tugging her forward.

Sallie kept her eyes on his face, not daring to look down. Maybe they'd defanged the snakes, milked out the venom. Maybe it was hocus-pocus, theatre. Maybe they wouldn't bite. Sallie took a step.

'Walk,' Ruth cooed.

Sallie took another step.

'Walk.'

Sallie felt a snake slide across her foot, and she bit her tongue to keep from screaming. But she kept moving. Drawn by Ruth's eyes, and hand, and voice, Sallie kept moving. Step, by step, by step. Until she made it through.

Ruth helped her up on the platform, and raised her hand in the air.

'Praise God! Praise God!' the congregation wailed.

Sallie tried to smile, but her lip trembled.

Ruth squeezed her hand as he held it aloft. 'I *knew* you could do it,' he said triumphantly. 'Praise God.'

Sallie smelled that sweet smell again and felt another tingle. But this one was an earth-shaker. 'Praise God!' she screamed.

And the crowd went wild.

Sergeant Joe Brown arrived at County General hospital at 10 p.m. He'd been out in the field, working a case when the call came in: his father had collapsed. A stocky fifteen-year veteran of the police force known as 'Brownie' to his friends, the officer was a master detective and crime lab chief, an intelligent, deadly stalker of criminals when he was on the job. But tonight the call was personal.

Brownie's mother greeted him as he rushed into the waiting area, but her eyes said he was too late.

'Daddy?'

Althea Brown put her arms around her son. 'Gone,' she whispered.

Brownie hugged his mother in silence as a collection of relatives gathered close. Then he turned to see his mother's face. She was trying to be stoic, but the pain was immense. 'How?' he asked.

'Heart gave out coming back from checker club.'

Brownie could hear his dad chuckling as he pulled off a quadruple jump on the board. 'Where?'

'On the path by Cutler Road. He tried to make it home in the dark . . .'

'Dark?' Checkers usually ended by 5 p.m.

'Yes.' Althea lowered her eyes.

'So he was *late* coming home.'

'A little . . . yes.' Althea's voice was barely audible.

Brownie stopped talking. No use getting into old business

now. He hugged his mother in silence, acknowledging several relatives and local clergy with a glance over her shoulder. Reverend Taylor had formed them into a circle, and they were praying. The Brown family was strong. They always came together in a crisis. 'When did it happen?'

'Seven, eight o'clock, not really sure. Someone called 911...'

'Who?'

'Don't know exactly. They found him on the road and called an ambulance...'

Brownie kissed her damp cheek. 'Where is he?'

Althea pointed to a curtained-off section of the emergency room.

Brownie gently removed his arms.

'Son?'

'I've gotta see him.'

Althea moved to the prayer circle as her son stepped to the curtain.

Brownie hesitated as a thousand victim gurneys reeled through his mind. Then he held his breath and went in.

Joseph lay under a white sheet, and Brownie slowly lifted it. Daddy's eyes were closed, his face frozen in a scream.

'Jesus, oh, Jesus,' Brownie gasped. Daddy looked like an asphyxiated fish. His lips were contorted, his skin taut against his skull. 'Jesus,' Brownie moaned. He must have *suffered*.

Brownie tried to smooth out the lines, but they were set in the flesh. The skin was cool, leathery. Brownie took his father's hand. It was stiffening as the death process went through its checklist.

'Daddy,' Brownie sobbed. 'Daddy...' He knelt by the bed and placed his head against the sheet.

'Come on, Joe!' Daddy called. He was standing by the ferris wheel at the county fair, reaching out for his son.

'Don't want to,' little Joe replied.

'Yes you do. It's gonna be fun.'

The line was moving forward, filling the red metal baskets as they rotated down from above.

'No,' Joe said.

'It's OK,' Althea urged. She was standing outside the chain, holding the baby. She wore bright red lipstick and a wide-brimmed hat.

'You too.' Joe pointed at her. 'Bring him.'

'Too little. Next year for sure.'

'Come on!' Daddy appealed.

'Go!' Mama said.

Joe ran forward and entered the cart. The attendant slammed down the bar and engaged the gears, and soon they were wooshing up, into the purple summer sky.

'Ohhhhhhh!' Joe screamed as they accelerated over the top.

'Wheee!' Daddy laughed.

They roared earthward in the fragrant air. And then they were skyward again, rocking into space. Joe snuggled next to Daddy, hollering and clutching his giant hand. And he didn't let go the rest of the night.

Brownie blinked back tears and started to place Joseph's hand under the sheet. Suddenly he stopped. He'd seen something through the salty fog. He wiped his eyes and examined the wrist. Then he lifted the sheet and checked the rest of the body: head, neck, chest, arms, and legs. Finally, he rolled the sheet back into place. 'Mama,' Brownie yelled. 'Mama, come in here!'

Althea entered expectantly.

'Did you see this?' Brownie raised an arm.

Althea didn't understand.

'Look!' Brownie pointed to a small straight-line mark on the wrist.

Althea shook her head.

'Did he have that before he left home?'

'Uh, I don't know. Don't remember...'

'There's one over here too.' Brownie lifted the other arm.

Althea was still dazed.

'Mama, get the doctor.'

She nodded listlessly and returned moments later with a young Middle Eastern man. His green robe was stained with blood, and his name tag said 'Gibouthi'.

'Did you work on my father?' Brownie asked.

'Yes, sir.'

'What was the cause of death?'

'Massive coronary.' The doctor pointed to an entry on the chart.

'Did you see these marks?' Brownie raised the wrists.

The doctor bent down. 'Yes. They were like that when he came in.'

'Do you know how he got them?'

'When he fell, probably. They're just minor abrasions.'

'They look like rope burns to me,' Brownie said, 'like his hands were tied.'

'I'm not familiar with that. Whatever caused the cuts had nothing to do with his death.'

'How can you say that?'

'His medical history. Past heart problems. By the looks of it, a coronary was inevitable.'

Brownie stared with disbelief. 'I want him re-examined.'

The doctor shrugged. 'I'm not qualified for pathology.'

Brownie pulled the chart from the doctor's hands. In the section headed 'Disposition of the body', the 'Transfer to funeral home' block had been flagged. Brownie crossed it out and checked another block: 'Autopsy'.

'I want to know exactly how he died,' Brownie said. Then he returned to the gurney, placed a finger in his father's mouth, ran it along his lip and smelled it. 'Did you do a blood-alcohol analysis?'

'No. Didn't think it was necessary.'

'Do one.' Brownie suddenly noticed his mother backing out of the room. 'Sorry, Mama. Something's not right here.'

Althea didn't reply. She returned to the mourners in the hall.

'It was a heart attack,' the doctor insisted.

Brownie shoved the clipboard against his chest. 'That's what *you* say. *I'm* not so sure.'

CHAPTER 2

Dawn came quickly to the mountain valley. The sun sneaked over the southern ridge line and raced across the meadows and woods to a grey two-bedroom townhouse on the outskirts of the central village. Jennifer rose at first light, as usual, stretch-exercising and drinking her coffee before Gardner rolled down the stairs, bleary-eyed, grumpy, and sore. He was favouring his leg, and hadn't slept well. Another day of work in the prosecution fields lay before them. And soon they were speeding through the morning mist, towards the golden dome of the courthouse that ruled the miniature skyline like St Peter's Basilica.

Lieutenant Harvis of the county police was waiting in the reception area of prosecution headquarters when they arrived. 'Got some bad news,' he announced.

Gardner ushered him into the inner office. Jennifer followed, closed the door, and the three of them were alone.

'Hit me,' Gardner said anxiously. This didn't sound good.

Harvis placed a file on the desk. He was a twenty-year

27

veteran of the force with a regulation haircut and ice-blue eyes. 'Brownie lost his dad last night.'

'God, no,' Gardner moaned. 'What happened?'

'Heart attack on the way home from the senior centre.'

Gardner pictured Joseph on his front porch, telling stories on a lazy Sunday, a kindly, gentle old man. 'How's Brownie taking it?'

'Not good. He was still on the Payson case, finishing up at the farmhouse when it happened. Didn't make it to the hospital till after his dad was dead. Stirred up some trouble in the emergency room.'

'Trouble?' Gardner looked at Jennifer.

'He hassled the doctor, insisted there was a problem with the diagnosis, ordered an autopsy.'

Gardner frowned. Autopsies were only performed in suspicious death situations. 'You said heart attack.'

Harvis nodded. 'That's what the doctor told Brownie, but he found some scratch marks on his father's wrists, something like that. I only got it second hand. Brownie thinks there might have been foul play. He asked for a departmental investigation. Wants me to assign *him* to do it.'

Gardner clasped his hands. 'You can't *do* that, of course.'

'Of course.' The department had a policy against personal involvement in a case. It was classic conflict of interest.

'So who are you assigning?'

'Frank Davis was in that sector when the ambulance call came in. He went to the scene and did some preliminaries, then volunteered to do a follow-up. I'm assigning *him*.'

'*Davis*?' Gardner rose up in his seat. 'He's a damn troublemaker.'

'Don't start with that again. He's a decent officer and not a half-bad investigator. Besides, he's already begun. I'm not taking him off now.'

Gardner did not respond. Davis was an abrasive cop with an attitude problem who'd been passed over for promotion four times. 'Don't you have anyone *else*?'

'No. Not at the moment. We're short-handed now, and if Brownie goes out, we'll have to use the other investigators to pick up his caseload.'

'So you're giving him administrative leave?'

'I'm going to offer it, but he doesn't have to take it.'

'Knowing Brownie, he won't.' Gardner said.

Jennifer had been reflecting on her own memories of Joseph. She'd spent time on the porch with Gardner, and Brownie, and his dad. She'd played checkers, and listened to his stories. '*Who* would want to kill him?' she finally asked.

'It's not certain he was *killed*,' Harvis replied, 'not certain at all.'

'But *Brownie* thinks so,' Jennifer said. 'Was there anything other than scratches? Any bruising, money taken, anything like that?'

Harvis glanced at the preliminary report. 'No. Davis came up clean on the first sweep, and there was nothing else amiss as far as we know.'

'Have *you* talked to Brownie yet?' Gardner asked.

'No. He took off after he left the hospital, faxed me the investigation request, and disappeared. We haven't been able to reach him by phone.'

'So he doesn't know about Davis being assigned?'

'No.'

Gardner put his hands on the desk and drummed his fingers. 'Brownie is not going to sit by and let someone else, especially *Davis*, run this investigation. You know that, don't you?' Brownie was an investigating machine that *never* shut off.

'Yes, I know.'

'So what are you going to *do*?'

'That's one reason I came over here. I thought maybe you...'

Gardner drummed his fingers faster. If there was such a thing as a 'best' friend, Brownie was it. 'You want *me* to tell him he can't investigate the death of his own father?'

'He listens to you.'

Gardner stopped drumming. Brownie was like a snapping turtle. When he got his jaws around a case he never let go.

'Will you do it?'

Gardner looked at Jennifer. She was shaking her head no. The police had to control their own. It wasn't Gardner's job.

'Will you?' Harvis repeated.

Gardner apologized to Jennifer with his eyes. 'I'll try,' he said.

'Spool it up again,' Brownie said. It was 9 a.m., and he was at the emergency dispatch centre in the fire station, listening to the tape of the 911 call that had come in on Joseph. He'd been up all night, pacing, driving, drinking coffee, crying, screaming. He'd wrung out a lot of sorrow. And now it was time to get back to work.

Dispatcher Sarah Little threw a switch, and the massive tape reel whirred into rewind. Brownie had heard it four times already, but under the circumstances, Sarah didn't mind doing it again. 'OK, we're set,' she said. The tape counter showed they were at the right spot.

Brownie gave the go-ahead signal, and Sarah pushed the play button.

There was some static, then the voice of the night-shift dispatcher:

'Emergency.'

'Yeah,' the voice said. 'You got a sick man on the pathway by Cutler Road.'

Brownie put his ear close to the speaker.

'What's his problem?'

'Passed out, needs help.' The words were muffled, unnatural.

'What's his exact location?'

'Mile or so from Cutler, in the woods.'

There was a pause, then the dispatcher spoke again. 'A unit is on its way, sir. May I have your name, please?'

No response.

'Sir? Are you still there?'

Brownie nodded, and Sarah stopped the tape. 'He was trying to disguise his voice.'

'Sounds like it.'

Brownie's eyes were red, and his stomach ached. 'Pull up the number reference.'

Sarah went to another console and keyed a command.

The screen scrolled data, then displayed a set of numbers. 'The call came in at 20.23,' she said. '8.23 p.m.'

Brownie looked over her shoulder. The system was programmed to print out the number of the telephone that made the call. That was because the caller could not always speak. The number *and* address let the dispatcher know where to send help if the caller was disabled.

Sarah ran her finger down the screen to the spot where the number and address should be have been. It was blank.

Brownie grimaced. 'A no-show.'

The dispatcher swivelled her chair. 'Must have been a cellular call. They don't print.'

Brownie nodded. The system was not designed to register cellular calls. There were too many transmission variables to make it viable.

'There's no way of knowing who the call came from,' Sarah said, 'unless you run the records of every cell phone customer on the east coast.'

Brownie looked up. 'Or know which system he's on.' The phone company's airtime log would show a call to 911 at 20.23 hours on September 20. But he'd need the right cellular company and their customer list. And there were millions of cell phones in the area.

'I'm sorry about your father,' Sarah said. 'Too bad we don't know who called.'

'Too bad,' Brownie replied. His eyes were as blank as the space on the screen.

'I know you'd like to thank him.'

Brownie blinked. 'Thank him?'

'For tryin' to save his life.'

'That's not what happened.'

'What do you mean?'

'The man wasn't a good Samaritan.'

Sarah looked confused. 'What *was* he?'

Brownie clenched his fist. 'Daddy's *killer*.'

Sallie Allen did not want to get out of bed. She pulled the pillow over her head, and shifted her body in the bunk. It was 9.30 a.m., and the dormitory was empty. The other women had gone out to do their chores.

Sallie closed her eyes and re-ran the images of last night. The CAIN people were crazy. Totally, beyond redemption, beyond belief, crazy. The scene had been bizarre to the max. She had been simultaneously terrorized, turned on, and, she had to admit, exhilarated. Ruth was a doll, a big, scary, hunky doll. But he'd disappeared soon after the ceremony and left her on the platform, shaky, wet, and a little disappointed.

Sallie Allen, former high school cheerleader, former college gymnast, was a natural go-getter. Growing up in a wealthy household in Georgia, she always got what she wanted: men, cars, attention. She was smart enough and pretty enough to move to the head of the line in any endeavour she chose. And her sights were set on a star in the journalistic walk of fame.

Sallie rolled over and sat up. She scouted the room, slipped her arm under the mattress, and pulled out her recorder and notebook. She switched tapes, and checked her notes. Today she would try to find what secrets lay behind the camp's closed doors. They'd kept her on a tight rein so far, restricting her access to most of the buildings.

Suddenly, there was a noise on the steps. Someone was coming! Sallie jammed the book and recorder under the mattress and stretched languidly, trying to look nonchalant.

'You're awake.' It was Alva, one of her roommates. She was a horse-faced woman in her early twenties with kinky blonde hair and hazel eyes. 'Did you sleep OK?'

'Like a baby,' Sallie lied. Visions of Ruth and the snakes had kept her up most of the night.

'You did great yesterday.'

The reporter smiled. 'You mean my *walk*?'

'Yes. I know you were scared, but you hung in there.'

'Has anyone ever been bitten?'

'Thomas wouldn't allow it.'

Sallie cocked her head. 'So the act is rigged?'

Alva looked puzzled. 'Rigged?'

'The snakes don't really bite...'

Alva put her finger to her lips. 'It's a test of faith. Leave it at that.'

Sallie took the hint and moved on. 'Thomas is wonderful, isn't he?'

'Yes.' Alva's eyes sparkled as she spoke.

'What does he do when he's not preaching?' Except for prayer meetings, Ruth was invisible.

'I don't really know. He leaves the camp a lot.'

'Where does he go?'

Alva pointed east, beyond the barbed-wire fence. 'Out there.'

'Do you ever go with him?'

'*Me*?' Alva blushed. 'No. Not me.'

'Someone else?'

34

'No one as far as I know. He spends most of his time alone.'

'I didn't mean to embarrass you,' Sallie said. Alva would follow Ruth to the moon if he asked her, that was obvious. 'I'm just trying to learn the ropes. The "do's" and the "don'ts" around here.'

'That's OK. I know what you're asking...'

Sallie tried to stay cool, keep her conversation glib. 'What's that?'

Alva blushed again. 'You want to know if he has a girlfriend.' She'd seen the sparks fly on the dais last night.

'No...' Sallie protested coyly.

'He *doesn't* as far as I know.'

Sallie pondered the words. Ruth was attractive enough, and man enough, but sex did not seem to be a part of the programme. That in itself was strange. He could have any woman he wanted.

Sallie began dressing. 'How long have you been here?'

Alva helped her on with her blouse. 'Two months.'

Sallie buttoned up her front. 'And how much money did you contribute when you joined?'

'All I had.'

'How much was that?'

'Six thousand dollars and my car.'

Sallie looked out the window. The church had quite a fleet of vehicles out there. '*Why* did you come here?'

'To be saved.'

'Saved from *what*?'

'Evil.'

Sallie was searching for an angle, a 'hook' for her story. '*Who* do you consider evil?'

'Who?'

'Do you see evil as a person or a thing?'

'The devil takes all forms.'

'So you see it as a *person*.'

'I guess so.' Alva gave her a sceptical look.

'There are no *black* people in the congregation. Is there a reason for that?' Sallie's research had uncovered a central theme in a lot of escapist cults: race. Hatred in the name of the Lord.

'No!'

'So blacks can join CAIN if they want to?'

Alva hesitated. 'Uh...'

'Yes or no?'

'I don't *know* about that. We don't discuss it.'

'But no blacks have ever joined, right?'

'Right.'

'What's *your* opinion of black people?'

'My opinion?'

Sallie was trying to smoke out a quote. 'Do you dislike them?'

Alva's jaw tightened. 'I don't *dislike* anyone.'

'How about Thomas Ruth? Does *he* ever preach about race?'

'Never!' Alva frowned. What was this?

Sallie smiled defensively. She had pushed it right up to the line. Time to back off.

'We're into *love* here, Sallie. *Love*. That's *it*.'

Sallie sighed. The race angle would make an ideal 'hook' for her story: white fundamentalists preaching bigotry, brandishing snakes in their upraised hands. That would put her article over the top. But the words she needed weren't being said. And if they didn't come up with some flaming rhetoric soon, she just might have to make it up.

Blocktown was a suburb of the county seat. A generation before the Civil War the land had been owned by William Block. He'd raised cattle, corn, and seed crops on the huge estate and shipped them down the Potomac to Washington. It was a prosperous venture, and Mr Block had become rich. But, as the legend went, he was tormented by the guilt of slavery, unable to enjoy his wealth. One day he summoned his slaves to the great house and set them free. And then he divided up his property and gave them each a share.

Joseph and Althea Brown's house lay on the border of Blocktown. It was a red brick house on a wooded street, flanking the valley and the forest that continued westward to the rocky ridge. Most Blocktown residents had one thing in common: they were descendants of the men and women who stood on William Block's lawn that sweltering August day, cheering, and weeping, and throwing their straw hats in the air.

'Thank you, Reverend, thank you,' Althea said. She was sitting in her parlour, robed in black, nervously stitching a quilt.

'In times of sorrow, the Lord extends his comfort.' Reverend Taylor's deep baritone filled the darkened room. 'This, too, will pass, the Saviour said.'

Althea put down her needle and touched her chin. Her lips twitched like she was going to cry again.

Taylor quickly stood and crossed the room. Handsome and nattily turned-out in a blue three-piece suit and spit-shined shoes, he was 'on the job'. He was the newest cleric in town, but he was fast becoming the most popular. He'd opened his 'TEMPLE OF THE WORD' in a converted farm supply depot just three months ago, and now hundreds flocked to the cinderblock building under a blue neon dove to hear him raise the roof each Sunday.

'Take my hand,' Taylor said. His teeth were polished ivory, his hair close-cropped.

Althea looked up shakily from her chair. 'What?'

The reverend extended a set of manicured fingers. There was a diamond ring on one finger, a gold chain on his wrist. 'Take my hand.'

Althea reached out as the reverend pulled a small wooden side-chair next to hers and sat down. 'Hold tight,' he said.

Althea grasped his hand. It was strong, empowering.

'Pray with me,' Taylor said.

Althea blinked a tear and weakly nodded her head.

'Comfort this woman, Lord! Comfort and protect her! Put your mighty arms around her and *squeeze* her to your bosom!'

There was movement in the hall as several relatives left the kitchen and went to the parlour. 'What's going on?' an aunt whispered.

'Taylor's praying with her,' a sister answered.

'Embrace her with your love! *Squeeze* out the pain!'

The relatives all gathered in the doorway and watched. Althea was rocking in time to the reverend's words, her eyes closed.

'Reach across the icy void and touch this woman's heart! Give her the strength she needs to keep movin' on, Lord...'

Althea opened her eyes. 'Joseph?' she asked.

Taylor paused for a second, then it clicked. 'While you're embracing, Lord, embrace the soul of this woman's departed husband! Guide him to you! Show him the way! Give him the key to paradise!'

Althea closed her eyes again, her fingernails digging into Taylor's palm.

'Keep Joseph by your side, almighty Jesus! At your right hand, in the place of the righteous. Keep him, and protect him, from now, until these two souls shall join again, and hold them together for all eternity ...'

Althea's face relaxed, but she still clutched Taylor's hand. He moved closer and cradled her head against his chest. They sat that way in silence for several minutes. Then Taylor began to sing.

'A ... ma ... zing Grace ... How sweet ... the sound.' Taylor's voice was soft at first, then louder, resonant and mellow: 'That saved ... a wretch ... like meeeee!'

The relatives looked at each other with surprise. No one had ever heard him sing before.

'I ... once ... was lost ... And now ... I'm found!'

An aunt began to hum.

'Was blind ... and now ... I seeeee!'

The relatives entered the room and formed a ring around Althea's chair.

'T'was grace ... that taught ... my heart ... to fear ... And grace ... my fears re ... lieved!' Taylor quavered.

'How pre ... cious ... did that ... grace appear ... the hour ... I first ... believe ... ed!'

'A ... ma ... zing grace ... how sweet ... the sound,' the family sang along. 'That saved ... a wretch ... like me!'

The aunts, sisters, and uncles joined hands.

'I once ... was lost ... and now ... I'm found ... was blind ... and now ... I seeeee!'

The song suddenly faded, and the room was silent. Only the beat of Althea's steady breathing rippled the air. Her eyes were still shut, but she looked at peace. Reverend Taylor held her tightly against him. And then he whispered something in her ear.

Officer Frank Davis walked down the steps of police headquarters towards his squad car. It was late afternoon, and the light was waning. Soon the sun would drop behind the ridge, and the evening chill would begin.

Davis was a lanky West Virginia boy who'd moved to the state ten years ago. His sandy hair, slow swagger, and slight drawl made him out to be a rube. But he wasn't. He was sharp-witted and ambitious. He'd worked a dairy farm and driven an eighteen-wheeler, but those vocations hadn't rung his bell. Then he tried law enforcement. That profession, he decided, was a keeper.

Davis had just hit the bottom step when he encountered Brownie on the way up. '*Sergeant*.' No Brownie. No Sarge. Just *Sergeant*.

Brownie stopped, but didn't reply. He was dressed in jeans and a denim jacket, unshaven and unkempt.

'Sorry about your *loss*,' Davis said.

Brownie glared at him through bleary eyes. 'Thanks for your concern, *Frank*.'

'Thought you were on leave.'

'Does it look like I am?'

Davis didn't answer.

'I've got work to do.' Brownie mounted a step. 'Nice chatting with you.'

Davis let him pass, then called out from behind. 'Don't worry about the case.'

Brownie stopped and turned around. '*What* case?'

'Investigation of your dad's, uh ... *death*.'

Brownie grabbed the rail for support. 'What are you *talking* about, Frank?'

'Lieutenant gave it to me.'

'What?'

'I'm on it. Don't worry.'

'You?'

'Yeah. Apparently there's no quota system on cases. They decided to give the white guy a chance.'

Brownie's nostrils flared.

'You're not the only Sherlock Holmes around here.'

Brownie wanted to rush down and deck him, but the bastard wasn't worth it. He was just a mouth. No brain. Just a mouth. He turned and ran up the stairs.

'Don't worry!' Frank yelled. 'I'm on the *case!*'

But Brownie had already passed through the front door on his way to see Lieutenant Harvis.

Davis parked his squad car at the Blocktown senior centre. It was almost dark, and lights were flicking on along the narrow commercial strip. In the west, the mountain range arched against the amber sky like a slate tsunami.

Davis walked to the centre and knocked. He was greeted by an elderly black gentleman and admitted into the outer hall. The man wore glasses and a hearing aid. He looked about eighty.

'Are you Ernie Jones?' Davis asked.

'Yes, sir.'

'I'm here about Mr Brown.'

Jones lowered his eyes.

'You were with him yesterday?'

'Yes, sir.'

'What time was that?' The officer removed a pad from his breast pocket.

'Afternoon.'

'What *time*?' Davis tapped his watch.

'Two o'clock. 'Round two o'clock.'

Frank wrote it down. 'And what time did you *last* see him?'

'Playin' checkers,' Ernie replied.

'When did you *stop* playing checkers?' Davis raised his voice.

'I went home 'bout four-fifteen, four-thirty. Bus picked me up.'

'And where was Mr Brown at that time?'

'He left out . . .'

Frank took a breath. 'What *time*? What time did he leave out of here?'

'Before me. We finished the last game after he left out.'

Davis wrote 'plus or minus four-thirty' on the pad. 'Do you know where he went?'

Concern flickered in Ernie's eyes. 'No. I don't know a thing about *that*.'

'He went somewhere,' Davis said. 'He didn't go *home*.' According to his calculations, the last four hours of Joseph's life were still unaccounted for. 'You *know*, don't you?'

Ernie took a step backward. 'No, sir. I don't.'

Davis moved towards him. 'Don't *lie* to me, Mr Jones. What kind of hanky-panky was he up to?'

Ernie took another step backward. 'Nothin'. He never done *nothin'*!'

Frank gave him a sceptical look. The man was protesting too much. Maybe there was something here after all. The doctors insisted a heart attack took old man Brown out. But maybe Sergeant Shithead was right. Maybe there *was* something else involved.

CHAPTER 3

Gardner entered the lab at police headquarters without knocking. Lieutenant Harvis had just phoned him that Brownie was on the premises, so Gardner rushed right over to pay his respects. It was 7.15 p.m.

Brownie stood up behind his desk when he heard the door open. 'Gard...'

'Brownie, I'm so sorry...' Gardner grabbed his friend's arm. 'Sorry, man.'

'Gard...' Brownie touched his hand.

'Anything I can do?'

'No. It's under control.'

'You're sure?' Gardner remembered the chaos of 'arrangements' when his own father died six years ago. The details were hell.

'I'm sure.' Brownie leaned against the desk.

'You shouldn't be here,' Gardner said. 'You should be on leave.' Brownie looked exhausted.

'No. Too much to do...'

'Take your leave.'

'No.'

'Brownie...' Gardner had been afraid of this. 'Let's get

out of here, go up to Paul's, have a few drinks, sort things
out...'

'No, Gard. I've got work to do...'

Gardner drew a breath. The man was stubborn.

'...Phone calls to make, reports to read ... And I
wouldn't be good company, not tonight.'

'Jeez, man. I don't give a damn if you sit there and spit
beer in my face. You need to be with somebody right now.
It's not good for you to be alone, especially here.' The lab
reeked of death.

Brownie tried to smile. 'Thanks for the offer, but I can't.
Not right now.'

Gardner looked at a report on the desk. 'What are you
working on?'

Brownie covered it with his hand. 'A case.'

'What case?'

Brownie didn't reply.

'We need to talk about it,' Gardner said.

'What?' Brownie was playing dumb.

'Your *suspicions*. Harvis told me.'

Brownie sat down.

'What do you think happened?'

Brownie closed the report's cover. 'I think he was
roped.'

'What did the doctors say?'

'They don't know shit.'

'But what did they say?'

'Coronary.'

'And you don't agree.'

Brownie looked up. 'That was part of it, but not everything. Someone was with him when he went down, made

the 911 call on a cellular phone, disguised his voice, then disappeared. Obviously didn't want to be identified. And Daddy had cuts on his wrists.'

'Cuts?'

'Ligature marks, I'm almost positive. Seen enough of those bastards to know what they look like.'

Gardner crossed his arms. Brownie did know the difference between a fall-down abrasion and a rope burn. 'But *who*?' he finally said. 'Who would hurt Joseph?' Nobody from Blocktown, certainly.

'That's what I'm trying to find out.'

'Do you have any leads, any evidence?'

Brownie lowered his head.

'What do you have?'

Brownie's eyes came up. 'Nothing ... *yet*.'

Gardner felt a chill. 'Take it slow, Brownie.' A bereaved cop with an itchy trigger finger could be dangerous. 'Let the Department handle it ...'

Brownie clenched his teeth. 'You mean *Davis*, the hillbilly pin-head?'

'I asked Harvis to assign someone else.'

'But he didn't do it, did he?'

Gardner shook his head.

'They don't fuckin' believe me. *That's* why they assigned Davis. They think I'm overreacting, that there's nothing there. They'd never give Davis a real case.'

'But you just admitted that you don't have any evidence.'

'This isn't about evidence, Gard.' Brownie thumped his chest with a fist. 'This is about my instinct, my feeling. I don't just *think* there's something wrong here. I *know* it.'

Gardner went silent. If Brownie's instincts could be

patented and bottled, they'd be billionaires. His instincts were uncanny and most times on the money. But they still needed proof. 'You're too close right now,' Gardner finally said. 'You've just taken a hell of a hit. You can't be objective. You have to let it go for a while...'

Brownie stood up. 'I'm not going to allow Frank Davis or anybody else to tell me how Daddy died. I'm going to find out for myself. With or without your *permission*!'

'Take it easy,' Gardner cautioned.

'I can't. Please try and understand. Someone *killed* my old man!' His voice cracked and his jaw trembled.

Gardner grabbed him in a hug. 'Let it *go*, for God's sake, let it go...'

Brownie tried to pull away, but Gardner held him tight. And then the façade cracked, and the anguish poured out.

Thomas Ruth drove his car out of the quarry gate and turned west, towards the secluded spot on the ridge where he could park and communicate in privacy. He felt tired. The snake routine had gotten him 'up', but then there was the depressing slide from elation into darkness later. Last night he'd got a real buzz. But then came the pounding in his head that lasted until dawn. He'd spent most of the day sleeping it off, and now, at evening, he felt a little better.

The countryside swelled from the lowland to the mountaintop. It was mostly rocky farmland and groves of trees stippled with dusty turn-offs that led nowhere. After six months out here, he really knew the terrain. Every boulder, every tree: he knew them all.

Ruth checked the rear-view mirror for traffic and caught a glimpse of himself in the glass. There were dark rings under his eyes. He smoothed his hair and looked away. It was finally catching up with him. There were too many bodies, too much pain. His eyes had seen too much. Armageddon, the fall of empires, the slaughter of innocents. Enough blood to fill a sea.

The road was clear, no headlights in either direction. Ruth turned off between two tall pines onto a hard-packed dirt road, and soon the car was enveloped in timbers. Slowly he made his way forward until the vehicle nosed out into a clearing. He released the accelerator and tapped the brake. And the car stopped a few feet from the rim of a 500-foot cliff.

Ruth shut off the engine and the lights and leaned back in the seat. The sky to the east was black. At this elevation there was no horizon. Heaven and earth blended together, and there was no difference between the dots of light that were stars and the ones that were electric. From this perspective they were all the same: torches in the night.

Ruth savoured the solitude. There was too much noise at the camp, too many people. Silence was better.

He unlocked the glove compartment and removed a cellular phone. It chimed as the numbers were keyed in.

After four rings there was an answer. 'This is the voice of TRUTH,' he said to the person on the other end.

'How is it going?'

'It goes.'

'How are you feeling tonight?'

'Physically or spiritually?'

'Don't fuck around. Are you all right?'

'I *live*.'

'Are you taking your medicine?'

'As the lamb doth suckle the ewe.'

'Cut the bullshit. Are you popping your pills?'

'*Yes*, master.'

'How's your supply?'

Ruth reached into his pocket, grabbed a plastic bottle, and rattled it. 'The coffers are full.'

'When you need more, let me know.'

'As you wish ...'

'It's not as I *wish*. You have to stick with the programme. Six a day. *Every day*.'

'I know.'

'OK. It's almost time for a cash drop. You know what to do.'

'Yes, of course, my Saviour.'

'Don't call me that.'

Ruth didn't respond.

'Hey! What the *hell* is wrong with you?'

'I grow tired ...'

'Well, drink some coffee and take your pills. We've got work to do.'

'Thy will be done.'

They talked some more, and finally Ruth pushed 'end' on the phone unit. Contact points, cash drops, pill supplies. It was all so familiar, yet so strange. When he talked, there was another person talking. When he listened, no one was there. Ruth's head pounded, and the screams began again, the anguish of the dead, wailing beneath his skin. He jammed a capsule into his mouth and swallowed it dry. Then he put his hands over his ears, lay back against the seat, and tried to focus on the shimmering lights that began at the base of the cliff and went on forever.

* * *

Frank Davis was on the move. He'd worked the Joseph Brown case all day, interviewing the other feeble-minds at the senior centre who had had contact with the deceased the day he passed from the earth. Except for the run-in with Sergeant Brown at the station, he'd hardly had a break. Now his squad car was parked outside the centre again.

This was the hardest he'd ever worked on anything. But this case was the 'big' one, his ticket by that fat-ass Brown. If he could solve it, he'd move up the ladder. And Brown would have to eat his dust.

Davis drove his car slowly up Mountain Road, past the centre. Every checker player there had sung the same tune: Joseph was a saint who never strayed from the straight and narrow. He didn't smoke, and he didn't chew, and he didn't mess with the girls who do. But the hospital records revealed that the 'saint' had a blood-alcohol content of 0.14 per cent at the time he died. And that was sinner's level: legally 'drunk'.

It was dark now, after eight-thirty. Davis panned his spotlight up and down the side of the road. How far could Joseph have walked after checkers? Alcohol was forbidden at the centre, and his house was 'dry' according to his wife. To run the BAC level up that high, he must have consumed the liquor just before he started down the trail. But there were no taverns in the area, or liquor stores either.

Davis was approaching 'Shantyville', a short strip of abandoned migrant worker shacks. When the tobacco industry left town a decade ago, the workers did too. The county had planned to tear them down, but there was never enough money in the budget. He dimmed his headlights and switched off the search beam. Everything seemed quiet. He lowered his window. A dog barked in the distance, and a car went by. But Shantyville didn't stir.

Suddenly, he saw a reflection in one of the cracked windowpanes, a light that flared and went out. He turned off the engine and exited the cruiser.

There were two rows of shacks, one along the road, the other behind. The light he'd seen had come from the second tier.

Davis gripped his flashlight and moved cautiously towards his target, stepping over rusted cans and discarded tyres as he went.

He moved into place beside the door of the last shack in the row. It looked sturdier and in better repair than the others. And there were footprints in the dust around the porch.

Davis clicked on the light and put his hand on his service revolver, but didn't unholster it. 'County police,' he called. 'If there's anyone inside, come out!'

Silence.

'This is the police!' he repeated. 'Come out!'

The door opened slowly. 'OK,' a female voice said, 'I'm coming out. Please don't shoot!'

Davis shone his light in the face of a young black woman.

'I'm not doing anything wrong,' she protested.

Davis directed the beam inside the shed. It was set up like an apartment, with a cot, a camper's stove, tables, and chairs.

'I live here,' she said. 'That's not a crime.'

'Stand over there, keep your hands up, and your mouth shut!' Davis barked.

The woman padded out into the dust in her bare feet.

'Is there anyone else inside?'

'No.'

'There'd better *not* be.' Frank raised his weapon in the ready position, and stepped into the shed. There was a sharp odour of burnt food in the air, and he covered his mouth.

'I'm getting *cold*,' the woman said.

'Keep quiet!' Davis was busy surveying the room. Just then the light landed on a bottle of rum by the sink. He looked closer and saw that it was almost empty.

He reached into his pocket, pulled out a picture of Joseph Brown and stepped back outside.

'Ever see this man before?' He shoved the picture into her face. The woman didn't react.

'If you know him, you'd better fuckin' tell me. The sonofabitch is dead.' Davis shone his light on the photo.

The woman looked at the picture and closed her eyes. And then she shook her head and began to cry.

Joseph Brown lay on a table at the Medical Examiner's office, awaiting autopsy. There had been a delay after the body came in because none of the pathologists wanted to open him up. They all knew Brownie and couldn't face the task. A replacement had to be called in, and now, at 8.45 p.m., he was here and ready to go.

Doctor Anthony Bellini stood at the head of the aluminium trough and dictated into a suspended microphone. He was thirty-eight and handsome, with curly black hair and a square jaw. He was sometimes used as a replacement examiner in situations like this.

'The body is that of a well-nourished African-American male,' Bellini said, 'younger in appearance than his seventy-six years.' He placed a latex-gloved finger in Joseph's mouth. 'Teeth are all natural, and in good condition.' He shone a light inside. 'Palate normal. Throat clear.' He rolled back the eyelids. 'Pupils normal and dilated, irises clear.'

Bellini proceeded down the body, noting his findings. 'Clear.' 'Unremarkable.' 'Normal.'

He picked up a wrist. 'Small abrasion on the under portion of the right wrist.' He placed a ruler next to it. 'Approximately seven centimetres in length. Straight line cut, with serrations on each side.' Bellini adjusted his headband magnifier and bent close to the arm. 'Several fibres imbedded in the wound.' He picked up a pair of forceps and carefully extracted the tiny hairlike strands. 'Samples removed for analysis.' He placed them on glass slides and sealed the slides in plastic.

'Similar markings on the left wrist,' Bellini continued. 'Four-and-one-half-centimetre abrasion, uneven edges, and...' He eyed the wound through his magnifier. 'Similar fibres affixed.' Again he removed samples.

Continuing down the body, Bellini found no other marks or wounds. Everything was 'clear, normal, and unremarkable'.

'Exterior examination complete,' Bellini said. Now it was time to see what lay inside. He picked up a scalpel.

Just then, the phone rang. He picked it up. 'Bellini.'

'Who?'

'This is Dr Tony Bellini. Who's calling?'

'Uh, Sergeant Joe Brown. County police.' Brownie was

caught off-guard by the unfamiliar voice. He had been told there would be a delay until tonight, not that there was a roster switch.

Bellini suddenly realized who was on the line. 'Sergeant,' he said.

'Have you started yet?' There was apprehension in his voice.

'Just the external.'

Brownie hesitated. This was hard, real hard. 'Did you check his wrists?'

'Yes.'

'What did you find?'

Bellini thought for a moment. It was not proper to discuss findings midstream, not even with next of kin. 'Are you sure you want to talk about this now?'

'Yes,' Brownie said. 'I have to know. What's your reading on the abrasions? I thought they looked like ligature wounds.'

'They're minor cuts,' Bellini said, 'but they did contain embedded fibres.'

Brownie swallowed. That was consistent with a rope burn. 'So his hands might have been tied?'

'Can't say for sure, but the marks could be consistent with that, yes.'

'Did you find any other marks or wounds?'

'No. Except for the wrists, there were no other injuries.'

'You're sure?' Maybe he'd missed something when he'd checked the body himself.

'Yes. I went over him very carefully. He was clean.'

Brownie went silent for a second. 'I would like you to run a fingerprint test,' he said at last, 'on his skin.'

Bellini looked at his admission document. Any tests beyond normal autopsy had to be enumerated on the form. 'It's not on the chart,' he apologized.

Brownie sighed. 'Do you have the equipment available? The spray and the UV lamp?'

'Just a minute.' Bellini checked the supply cabinet and returned.

'Yes.'

'Are you qualified to lift prints from human skin?'

'Yes, I am.'

'Run the test,' Brownie begged. 'Please.'

Bellini looked at the chart again, then at the body of Joseph Brown. He hadn't done one of these in quite a while, but Brownie's tone of voice made it hard to refuse. 'OK,' he conceded. 'I'll do it.' He could always pencil in the request authorization after the fact.

'Thank you,' Brownie replied. 'I'm very grateful. Let me know if you turn up any prints.'

'Will do,' Bellini said. Then he hung up the phone.

Bellini rolled Joseph on his stomach and extended his arms away from the body.

Several years earlier a fingerprint examiner for the San Diego police department had conceived a method for developing fingerprints on human skin. It was a controversial process utilizing aerosol spray and ultraviolet light. Similar to a neutron test for gunpowder residue, the test was successful in detecting fingerprints on skin in about ten per cent of the cases.

Bellini checked the date on the developer spray can to see if it was current. Expiration was a year away. He removed the cap and began spraying the body, beginning with the arms, then moving to the face and neck, covering the exposed skin with a fine sticky mist.

He looked at the checklist printed on the can. 'Allow mixture to remain on the skin for three minutes before exposing to UV light.'

Bellini checked his watch and hooked up the black lamp. 'Three minutes,' he said aloud. Then he extinguished the overhead light, and switched on the lamp.

The upper half of Joseph's body glowed purple under the rays. Discounting the paramedics and doctors who always wore gloves, anyone who touched Joseph within the past forty-eight hours might have left a fingerprint on his skin. Bellini scanned the lamp towards the head, looking for a white oval mark that signified a print. Each arm was scanned. Nothing. Then, up to his shoulders. Again, they were clean.

Bellini played the lamp across Joseph's neck. 'Huh?' he gasped. He moved the lamp closer, then away.

'What the hell?' He was looking at a strange jagged pattern that had suddenly appeared across the back of the dead man's neck.

Bellini put down the lamp and felt his way to the closet, fumbling inside until he located a camera filled with special film.

In a moment, he was back. He raised the lamp with one hand and the camera with the other, clicking images of the unusual lines from every angle. He'd run a lot of these tests before and developed fingerprints on skin. But in all the tests he'd ever done, he'd never seen anything like *this*.

Jennifer sat at the counter of Russel's Deli waiting for

Gardner. The restaurant was a block down the street from the courthouse, a culinary secret in a brownstone building. Jennifer checked her watch. It was almost 9.00 p.m.

After their meeting with Lieutenant Harvis, Gardner had put her back to work. A string of felony cases needed indictments drawn up. Could Jennifer do it? Of course. Plough-horse Jennifer could do it all: try cases, interview witnesses, draw indictments, even run for coffee. Gardner had taught her well, and she'd been a great student. Her own work ethic demanded no less. Work, work, work, day and night. The fight song of the law profession.

'More milkshake?' Ida Russel asked. The hefty proprietor lifted a metal cup and poured chocolate into Jennifer's glass.

The prosecutor shook her head. 'I'm full, Ida. Thanks.' She'd had one of them today already, and *that* was over her limit. She was as concerned about keeping fit as Gardner, but every now and then she craved a sweet. Jennifer swivelled her stool, and looked out at the empty street. Suddenly, she was struck by a déjà vu. She'd been in the same spot earlier, at lunch. And she'd swivelled her stool the same way...

It was bright outside. The sun had painted gold streaks across the plate-glass window. The door opened and a young woman entered. She was pregnant, holding a young child's hand, pushing a stroller. Blonde and pretty, she was a suburban superwoman. Jennifer studied her face. It was flushed and anxious as she struggled to keep her toddler under control.

'Can I, Mom?' the boy asked in a whiney voice. He pointed to the candy counter. The mother dug into her purse and handed a quarter to Ida. Then the infant in the stroller began to cry. As the boy sucked a lemon stick, the woman rocked the tiny one gently against her chest.

Molly. The baby looked like Molly. Jennifer turned away suddenly, grabbed her sandwich and took a bite. The baby looked like Molly: a little round face with big round eyes and a fluff of red hair. Jennifer's law books had blocked her out, and then the cases, and then Gardner. Work, work, work. The little face had been covered up, obscured. But lately, it had come back. Lately, it was everywhere.

Gardner was a photo nut. He had album upon album of frozen memories. Granville in every conceivable position and pose, a glossy chronology of his life. One evening they were perusing a set of prints from the vacation at the lake.

'Look,' Gardner had said proudly. There was a time-sequence series of Granville leaping off the dock. First he was crouching, then in midair, then at the water, then splashing the green surface. His expressions changed with each shot: anticipation, fear, bravado, triumph. 'What do you think?'

'Cute,' Jennifer had replied. Granville was a wonderful kid, full of life and unbridled energy. Full of surprises, full of love.

Gardner had put down the pictures. 'You know, Jen, I've never seen any of *yours*.'

'My *what*?'

'Your pictures. When you were in high school, college ... When you were a kid.'

'I don't have any.'

'No?' Everybody kept pictures. 'Why not?'

'My dad wasn't into it, and my mom was, uh, you know, sick most of the time.'

'So you don't have *any* photos of your childhood? None at all?'

'No.'

'That's too bad.' Gardner had turned the album page. There was Granville again, mugging in a big hat. 'Too bad...'

Jennifer had looked over his shoulder but couldn't focus her eyes. What she'd said was not entirely true. She *did* have pictures. But her pictures weren't the normal kind. They weren't printed on paper, they were printed in her mind. Molly in her crib. Molly in her highchair. Molly on her bike. Molly in her coffin. Jennifer *did* have pictures. But she'd spent most of her life trying *not* to look at them.

'Jen?'

She glanced up. 'Gard!' The prosecutor had sneaked into her reverie.

'Ready?'

Jennifer stood up from the stool and stretched. 'Yes.'

'You OK?'

'Uh huh. I ... was just waiting for you ...'

'Sorry. It took longer than I'd expected.'

'How's Brownie?'

'Not good, really messed up.'

'What's he doing?'

'*Working*. On his father's case.'

'He's not supposed to.'

Gardner shrugged. 'Right. But who can stop him? You know Brownie. He investigates in his *sleep*.'

'Did you try?'

'I tried.'

'And?'

'I don't know. He's got to rest soon. He can't go on like this.'

'Speaking of rest...' Jennifer said plaintively. 'Can we *leave* now?'

Gardner looped her arm. 'Sure.' It had been a long day for them both. 'Let's go home.'

CHAPTER 4

The day of Joseph Brown's funeral was miserably hot. A front had moved in from the Gulf, and the air was heavy as Gardner drove to Smith's Mortuary in Blocktown. The leaves on the trees dangled listlessly, and a hush filled the streets. No mothers hung out wash, no children played. The town was in mourning. Life was on hold until brother Brown was laid to rest.

Gardner tugged at the collar of his shirt as he parked in the lot. He was sweating, and his back was damp. Brownie had asked him to be a pallbearer. He'd dropped Jennifer off at the church, and now he was ready to do his duty.

Brownie greeted him at the door. He was dressed in a dark blue suit. 'Hey, Gard,' he said softly.

Gardner squeezed his hand.

'Like you to wear these.' Brownie handed Gardner a pair of white silk gloves like the kind he was wearing. Gardner tugged them on.

'Almost ready,' Brownie said. 'Just waiting on one more pallbearer.'

They walked down a dim corridor past a bubbling fish

tank to the viewing room. Several black angels frolicked in the seaweed, and the odour of flowers choked the air. Inside, several men talked quietly by the bronze casket as Joseph listened silently from his white-tufted bed.

'Like you-all to meet Gardner Lawson,' Brownie announced, 'County prosecutor.'

The men lined up, and each pressed his gloved hand against Gardner's.

'Sam Ellison, Ernie Jones, Harry Dugan,' Brownie said in turn.

'Glad to meet you,' Gardner replied. The men all looked like Joseph: dignified and proud. But today there was no laughter, no story, no joke. They were as solemn as the mortician who stood at attention by the door.

Gardner knelt on a cushion beside the casket. To the rear lay a massive floral arrangement: roses, carnations, and lilies. Gardner closed his eyes. Suddenly a sharp pain skated across the surface of his heart. Suddenly it was *his* dad in the metal box. *His* father, lying cold and still. He'd just kissed his wooden cheek, tucked a linen handkerchief in his pocket, and gagged on his own tears.

Gardner opened his eyes. Joseph's folded hands were inches away. Gardner studied them, trying to fight his memory. He wasn't dead. He was just sleeping. Gardner kept his eyes open and said a prayer. Just then, there was a noise by the door.

'Let's move,' a voice said.

Gardner turned around. Another man had just entered the room. Heavyset and dark-skinned, he looked like Brownie, but he wore a tribal African cap and a striped scarf over his suit.

One of the elders handed him a pair of gloves. Brownie walked over to the prosecutor.

'Who's that?' Gardner whispered.

'My *brother*.'

'*Brother*?' Gardner was shocked. He knew nothing about a Brown brother. 'You have a *brother*?'

Brownie shook his head. 'Not really.'

Gardner waited for an explanation, but Brownie stopped talking.

'Let's go!' The brother demanded.

'This man here is still praying.' Brownie pointed to Gardner, and the prosecutor started to rise. 'Take your time,' he whispered.

Gardner dropped back down to his knees.

'Yeah,' the brother said. 'Take your time. *He* isn't going anywhere.' He pointed to his father's body.

'Watch your mouth,' Brownie warned. 'Show some respect.'

The elders moved between the two men.

'I got respect, Mr Detective. Whole hell of a lot of *respect*.'

Gardner stood up.

'Don't rush,' Brownie said.

'That's OK, I'm done.' Gardner was getting uncomfortable.

One of the elders led the brother back towards the door.

'What was *that* all about?' Gardner asked.

'Nothing.'

'Nothing?' He'd seen less friction between heavyweight fighters.

'*Nothing*,' Brownie repeated. 'And now, as the man said, it *is* time to go.'

Brownie signalled the funeral director to wheel the casket towards the door. Silently, the six men took their places. The brother and an elder were up front; two elders held the middle; Gardner and Brownie carried the rear.

'You OK?' Gardner whispered.

'Yeah.'

'I'm right beside you.'

Brownie nodded.

They marched to the door.

'On my signal, lift,' Brownie said. 'One, two, three!' The casket came up from the trolley, and the bearers carried it through the threshold and down the steep steps.

Gardner strained under the weight, his gloved hand slipping against the polished handle. He glanced at the casket shimmering in the heat. Then he noticed Brownie's reflection in the shiny surface. From that perspective, it looked like he was screaming. But no sound was coming out.

Frank Davis stopped his cruiser outside of the quarry gate. There was a sign attached to the bars: 'CHURCH OF THE ARK, INC., CAIN, NO TRESPASSING'. The rest of the department was at the funeral, but he'd declined. His investigation was more important than sucking up to the chief of the crime lab.

The inquiry was rolling right along. It turned out that the checker boys at the senior centre were jumping more than game chips in their leisure time. They'd set up a regular little 'love shack' in the back row of Shantyville. The black bitch he'd rousted was a homeless gal who'd hitch-hiked out from the city. The old guys had chipped in and set her up with a place to stay. And when the mood struck, they'd amble over for some grab-ass and some hooch.

But that didn't solve the mystery. It might explain the scratches on Joseph's wrists, but then again, it might not. The slut refused to explain what went on in her greasy cot. So Davis went back to the 'crime' scene, the place where Joseph fell. As with the first time out, there was nothing definitive, no physical evidence to speak of. The only thing he found was a rub mark on a tree and some broken twigs off the trail. But a deer's antler could have caused the rub, and the paramedics could have crushed the twigs. So he didn't have a 'lock' on any proof at the moment.

The entrance to CAIN was blocked by a heavy gate. On either side, a ten-foot wire fence ran for a hundred yards, turned ninety degrees, then ran a mile back to the woods. The camp was secure on all sides. Davis sounded his horn.

He'd been trying to figure out motive since getting the case. If someone *had* whacked Brown they had to have a reason. It wasn't robbery, that was certain. His gold watch, wallet, and cash were still on him. And it didn't appear to be jealousy or revenge. The old lady was in a state of denial about his drinking and his catting. To her and everyone else around town, the fucker *was* a saint. So it had to be something else. Davis had put out the word with his roughneck street network: any strangers in town? Any

Klan activity brewing? Any rumours making the biker-bar rounds? Maybe this was a race thing. Maybe someone decked old man Brown because they didn't like the colour of his skin.

And that's what led him to CAIN. 'Some weird shit going on out there,' Wally Pete told him. 'They got a lily-white preacher, a bunch of babes, and they're buying up ammo at the hardware mart like crazy.'

That got Frank's attention. He checked the tax map and found something else interesting. The quarry property backed up to Cutler Road. There was a stretch of woods in between, but a path connected the two sectors: the same path where Joseph Brown died.

Davis found a phone listing for the church and asked the dispatcher to call and say the police were on their way. Except for CAIN, the rumour mill was silent. But it *was* a lead. And it *was* worth checking out.

Frank lowered his window. The air was still, and soggy heat rolled into the car. Suddenly, a man appeared at the top of the rise beyond the fence. He ran down and unfastened the lock. Then he waved the vehicle forward, stopping it at the boundary.

'You're here to see Thomas Ruth?' the man asked. He was dressed in jeans and a T-shirt, his hair tucked under a baseball cap.

'That is correct.'

'Do you have a search warrant?'

Davis shook his head. 'No, I do not, but I would like consent to enter the premises.'

'May I ask what this is about?'

'I'll take that up with Mr Ruth.'

'OK, but would you mind telling *me* in the meantime?'

Frank studied the man. Tall and conditioned, he was probably a security guard. 'OK. We had an incident earlier this week over in Blocktown...' He pointed towards the woods.

'What kind of incident?' The man didn't look like the fundamentalist freaks they grew back in West Virginia. He looked like a high-school teacher.

'Father of one of our police officers died under strange circumstances. We suspect foul play.'

'Died?' The man looked alarmed.

'Dead as last year's tick. We think someone tied him up, tortured him to death.'

'Who did it?'

'That's what we're trying to find out.'

'Do you think Thomas Ruth was involved?'

'We're not ready to make formal accusations. We're just checking on a few things. If Ruth was *not* involved, he's got nothing to worry about.'

The man stroked his chin and squinted into the bright sun.

'I'd like you to take me to him,' Davis said.

'You're with him now,' the man finally replied. '*I'm* Thomas Ruth.'

Ruth entered the cruiser and directed Davis into the compound a half-mile beyond the gate. 'Sorry about the deception,' he said as they drove. 'I make it a practice to learn the agenda before I talk with people I don't know. Please forgive me.'

'No problem.' He sounded sincere.

As they drove, Frank made mental notes of the layout.

Everything was like the schematic in the land records plat: a wide-open space, a dirt road, several buildings, and a giant granite pit.

They parked by the administration building and exited the cruiser. Davis looked around. There was no one in sight. 'Where are all your people?'

'Chores, prayer, meditation. I thought you were here to see *me*.'

'I am. You got a cool place we can talk?' The sun was burning through his uniform cap.

Ruth motioned to a covered porch.

They stepped into the shade. Pin-holes in the rusty roof let a shotgun spray of light through, but it was cooler. Davis removed his notebook. 'Where were you three nights ago, between 8.00 p.m. and 12.30 a.m.?'

'Here.'

'You were at the quarry all night?'

The preacher nodded.

'Got anyone who can verify that?' Davis scanned the empty street.

'Is it necessary?'

'I can rule you out as a suspect if you substantiate your whereabouts that evening.'

'I was here.'

'OK . . . Give me the name of a person who can vouch for you.'

'We have a rule of confidentiality in this church. Members are assured their privacy will be guarded when they enter these gates. I intend to honour that commitment.'

'But they could clear you of suspicion.'

'I understand that, but as I told you, I've done nothing wrong.'

Davis began to speak but held back.

'I am in solitude most of the time anyway,' Ruth continued. 'I'm not sure *who* I could get to give me an, uh, alibi...'

Davis made a note. 'Alibi' was a strange choice of words for a preacher.

'Did you leave the quarry at *any* time that day?'

'Which day?'

'September twentieth.'

'I don't remember. I go outside a lot but can't say for sure if I did then.'

'Do you keep a diary, a log of your schedule?'

'No. The Bible is my only schedule.'

'Under the circumstances, I *do* need to interview some of your people.'

'I cannot allow you to do that. My lambs are here to escape the evils of the world, and it's my job to protect them.'

'It could only *help* you to permit it.'

'The word of the Lord is sufficient unto itself. I have done *nothing* wrong.'

'But it's not the Lord's word I'm questioning. It's *yours*.'

Ruth pressed his hands to his temples. 'Forgive him, Lord.'

Davis decided to move on. He walked over to several vehicles on the lot. 'Which one do you drive?'

Ruth pointed to a late model Lincoln Continental.

'Mind giving me your car phone number?'

'775-2828.'

'What cellular company do you use?'

'Mountain Bell.'

Just then, a bearded man ran up the street. He was dressed in a linen robe and sandals. 'What's going on?' he asked, eyeing the uniform.

Ruth tried to take him aside, but he resisted.

'What's your name, sir?' Davis asked.

'What's going on?' the man persisted.

'I'll handle this,' Ruth told him. 'Go back to your cabin.'

'What's your name, sir?' Davis repeated.

'Your cabin!' Ruth ordered.

The man turned around and began to leave.

'Wait a minute, sir!' Davis called, trying to catch him.

Ruth grabbed Frank's arm. 'Stop.'

Davis halted and looked at his arm. Ruth had it in a death grip.

'Let go, Mr Ruth!' He reached for his holster.

Ruth released and stepped back, but the intruder was gone.

'You just made a *mistake*,' Davis said coldly.

'I don't think so.' Ruth's eyes looked like they could cut steel. 'Get off this property and get off *now*.'

Davis took a step backward. The guy was about to lose it.

Ruth put his hands to his head again. 'Vengeance is mine, sayeth the Lord!'

Davis unsnapped his weapon and backed to his car. He opened the door and got in.

Ruth was still in the street. 'And the unrighteous shall perish!'

Davis watched for a moment as he started the engine.

'I'll see *you* later,' he said. Then he peeled out in a cloud of yellow dust and raced towards the gate.

Joseph Brown's funeral had just begun at the Blocktown AME Church. A traditional sect, its members were men and women of Joseph and Althea's generation too set in their ways to switch allegiance to Reverend Taylor. The small clapboard building was packed with mourners, and the overflow thronged the yard, listening on loudspeakers: townspeople, relatives, and a hefty contingent of cops. They'd all loved the old man.

Inside the main hall it was unbearably hot. There was no air-conditioning, and the crowd fanned themselves with programmes and hymnals as Reverend Boyd prepared to send Joseph into the heavens.

'We haven't come here for a funeral,' the white-haired preacher said. 'This is a celebration.'

'Yes, sir,' a voice hollered from the balcony.

'The joyous celebration of a man's life...'

'That's right!' another voice replied.

'Brother Joseph lived a good man, and he died a good man!'

'Amen!'

Gardner and Jennifer sat in the second row. Ahead were Brownie, Althea, and the long-lost brother. Dour and sullen, they flanked their mother like ebony columns. Althea sobbed intermittently into a handkerchief, and the sons alternated in comforting her. She was the no-fly zone in their silent war, and it showed.

Gardner tried to swallow but couldn't. His throat was too dry. He gripped Jennifer's hand. She gripped back.

'God called Joseph to him, and Joseph went,' the preacher cried. 'Yes, we'll miss him! Yes, we'll be sad when we see that empty chair! But, my friends, understand that he's in a better place right now than we are!'

'Amen!'

'So we celebrate! We do not mourn! We praise! We do not despair!'

The crowd quieted.

'Joseph Brown was a good man, an honest man, a peaceful man! He was a family man.' The reverend pointed to the Brown delegation. 'He was a kind man, a loving man, an intelligent man! Are you picking up the *word* here, friends? As we celebrate the life of Brother Brown?'

'Yes, sir!'

'Joseph Brown was a *man*!'

'Praise God!' a woman called.

'He had some warts, like all mortal *men* ... Only one man in the history of the universe didn't have *any* warts, and that was Jesus Christ. But Brother Brown didn't have *many*, and that's why he sits by God's side, and the rest of us sinners still labour in the heat of the world!'

Brownie looked at the preacher and tried to listen to what he was saying, but the words seemed to fade away as soon as they came out of his mouth. It was hot, but he didn't feel the heat. It was bright, but he didn't see the light. All he could see was his father's face, alive, and strong, and in another time.

When Brownie was fourteen, his dog died. He was only a mixed-breed, but he was gentle, and Brownie loved him. 'Can we get another, Daddy?' he asked.

74

'Yes, son,' Joseph agreed.

So they searched the papers for a give-away and found one: 'Eight-year-old male collie. Free to good home.'

'325 Sedgewick Place,' Brownie said as his father manoeuvred the old Chevrolet towards the other side of town. They crossed hills, meadows, and woods, and emerged on a development of stone ranch houses. 'Sedgewick Estates,' the sign read.

'325,' Brownie said.

Joseph turned onto the main street and slowed.

'325,' Brownie repeated.

Joseph entered a driveway. '325. This is it.'

They walked to the door and rang the bell.

'Yes?' A plump, fortyish white woman answered the door.

Joseph removed his hat. 'We're here about the dog.'

The woman hesitated, and a man suddenly appeared at her side. 'These people are here for Pete,' she told him.

Brownie looked into the yard. Behind the fence was the most beautiful dog he'd ever seen: a fluffed-up collie, just like Lassie. He smiled, and the dog wagged its tail.

'You're too late,' the man said abruptly. 'We already gave him away.' Brownie looked up.

'We called about it,' Joseph said.

'Sorry.'

Brownie grabbed his father's arm. 'But...' He was pointing at the yard.

'Wouldn't happen to have another, would you?' Joseph asked.

'No, I don't. Not to give away.'

'Daddy!' Brownie was still tugging at his arm.

'Thank you anyway,' Joseph replied, replacing his hat and turning towards the car.

'Daddy!' Brownie persisted.

'Get in the car, son.'

Brownie slammed the door and stared at the collie peering through the fence. 'They had the dog!'

Joseph kept silent as they drove back to the highway.

'Didn't you see, Daddy? They had the dog!'

'I saw it, son.'

'So why didn't you do something?'

'The man didn't want to give it to us. That was his right.'

'Why not? Because we're black?'

'Maybe. But it was still his right. He can give the dog to anyone he wants.'

'As long as they're white,' Brownie said under his breath.

They were out of Sedgewick Estates now, in the countryside. Joseph pulled off the road and stopped the car. He put his hand on Brownie's shoulder and looked into his eyes. 'I want you to calm down, son,' he said. 'You can't go through life bein' a hater.'

'But they *were* haters!'

'Yes, they were. That's their problem. We don't have to be like them.'

Brownie's eyes filled with tears. 'But we didn't get the dog!'

Joseph rubbed his son's neck. 'Plenty of dogs in this world, Joe, at least as nice as that one.'

They sat for a moment in silence. Then Brownie leaned over and hugged his dad. When he pulled away, his tears had dried, and he was trying to smile. 'Probably had fleas, anyway,' he said.

* * *

Brownie fought back a tear and looked up at the pulpit.

'Friends,' Reverend Boyd continued, 'a prominent member of our community is here today to join this celebration. He has asked to say a few words, and I'd like him to come up now, if he would...' He pointed to the back of the church, and Reverend Taylor hustled down the aisle and ascended the steps. Preened and resplendent in black, he was ready to preach.

'Thank you, Reverend Boyd.' His smooth voice poured into the pews and flowed from the speakers. 'I knew Joseph Brown, as we all did, and I agree with most that's been said so far. Joseph was a good man, a kind man, a peaceful man. He was a man in every sense of the word ... but I must respectfully disagree with one thing Brother Boyd told you here today...'

The congregation hushed.

'Maybe God did *not* call Brother Brown to him just yet.'

Several mourners looked around, and Taylor paused for effect, his heavy breath rumbling over the p.a. system.

'Maybe Brother Brown was *sent* to the Almighty before his time.'

Gardner stared up at the altar. This didn't sound like a eulogy.

'This life may not compare to the one God's got waiting for us in the hereafter,' Taylor continued, 'but it's a life.'

'Un huh,' someone said.

'God gives us life, and life is precious.'

'Amen!'

'God doesn't *want* us to come to him until our job here is done!'

77

'That's true!'

Taylor stopped suddenly and looked out across the room. 'We honour Joseph Brown here today, but we don't accept the fact that his time had *come*!'

'That's right!'

'We don't let any man tell us that our *time* has *come*!'

'Amen!!'

Gardner stirred in his seat. Taylor was inciting the crowd, and the inference was clear: someone had *killed* Joseph Brown. In truth, it was just conjecture, Brownie's hunch. But Taylor's words were making it fact.

'What's happening?' Jennifer whispered.

'I don't *know*,' Gardner replied over the din. This had come out of nowhere.

'God can *call* us,' Taylor yelled, 'but no man on this earth can tell us it's time to go!'

'Hallelujah!'

'Death comes when *God* decrees it!'

'Amen!'

'Death waits on *his* commandment!'

'Yes, sir!'

'But in the case of Brother Joseph, dear friends, God did not issue the call!'

The crowd went quiet again.

'No, dear friends, God was not yet ready to take our Joseph ...'

Gardner squeezed Jennifer's hand.

'*Someone* among us decided to do God's work *for* him!'

Gardner looked at Brownie and his brother. They were no longer immobile. Each time Taylor uttered a word, their heads moved.

'No *man* has a right to take a life!' Taylor yelled.

The heads moved again.

'No *man* can wield God's sword!'

'Amen!'

'We may have to accept the fact that he is *gone*, but we don't have to accept the reason *why*!'

Another hush.

'No *man* can do this evil deed and walk away!'

'Amen!' Brownie yelled.

'No *man* can escape God's wrath!'

'That's right!' the brother called.

'No *man*!' Taylor signalled for a reply.

'No *man*!' the mourners roared.

'No *man*!'

'No *man*!' The church rocked. And the voices of the brothers Brown were the loudest of them all.

Sallie Allen was nervous. Thomas Ruth had put the compound on alert because a police officer was coming for a visit. 'Stay in the dining hall while I deal with him,' he'd ordered. And the flock had obeyed. Without question or hesitation, they'd all marched to the oblong building and disappeared inside, Sallie included. It was like a nuclear attack drill: a room full of silent people, their heads down, their hands clasped, waiting for the fatal flash.

Finally, the 'all clear' sounded, and things returned to normal. They were allowed to venture outside. But in the dining hall, they'd covered the windows with sheets, so Sallie had not been able to peek. She was dying to know what the police wanted.

Since her first day in the compound, Sallie had been

reconnoitring. How many CAIN followers were there? Fifty, as far as she could count: thirty men and twenty women. Their backgrounds? Diverse: mechanics, salesmen, housewives, drifters. Their financial resources? Substantial: a fleet of cars, walk-in refrigerator, cache of food, and state-of-the-art computer. Armaments? That was still a question mark. The restriction on her movements made that a tough one. But Sallie wasn't about to give up. She still needed a 'hook'. And an arsenal of weapons would do nicely.

The followers had now fanned out to complete their chores. Sallie was on meal preparation duty, and she waited in the dining hall for the cook to tell her what to do. Standing by the window, she could barely see the administration building through the waves of radiating heat. She wiped a tickle of moisture from her hairline as a dust-devil swirled in the roadbed and died. Sallie knew her time was short. In the next twenty-four hours she had to get what she needed and get out. Her deadline was approaching. The first draft was due day-after-tomorrow.

Suddenly she saw Thomas Ruth rush from the administration building. He leaped from the porch and ran to his car. Then he backed out, sped towards the front gate, and disappeared.

'Sister Sallie,' the cook called, 'can you help me?' She was a middle-aged runaway from an eastern city, a mom who discovered 'religion' and abandoned her husband, kids, Volvo, and ended up here. Her name was Dorothy. She was dressed in traditional CAIN garb: jeans, T-shirt, and flip-flops. Her brown hair was cinched back, and she wore no make-up or jewellery – as decreed by Thomas Ruth.

Sallie turned from the window. 'Sure.'

Dorothy handed her a list. 'Bring these items from storage please.'

Sallie took the paper. 'Right away.'

The storage room was in a small garage behind the administration building. Non-perishables such as canned goods and spices were kept there. Their appearances may have been plain, but they ate well. No vegetarians allowed.

Sallie walked up the street. She'd been inside every building in the compound but the men's dorm, the administration building, and a padlocked shed down by the quarry. She'd made diagrams and notes as to what was where and what it was used for. 'Eating.' 'Sleeping.' 'Preaching.' The days and activities were structured, and each activity had its time and place. The followers droned through the hours in quiet obedience, their wills forfeited to Ruth just like their possessions. The preacher kept the schedule tight, kept them busy so there was little chance to reflect on their isolation from the outside world. *Ruth* was their world now. And the woods beyond the quarry fence were as far away as the sun.

Sallie passed the men's and women's dormitories, former stone-worker's bunkhouses. They slept on Spartan cots arranged in open rows, and ate and bathed in same-sex shifts. Ruth had a thing about interaction. Men and women only came together when they prayed.

Sallie cautiously stepped up on the porch of the administration building: the headquarters where Ruth 'meditated' and 'slept'. Sallie had never seen anyone but Ruth and a few trusted males go inside. Ruth had 'strictly forbidden' access to anyone else, and there was a sign on the door:

'PRIVATE'. She glanced in a window. The room was empty. She moved to the next one. This, too, was empty. Sallie approached the front door and glanced over her shoulder at the street. No one was in sight. By now she'd reached the entrance. Ruth was gone, and the place looked deserted. She tried the door handle. It was unlocked!

Sallie slipped down the darkened hall to a room at the far end. She'd spotted the computer equipment through the window a few days ago. Now she could check it out up close.

Her heart was racing as she entered the room. 'Woah!' she whispered. Ruth had an IBM subsidiary in there. She'd seen some of it through the window, but not all this. There were keyboards, mainframes, modems, printers, scanners, copiers, and fax machines.

Sallie hurried to a console and threw the power switch. The computer vibrated as it prepped for operation. Finally the electronics had sorted out, and the blinking cursor came to rest. 'PASSWORD?' the screen asked.

Sallie keyed in 'CAIN'. It was as good a guess as any.

'INVALID COMMAND', the screen replied.

Sallie typed in 'RUTH'.

'INVALID COMMAND'.

Sallie tried 'THOMAS'.

'INVALID', again.

Sallie didn't have much time. If she got caught they'd throw her in with the snakes. She shuddered and tried another variation: 'T.RUTH'.

The letters faded for a moment, then began to blink. It had worked. She was in!

Sallie keyed 'dir/p' on the console, a command that would display the files in memory. The screen responded with a list of phrases. 'STRIKE ANY KEY TO CONTINUE', the prompt said.

Sallie hit a key, and more file names rolled into view. She scanned hurriedly, looking for buzzwords.

'STRIKE TO CONTINUE', the prompt reminded.

Sallie hit another key. Suddenly, there was a sound down the hall, footsteps approaching.

Sallie glanced at the screen as another set of files was revealed. Then she shut off the power and ran to the window, opening it and squeezing through as fast as she could.

Sallie hit the ground running and didn't look back until she turned the corner. By now she was at a walk, and she casually approached the storage room. Her heart was beating wildly, but it wasn't just fear. She was pumped up because she'd seen something: several filenames in the mix. The computer was Thomas Ruth's alter ego, a visual insight into his complex mind. And now, something on his mind had come to light, reflected by two of his files. 'CONTINGENCIES', the first one read. And that was followed by a sub-directory: 'DEATH'.

CHAPTER 5

Gardner sat in his townhouse kitchen staring at a glass of iced tea. It was midnight, and he was tired, but he'd probably lie awake if he went to bed. He sloshed the tea and took a half-hearted sip. Storm clouds were building, and he was worried.

Jennifer descended the stairs and entered the room. She was dressed in blue silk pyjamas; her face was scrubbed, her hair pulled back and tied with a 'scrunchie'.

'You're brooding,' she said.

'I'm not brooding.' Gardner didn't look up. 'I'm thinking.'

'Sometimes it's hard to tell the difference.'

'Huh?'

'You don't *think*, you *agonize*.' Jennifer sat down at the table.

Gardner finally raised his head. 'Today was a bitch. A first-class bitch.'

'The funeral.'

'If you can call it that.'

'Reverend Taylor certainly electrified the crowd.'

'Yeah.' Gardner drank another sip. 'Amazing what a person can do with a well-turned phrase.'

'You're concerned about the Brown case.'

'Yes, I am. Who the hell told Taylor about the investigation in the first place? It was supposed to be confidential...'

Jennifer went to the refrigerator, poured some tea for herself, then returned to the table. 'Brownie, maybe?'

'Maybe. But that's not important now. The cat's out of the bag, and Blocktown's mobilizing for pay-backs, thanks to Taylor. This is how it starts, Jen. Rumours fly, innocent people get hurt. And for what?'

'Joseph Brown's murder.'

'What *murder*? You read the reports. It was a heart attack. That has never been disputed. Natural causes do *not* equal murder.'

'What about the scratches on his arms?'

Gardner brushed back a stray hair. 'God, Jen, the man was drinking and carousing just before he died. You know what Davis uncovered. Maybe the Shantyville woman, uh, Jackie Frey, tied him up. Maybe they were into some kinky stuff. Maybe *that's* what killed him.'

'Brownie doesn't think so.'

'No, he doesn't. But we have to deal with reality here. We have to stay objective, keep our heads cool, even if no one else does. Right now this thing is being fuelled with innuendos based on a false premise, and that's bad.'

Jennifer put her glass in the sink and returned to the table. 'So you don't believe there was any foul play in Joseph's death at all?'

Gardner shook his head. 'Not from what I've seen so far. Davis is still digging, but unless he finds some hard evidence soon, I'd say it's just about done.'

'What if *Brownie* comes up with something?'

'Pray that he doesn't.'

'Why? He has a right to know what happened to his father.'

Gardner frowned. 'You saw him at the church. He was sucked in by Taylor like the rest of the crowd. If he had any objectivity before, he sure-as-shit doesn't have any now. That was a lynch-mob forming in there today, and Brownie was ready to lead the charge.'

'He just lost his dad. What do you expect?'

'Nothing less. That's why he has to back off till he cools down.'

They stopped talking.

'Now there's a definite *brood*,' Jennifer said. 'I wish I had a mirror.'

Gardner tried to smile. 'I have to make a decision.'

'That's obvious.'

'Do I place Brownie on temporary suspension or ...'

Jennifer watched Gardner for a moment. 'You're having trouble deciding. Nothing *new* about that.' There was sarcasm in her voice.

'What do you mean?'

'You can't decide *anything* lately.'

Gardner sensed danger. The professional/personal line was about to be crossed. 'Jen ...'

'We can't keep putting it off,' she said suddenly. 'There's always going to be a case, always an excuse ...'

'Please, Jen,' Gardner protested, 'not now, please ...'

'Now.'

Gardner hated this. Jennifer had caught him in a pensive

mood, and now she was trying to shift the agenda. 'Please...' he begged.

'I want to talk.'

'OK ... OK.'

Jennifer looked into his eyes. 'How old am I?'

Gardner frowned. 'Uh, how old?'

'My age, Gard. What is my age?'

'Thirty-one.'

'Thirty-*three*. I'm thirty-three years old!'

Gardner reddened.

'I want to get married. I want a child. I want permanence...'

'No...' Gardner moaned. Not *this* again.

'*Yes*. You have to listen to me, try to understand.'

'I do understand, Jen, it's just ... it's just...'

'You've *had* your life. You have a son. You don't want to start over.'

'That's not it.'

'What *is* it, Gard?'

'Things are heating up right now ... It's hard to think.'

'It's *always* hard to think when it comes to this. You *never* want to talk about it. You're always putting me off.'

Gardner sighed. Here they go again. Everything is smooth for a while at the office, in the bedroom, and then *wham*, it hits.

'I want to get *married*,' Jennifer went on, 'like normal people. We've been living together for four years, and it's been great, but...'

'It *has* been great,' Gardner interrupted. 'We get along.

We have the same interests, the same profession. You love Granville...' What's to change? It was a great arrangement, convenient, comfortable.

'I want *more*. My own family.'

'But you, me, and Granville *are* family.'

Jennifer adjusted her glasses. 'It's not the same.'

'But I thought you loved him.'

'I *do*. But he's not mine. He's *hers* and always will be. I want something that's a part of *us*, a part of you and me alone!'

Gardner looked down at the table.

'I'm tired of this arrangement, Gard.'

'I know.'

'You have to do something about it.'

'I know.'

Jennifer stood up. 'I'll wait a little longer, but I can't wait forever.'

'I understand.' Gardner's head was still lowered like a petulant kid.

'I *won't* wait forever.'

'I...' Gardner's reply was lost in the sound of Jennifer's footsteps retreating up the stairs. He picked up his glass and pulled back his arm like he was going to throw it against the wall. Then he stopped and placed it on the table.

'Marriage is sacred,' his mother said. 'You marry for life.' They were sitting on the dock of the three-acre pond on the family estate. It was a blue-sky summer afternoon, and Gardner was twelve years old. A pair of wild geese paddled silently across the still water as he dangled his legs over the edge.

Gardner looked at his mom. She wore a yellow towel on her head, and her bathing suit was still wet. Her toenails were painted crimson.

'Your father is the only man I've ever loved,' she continued. 'We met, courted, got engaged, married, and we're still together.' She looked past the pond, past the trees, to a brick mansion on the far hill. 'It's important to stay together, son. Men and women need each other. And marriage is the glue. You will get married, one day, Gardner, to a beautiful young woman. And you'll stay married forever...'

Gardner got up from the table. 'Stay married forever...' He'd been there, done that. 'Marry for life...' What a joke. Carole had been his beautiful woman. They'd met, courted, engaged, married. But the tides had destroyed their sandcastle world. Inside forces, outside forces, a combination of both. It didn't matter, really. The strongest glue in the universe eventually came apart. And that was the problem.

Gardner turned off the kitchen light and walked into the hall. Then he slowly climbed the stairs to his room.

Brownie stood by the examining table in the crime lab, staring at the documents he'd laid out. It was late, but he wasn't going home, not tonight. Mama was with the family, at the wake. Brownie had put in an appearance, then retreated here where he could be alone. A dead father and a live brother were more than he could handle in one day.

The funeral had been tough. Mama's tears had eaten him up. Faults and all, she'd adored the old man. But nothing had prepared him for the burial. When the casket went into the vault, Mama screamed and tried to jump in with it. Then she fainted, and the aunts collapsed around her. There were limp bodies everywhere, and the wails of the other mourners cut down to the bone. It was a living, dying hell.

Brownie shivered and tried to stifle the thoughts. Then he opened Frank Davis' latest report, the one that had just come in this afternoon. Amazingly, the fuckhead had turned up a lead. He'd stumbled onto a possible suspect: a fundamentalist freak-o named Ruth. Brownie had already reviewed the report three times, but now he sat down to read it again, circling the important sections in red ink: 'CHURCH OF THE ARK, INC., ABBREVIATION: CAIN.' 'NO ALIBI.' 'CAR PHONE.' 'MOUNTAIN BELL.' 'SUSPICIOUS BEHAVIOUR.' 'EVASIVE DURING QUESTIONING.' 'DENIAL OF CONSENT SEARCH.' 'ANTAGONISTIC.' 'COMBATIVE.' 'PROXIMITY TO CUTLER ROAD.' 'POSSIBLE WEAPONS VIOLATIONS.' At the bottom of the page was Davis' preliminary conclusion: 'INSUFFICIENT PROBABLE CAUSE TO JUSTIFY SEARCH WARRANT OR ARREST. INVESTIGATION CONTINUING.' Brownie underlined that part with his pen.

There was a supplemental report attached which Brownie had not highlighted. In it Davis meticulously set out in writing what the Brown family had kept quiet for years: Joseph had a taste for liquor and ladies. He was a 'good man, a kind man, a gentle man' like the reverend said, but he did have his faults. Brownie had brought him home in a squad car more than once, but the family had always managed to cover it up. And now, redneck Davis had dug it out and written it up, the sonofabitch. Brownie tried to restrain his anger as he scanned down to the final paragraph of the report. 'NO CLEAR CORRELATION BETWEEN THESE ACTIVITIES AND THE MANNER OF DEATH. INVESTIGATION CONTINUING.' On that point, at least, he and Davis agreed. Daddy was a rake at times, but he was pretty normal in his needs. Bondage wasn't his thing. The Frey girl didn't cause the scratches, he was almost certain.

Brownie moved to another file. 'Thomas Ruth,' he said aloud. 'What the fuck kind of name is that?' Davis had run a background check on the man as soon as he returned to the station. There was no criminal history listed for 'Thomas Ruth'. Checks into his family, educational, and employment history had drawn blanks also. 'Who are you?' Brownie asked, walking to a bookshelf. He picked up a copy of HATEWATCH, and turned to the index. Hatewatch was a public interest foundation that tracked cults. They updated the whereabouts and activities of reclusive groups on a monthly basis. 'C,' Brownie said. 'CHURCH OF THE AGONY, CHURCH OF THE ANGELS, CHURCH OF ANTHONY.' But there was no 'CHURCH OF THE ARK, INC.,' No 'CAIN'. Brownie checked the date. SEPTEMBER, current year. He flipped to the index. 'CUMULATIVE LISTING OF ANTISOCIAL CULTS,' it said. But there was no 'CAIN.'

Brownie put down the book. Then he leaned back and closed his eyes. The wails at the graveside were echoing in his mind again. He tried to fight them, but he couldn't. '*Joseph!*' Mama screamed.

'*Joseph!*' The jaws of the grave were gaping.

'No,' Brownie groaned. 'No...' Another deluge was coming.

'*Joseph!*'

Brownie's body spasmed, and the tears gushed. And there was nothing he could do to stop them.

Brownie sat up, wiped his eyes, and looked at the clock. It was almost midnight. He stood and shook out his legs. The coffin was in the ground, and Daddy was gone, buried, never coming back. He'd have to accept it: Joseph was *gone*. Davis had tagged him a drunk and runaround, but Davis didn't know shit. The fact remained that Daddy was gone. And *someone* had ended his life.

Brownie slowly stacked the reports. The evidence wasn't conclusive, but that didn't matter. A good detective didn't need evidence. A good detective could get the job done on instinct alone.

Brownie walked to the door and turned off the light. He had a new lead to check out. And time was short.

Althea's house was filled with family and friends. It was well into the night, and the wake was still in progress. Ham, biscuits, and fruit were laid out on the table in the dining room. The uncles were in the kitchen smoking and tipping glasses of whiskey. The aunts and nieces sat in the flower-papered den. And Althea was upstairs, attended by a nurse. She was sedated in her bed, propped with pillows, corpse-like, very still. The day had flogged her soul, and she was exhausted.

On the porch, two men conferred. They spoke in

whispers as the sounds of the mourners drifted through the house.

'Hell of a job you did today,' Brownie's brother said.

'Thank you,' Reverend Taylor replied. He'd arrived late and missed consoling the widow. 'Your pop was a good man.'

Paulie Brown leaned his elbows against the wooden rail. 'That's what they say.'

Taylor sensed anger. 'You know about the woman thing?'

'Doesn't everybody?'

Taylor crossed his arms. 'Poking some strange stuff every now and then doesn't make a man bad. We're *all* human. Don't blame your dad for what he did wrong. Praise him for what he did right.'

'We're not in church.'

'Didn't mean to offend, Brother,' Taylor replied. 'What religion do you practise?' The African outfit signified something.

'I follow the old ways ...'

Taylor nodded. This Brown was odd, nothing like the policeman.

'Who killed my daddy, Rev?' Paulie asked suddenly.

'Who?' Taylor seemed surprised.

'You were bustin' a hell of a move up front today. Like you know what happened out on the road.'

Taylor glanced around nervously. 'Your brother has the details,' he said. 'Why don't you ask him?'

'We don't exactly talk. I want you to tell me. Who's behind this?'

Taylor moved closer. 'I don't know.'

'Well who the fuck were you talkin' about today?'

'Calm down.'

'I want to know!'

'Have you *ever* been to church, Brother?'

'Yeah. Of course I have.'

'Then you know you can't place a literal interpretation on what a preacher says. I was being allegorical...'

'Bullshit!'

'Take it easy, my man.'

'You had no right!'

'Hey! Get it under control. What I said, I *meant*. It was not your daddy's time...'

'So who cut it short?'

'I said I don't *know*. I got my suspicions ... But I don't know.'

Paulie adjusted his hat. 'OK,' he said.

'Let's keep it together, Brother. We're on the same side.'

'Yeah.'

Taylor buttoned his coat and prepared to leave. 'I've got to be going. You can get back to your folks.'

Paulie didn't move.

'Please tell your mama that I was here. I'll call again when she's feeling better.'

'Yeah,' Paulie muttered, his head down.

The reverend walked off the porch towards his car. Suddenly, he turned. 'Brother Paul?'

Paulie raised his head.

'Vengeance is *mine*, sayeth the Lord. Remember that.' Then Taylor drifted out of the light, and left Paulie alone in the shadow of the house.

* * *

Frank Davis put his feet up on the cluttered desk in his mobile home, and kicked over his girlfriend's photo. The cheatin' whore wasn't returning his phone calls. Things had been rocky with the chunky brunette waitress for the past few months, and now the picture was clear: she was seeing someone else.

Davis popped a beer can and surveyed his domain. A two-bedroom trailer on lot 32 of the Greenhills mobile park, it was furnished with yard-sale rejects and West Virginia hand-me-downs. What a shit-hole. No wonder he couldn't keep a steady 'squeeze'.

By this time in life, he'd contemplated more. A real detached house, on a real detached lot. But on a patrol-man's salary, that couldn't be. And until he made the big score, this was where he'd stay.

Davis threw Donna's picture in the trash, and opened the Brown investigation file. It was the only thing at this point to take his mind off the two-bit reality of his life.

He was spitting out reports as fast as he could, turning them into the Lieutenant as soon as he came in from the field. That should keep the pump primed.

A cassette tape fell out of the folder. 'INTERVIEW WITH JACKIE FREY', it was labelled.

Davis placed it in his recorder and fast-forwarded. Then he hit play.

'Go over it again,' he heard himself say. 'What time did Mr Brown leave?'

'Just about dark,' Jackie answered. Her voice was weak, barely audible.

'Speak louder.'

96

'Dark.' Her voice level was the same.

'Which direction did he walk?'

'Don't know.'

'How drunk was he?'

'Don't know.'

'What sexual activities did you perform?'

Silence.

'I know you screwed him. Describe what happened.'

Silence.

'Jackie, I have a vagrancy charge just waiting to file against you. The only way to stop it is to get your damn mouth in gear. Now tell me about the sex!'

There was a blubbering sound on the tape, and Davis hit the stop button. 'Nigger bitch!' he snorted. Then he crumpled the beer can, popped another, and pulled a county road map out of his desk drawer.

'Quarry,' he said, tracing his finger along mountain road until he found the CAIN compound. Then he took a marking pen and circled several spots along the route west. Maybe Thomas Ruth did fuck up old man Brown, and maybe he didn't. Only him and the Lord knew for sure. But there was more than one way to get the bastard to talk. He'd tried one approach out at the quarry. Now it was time to try something else. Now it was time to improvise.

Sallie moved quietly in the darkness, trying not to awaken her bunkmates. It was 2 a.m., and the camp had slipped into silence. She eased open the screen door and stepped down into the street. Tomorrow was her last day. Her research was almost complete. It was time to wrap it up.

Sallie tiptoed beside the dorm and ducked behind a bush.

From there she had a clear shot of the administration building and parking lot. A pole lamp lit the scene with a cone of yellow light. She counted the cars in the lot: eight, all accounted for. Everyone was tucked in for the night.

Sallie kept low and walked towards the granite pit. She'd put most of the pieces together by now, but the weapons question was still open. She'd observed some strange activities down there the last few days: a van backed up to the shed several times. But she couldn't see what they were doing or why. Tonight she was going to try to find out.

The air was chilly, and the dew lay heavy on the grass. The sky was clear and moonless, the stars intense. There was just enough contrast for Sallie to discern the jagged blocks of stone that lay on either side of the path.

The story was partially outlined in Sallie's mind. The CAIN cult was destined for destruction. They talked peace and love, but that was just a cover. They were bigots at heart, bigots with a sinister leader, a sinister mission. They were dangerous as hell.

The path began to steepen, and Sallie knew she was close. The shed was at the end, in a flat area on the lip of the giant pit. Just beyond was a dizzying plunge into the quarry lake. Sallie slowed.

The outline of the shed suddenly emerged. Sallie stopped and listened. All was silent.

She took a step.

'Halt!' a voice ordered.

Sallie froze.

'Who's there?'

Sallie gulped. She'd been caught.

'Identify yourself!'

Sallie considered her options. None was any good. '*Me*,' she finally ventured. Maybe she could plead ignorance.

'*Sallie*?'

'Uh huh.' Her heart was palpitating.

'These cliffs are dangerous.'

Sallie suddenly recognized the measured cadence. 'Thomas Ruth?' She tried to sound calm.

'What are you doing out here?'

Sallie's instincts took over. 'I couldn't sleep, thought I'd take a walk...'

'Really?' Ruth sounded sceptical. 'You *know* that's forbidden.'

Sallie could now make out a human form on a rock outcropping above.

'I ... I forgot. Please don't be angry.' Sallie saw a hand reaching down. She grabbed it, and Ruth pulled her up.

'Careful,' he said, 'a fall could be fatal.'

She made it, and soon she was beside Ruth on a narrow ledge of stone extending over the lake.

'You really should not be out here.' Ruth sat and wrapped his arms around his knees.

'Sorry. I couldn't sleep.'

'I couldn't sleep either.'

Sallie sensed sadness. 'No?'

Ruth didn't reply.

Sallie studied him in the starlight. He was still an enigma. Stand-offish and private, everything about him was a contradiction. There was no vacant stare in those bright blue eyes. The man had depth. He'd obviously seen a lot in his life, done a lot. But what?

They sat in silence for several moments.

'Peaceful, isn't it?' Sallie finally said. As long as she was here, she might as well be a reporter.

'Peaceful,' Ruth repeated.

Sallie held her breath. It *was* silent up here. There were no creatures chattering, no wind sounds, no sounds at all. She could almost hear her heart thumping. 'Can I ask you something?'

'Ask.'

'Why were the police here?' There had never been an official announcement, only rumours about 'trouble'.

'It's ... nothing, a misunderstanding.'

'Want to talk about it?'

'No.'

'I could help you resolve it.' Her tone was silky. The sex lure was out.

'The *Lord* is my shepherd.' His hands still gripped his knees.

'*I'm* a good listener too.' That was more throaty, more sensual.

Ruth didn't stir.

Sallie gritted her teeth. The man was dead below the waist. She decided to try again. 'Tell me what you want. I'm *very* flexible...'

She touched his back. The muscles were tense, taut.

'*Don't*,' Ruth said.

Sallie quickly withdrew her hand. Three strikes, that was it. Time to switch to religion. 'When did you receive your calling, Thomas Ruth?'

'My calling...' His words drifted over the ledge.

'To establish your church.' Sallie's 'background' file was blank. The group had sprung out of nowhere.

100

'The Lord spoke to me.'

'When?'

'In a dream...'

'What did he say?'

'To strike out in the wilderness like the tribe of Israel, to seek out evil...' His voice dropped off.

Sallie waited, but the master had stopped. 'Where did you get the money?' The Lord might have told him what to do, but the cash came from humans.

Ruth's body suddenly went rigid and he lowered his arms. 'Who *are* you, Sallie?'

Sallie's heart began to race. Shit! She'd just committed journalistic suicide: one question too many. 'Who?' she asked shakily.

'You're *not* a believer!' Ruth was out of his 'trance'.

'I believe.'

'Your eyes betrayed you in the valley of death. You do *not* believe.'

'I was afraid.'

'Why are you asking questions, sneaking around? Why are you *here*?' Ruth's voice was threatening.

Sallie tried to stay cool. This was an unexpected turn. 'I want to be part of CAIN.'

'No, you *don't*! You have another reason for being here. What is it?'

Sallie tried to stand up. 'No. I told you. I want to follow CAIN.' She felt for the edge of the rock with her toe.

Ruth seized her arm. 'Where are you going?'

Sallie tried to twist away, but the grip was like iron. 'Back ... Back to my cabin.' She was still twisting like crazy.

Ruth held firm. 'Have you ever been *baptized*, Sallie?'

101

Her heart did a cartwheel. 'Uhhhh!' she screamed. The closest water was three hundred feet below.

'God washes away sin!' Ruth pulled her towards the precipice.

Sallie fell back, kicking with both feet. That forced Ruth to release her arm. She rolled across the ledge and leaped down to the trail. Then she took off through the rocks.

'Sallie!' Ruth called from the darkness.

She froze mid-step.

'I'm *talking* to you, Sallie!'

She held her breath.

'Goodnight!'

Sallie gasped and ran down the path at full speed, bouncing off stone walls, slipping, falling. Ruth was a psycho. A mysterious, *dangerous*, psycho. He'd psyched out her intent and almost dumped her in the lake. To hell with leaving tomorrow. She was escaping this loony bin tonight!

CHAPTER 6

A strategy session convened at 7.00 a.m. sharp at the State's Attorney's office. After the fireworks at the funeral, Gardner wanted to assess the status of the Brown case. Present were Gardner, Jennifer, Lieutenant Harvis, and Officer Bobbie Thompson, a black cop who patrolled Blocktown. Gardner stood by the drawing board, readying his chalk.

'Before you get started,' Lieutenant Harvis said, 'you need to know something. There's been a new development.' He handed Gardner the latest Davis report. 'Frank's located a possible suspect.'

Gardner scanned the four page document. 'Ruth?'

'That's the name he goes by,' the Lieutenant replied.

Gardner walked back to the conference table, sat down, and read the report more carefully. Then he passed it to Jennifer.

'This is mostly speculation,' he said. 'I don't see any direct tie-in to Joseph Brown.'

The Lieutenant withdrew another report from his folder. 'There's more.' He shoved it across the polished mahogany. 'Frank confirmed the purchase of shotguns, long guns,

103

ammo, and a whole lot of rope from the Dixie Hardware Mart. All signed for and paid for in cash by one "Thomas Ruth".'

Gardner scratched his ear. 'I still don't see the *connection*, the tie-in to Joseph's death.'

Harvis laughed. 'You're making a joke, right?'

'No.'

'*Rope*? Tie-in?'

Gardner got the picture. 'Jeez, Harv ...'

'We got a group of flaming holy-rollers, *all-white* holy rollers, stocking up on weapons and *rope*. A weirdo priest with a cellular phone, an attitude problem, and no alibi, and a secret hide-out that just happens to back up to the spot the old man died. In *my* book that's a connection...'

'It's still speculation,' Jennifer interjected. She'd just finished reading the report. She looked at Gardner.

'She's right,' Gardner said. 'There's no direct evidence of any kind, as far as I can see, that ties, uh, connects this Ruth person to Brown. No witnesses, no physical evidence. And there's no *medical* confirmation that the heart attack was somehow induced.'

'So what are you saying?'

Gardner stood and returned to the chalk board. 'I'm *saying* we still have nothing as far as launching a prosecution is concerned. Suspicion? Yes. Speculation? Yes. But the level of proof we have so far doesn't even reach probable cause. Davis said that himself. In his report.'

'So we hang it up?' Harvis looked disappointed.

'No. You keep investigating...'

Harvis sensed a 'but' coming.

'But you have to, uh, *we* have to keep security tight. If the word gets out who we're looking at, there could be trouble. You saw the emotion at the funeral. We could get a real nasty backlash out of this.' He turned to Officer Thompson. 'What's happening in Blocktown, Bobbie?'

'Quiet now,' Bobbie said. 'They had a meeting at the church about 6 p.m. ... Broke up about eight.'

'Taylor's church?'

'Yes, sir.' Bobbie had been on the force for nine years. He was tall and thin, and well-liked by other officers and the community. In Blocktown they'd nicknamed him 'the whip'.

'Any idea what went on at the meeting?' Gardner wrote 'TAYLOR' on the board.

'No, sir. I was patrolling.'

'Any activity *after* the meeting?'

'Taylor and about ten others hung around in the parking lot talking. The rest went on home.'

'Bobbie,' Gardner said solemnly, 'I want you to be brutally honest. You know Blocktown. What's the mood out there?'

The officer shook his head slowly. 'Tense,' he said. 'Never seen it quite like this. They're setting up a neighbourhood "watch" programme and buying guns.'

'Guns? What kind of guns?'

'Handguns.'

Gardner grimaced. That was great. 'Where are they getting them?'

'The church. Taylor's hawking them out of his basement.'

'*Taylor*? The preacher?'

'That's what I understand.'

'Is that legal?' Jennifer asked.

Gardner leaned against the chalk board. 'It sure as hell *isn't*.' He looked at Bobbie. 'Where are the guns now?'

'People already bought 'em as far as I know.'

'So the deed is done?'

Bobbie nodded.

Gardner slapped chalk off his arm. 'That makes it tough. If we make an issue of it, it'll look like *we're* the bad guys, that we don't want them to protect themselves.' They were boxed in. 'Have you heard any rumours?' he asked Bobbie. 'Anything about who *they* think might have killed Joseph?'

'No. All I heard was that they think he got, uh, kinda *lynched* by somebody. Haven't heard any names mentioned.'

'Do they think it was a racial attack?'

Bobbie looked down. The county thrived on racial harmony. Everybody got along great.

'Bobbie?'

'Yeah,' he said. 'That *does* seem to be the attitude.'

Gardner crossed his arms. So that was *it*: supposition on speculation on innuendo on rumour, and they had a potential race riot on their hands. This was *bad*.

Gardner turned to Lieutenant Harvis again. 'So Davis got nothing out of Ruth. Nothing at all?'

'Correct. He was evasive as hell, impossible to interrogate.'

'What about a background check? You ran one, right?'

'*Attempted* is a better word. We ran name checks, social security checks, driver's licence checks, the whole ball of wax.' He opened another folder. 'Thomas, no middle name Ruth, birthdate unknown, current address: 8890 Quarry Road, current telephone number: 599–6664, prior address: unknown, prior employment: unknown, prior everything: unknown.' Harvis shut the folder.

'What about fingerprints? Did you run his prints through the computer?'

Harvis frowned.

'Frank *did* ask Ruth to submit to a print check...'

Harvis twisted in his seat. 'No.'

'No? Why not?'

'Because it's not *normal* procedure. We usually get identification information through other channels ... didn't think we'd have this much trouble. Frank was not directed to get prints.'

'So we don't know who this character is, and we don't have fingerprints so we can find out?'

Harvis nodded.

'They could go back and get them,' Jennifer suggested.

'He'd refuse,' Gardner replied. 'Judging by his attitude he'll stonewall any further investigation. Without a warrant or formal charge we have no authority to force him to submit to fingerprinting...'

'They can always *try*,' Jennifer persisted.

Gardner walked from the board, and sat down at the table. 'No,' he finally said. 'We have to figure another way.'

'I told Frank to do what it takes,' Harvis declared suddenly. 'I told him to keep on Ruth till he got something.'

'Great move, Harv,' Gardner said sarcastically.

The Lieutenant frowned.

'Giving Davis a blank cheque could be dangerous.'

'You have a better idea?'

'Put someone *else* on it.'

'No. Frank's gonna come through. You'll see.'

'Watch him, Harv,' Gardner replied. 'Watch him like a goddamn hawk.'

The meeting continued for another twenty minutes, then broke up. The only conclusion they were able to draw was that they were on a tightrope. At one end was truth, the other, logic. Below was chaos.

Gardner and Jennifer sat alone at the table. 'This is a lot worse than I thought,' Jennifer said.

'You noticed.'

'I understand what you meant last night about how riots start. It *could* get ugly.'

Gardner nodded.

'We can get through this.' She touched his hand.

Gardner perked up. Maybe the storm was over. Maybe Jennifer had backed off the hard line. '*We* can,' he said.

Jennifer read his mind. 'You're not off the hook,' she warned. 'Don't misinterpret the show of support.'

Gardner smiled and kissed her cheek. She *really* didn't mean it.

Brownie raised his head from his lab table and rubbed his eyes. Then he checked his watch: 8.15 a.m. He must have dozed off after coming back here early this morning. His neck hurt, his stomach gurgled, and his eyes were crusted. He was a mess.

Brownie packed up his papers and put them in his desk drawer. Just then the door opened.

'Brownie!' It was Lieutenant Harvis. 'What the hell are you doing here?'

'I work here.'

'I told you to take time off.'

'Didn't know it was an order.'

'It wasn't an order. It was a *suggestion*.'

'Then I respectfully decline.'

Harvis hesitated, rubbing a sheet of paper between his fingers. 'I just came from the State's Attorney's office. We've been going over your father's, uh, case . . .' His eyes became apologetic.

'You still planning to leave *Davis* in charge?'

'Yeah. 'Fraid so.'

Brownie's eyes narrowed.

'But in the meantime . . .' He handed Brownie the paper. 'Sorry I have to do this, Brownie. You are officially relieved of *any* involvement with the case whatsoever.'

Brownie read the document, then he folded it sharply.

'We have to avoid even the *appearance* of impropriety here, please understand.'

Brownie crossed his arms like a Russian Bear. 'The directive says "formal" involvement. What about *informal*?'

'*No* involvement,' Harvis replied. 'This is to protect *you*, in case things heat up.'

'You mean in case I decide to go out and roust the *suspects*.'

Harvis frowned. The Davis report was supposed to be an internal memo, confidential. Not even Brownie was supposed to know about it.

'You've seen the report?'

'Yeah.' Brownie had a lot of friends in the department:

109

clerks, cops, secretaries. Nothing escaped him.

'Then you know what I'm talking about. You're the *last* person who should go anywhere near the quarry. This thing is a powder keg, and you're the match.'

'I take it this isn't a *suggestion*.'

'No. This is an *order*.'

Brownie did not respond.

'This you *cannot* respectfully decline. You don't have to take leave, but you are totally, and absolutely off the case. Understood?'

Brownie remained silent.

'An *order*,' Harvis pointed his finger in Brownie's face. Then he left the room.

Brownie did a slow burn after Harvis left. Then he picked up his phone and dialled.

'Tony Bellini.'

'Doc, this is Joe Brown.'

'Sergeant.' There was sympathy in his voice.

'I was checking on the autopsy report. Haven't received it yet.'

'Still in processing. It's done, but our typists are backed up. Should be out in a day or two.'

'What about the print test? Is that going to be attached?'

Bellini cleared his throat. 'I was meaning to ask you about that when I gave you the results the other day. I still haven't inked the form to indicate the test was performed. What do you want me to do? As I told you, the test was *negative* for fingerprints.'

'But there were some other marks,' Brownie said.

'Yes. They show up in the photos real well. My guess is

that there was contamination that caused the spray to react. There were no corresponding cuts or abrasions on the neck that I could tell.'

'I want to see the photos.'

'Fine. Do you want that included with the autopsy packet or separate? It's your call.'

Brownie thought for a moment. The autopsy report would go straight to Davis and then to the Lieutenant. 'Send the print report and the pictures to me, uh, at my home. And don't itemize them on the autopsy file.'

'Done,' Bellini said. 'Uh, any progress with the investigation?'

'No,' Brownie replied. 'Not at the moment. But there will be soon.'

Sallie Allen was in a motel room on the Pennsylvania Interstate. Her laptop was set up on the small desk, and her fax-phone was plugged into the wall jack. She was clicking away on the keys, roughing out her story.

Last night had been hell. After the scene with Ruth, she'd wasted no time getting out. She retrieved her notepad and tape recorder from her cabin and raced for the gate, envisioning her head being stuffed in the rattler barrel the whole way. When she reached the entrance, she found it locked. Then she saw headlights approaching from the compound. She scrambled into the bushes, cutting up her legs. The car took a turn by the gate, then bounced down a dirt road paralleling the south fence. They were looking for her!

Sallie ran to the wire, and started to climb, gasping and clawing her way to the top. She threw her leg over the barbs in time to see the headlights coming back. Then she flung herself off the other side, hitting the ground hard, rolling, and running for the woods.

The rest of the night she intermittently ran and rested, putting as much distance between herself and the quarry as she could. Ruth had really scared her. His alluring exterior was deceiving. Underneath that blond fluff he was as venomous as his snakes.

By dawn, she was finally able to make it to town. Thanks to a grizzled farmer in a flat-top truck she caught a lift to an auto rental shop and picked up a car. And now, here she was, fifty miles away, scared, and nervous, and tired. Piecing together her masterpiece.

Beside the word-processor lay a police teletype, faxed in from New York. Sallie had phoned her publisher and asked them to check any police activity involving CAIN. The news blackout at the quarry had kept her in the dark as to the mystery beyond the fence. And now it was clear: there was a suspicious death incident under investigation. The details were spare, but it filled her blanks. A black man had died and the cops were checking it out. Ruth and CAIN *had* to be involved.

Sallie played her keys '...HE SPEAKS OF LOVE AND THE WORD OF GOD, BUT HIS HEART IS EVIL' ... 'HIS SUBJECTS FOLLOW AND OBEY, MESMERIZED BY HIS POWER AND HIS CHARM...'

Just then the phone rang. Sallie clamped it against her neck.

'Yeah?' Her hands were busy.

'How's it going?' It was her editor, Phyllis Downs.

'In progress.'

'How soon can we get copy?'

Sallie hit the enter key and jumped to a new paragraph. 'Today. This afternoon.'

'Good. Staff might give you the cover if it's up to snuff.'

Sallie stopped typing. 'Cover story?' That was a huge step up for her. She was usually filler.

'Make it good, and we'll see.'

Sallie smiled and rubbed a sore spot on her knee. 'Get the artwork ready,' she said. 'This one's a doozy.'

'Can't wait.'

Sallie hung up the phone, and went back to her keys. The words and images were flowing fast, and she could hardly keep up with herself. Her first cover! It was a dynamite piece, a blockbuster. This was a story that no one would ever forget.

Paulie Brown stood in the backyard of his aunt's house and looked across the Blocktown valley. He had Brownie's wide face and heavyset muscular physique. But light years separated their souls.

Paulie had abandoned his surname and hometown long ago. He had adopted the Africanized 'Katanga', and moved to Washington DC where he worked at a drug rehabilitation centre in a run-down ward. He dressed tribally and read revisionist history. And he distrusted white people big time.

'What you doin', Paulie?' his aunt asked. She'd never gotten used to the name change.

'Looking at your town, Aunt Gladys.' His mother's

youngest sister was his favourite relative. Slim and bespec-
tacled, she was a devout, kind-hearted woman. And her
cooking was superb.

'Thinkin' about Daddy?'

Paulie turned. 'Yeah...' He and Joseph had had a rocky
relationship too, over a cloud of issues. But Joseph was
blood, and his passing hit hard.

'I wish you and Joseph junior had done better,' she said
sadly.

'Don't start on that.'

'You are *brothers*.'

Katanga smirked.

'You need to talk,' Gladys suggested.

'No, we don't.'

Gladys put her hand on his thick arm. 'Daddy hated
this thing with you two. Could never understand what
happened...'

Katanga stared into her eyes. 'Yes, he *did*.'

'Can't you let it go? *Now*? After all this time? As a
tribute to Daddy?'

'My Daddy is *dead*. Killed. Snuffed. Drive-byed. Iced
... Haven't you heard?'

'Don't listen to Reverend Taylor. He's a troublemaker.'

'Yeah?'

'He's been riling things up since he come out here.
Daddy didn't think much of him. Refused to join his
church.'

'Yeah?' Strange how he was the keynote speaker at the
service.

'We got to move on,' Gladys said. 'Start puttin' things
back together. Stop talkin' nonsense.'

'You people amaze me,' Katanga replied. 'You live on the slave plantation, and you still have a slave mentality!'

'Don't talk that way.'

'Why don't you wake up? Why don't you see what is really happening to your lives? Why do you keep making excuses for yourselves?'

Gladys shook her head. 'Please, Paulie ...'

'Daddy is dead because *someone* killed him. Some white-skinned slave master ...'

'Please,' Gladys begged. 'That's not true. It was his poor old heart!'

'It might'a been his heart, but *someone* helped it along.'

'No ...'

'And *you* and your God-loving brother this, and sister that, deny it. You accept what the man dishes out like you always have. A hundred years, and nothing's changed!'

'Paulie ...' Her voice was trembling.

'But *I* don't have to accept it!'

Gladys put her arms around her nephew and held him.

'I'll *never* accept it!'

'Please, Paulie.'

'*Never*!'

'Don't do nothin',' Gladys whispered. 'Please ...'

But Katanga ignored her. He was looking towards the meadow and the woods, north, where two miles distant there was a giant gash in the earth enclosed by a stretch of metal fence.

Thomas Ruth was agitated. Sallie's defection had set the camp on edge. He'd been warned about intruders, spies in their midst, but this one had slipped through despite the screening procedure. He'd suspected Sallie earlier, but her willingness to walk the valley had temporarily convinced him she was OK. And then she was seen poking around in places she had no business in. Whether she was a cop, private investigator, or something else, it really didn't matter. There was *nothing* in the quarry to see. He'd made sure of that. Whatever Sallie was up to would not pan out. They were *clean* from top to bottom. But the deception still bothered him.

Ruth unlocked the gate and drove out of the compound. It was late afternoon, not exactly the best time, but he had to get out and make contact, explain the situation.

He turned right and headed west, towards the retreating sun. The sharp rays hurt his eyes, despite his dark glasses, and he slapped the visor down to block them. His head was pounding again. After another no-sleep night and a half-dozen extra pills, his brain still felt like it was on fire. Thanks to Sallie, no doubt. He'd only tried to scare her up on the ledge, shake her up a little, teach her a lesson. He'd never have thrown her over the edge. That wasn't his style. But she'd still got to him, got inside his throbbing skull.

Ruth continued driving, checking his rear-view for traffic. The cut-off was a half-mile up, and he didn't want anyone to see him make the turn. He slowed through a tunnel of overhanging maple trees, cutting past the dancing shadows that the leaves made as they swayed in the wind. For a second, he flashed back to a scene a life ago. He felt panic in his throat, saw muddy boots, heard voices. Ruth swallowed and the car came out of the trees. He took several deep breaths and tried to stabilize. His head was still pounding.

The turn-off was just ahead. Ruth checked the mirror again. 'Shit.' There was a car coming up behind him. He slowed to let it pass, not wanting to overrun his secret road.

The car kept coming but didn't move over to the other lane.

'Pass,' Ruth said.

But the car slowed and pulled up close behind.

'Shit!' Ruth repeated.

The car was very close now, almost on his bumper. Close enough for Ruth to see the blue-and-red bubble lamp spinning angrily on its dashboard.

CHAPTER 7

Attorney Kent King removed a financial ledger from his office desk, flipped it open, and examined the last two months' billings. Client names and case numbers filled the left-hand margin, and retainer balances were recorded in a column on the right. He ran his finger down the page, to the current status of his income account. A hefty five-digit cash available figure lay on the bottom line.

King smiled and shut the book. Business was good, and fees were at an all-time high. He could coast a while if he wanted to, or take a sabbatical. There was no pressure to keep rooting clients out of the county's underworld.

King was a predatory litigator, the wild man of the local bar. Tall, darkly handsome, and well built, he had a penchant for sports cars and designer suits. And he was constantly searching for the ultimate 'gotcha' against Gardner Lawson. King had risen from the Baltimore slums, and Lawson had been born to privilege. King was 'street', and Lawson was 'country club'. King defended 'evil', and Lawson represented 'good'. And that made them book-ends from Hell.

The intercom buzzed, and King depressed the lever. 'Yeah?'

'You have a visitor,' his secretary said.

King glanced at his appointment book. No clients listed this morning. He was scheduled to play golf in about twenty minutes. 'Who is it?' he asked.

'A Mister Thomas Ruth.'

King rubbed his chin. He'd heard about Ruth through his information highway, the defence attorney scuttle-but channel. 'Send the gentleman in,' he said.

The door opened and Thomas Ruth entered. He was dressed in a black shirt and pants. His face was grim.

King shook hands and pointed to a chair.

Ruth sat down. 'Thanks for seeing me without an appointment,' he said softly.

'No problem. I'm glad you came in. How can I be of service?'

Ruth leaned forward. 'I need advice.'

'I'm in the advice business,' King replied. 'Would this be about a man found dead on a country road?' He knew about the investigation and all its implications.

'I'm not involved in that,' Ruth protested.

King eyed him sceptically. Criminals sat there every day and declared their innocence. 'I'm not a judgemental person, Mr Ruth. I don't give a damn if you were, or you were not. It makes no difference to me. I'll defend you either way...'

'CAIN, uh, my church, Church of the Ark, is a peaceful, law-abiding organization. But...'

King cocked his head.

'Someone else may have committed the crime, someone

120

outside of CAIN, without my knowledge or approval...'

'Hold it,' King interrupted. 'You are either involved in these activities or you're not. Which is it?'

'I have done nothing...'

'But?'

'But I might know who did.'

King picked up a pen. 'You might know or you do know?'

Ruth leaned back. 'Might know.'

'And did you facilitate the activities in any way? Did you aid them or abet them?'

'No.'

King made a note.

'What if someone was killed, uh, and what if I knew about it? Does that make me criminally responsible?'

'I cannot respond to generalities, Mr Ruth. You have to spell it out for me. Who got killed and who did the killing?'

Ruth looked down.

'You have to tell me if you want my help.'

Ruth reached into his pocket and pulled out a small plastic bottle. He opened the cap, and popped something into his mouth. King tried to read the label, but it went back into the pocket too fast.

Ruth took several deep breaths and closed his eyes.

'You OK?' King asked. He didn't look well.

'Hypertension,' Ruth said. 'Sorry. Uh, I have another problem. Another legal problem.'

King stared across his desk. 'What about the one we've been discussing?'

'I can't tell you any more about it. All I can say

is that I would never kill anyone. I detest killing. I was afraid that I might be held accountable just by knowing.'

'If you took no action to aid and abet, and you have disassociated yourself from the criminal enterprise, you're in the clear. Mere knowledge of a felony is not a crime. But if you did more than know, if you conspired in some way to make it happen, you're as guilty as the actual perpetrator.'

Ruth listened silently.

'That's all I can advise under the circumstances. Unless you tell me more, I'll have to leave it there. I don't deal in hypotheticals. I deal in reality.'

'I understand.'

'What's the other problem?'

Ruth didn't answer.

'The other problem?' King's tee time was approaching.

'My life has been threatened.'

'By whom?'

'A police officer.'

King's eyebrows arched. 'County police?'

'Yes.'

'What exactly did he do?'

'Pulled my car over; cursed me; harassed me; said I'd committed a crime; said I'd be executed for it...'

King jotted more notes. 'When and where did this take place?'

'The past few days. On Mountain Road.'

'Anyone witness this?'

'I don't think so. The area's isolated. Can you make him stop?'

King smiled. 'Absolutely. I can file a restraining order

requiring the officer to cease and desist all contact with you unless he lodges a formal criminal complaint.'

Ruth closed his eyes and put his hand over his face.

'Mr Ruth?' He didn't seem to be listening.

The hand came down, but the eyes stayed closed.

'With an emergency petition in civil court I can obtain a hearing in a couple of days. The judge will get him off your back.'

Ruth opened his eyes and nodded in slow motion.

'This doesn't mean they'll quit,' King warned. 'They could still come at you with another cop. But this particular officer will have to leave you alone.'

Ruth gazed towards the ceiling. 'And the Red Sea parted and swallowed the chariots...'

'Huh?' King didn't follow.

'And the waters consumed Pharaoh's men...'

King finally got it. 'At least one of Pharaoh's men, anyway.' He wrote 'RESTRAINING ORDER PETITION' on his pad.

Ruth began to stand up.

'Hold on,' King said. 'I still need information.'

Ruth wavered on his feet. His forehead was perspiring.

'Got to get some air.'

'OK,' King answered, 'one second. I have an additional question, then you can take a breather.'

Ruth steadied himself against the chair.

King looked him in the eye. 'I need to know the officer's name.'

Jennifer raced into Gardner's office and threw a magazine on his desk. It was midday, and she'd left for lunch at

Russel's ten minutes ago. But now she was back, red-faced and huffing. 'Look,' she gasped.

Gardner put down his dictaphone and picked up the magazine. It was folded open to the centre, but he recognized its format: *Interview*, an exposé-type glossy with worldwide circulation. There was a picture of the granite quarry, and a bold-type headline: 'THE RISE OF CAIN'.

Gardner looked at Jennifer. 'What is this?'

'Read it,' she replied, sitting down to catch her breath.

'A remote county in western Maryland is the setting for a most profound tragedy,' Gardner quoted. 'In that pristine locale, a smooth-talking hate salesman named Thomas Ruth is purveying the latest in lunatic fringes: THE CHURCH OF THE ARK, INCORPORATED. This so-called religious organization, which goes by the sinister acronym CAIN, is secluded in a granite fortress, plotting acts of terror...'

Gardner looked up. 'Christ.'

'Keep going. It gets worse.'

'The preacher uses the Bible to conceal his true intent. He talks of faith and love within the compound fence, but across town, in the African-American community, a man lies dead. Tied up and tortured, the elderly gentleman's heart gave out. Sources say CAIN was involved, but they will neither confirm nor deny to what extent...'

'Jesus Christ!' Gardner couldn't believe it. This was a disaster.

'Keep reading,' Jennifer said.

'CAIN draws its followers from society's inventory of throwaway lives. To ensure their loyalty and commitment, Thomas Ruth forces them to walk barefoot through a pit of

124

rattlesnakes...' Gardner put the magazine down. 'How in God's name did this happen?'

'Undercover reporter.'

Gardner turned the page.

Jennifer pointed to a boxed-in segment. '*Sallie Allen, Investigative Daredevil,*' it said. '*She Goes Anywhere for a Story.*' There was a picture of Sallie in the cockpit of a jet fighter.

'Reporters,' Gardner groaned. His hatred of the fourth estate was legendary. They always screwed up the facts.

'Read the rest,' Jennifer advised. 'They even mention us.'

Gardner scanned the remainder of the article. 'The county police and State's Attorney's office have been powerless to stop the spread of CAIN. A spokesperson for the prosecutor would only say the matter is under investigation.' Gardner let the magazine flop down. 'Spokesperson? We don't even have a spokesperson!'

'No kidding.'

'This is awful...' Gardner wrung his hands. 'What a fucked-up mess.'

'You have to do something,' Jennifer said.

'Do what? Manufacture evidence? We still don't have anything concrete on anybody, much less Ruth!'

'What about this?' Jennifer pointed to the article.

'What about it? It's nothing but hype, media BS. There isn't a straight fact in the whole damn piece.'

'You could convene the Grand Jury; summons the reporter; try to build a conspiracy case...'

'No way. Their first amendment lawyers wouldn't let her near the place. Protected sources, all that bullshit...'

The phone rang, and Gardner picked it up. 'Lawson.' His face paled, and he made some notes. 'Uh huh. Uh huh. OK.'

Jennifer tried to read the words upside down, but couldn't.

Gardner hung up. 'That was Harvis. Someone just used the CAIN sign at the quarry for target practice.'

'Do they know who did it?'

'There's more guns in Blocktown right now than there are in the Armoury. Take your pick.'

'Anyone hurt?'

'No. Not at the moment.'

'You have to do something, Gard, and you have to do it now.'

'Thanks a lot Sallie!' Gardner threw the magazine on the floor.

'No use blaming her now,' Jennifer said. 'It's too late.'

'Yeah. You got that right. Too damn late.'

'So what's it going to be? What's your decision?'

Gardner started to reply but stopped. The escalation they'd feared had begun. The first shots were off the mark, but the next ones could be fatal.

'Well?' Jennifer was waiting.

'We'll do it,' he said.

'Do what?'

'We have no choice now. With or without evidence, we have to remove one factor from the equation to defuse the bomb. We have to bring in Thomas Ruth.'

Brownie rubbed his eyes and stared at the top of his lab table. It was 2 p.m., and he'd been in a fog all day. Last night had been rough. Exhausted as he was, he couldn't sleep. He'd wrestled his pillow well into the morning, then drifted into a half-conscious state of fragmented dreams. His pillow was soaked when he arose, and his head ached. And he was more exhausted than ever.

Brownie examined the stack of files on his workspace that he'd bootlegged from other cops. The Ruth investigation was off-limits, the Lieutenant said. But there were ways around that. His buddies had loaned him their case files. That would keep him up to speed until he made his next move.

A copy of *Interview Magazine* lay next to the files. Brownie picked it up and re-read the CAIN article. He'd circled several words in red ink, and he reviewed them again: 'HATE', and 'RATTLESNAKES'. He studied the page, then turned to the author's insert. Something was wrong here. The woman was billed as an investigator, but her investigation was all conclusion. Where were the facts? Where was the smoking gun? The puff piece on Sallie Allen was as lengthy as the story itself. She was part of the story, and that made the whole process suspect.

Brownie studied the text. The only meat in the entire piece was her description of the snake-walk through the valley of death. *'The rattlers are kept in a wooden barrel,'* Brownie read. *'They are released on the floor, and arrayed in two rows. The initiate is then required to walk through the squirming mass while the congregation chants in the background...'*

Brownie dropped the magazine. The words had triggered a memory.

* * *

'Daddy, look at this,' Brownie called from the backyard. It was late summer, and he was out trimming weeds along the back fence. That's when he saw it, wrapped around the wire.

'Daddy!' he called, grabbing it behind the head and wrestling it off the rusted strand.

'What is it, Joe?' Daddy ambled out to the porch, newspaper in hand.

Brownie held his arm behind his back and walked towards the house. 'Got something for you,' he teased.

Joseph raised his reading glasses. 'What do you have, son?'

'This!' Brownie laughed and whipped his arm forward. There was a three-foot black snake wrapped around it.

'Joe!' Daddy screamed. He fell backward, and almost hit his head on the post. 'Joe!' His eyes were white, his feet jumping.

'What's wrong, Daddy?' Brownie hadn't expected this.

'Get it out-a here! Out-a here!' Joseph barricaded himself behind a chair. 'Out-a here, Joe!'

Brownie backed away, and tried to untangle the beast from his arm. Daddy covered his eyes. 'Hurry!' he yelled. 'Hurry!'

'I'm hurrying,' Brownie said, opening the back gate and running down towards the stream. He finally got it off when he reached the water. And there he bashed its little arrow-shaped head in with a rock.

'Don't ever, ever, ever, do that again, Joe.' Daddy said later. He was still nervous, shaky.

'I won't, Daddy,' Brownie promised. He hadn't meant

any harm. Daddy had never mentioned being scared of anything.

'Just something I have,' Daddy explained.

'I understand,' Brownie said. And he never did it again.

Brownie suddenly came to and leaped up from his chair.

'Shit!' he yelled. 'Oh shit!' He rifled his briefcase and yanked out a folder. It was the autopsy print results, delivered yesterday. He'd reviewed the photos, and grudgingly accepted Bellini's conclusion that the marks on Daddy's neck must have come from a chemical reaction of some kind. There were no injuries to the neck whatsoever. None. The marks that showed up under the ultraviolet light were just a freak anomaly, of no real significance.

Brownie hurriedly removed one of the black-light photos. Joseph's head was barely visible in the darkened print, but his neck area was clearly outlined in white. Brownie tried to remain calm, detached. This was not his father, it was another case.

He squinted and raised the photo. Across Joseph's neck was a clear pattern of criss-crossed lines. He grabbed his magnifier and adjusted the focus.

The lines enhanced under the lens. They were uniform in length, about an inch to an inch and a half each. Brownie studied them carefully, moving left to right. Suddenly, he stopped. In the lower portion of the neck, four lines intersected, forming a box. Brownie sketched the image on his pad. Then he sketched an identical one next to it, and another, and another, until he'd created a chain.

Brownie gasped when he realized what he'd drawn. 'My

God, no!' Brownie stared at his sketch. Daddy did die of a heart attack, no doubt about it. But it wasn't a natural event. Something had caused it. Brownie circled the word 'snake' again in the article. Oils from its skin must have triggered the chemical reaction. That's what left the marks!

Brownie stood up on shaky legs. It was finally clear. He knew what had happened to Joseph. He grabbed his jacket and rushed for the door. Brownie knew what had happened. And now he knew what he had to do about it.

'Reverend Taylor!' Mrs Driver called.

The reverend pressed his brake and slowed the car. A woman in a lemon-coloured derby was flagging him down. He waved back and pulled into the parking lot of the Blocktown pharmacy.

He lowered his window, and she thrust herself forward.

'Gotta talk to you,' she said hurriedly. There was a copy of *Interview Magazine* in her hand.

'I saw it,' Taylor said. He looked worried, tense.

'You need to have a council meeting. There was a shooting out at the quarry today just after that story came out. I've been trying to reach you...'

'Sorry. I was busy.'

'This is serious,' she continued. 'You got everyone carrying guns, and now they're using them. The children are scared to go outside, and the old folks are locked in their room...'

'I'll take care of it,' Taylor said. He wasn't wearing his usual suit. He was dressed in overalls and a leather jacket.

'Please call a meeting.'

'I will. Don't have time to do it right now, but I will.'

Mrs Driver checked to make sure she'd stopped the right car. This didn't sound like the take-charge Taylor she knew, didn't look like him either. This man was preoccupied.

'When?' she persisted.

Taylor looked at his watch. It was 3 p.m. 'Tonight, maybe. Possibly tomorrow. I'll have to let you know.'

'The devil is roaming free out there,' Mrs Driver said. 'I don't think we can wait.'

'We'll have to,' the reverend replied. 'Right now I got something to do.' He nodded politely and raised his window. Then he pegged the accelerator, and roared off down the road.

Frank Davis adjusted his radio receiver. 'Say again, dispatch. Your transmission was garbled.' He was behind the ridge at the north end of the county, not the best spot for reception.

'The chief has just issued a pick-up order on Thomas Ruth.'

Davis turned the volume all the way up. 'Has a warrant been issued?'

'No warrant. Detain for questioning.'

Davis spun his car around and headed down the hill. He'd been looking for Ruth all day, but the bastard had somehow eluded him. Now he was official 'meat', and he was nowhere in sight.

Davis checked his map as he drove south. Ruth had been a no-show all day at his usual haunts. His car had left the quarry and hadn't returned. That much he knew.

The sky was a deep grey now, and the clouds looked like

icebergs in an arctic sea, glinting on the horizon. Davis increased his speed. It would be night soon, and he had a stop to make. Thomas Ruth was up for grabs. And Davis had to get to him first.

'Where is Thomas Ruth?' a follower asked. The CAIN congregation was assembled under the tin roof of the shed for a 9 p.m. prayer meeting, but the leader wasn't there. Two men approached the platform. But neither was Thomas Ruth.

'I have an announcement,' Nicholas Fairborne said, mounting the dais.

The flock came to attention.

'The meeting for tonight is cancelled.'

A moan drifted up from the gallery.

'Please return to your dorms.'

The followers stood and filed out, leaving Fairborne alone with the other man.

'Why didn't you tell them?' the man asked.

'No need to cause alarm at this stage,' Fairborne replied.

'What happened between you two earlier?'

'What?'

'I thought I heard Thomas yelling. Were you having a disagreement?'

Fairborne looked over his shoulder. 'No.'

'Sure sounded like it.'

Fairborne shook his head. 'It was nothing.'

The man put his hands on his hips. 'So what do we do now?'

Fairborne pointed to the administration building. 'We try his car phone again. Maybe it's back on the air.'

'And if he still doesn't answer?'

'Then we sound the alarm.'

The Allegheny State Park cut diagonally across the northern end of the county. It was a lush swath of pine forests, rock gorges, secluded meadows, and rushing streams. Hikers and campers trekked its trails day and night. And they always got a workout.

Randy Allison and his two sons had driven up from Baltimore. They'd arrived at the park's south entrance at 8 p.m., signed the register, and begun hiking to the campsite they'd selected on the map. The trail was steep and demanding. It wound over two high ridges, past the electrical substation, and down a sharp grade into a hidden clearing. Most campers avoided the route as too dangerous. But Randy wanted his fifteen-and sixteen year-old sons to exert themselves, so he'd picked the most challenging path.

They'd been out for over an hour. The trail was very dark and deserted, and they'd seen no one since they'd left the parking area. Tom and Brett Allison were up front with the flashlight, and Randy was labouring behind. This was much harder than he'd anticipated.

'Power station,' Tom called. It was a checkpoint on their route.

'OK,' Randy replied, as the light disappeared over a rise. He was proud of the way the boys were taking to the trip.

'Dad!' Tom suddenly screamed from the darkness ahead.

Randy ran forward, stumbling and slipping against the rocks.

'Dad!' It was a cry for help.

Randy crested the rise and raced down towards his boys.

They were standing by the deserted substation, staring in.

'Dad, look!' Tom hollered. He shone his light through the open gate.

Randy was breathless from his run. He wiped the sweat from his eyes and tried to focus on the spot where his son had rested the beam. 'My God,' he gasped.

A man was slumped against the high-voltage panel, handcuffed to the sparking grid. He was tall and shoeless.

And he was dead.

PART TWO

CHAOS

CHAPTER 8

A chainsaw ripped the pre-dawn air as the police team cleared a pathway to the power station. The Allisons had fled to the parking area and alerted the authorities after encountering the body. And that set into motion the response sequence: a patrol officer first, then a medical unit, then the backup cops. Now, finally, at 5 a.m. they were working the lab van and paramedic truck closer to the rocky site.

Officer Billy Hill had been the first man to answer the call. He'd met with the Allisons and instructed them to remain at the ranger shed. Then he'd sprinted out alone to find the body. Hill was a low-time man on the force, a freckle-faced twenty-four year old strong on enthusiasm but weak on experience. When he reached the grid he'd tried to follow procedure: confirm the condition of the victim, secure the scene, locate evidence. He was moving fast, trying to get it all right. But this was his first encounter with a corpse.

Hill had radioed the power company to shut down the electricity. The grid was still smoking and spitting out sparks, making access to the body impossible. The juice was cut, and the fireworks stopped. Then Hill lowered the dead man to the ground before anyone else had reached the site.

Gardner and Jennifer held hands as they struggled over the slippery stones. They'd been alerted and advised to come out to the scene.

In the darkness, the trail was hazardous. The slimy dew had made the flat shale as slick as ice. They skated across the slate and soon saw the glow of portable floodlights beyond the rise.

It looked like a movie set. Five beacons lit the empty grid with harsh white beams while police, medics, and park rangers milled in and out of the shadows. Gardner spotted Lieutenant Harvis on the periphery, talking to Frank Davis.

Harvis ran over when he saw the prosecutors.

'What's the word?' Gardner asked.

'Pretty sure it's Ruth,' the lieutenant replied. 'Davis has ID'd him, but there's some charring on the body and the face is messed up. We're waiting on someone from CAIN to make a final identification.'

Gardner glanced at Davis. The officer shrugged sheepishly as if he'd screwed up his assignment. 'When did *he* get here?'

'Frank arrived when we did. Billy Hill was first on site, Davis and the rest of us got called in when they ran the alert roster.'

Gardner looked towards Davis again, but he'd wandered off. 'Where's the body?'

Harvis pointed into the darkness. 'Medics have him. They cut an access path on the south side so they could drive up. They'll hold him until we get a confirming ID, then transport to the Medical Examiner's for autopsy.'

'Who removed the body from the grid?'

'Hill. He shut off the power and laid him down.'

Gardner looked at Jennifer. The rule was to leave the body in place until the investigators completed their preliminaries. 'Did Hill take photos?'

Harvis shook his head. 'No.'

'No photos?' Exact body position was crucial in determining what happened.

'Sorry.'

Gardner sensed irony. 'Really? You don't seem sorry.'

Harvis checked around for eavesdroppers. 'This isn't a *normal* situation. There's a complication . . .'

'What?'

'Looks like an *inside* job.'

'Inside the church?'

Harvis looked over his shoulder again. 'No. Inside the *department*.'

Gardner's eyes met Jennifer's then moved back to the lieutenant's.

'What do you mean, Harv?'

'I mean we might have a problem here. A real *problem*.'

Gardner suddenly understood. 'An officer is implicated?'

'It's possible.'

'What evidence do you have?' Jennifer asked.

'One item in particular. Take a look at the body.' Harvis motioned towards the grid with his chin.

'What *item*?' Gardner asked.

'You'll see,' Harvis replied.

* * *

The body had been placed in a plastic bag before being laid on the gurney. It was unzipped, awaiting the arrival of a person from CAIN who could confirm its identity. The prosecutors approached quietly.

Gardner stared at the gruesome face emerging from the dark green bag. The sky had lightened now, and the features were visible. There was charring on the forehead and cheeks, and the pale hair had been burned away leaving a mohawk of blackened scalp down the centre of his skull.

'Ugh,' Jennifer groaned.

'That's what a couple hundred thousand volts will do to you,' Gardner said solemnly as he zipped the bag open. The zipper was at waist level now. 'Look.' Gardner lifted the plastic.

Jennifer glanced inside the fold. The hands were laid across his abdomen, and the wrists were handcuffed. The logo of the county police department was imprinted in the shiny metal.

'County cuffs,' Jennifer said.

Gardner quickly zipped the bag back up to the neck.

Voices suddenly echoed behind them. 'Over here, sir.'

Gardner and Jennifer moved aside as two officers escorted a man to the gurney. He was about Ruth's age, bearded and dressed in denim. As soon as he saw the ravaged face, he nodded. 'That's him.'

'You're certain?' an officer asked.

'Yes, no question.'

Gardner introduced himself. 'When's the last time you saw him?'

Nicholas Fairborne eyed Gardner cautiously. 'Yesterday morning.'

'When did he leave the quarry?'

Fairborne stared. 'I'm here to identify a body, sir, not to be interrogated.'

Gardner was surprised. The man was being uncooperative, almost defiant. 'Don't you *want* to help?'

Fairborne turned away.

'Don't you want to help?' Gardner repeated.

Fairborne continued walking.

'Want me to detain him?' one of the cops asked.

'No,' Gardner finally said. There was no sense pushing it.

'What's his problem?' Jennifer asked.

'Maybe he *knows* something.'

'You think they killed their own leader?'

'It's happened before. Cults are dangerous businesses...'

Jennifer studied his face. 'But you don't think that's what happened here. You think one of our cops might be involved, like Harvis said.'

'Could be,' Gardner whispered.

'That's why they're buttoning down the investigation. No photos, no rush to judgement.'

'Yeah.'

'So who do you think did it?'

Gardner put his lips to her ear. 'There's only one cop on the force with a motive...'

'Brownie?'

Gardner nodded.

'Brownie couldn't do it,' Jennifer said, 'wouldn't do it...'

Gardner looked east. The sun had just breached the horizon and filled the forest with saffron light. It was the beginning of another stunning autumn day. But Gardner barely noticed.

Nicholas Fairborne sat at a computer terminal in the CAIN administration building, feverishly fingering the keys. He was running the files of Thomas Ruth, looking for references to money.

Fairborne selected a title from Ruth's personal menu: 'CASH'. He keyed the filename and hit 'enter'.

The 'CASH' file booted up, and Fairborne scanned the page.

'CASH IS ESSENTIAL TO COMMERCE, BUT IT HAS NO PLACE IN THE REALM OF SPIRIT. "RENDER UNTO CAESAR" JESUS TAUGHT. FEED THE HUNGRY. PROVIDE FOR TRANSPORTATION, COMMUNICATION, CLOTHING, AND SHELTER. INVEST WISELY. CD'S AT 7 AND 1/4 PERCENT. BUY WENSCO INDUSTRIES AT 12 SELL AT 18...'

Fairborne skipped to the bottom and scrolled the next three pages until the file said, 'END'. It was more of the same: fragmented musings, Bible quotations, investment strategies. But there was no banking information, no account number. Ruth had taken CAIN's finances with him to the grave.

The 'CASH' file was still on the screen. Fairborne hit the print mode, and printed it. Then he ripped out the pages and slapped them on the desk.

This was a disaster. Ruth had promised to bring him up to speed on the money, but each time the subject came up, it was artfully dodged. Fairborne slowly rubbed his beard. He'd lost his own business three years ago, a string of inner-city liquor stores that had been robbed and shot-up and vandalized so many times his insurance lapsed and he went bankrupt. Then his wife left him, his house and car were repossessed, and he was set adrift in the world of the middle-aged, broke, angry, and alone. Then he met Thomas Ruth.

Fairborne was CAIN's unofficial second-in-command. He was smart and well-organized, and Ruth had included him in the inner circle soon after his arrival five months ago. Ruth had shared some secrets, pledged untold power and wealth. But in the end, he hadn't delivered.

Fairborne scanned more files, until 'FILESEARCH COMPLETE' flashed on the screen. Nothing even hinted at the whereabouts of the cash. He returned to the main menu and selected 'ERASE FILES'. Then he dumped Thomas Ruth's ramblings into electronic oblivion.

Suddenly the door popped open, and a woman ran in. 'Nicholas!' she called.

He stood up. 'What is it, Dorothy?'

She was crying. 'They won't let us have the body!'

'What?'

'I called to find out when we could pick Thomas up, and . . . and . . .' Her voice choked off.

'Take it easy,' Nicholas steadied her with his hand. 'Start over.'

Dorothy took a breath. 'They said we can't have Thomas Ruth's body back after the autopsy. Don't *we* have a right to bury him?'

'I don't know. What exactly did they say?'

'The Medical Examiner's office told me that we could not take him because the body has already been claimed.'

'By whom?'

'They wouldn't say. Can't *you* do something?'

Fairborne gritted his teeth. Ruth was dead, the money was missing, and he was in charge.

'Can't you do something?' Dorothy repeated. The remains of Thomas Ruth belonged to the church.

'I'll try,' Fairborne said. Right now there were more important things at hand than an electrocuted corpse.

'Please!' Dorothy begged.

'I'll try,' the new leader snapped. First he'd have to find the money. And *then* he'd attend to the arrogant jerk who'd hidden it.

The Blocktown elders were gathered in Reverend Taylor's church. After Joseph Brown's funeral, more of Reverend Boyd's faithful had defected to Brother Taylor. He was now the religious king of Blocktown.

Taylor presided at the meeting. 'The *man* is dead,' he said solemnly.

'Amen,' came the refrain

'He raised up his evil head, and God cut it off.'

'Praise the Lord.'

'So now we must be vigilant.' Reverend Taylor looked in each person's face. 'We must be prepared for the consequences. We must protect God's warrior, the one who carried out his word.'

The group fell silent.

'You *know* what we must do. When they come knockin' at the door asking questions.'

'Don't let them in.'

'Say what?'

'Don't let them in.'

'I hear you,' Reverend Taylor was subdued tonight, quietly making his point. He slipped his hand into the breast pocket of his three-piece suit. 'But they may try to bust *down* the door.'

Silence.

'They may force their way in, but they don't have to *find* anything when they get inside.'

'They ain't come yet,' an elder declared.

Taylor leaned on the podium. 'Any news on the street?' They all shook their heads 'no'.

Taylor clasped his hands in front of him. 'The deed was done in the dark, and nobody *saw* a thing.'

'That's right.'

'And nobody *knows* a thing.'

'Amen.'

An elder stood. He was Officer Bobbie Thompson's uncle.

Taylor pointed to him. 'Brother Richard?'

'The man might not come, Reverend.'

'Why not, Brother?'

'I heard say a cop might'a done the Lord's work this time.'

There was a stir, and the Reverend raised his hands. 'Speak on, Brother.'

Richard stood. 'It's supposed to be, uh, confidential, a secret, but I heard it through Bobbie. Rumour is a cop took out the snake man.'

Taylor narrowed his eyes. 'Is that why it's so quiet?'

Richard shrugged.

'That won't be the last of it,' Taylor said. 'If a cop did do it, they might point the finger of suspicion at Blocktown anyway.'

Heads nodded.

'They might come around lookin' for a chump to lay it on.'

More heads moved.

'They might try to shift suspicion away from their own selves.' Taylor glanced around the room. 'But they won't find anything, will they, Brothers?'

'No *sir*.'

'The cupboard will be bare.'

'*Amen*.'

'No clothes in the closet.'

'*Uh huh*.'

'No shoes under the bed.'

'*That's right*.'

Taylor raised his arms in the air and closed his eyes. 'We have been delivered from evil, my friends. We must praise the Almighty ... Please join hands and say a prayer of thanks for the benefactor, God's faithful unknown soldier...'

There was a networking of hands around the room.

'Lord, you've seen fit to embrace our little town,' Taylor began. 'You sent us a deliverer, a warrior in the night. Shield him, Lord, from the vengeful wrath of men, and bless his soul ... Amen.'

The hands disconnected silently. Then all eyes turned to Reverend Taylor. His face was taut; tears streamed down his cheeks.

'Reverend?' The elders had never seen him like this.

Taylor removed a handkerchief and cleaned himself up. 'Sorry, brothers,' he said self-consciously. 'The spirit suddenly came on me . . .'

It should have been a joyous occasion. The *man* was dead. But Reverend Taylor looked like he'd just lost his best friend.

Brownie crouched in the darkness and looked over his shoulder. It was late at night and the woods were quiet. But he had to make sure he was alone. He couldn't be seen out near the power station, especially not now. The Lieutenant had restricted him to house duty after the word had come in on Ruth. He could work cases in the lab, but the murder investigation was strictly forbidden. Brownie had agreed to keep out of it. But he had lied.

The death reports on Ruth had been easy to obtain. Fellow cops had dropped them in the lab long enough to run copies. And then they'd supplemented the information with whispered conversations and bathroom meetings. Now he was as current on the case status as anyone on the force.

Brownie lowered himself into a narrow trough between the rocks. The deep shadow of the power grid lay fifty yards away, lurking like an oil rig in the depths of the sea. Brownie pictured Ruth pinned to the panel, spasming and convulsing as the current coursed through his body, gasping, choking, burning, and dying.

Brownie looked into a hole and poked around. A white object illuminated. He pulled it out. A candy wrapper!

Brownie tossed it on the ground. 'Where are you?' he asked, moving to another rift in the stone. 'Where the hell are you?'

In studying the police reports, Brownie had encountered a glitch in the investigation: not all of Ruth's personal effects had been found in the crime scene search. Two crucial items were still missing. And those items were crucial enough to crack the case.

Brownie pointed his light into a crevice, and something moved. He shuddered and jerked away. Maybe it was a snake, hiding in its den. 'Snake!' he moaned, fighting the image of Joseph screaming and struggling as the serpent encircled his neck.

Brownie slapped himself in the face to stop the vision. 'Goddamn it!' he cursed, smacking himself again, the words echoing off the trees.

He took several breaths and tried to relax, but the vision still flickered. A man was writhing in torment, but it wasn't Joseph. Now it was Thomas Ruth.

Brownie switched off his flashlight and sat on a rock, pulling his knees up to his chin and hugging his legs. He had to get himself under control. He had to ride out the storm.

Slowly the images faded, and the screams evolved into noises of the night. Finally, he was calm. It was time to get back to work.

Brownie resumed his search, checking more cracks and crevices without success. Then he moved to another sector, well below the grid. There was a layer of slate cut into the side of the hill off the path. Several ledges jutted out, and there were holes and crannies underneath.

Brownie scouted the outcropping first, playing his light in a tight search pattern. On one sweep, his eye caught something.

Brownie approached, and knelt down. There was a small thatch of threads caught between the rocks. He pulled a pair of forceps and plastic evidence envelope from his pocket. Then he sealed the tiny piece of cloth in the bag.

For the next hour the search continued up and down the vine-tangled slope. Finally, there was one more hole to check, one more rock crevice in an almost inaccessible overhang. Brownie shinnied out on the ledge and pointed his light into the crack.

'Yeah!' There they were: Ruth's missing effects, tucked away where no one was supposed to look.

Brownie cautiously reached into the fissure and removed a pair of brown shoes. Then he slid off the ledge, extinguished his light, and faded into the darkened woods.

Gardner snapped upright in his bed. The clock glowed 4.25 a.m.

Jennifer stirred and awoke. 'Gard?'

He was sitting in place, silent and immobile. 'Huh?'

'You OK?'

'Yeah.'

'What's wrong?'

'Can't sleep.'

Jennifer switched on the bedside lamp, and Gardner shielded his eyes. 'Brownie?' she asked.

'He won't return my calls. He's dropped out of sight, and the cops say they don't know where he is.'

'Try not to worry,' Jennifer said.

'Can't help it. He's never done this before ...'

'I'm sure he's fine.'

'*You* are, but I'm not.'

'Stop it,' she finally said.

'What?'

'Stop thinking what you're thinking. Brownie is *not* involved in Ruth's death.'

'The cops have clammed up, and he won't speak to me. It's like they know something that we don't.'

'I'm sure there's a good explanation.'

'There'd better be. I'm starting to worry big time.'

'He didn't *do* it,' Jennifer said firmly. 'Go back to sleep.' She kissed him on the neck and turned off the light.

Gardner lay awake, remembering a foggy April night four years ago. Renegade bikers had set up a drug processing plant in an isolated farmhouse near the ridge line. The undercover narcotics squad had made several 'buys' of PCP and obtained a search warrant. Brownie was assigned to head up the bust, and Gardner was along as an observer. They drove to the lonely site in a pissy little rain and set up a perimeter on the muddy road. The SWAT team was supposed to strike first, smash the door, and secure the scene. Then the rest of the crew could enter and search.

Brownie and Gardner stood by their car as the assault commenced. There was an explosion and shots, and a man ran out of the door firing an automatic weapon. He made it past the first wave and raced towards Gardner and

Brownie, blasting away with his burp-gun. The rounds whistled through the rain and blew out the windshield.

Brownie threw Gardner to the ground and lay on top of him as he returned fire with his sidearm. The man was still on his feet, still approaching, still shooting. Bullets splashed the mud and stitched the side of the car. He was ten feet away when Brownie finally dropped him with a head shot.

Gardner stood up and wiped the grime from his face. That had been close. He wasn't wearing a bulletproof vest like the SWAT team, and he thanked Brownie for protecting him. Then he noticed that Brownie wasn't wearing one either.

Gardner rolled on his side and hugged Jennifer's back. Brownie was in trouble. He could feel it. And somehow he had to help.

CHAPTER 9

Police Chief Larry Gray paced the floor of his office. An appointee to the top cop position a year ago, he was usually a calm, hardworking professional. But today he was uptight.

Gardner and Jennifer sat on the other side of his wide desk. They had just asked 'the' question. Was anyone on the force implicated in the death of Thomas Ruth?

'I don't know,' the chief said, spiking the bristles of his short silver hair with the palm of his hand. 'The whole department is whispering about it, but so far we don't have any direct proof.'

'*Direct*?' Gardner asked. 'You do have some proof then.'

Gray opened his drawer and removed a plastic bag. Inside were the handcuffs Ruth was wearing when he died. 'These are definitely ours,' he said, dumping the cuffs out. They jangled and hit the mahogany with a 'thunk'.

Gardner glanced at Jennifer.

'They were registered county property, not available on the commercial market. They belonged to someone on the force, that much is certain.'

153

'Is there a serial number?' Jennifer asked.

'Not on this particular model,' the chief replied. 'But we can narrow down a time frame when they were issued. This handcuff series came out in the late seventies and was discontinued in 1981. Any officer who joined the force after that time would not have had them.' He pulled out a folder and withdrew a piece of paper. 'That limits the exposure to these twenty-five officers.' He handed the paper to Gardner.

Brownie's name was at the top of the list. 'Why are you going through this bullshit, Larry?' Gardner asked. 'Order the men to turn in their cuffs. That should isolate the one who owned these.' Brownie could not have done anything so stupid, he kept telling himself.

'It isn't that simple,' Gray replied. 'When the new model came out, we issued it to *all* officers. The older set,' he gestured to the cuffs, 'we allowed the men to keep as a backup. All we know is that twenty-five officers now on the force had sets of these cuffs in '81.'

'So call them in and demand an accounting.'

The chief shook his head. 'That won't work. These men are tight. They'll never put one of their own in jeopardy. They'll cover for each other until the end, say they all *lost* their backup sets.'

'Does that include Davis?'

'Davis never owned cuffs like these. He joined too late.'

'He could have picked them up from another cop.'

The chief frowned. 'Frank Davis didn't kill Ruth. The Medical Examiner said that Ruth died at approximately 6 p.m. Frank was at the Mountain Road station servicing his cruiser at that time. That has been verified.'

Gardner and Jennifer exchanged glances. Medical examiners were notorious for miscalculating the exact moment of death.

'Anyway, I wish you'd get off Frank's back. He's a good officer. Harvis is assigning him to head up this investigation.'

'Davis?' Gardner was stunned. 'He's not even a detective.' It was bad enough they put him on the Joseph Brown case, but this could be a disaster.

'He's the best qualified person at this point. He knew more about Ruth than anyone...'

'Maybe that's the problem,' Gardner said.

'Frank can do the job.'

Gardner and Jennifer shared another look. The chief had a right to manage his own personnel, and they were not going to win the loose cannon argument. 'So what are you planning to do next?'

Gray fiddled with the plastic bag. 'That depends on *you*.'

Gardner leaned forward.

'You know the rumour,' Gray went on. 'Someone in the shop iced Ruth...'

'More like "burned",' Gardner interrupted.

'Burned, iced, what the hell is the difference? The sonofabitch is dead. But now, under the circumstances, I need to know from you how far do we push it?' He stared into Gardner's eyes.

'Are you asking *me* what it sounds like you're asking me?'

Gray did not respond.

'You want *my permission* to shit-can the investigation?'

Gray shook his head. 'I'm not doing that,' he said. 'You

know me. I can take the heat. That's not where I'm coming from. I need your input on this one, your help. If we proceed, we may hurt *someone* we all care about. I just wanted to be sure that you knew the consequences before we went any further.'

Gardner reflected for a moment. If he gave the word, the wheels would stop right now, that's what Larry was implying. But that was unethical and illegal. They both had a duty to seek out the perpetrator of the violent crime. 'What is your next investigative step?' he finally asked.

The chief picked up the bag. 'These have not yet been processed for fingerprints. I can send them out to an independent agency, or have them done in-house.'

Gardner gritted his teeth. A fingerprint on the cuffs would produce an instant suspect.

'But, we still have to get something straight,' Gray resumed, 'before deciding about that.'

'How far we intend to go?'

The chief nodded grimly. 'Right. If we *start* the race, we have to finish. All I was trying to say before is that I see no reason to rush. Things are quiet at the moment. People in Blocktown are breathing easier. Ruth is dead, and the crisis is over. There is no reason right now to push. *Nobody* seems to give a damn that this guy is dead, not even the people out at the quarry. They won't even answer questions. All they seem to care about is getting his carcass back.'

That was strange, Gardner thought. Fairborne had been most uncooperative at the power station, and the CAIN church wasn't screaming for blood. An unusual response, to say the least.

'It's quiet now,' Gray continued, 'and we have time to think it through.'

'So you could hold the cuffs a while longer, *before* processing?'

'As long as no one is making a fuss, why not?'

Gardner considered the options. More time would give him a chance to contact Brownie and get his version. If he was clean, they could green-light a full inquiry. And if he wasn't, they'd have an opportunity to think of another plan.

'So what's it going to be?' the chief asked. 'Can I slow this thing down?'

Gardner took a deep breath. This was a solemn occasion, a circumstance that could later be called a conspiracy in the making or a cover-up.

'What's the word?' Gray prodded.

Gardner stood. 'An investigation *must* be conducted. There is no way around that. But the time frame is flexible.'

'You're taking your time as a precaution against error,' Jennifer suggested.

'Right,' Gray replied.

'You proceed, but *slowly*.' Gardner picked up his briefcase.

The chief nodded. 'So I can *hold* the cuffs? Delay processing them?' He lifted the bag.

Gardner hesitated at the door. If the handcuffs went to the lab now, and there was a print on them, they might identify the killer. But that was the question. At this point, did they really *want* to know?

Gardner turned and faced the chief. 'Hold the cuffs,' he said, 'until you hear from me.'

* * *

Kent King pulled the Thomas Ruth file from his desk drawer and laid it under his lamp. The petition he'd drafted after Ruth's visit was the only document inside. King studied it carefully and closed the folder.

He grabbed the phone and dialled an outside line. Court clerk Judy Field answered.

'Judy, this is Kent King. I need you to run down a paper I filed yesterday.'

'OK, what's the caption of the case?'

'In the Matter of Thomas Ruth ...'

'Thomas Ruth,' the clerk replied. 'As in "crispy critter"?'

'That's the one.'

'What do you want me to do with it?'

King doodled on his yellow pad. 'Pull it out and return it to me.'

'I have to log it in,' Judy replied. 'It's an official pleading.'

'Do not log it in,' King said. 'Put it in an envelope and send it back.'

'All pleadings have to be logged.'

'They do *not*,' King said firmly. 'I am withdrawing it before filing, just like it never arrived. The man is dead, and the petition is moot. Send it back please.'

'OK, Mr King,' Judy said.

'And no logging,' King added.

'Uh huh,' Judy replied. Then she opened the court docket and placed a notation in the MISCELLANEOUS section: 'PETITION *IN RE RUTH*, FILED ON 9/23, ABATED BY DEATH, WITHDRAWN BY ORDER OF K. KING, ATTORNEY FOR THE DECEASED.'

* * *

King put down the telephone. That was a close one. There was no use airing Ruth's complaints now that he was dead. That could lead to complications, especially if King somehow got drawn into the case.

King looked at a framed set of Chinese characters on his wall. It was the word for 'crisis' and it was formed by combining characters from two other words: 'risk' and 'opportunity'. King smiled. That simple concept had been the key to his success. With every crisis there *was* an opportunity. And he never let one pass him by.

In the mid-sixties, the Franklin brothers were the BMOCs of East Baltimore High School. Slickly handsome and wealthier than other kids, Nick and Zack Franklin commanded respect and reverence from everyone but a wiry junior named Kent King. The brothers drove a shiny roadster and courted cheerleaders. King lived behind the furniture warehouse and walked to school. And the Franklins razzed him mercilessly every chance they got.

'Hey, Clark Kent,' Zack hooted from his car.

'It's King.' He was on the sidewalk.

'You ain't no King,' Nick added from the back seat as the two blondes with them laughed. 'You're a fuckin' queen.'

'Fuck you.'

The car stopped. 'You want to try?' The brothers emerged and formed a muscled barrier. 'Come on, Supershit.'

But King knew better. Zack and Nick were a deadly tag team. Together they could pulverize anybody. 'Later,' he said, turning away.

'Chickenshit, Supershit,' the brothers called.

But King ran down the alley and jumped the fence.

Then King met Lilly Mandaro in a Little Italy restaurant. He was bussing tables, and she was with her parents. She was a dark-haired, dark-eyed goddess, and she was attracted to the slim good-looking fellow who kept her water glass filled. They struck up a friendship, then something more. She went to an uptown school. And she was more than willing to help King take on the Franklin brothers.

It didn't take long for Nick to go for the bait. While Zack was at wrestling practice, Lilly was in the stands of the basketball court, showing knee, and smiling, and flashing her seductive eyes. Nick bit like a bass, and they began a series of secret rendezvous. 'Don't tell anyone about us,' she made him promise. 'Not even your brother.' And Nick agreed. This girl was the sexiest babe he'd ever met.

Of course, secretly, Lilly was playing the same game with Zack. She'd cornered him in the record shop while Nick was at an away game. And it didn't take long for her to heat him up too. Soon both brothers were involved with Lilly. And neither of them knew it.

Then it was time to pull the plug. In a well-orchestrated 'sting' Lillie told each brother that the other was trying to 'hit' on her, and that it was getting her upset.

There was a confrontation in the school cafeteria.

'Liar!' Nick hollered.

'Back-stabbing bastard!' Zack replied.

And the fight was on. They went at it with fists, knees, and feet, filling the room with screams, spurting blood, and broken teeth.

And when the smoke cleared, the Franklins were history. And Kent King had Lilly on his arm and a smile on his face.

* * *

Brownie knocked on the door of his aunt's house, absently fingering a hole in the screen while he waited for her to respond. It was 4.00 p.m., and her car was in the driveway. She had finished her round of visiting local shut-ins for the day.

The door opened, and her face appeared. 'Joseph Junior!' she exclaimed.

''Afternoon, Aunt Gladys,' Brownie said softly.

She pushed the screen and allowed him in. As he entered he hugged her around the shoulders.

'Good to see you, boy,' she whispered.

They walked to the kitchen, and Brownie sat at the small table by the window. There was a valley view to that side of the house, and a ripple of mountain ridges beyond. The sun was dipping in that direction, casting a sheaf of rays into the room.

'How about some cake?' Gladys asked. The air smelled of butterscotch icing.

Brownie hesitated. His regimen of late had been lack of food, lack of sleep, and lack of human contact. 'OK,' he finally said. 'Small piece please.'

Gladys lifted the cover of her cake container and unveiled a sculpted masterpiece. 'Let you have a big one,' she replied.

Brownie smiled as she cut a large wedge. Then she placed it in front of him. 'Your mama asked if I'd seen you,' his aunt said.

Brownie took a bite of cake and shook his head. He'd been to see his mother twice since Daddy died, and each visit was bad. The emptiness of the house, Mama's crying, and his inability to comfort her had made things worse. Finally, he'd stopped going. The aunts and cousins would take care of her. Right now he couldn't help.

Brownie swallowed. 'How is she doin'?'

'Misses Daddy and *you*,' Gladys replied. 'I know it's hard, but we need to keep the family together. Right now you're the only man she's got.'

Brownie looked through the window and his mind wandered. Several youngsters had just hopped out of a school bus across the street. Chattering and roughhousing, they ran around the corner and disappeared. Brownie refocused on his aunt's yard. An old wooden swing hung from the oak tree, swaying slowly in the breeze. Brownie closed his eyes for a second. When he opened them the swing was new, and he could see two boys playing baseball. The younger one was trying to throw, and the older one was coaching him. 'Take your time and aim,' the elder said. The little one reared back and let loose a wild pitch that almost hit the house. The older boy retrieved the ball and tossed it back. 'Again!' he yelled. The ball flew off at another awkward angle. The elder patiently retrieved it. 'Again,' he said. 'But this time, *aim*.' The younger boy took a world series stance, set, wound, and unleashed the ball. It zapped through the air, homed on the target, and smacked into the centre of the catcher's mitt.

'Joseph?' Gladys asked.

Brownie blinked, and looked out of the window again. The boys were gone.

'You OK?' Gladys touched his forearm with her wrinkled fingers.

'Yeah,' Brownie replied, taking a deep breath. 'But I need to ask you something.'

Gladys adjusted her glasses.

'You seen Paulie this week?'

She shook her head sadly. 'Paulie...'

Brownie played with his fork. 'When did he go back to DC?'

Gladys stood, went to the refrigerator, and returned with a glass of milk that she set by his plate. 'Think it was day before yesterday.'

'So he was here the night the man got killed at the power station.'

Gladys nodded silently.

'He *was* staying with you, right?'

'Yes. He stayed here...' She was starting to get nervous. 'What's this about, Joseph?'

'Can you tell me what he did that night?'

Gladys put her elbow on the table. 'He was going over to see Reverend Taylor. That's what he said.'

'What time was that?'

Gladys looked at her watch, then at the clock on the wall. 'Evenin'. Around suppertime.'

'When was the next time you saw him?'

Gladys frowned.

'Do you remember what time you saw him later?'

'No.'

'How was he dressed?'

'Dressed?'

'Yes ma'am. Was he wearing the African outfit?'

'Why are you asking?'

Brownie stared at the table.

'Oh my God.' Gladys suddenly sat upright. 'I *know* why...'

'It's OK, Aunt Gladys,' Brownie said. 'Nothing is going to happen.'

'You're the boy's *brother*. How can you do this to him again?'

Brownie took her hand. 'I'm not *doing* anything. I'm just asking questions.'

'For the police,' Gladys replied.

Brownie squeezed her hand. 'No,' he repeated. 'This is not for the police.'

'You just got to be a policeman. Always a policeman!' Tears filled her eyes. 'Why can't you be a brother?'

'I *am*, Aunt Gladys. That's what I'm trying to be.'

'You got to *help* that boy! You can't keep tryin' to hurt him!'

'I'm *not* trying to hurt him. Please understand that. I just need to know what he was doing the other night.'

'For the police,' Gladys repeated.

'No,' Brownie answered. 'Not for the police. For *me*.'

Frank Davis scanned the hallway outside of the police lab and reached into his pocket for the pass key. He'd waited all day for his chance, and now the coast was finally clear. He inserted the key, slipped into the room, and re-locked the door.

Davis left the light off and went directly to Brownie's desk, trying several other pass keys until he found the right one. Soon the desk was piled high with purloined files.

The chief had issued a slow-down order on the investigation, confiscated the handcuffs, and told the force to belay the rumours. The lid was on. But Davis still had a job to do, and his ultimate goal was still in sight.

Davis screened several files and confirmed that Brownie had been a bad boy. He'd disobeyed the lieutenant's directive to lay off his father's investigation and he'd set up his own secret inquiry. It was all here: confidential reports, notes, and sketches.

Davis noticed an aerial map at the bottom of the stack. He pulled it out and placed it on the desk. It was an overview of the county, and Brownie had outlined two sections in red ink: Blocktown and the quarry. Then he'd drawn dotted lines between the locations, writing 'POSSIBLE ACCESS ROUTES TO CUTLER ROAD' by the markings.

Davis smiled. Brownie was a jerk, but he was a good investigator. He'd found the back-country passageway between Blocktown and the quarry that no one else had noticed.

Davis turned the page to an enhanced view of the sector. Brownie had put marks there as well. There were three circles along the route. Davis raised the page to see it better in the dark. Then he laughed out loud and put the page down. 'Got you, you black-assed bastard,' he declared. Inside the first circle was the fire tower, the second, the waterfall. But it was the third that made him laugh. Brownie had highlighted another spot where he might encounter Mr Ruth, and this one was very familiar. Inside the third circle was the notation: 'POWER STATION'.

The county circuit court judges were in their weekly

meeting. It was a private session, closed to the public and other officials. Every Friday they convened at 5 p.m. to discuss the events of the preceding days. They talked about cases and defendants, warned of deceptive lawyer tactics, and set the agenda for the future.

'New business?' Judge Danforth inquired. He was chief judge, and he looked the part: a mane of white hair and ruddy cheeks above a black robe.

'We've been receiving calls from the press about this CAIN murder,' Judge Harrold said. As administrative judge, it was his job to handle the media. 'They're asking about the investigation.'

'Refer to the State's Attorney,' Danforth replied abruptly. 'Do not comment.'

'But there's talk about a cover-up, police involvement...'

'Let Lawson handle it,' Danforth said impatiently. 'There is such a thing as separation of powers, remember? We're judicial. They bring us a case and we decide. The State's Attorney is executive. He investigates. He files charges. That's not our affair.'

'The reporters seem to think that it is.'

'It's not,' Danforth concluded. 'We say nothing, and we do nothing. This is Lawson's baby and he has to nurse it.'

'But what if the police are involved in the crime?'

Danforth tossed his mane. 'We're judges, not prosecutors. We stay out of it as I said. Next subject, please?'

Brownie's house lay on a secluded farm road south of town. A white two-storey wooden building, he'd bought it ten years ago, and renovated it himself. As a bachelor he had the time and energy to devote to the project. And, like most things Brownie tackled, the results were spectacular.

Gardner drove his car into Brownie's driveway. Bordered by maple trees, the crushed stones curved gracefully toward the front door.

'Both vehicles are here,' Jennifer said. Brownie's private auto was next to the lab van.

Gardner parked by the grape arbour that screened the walkway. The leaves were browning, and clumps of ripe fruit dangled beneath. The prosecutors approached, and Gardner knocked on the door.

'Hello,' Jennifer said. Gardner turned as Jennifer patted Brownie's collie, Jasper, on the head. He wagged his tail.

Gardner knocked again.

'Call him,' Jennifer suggested.

'Brownie!' Gardner yelled. There was still no answer. 'I'm going in,' he said, testing the door handle.

It was unlocked, so they entered. The living room was a mess. Dishes piled the coffee table, and newspapers were strewn across the floor. There was an indentation in the couch, in line with the TV.

'Brownie?' Gardner called again.

There were two doors to the rear of the room. One led to the kitchen, the other to Brownie's workshop. A buzzing sound was coming from the work area.

Gardner walked to the door and quietly opened it. The room looked like Brownie's lab at police headquarters, packed with test tubes, scanners, magnifiers, and electronics. Brownie was bending over a table, blowing something with a hairdrier.

167

'Brownie!' Gardner hollered.

The policeman jumped off his chair, dropped the drier, and pulled a cloth over the tabletop. 'Gard!' He was startled.

The two men looked at each other for a moment. Then Jennifer came in.

'Hi Brownie,' she said. He was unshaven and bleary-eyed. And he had lost weight.

'Jennifer.' Brownie was awkward, embarrassed. He hadn't expected visitors.

'We need to talk,' Gardner declared.

Brownie ushered them into the living room and closed the door to his lab. He motioned them to sit and began picking up newspapers and trash. Jennifer stacked dishes, while Gardner sorted magazines. On top was an issue of *Interview*.

Finally, Brownie sat down. 'I know why you're here. I'm afraid things got out of hand. I wanted to tell you, but I couldn't.' Brownie lowered his eyes. 'Not after what I did.'

'You have *something* to tell me?' Gardner asked shakily.

'His rights,' Jennifer whispered.

'No.' Gardner raised a finger.

'But...' If Brownie had erred he had to be given his rights. Friend or not, he was entitled to due process.

'Brownie is not in custody, and I'm not interrogating him,' Gardner said. 'Miranda warnings only apply to *custodial interrogation*. This is a private conversation.'

'But...' Jennifer protested. Brownie should not be allowed to incriminate himself, not even to a friend. That was in *Brownie's* best interest.

168

'It's OK,' Brownie said wearily. 'I *know* my rights. I should after all these years... I screwed up, man. It...'

'Hold it!' Gardner interrupted. 'Maybe it's better if you *don't* speak.' If he *knew* the truth, he'd have to do something about it.

'It's OK,' Brownie repeated. 'I know the rules, and I'm willing to play. I didn't kill the man. I sure as hell *wanted* to, but I didn't do it. I *talked* to him on that day. I was convinced he killed Daddy, and I was pissed...'

'What did you *do*?' Gardner asked.

'Stopped his car. Interrogated him.'

'Where?'

'Dunlop Road, just outside of town.'

'What were you driving?'

'Lab van. I had set up a surveillance.'

'So you were waiting for him.'

'Yeah. I knew his schedule.'

'How did you know that?'

'One of Davis' reports. He had a timetable and route map for Ruth plotted out.'

'And Dunlop Road was on it?' That was an odd location, just off the Interstate.

'No. I talked to old Gus at the Amoco station. He'd seen Ruth heading into town earlier in the day, and hadn't seen him come back. I decided to intercept him on Dunlop.'

'So you stopped him,' Gardner continued. 'On what pretext?'

'None. I just flashed the lights, and he stopped.'

'What happened then?'

'Asked him back to the truck.'

'Asked?' Brownie just said he was 'pissed'.

'*Ordered* him out of the car, brought him back to the van, stuck him in the front seat and told him I knew he used a snake on Daddy...'

Gardner and Jennifer looked at each other. Snake?

'Daddy was terrified of snakes, enough to cause a heart attack if he had one put on him. A skin fingerprint test showed marks on his neck that looked like scales. Ruth used snakes in his act. I put it together and made the accusation...' Brownie stopped talking.

'There was no skin print test in the autopsy,' Gardner stated.

'Yes there *was*. I ordered it.'

'Shit!' Brownie was way off base. 'So what happened in the van?'

'The man went nuts. Denied doing anything to Daddy, denied hurting anyone. Said he wanted to be left alone, he didn't hate anyone, why were people after him?'

'And then?'

'He started crying, quoting the Bible, talking nonsense.'

'What did you do then?'

'I let him go,' Brownie said.

'Let him *go*?'

Brownie nodded.

'What about the handcuffs?' Jennifer asked. 'He was handcuffed when he died.'

Brownie rubbed his face. 'They were mine,' he said under his breath.

'I cuffed him before I questioned him in the van. Used my extra set.'

'Why?' Gardner asked. 'Was he under arrest?'

'No.'

'So you put him in cuffs, asked questions, then let him go?'

'Yeah.'

'And you removed the cuffs.'

Brownie did not reply.

'You removed the cuffs,' Gardner repeated.

'No. I left them on.'

Gardner stood up. 'You released him *in handcuffs*?' That was insane.

'Yeah.'

'Please, dear God, tell me why?'

Brownie shrugged. 'I wanted to jack the motherfucker up. He was loosely cuffed in front. He could still drive. I just didn't want to make it easy for him. Let the fucker sweat for a while, find his own way out, I thought...'

'That's not going to hack it, Brownie!' Gardner snapped. 'No one's going to believe that explanation.'

'But that's what happened, Gard, I swear to God. I was gettin' ready to unlock the handcuffs, and I thought, "What the fuck?" Why not let him squirm? So I put the keys back in my pocket and turned him loose.'

'So what did *he* say?'

'He was blubbering some kind of scripture. But he did go back to his car. And he *did* drive away.'

'Still locked in *your* handcuffs,' Gardner said.

'Yeah.'

Gardner looked at Jennifer. There was enough circumstantial evidence against Brownie right now to support a murder charge. 'We have to keep this to ourselves,' he said. 'Until we get a lead on the killer, we have to keep this quiet.'

'I know it *looks* bad,' Brownie said.

'That's why no one can know,' Gardner replied. 'If the truth gets out of this room, *you're dead.*'

CHAPTER 10

Gardner and Jennifer were barricaded in the conference room of the State's Attorney's office. A battalion of reporters was camped outside the door, and the chief prosecutor had left word that he was unavailable. Sallie Allen's CAIN article had stirred a national interest in Ruth, and now that the man was dead, the dominoes were falling in the rest of the news world. Every paper and tabloid show in the country wanted a piece of the action.

'You have to say *something*,' Jennifer advised.

'I do *not*,' Gardner replied. 'The case is under investigation, and I am under no obligation to discuss it.'

'They're construing your silence as a cover-up. They've heard the rumours, and they're looking for a public denial. If you had nothing to hide, you would answer their questions. That's what they're thinking.'

Gardner swivelled his chair. 'I have a right to run this case the way I want. I don't have to answer to anybody.'

Jennifer picked up a file. 'Speaking of the case,' she said, 'what have you decided to do about Brownie?' Gardner had been in a state of shock since last night, barely talking since his friend confessed.

'What do you mean, *do*?'

'We have to find Ruth's killer, that's first priority. But what do we do with Brownie in the meantime?'

Gardner squinted. He was still ticked that Brownie had put himself in such a dangerous situation. If the handcuffs were identified as his, it would all be over. They'd never be able to keep that under wraps. Thank God Chief Gray was sitting on them. 'We keep him secluded while we follow other leads.'

Jennifer was studying the file. 'What leads?' So far *all* of the circumstantial evidence pointed to Brownie.

'There must be something else the investigators came up with, some other evidence.'

Jennifer shook her head. 'They didn't find anything at the scene. No physical evidence. And we know there were no witnesses. The cops exerted very little effort after they saw which direction it was heading.'

Gardner made an entry on his legal pad. 'Then it's up to us to get it back on track, in the *right* direction this time. Let's look at motivation. Who, other than Brownie, had a motive to whack Ruth?'

'Someone from Blocktown?' Jennifer asked. 'As a pre-emptive strike in response to the Sallie Allen article?'

Gardner nodded. 'Possibly. There was gunfire out at the quarry. That puts everyone in Blocktown in the kill column.'

'What about Reverend Taylor?'

'He's got the rhetoric down pat.'

'So do we include him as a suspect?'

'Yeah. Might as well . . .' Gardner noted his name.

'How about Fairborne? Like you said earlier, there could have been a power struggle within the church.'

Gardner added that to his list. 'No question. His attitude alone makes *him* suspect.'

'Davis?'

Gardner smirked. 'You heard the chief. He's innocent.'

'But you don't believe it.'

Gardner wrote 'FRANK DAVIS' on his pad. 'He was bird-dogging Ruth, and he hates Brownie's guts. That makes him a qualifier too.'

'But what would his motive be?'

Gardner put his pen to his lips. 'Motive...' There was something odd about Davis, something he couldn't pinpoint. The man was a schemer.

'Maybe he still wants that promotion,' the prosecutor finally said.

'So there are a lot more possibilities than just Brownie.'

'Right,' Gardner answered. 'Now all we need is some evidence to support the suspicions.'

'But Davis is still on the case, and the chief knows nothing about Brownie's true involvement. *Who* is going to investigate, dig out the proof. *Us*?'

Gardner was about to answer when the phone buzzed. Jennifer picked it up, listened for a moment, then re-cradled. 'Reporters are disrupting the office. They're trying to interview the secretaries and law clerks. You have to stop it.'

Gardner rubbed his eyes. He'd rather wrestle alligators than go out there.

'Give them a statement,' Jennifer said. 'Something pithy, noncommittal. Just get them out of there.'

175

Gardner stood up. He couldn't hide forever. Sooner or later he would have to face the press.

When the door opened, the reporters swarmed. They were gathered in the waiting area and the hall outside. 'Mr Lawson! Mr Lawson!' they called, elbowing each other for position.

Gardner raised his hand. 'Please. I have a comment to make, then I'll have to ask you all to leave.'

'Was it a police officer?' a reporter called.

Gardner stared her down as the others thrust their microphones forward. 'There's been a lot of speculation about the Ruth investigation,' Gardner began, 'but let me assure you now that there have been *no* conclusions drawn at this point. The case is still open, and there are *no* suspects that I can discuss publicly. When we have something conclusive, you will be notified. In the meantime, I have nothing further to say.'

'Is the suspect a police officer?' a reporter asked.

'Are you withholding evidence?'

'Is an officer on suspension?'

Gardner raised his hand again. 'I've said all that I can say. Please have the courtesy to vacate my office. Thank you.'

'Mr Lawson!' they called.

But Gardner retreated into the conference room and cut them off.

Outside the office, a reporter had set up for a remote broadcast. She was dressed in a silk blouse and wool skirt, her face freshly blushed. 'You've heard it from the man in charge, John,' she said to the camera. '"No conclusions."

That would support the rumours that are flying all over town. They say a police officer was involved in the death of Thomas Ruth, and the authorities are dragging their feet because they want to protect him.'

'Sounds serious, Susan,' the anchorman said.

'It *is*, John. The credibility of law enforcement is on the line. And I'm sure we haven't heard the last of it.'

'You stay on the story,' John said.

'I *will*,' Susan replied.

The light went dim and the camera clicked off. Down the hall, several other remote broadcasts were in progress. Gardner had asked the reporters to leave, but they were all still there. And that's where they intended to remain for the duration.

Kent King and Chief Judge Danforth were lunching at the Anderson Mountain Inn. It was a secluded mansion at the four-thousand-foot mark on the side of the ridge. The food was delicious, the view breathtaking, the clientele discreet.

The two men sat in a private alcove on the enclosed balcony. Below, the trees were turning colours, and Summer Lake cast a shimmering reflection in the distance. From that vantage point the county seemed at peace.

'The Ruth case is out of control,' King said. He and the judge were longtime golfing partners and unofficial 'buddies' away from the bench. Despite the fact that King was a regular in his courtroom, they often chewed the legal fat.

The judge sampled his broiled trout and put down his fork. 'Lawson has it covered,' he said.

King laughed. 'How long did it take you to get to your chambers this morning?'

'Normal time.'

'How many reporters did you have to climb over?'

Danforth smoothed his linen napkin. 'What's your point, Kent?'

'The media's swarming. Haven't you noticed?'

'I noticed. So what?'

'You don't *get* it, do you? They're playing hide-the-bad-guy with the investigation.'

'Stay out of it, Kent. It's not your concern. The State's Attorney has the ball. Lawson will get it resolved in due course.'

'Lawson is the *problem*.'

'He's honest,' the judge said. 'Pigheaded sometimes, but honest. I don't believe he'd do anything improper.'

'That's not the point. The integrity of his office has been challenged, and the appearance of impropriety is as bad as impropriety itself. That makes his judgement suspect.'

Danforth played with his fork. The county was definitely under attack. Allegations of cover-up, corruption, and conspiracy dominated the news. But that wasn't really a *judicial* matter.

'You can't let the fox guard the henhouse,' King said.

Danforth looked him in the eye. 'How would *you* handle it?'

King pulled a paper from his jacket and handed it across the table.

'What's this?' the judge asked.

King smiled. 'Article eighteen of the State Constitution,

and chapter twenty-nine of the county code, the enumeration of a certain power you were accorded recently. The statutes allow the court to take control of situations like this. Lawson does not have exclusive control over the Ruth case. You can bring in an independent contractor.'

'I can do *what*?' Danforth was unaware of the law. He read the document and folded it.

'Surprise!' King said.

Danforth shook his head. 'You never cease to amaze me, Kent.'

'I'm here to serve, Dan.'

Danforth put the papers in his pocket. 'How can I *ever* repay you?'

'I think you know,' King said. 'When you make the appointment, you're going to need a volunteer.'

The judge understood. 'You sonofabitch!'

King grinned. 'At your service.'

Brownie sat at the table in his home laboratory studying the fingerprint he'd just lifted from Thomas Ruth's shoe. It was the full thumb of a right hand, removed from the side panel of the footwear. The print was clear, and it was recent. Now all Brownie needed was a match.

After the meeting last night Gardner had ordered him to stay home and keep quiet. And Brownie had agreed. The prosecutor was rightly upset and angry, but that couldn't be helped now. Brownie had agreed to stay out of sight. But he had *not* agreed to stay out of the case.

He picked up the phone and dialled the number of the Medical Examiner, Dr Alva Charles, senior pathologist and old friend.

'Doc, this is Joe Brown,' Brownie said.

'Brownie! So sorry about your dad...'

'Thank you.'

'We all support you down here, you know that.'

'I know, thanks. Listen, Doc, I need a favour. You still have Thomas Ruth in the freezer, right?'

'Ruth? Electrocution victim?'

'Yeah.'

'He was one of our guests.'

'Is the body still there?'

'I think so. I'll have to check. A bunch of corpses were picked up this morning.'

Brownie shifted the latent print card in his hand. 'I need a copy of his fingerprints.'

'Ruth's prints.'

'Correct.'

Dr Charles paused. 'I can arrange that,' he finally said. 'How soon do you need them?'

'Immediately.'

'I'll do it this afternoon. Where do you want them sent?'

'Can you fax 'em to me at 576-8333?'

'Certainly.'

'And this is confidential,' Brownie added.

'I understand.'

Brownie thanked the doctor and hung up. He looked at the print he'd lifted from Ruth's shoe, an elongated pattern of lines under a piece of tape. The number one rule in fingerprint identification was to eliminate the prints of anyone who had known access to the object that was touched. Brownie traced the lines with his finger. If the print came from Ruth, he could relax. If not, he still had a problem.

Frank Davis had a hot lead. He'd canvassed the Mountain Road area from top to bottom, looking for witnesses. Had anyone seen Thomas Ruth driving on the afternoon he died, he wanted to know? That's when Amos Rudd told him that Brownie was asking the same thing on that very day.

Davis throttled back his cruiser and looked for the house on Clayton Avenue where Eunice Land lived. Amos had told him that both Ruth and Brownie had gone south on the 25th. South! No wonder Frank had missed him. He was working the back roads to the north. But there was only one major thoroughfare south, and that was Dunlop Road. Davis had set up out there for two days and copied tag numbers. Regular travellers on the route were easy to spot. They commuted, or car-pooled, or took that road shopping on a regular basis. He accessed the motor vehicle administration computer for the tags that repeated and obtained several names, addresses, and phone numbers. And that's how he located Eunice Land.

Davis parked on Clayton and walked to the door of a small Cape Cod with enclosed porch. He checked the street number again and rang the bell.

A small dog barked, and a woman appeared.

'Ms Land?'

She nodded her bleached head. 'Yes?'

'Frank Davis. County police.' He wasn't in uniform, so he showed his badge. 'We talked on the phone. May I come in?'

The woman opened the door and directed him to a damask-covered table in the kitchen. The room was bright, decorated with plants and ceramics. A Yorkshire terrier bounded in from another room and sniffed his ankle.

'Duchess,' the woman scolded.

'No problem,' Davis said, scratching the animal's head. 'I like dogs. Can I get your full name?'

'It's Eunice Land,' the woman replied, 'but most folks call me Eunie.'

'May I call you Eunie?'

'Sure. Can I get you anything? Coffee? Tea?'

Davis declined. 'I want you to tell me again what you saw the other day on Dunlop Road the afternoon of the twenty-fifth, what you told me on the phone.'

'I saw the man who died.'

'You mean Thomas Ruth.'

Eunie nodded. 'I didn't know his name at the time, but I recognized him later ... from the newspaper.'

'Where was he when you saw him?'

'Outside a police car.'

Davis wrote it down. 'What kind of police car?'

'Don't really remember. It was white, said 'POLICE' on the side.'

'Was it a *van* type vehicle?'

Eunie nodded again, and Davis wrote down 'LAB VAN'. 'Who else did you see?'

'There was another person with the man, but I didn't really get a good look at *him*.'

'It was a *him*?'

Eunie shook her head. 'Think so ... I can't say for sure. All I remember is the man who died.'

Davis withdrew a personnel photo from his pocket and showed it to her. 'Is this the person he was with?'

Eunie studied the picture. 'Could be...'

'You're going to have to do better than that, Eunie. We've got a murder investigation here. Was this, or was this *not*, the man you saw with the deceased?'

Eunie hesitantly looked at the face again.

'This is important,' Davis said. '*Very* important.'

'I think that's him...' Eunie ventured. 'But...'

Davis raised his hand. 'No "buts", Miss Land. This *is* the man.' Davis wrote 'POSITIVE ID' in the margin and had her sign her name underneath. Then he put the photo of SERGEANT JOSEPH BROWN, JR. back in his pocket and closed his notebook.

The courthouse was in an uproar. The judges had called a news conference for 10.00 a.m. and no one seemed to know what it was about. Judges *never* called news conferences. In fact, they rarely spoke to the press.

Gardner and Jennifer pushed their way into the door of courtroom one. They, too, had been caught off guard by the announcement. They'd been struggling with their private Ruth investigation for the past few days, with little success. The entire county had clammed up, so they were still in the starting blocks. At least the Brownie connection remained hush-hush.

The prosecutors fought through the throng of reporters, and found some empty spots in the front row. They sat down just as the judges entered.

Judge Danforth smacked his gavel and called for order. He was flanked by the rest of the circuit bench: Simmons,

Harrold, Kelly, and Hanks. The courtroom went silent.

'As you *all* know,' Danforth began, 'it has recently been suggested that the county police and prosecutor's offices have committed certain improprieties in the Thomas Ruth investigation. These allegations have impugned their reputations, and caused embarrassment to elected and appointed officials alike.'

'I don't like the sound of this,' Gardner whispered.

'Accusations of impropriety, even if untrue, can undermine the integrity of our system of justice. We are *absolutely certain* that there has been no improper conduct in this matter, but that does not change the public's perception. The circuit court judges, have, therefore, pursuant to authority granted by the State Constitution and article 18, chapter 29 of the county code, decided to intervene...'

Gardner turned to Jennifer. What the hell was going on?

'As of twelve noon this date, the State's Attorney will no longer have responsibility for the Thomas Ruth investigation. The case will be within the exclusive jurisdiction of independent counsel...'

The chamber's door opened, and a man entered.

'No!' Gardner breathed.

'Ladies and gentlemen, it is my honour to present the court's unanimous choice for this position...'

Gardner sprang to his feet. 'You can't do this, Judge!'

Danforth peered over his glasses, 'I believe I can, Mr Lawson. I have explicit authority to make the appointment, and I direct *you* to co-operate fully in implementing the transition.'

Gardner was speechless. This was the sleaziest sand-bag job of all time.

'Please sit down, Mr Lawson, so we can get on with the presentation.'

Gardner dropped into his seat and looked at Jennifer. Her face was ashen. She was stunned too.

'And now, I'd like to introduce our new special prosecutor,' Danforth announced, 'Mr Kent King.'

King took a bow. He was dressed in a new Armani suit, and his dark hair was slicked with mousse. Cameras flashed, and recorders whirred as the newly-appointed knight strutted his stuff.

'This isn't happening,' Gardner moaned.

'I will do my best to see that justice is done in this important case,' King declared, looking at Gardner. 'The guilty party will be apprehended and prosecuted. And no favouritism will be shown . . .' His eyes riveted the prosecutor's. 'No matter who the defendant turns out to be.'

Gardner and Jennifer left courtroom one and retreated to their office. The sudden turn of events had put them in the spotlight again. Reporters wanted to know why he had objected. Was there something improper about what the judge had done? Gardner had declined to answer, but not because he was stonewalling. He had declined because he didn't *know*.

'Check the law,' Gardner said as Jennifer unpiled a stack of books onto his desk. They were looking for the authorities Danforth had cited in making the appointment.

Jennifer opened the Constitution. 'This is just the jurisdictional statement.'

'Anything else?' Gardner asked. That was no big deal.

'That's it,' Jennifer said. 'The rest of the section talks about the right to jury trial, et cetera.'

'OK,' Gardner said, 'now check the code.'

Jennifer opened a thick volume of county laws. 'Here it is,' she said.

'Read it.'

'In matters involving impeachment or conflict of interest within the office of the State's Attorney, pursuant to jurisdictional authority in the State Constitution, the circuit court *may* take such action as it deems appropriate, including, but not limited to appointment of an independent counsel, interim state's attorney, or special investigative counsel...'

'Christ!' Gardner exclaimed. 'What is the date of enactment?' It must have been slipped in during some late-night legislative session and passed by a sleeping council. There had been no fanfare, no publicity.

'July first, two years ago.'

'Check legislative history.' Laws like that didn't come out of thin air.

Jennifer turned to the appendix. 'Amendment, amendment, amendment...' There had been a lot of changes, and she was searching for the right one. 'OK, got it.'

'Who sponsored the bill?' Gardner suspected how this had happened.

'Pat Caesar. It was an amendment to the farmland registry bill.'

'Sonofabitch.'

'He's one of King's cronies,' Jennifer said.

'They're tight all right. King told him to slip this one in, and the bastard did it. No one was notified, and no one knew to protest it. It just lay dormant like a land mine, right under our feet...'

'Can we challenge the way it was passed?'

Gardner studied the statute for a minute, then closed the cover.

'No. They did have a published agenda, and an open meeting. It was legal. The amendment was in small print, and no one noticed.'

'That's how King wanted it.'

'Exactly. He's always plotting something. And this plan was brilliant. He planted the mine and waited for the day we'd step on it.'

'And we *did*,' Jennifer said.

Gardner looked her in the eye. 'Yeah. We sure *did*...'

Suddenly there was a commotion outside the door. Gardner picked up the phone. 'What's going on?' he asked the secretary.

'It's Mr *King*,' she said.

Gardner looked at Jennifer. 'The *special prosecutor* is here.'

King was brandishing Judge Danforth's appointment order when Gardner and Jennifer entered the waiting area. 'Get out here, Lawson,' he said.

'What's the problem, Kent?' Gardner asked.

'Give me all your Ruth files.'

Gardner crossed his arms. 'By what authority?'

'*This*.' King dropped the order on the front desk.

Gardner skimmed the document. 'It doesn't say that in here.'

King smiled. 'You *know* I'm entitled to the files, now give them up.'

'We'll need time to comply.'

'That's not acceptable. I want them *now*, before they're tampered with.'

Gardner set his jaw. 'I will assemble them tonight, and you can pick them up tomorrow morning.'

'No. I want them *now*.'

The two men stood face to face, each unintimidated. 'I also need office space,' King added.

'What?'

'You are to provide me with an office.'

'Says who?'

'Danforth. If you'd stayed for the press conference, you would have heard it from *him*. I am to be given full backup support from your staff, including secretarial, telephone, fax, library, files, and an office.'

Gardner looked at Jennifer. All of their offices were occupied.

'Your girlfriend can move in with *you*,' King said, motioning behind them. 'And I'll take that one.' He pointed to Jennifer's private room.

Gardner held his breath. King was pushing him to the limit. 'Watch your mouth, Kent,' he said.

'Excuse me. Your *associate*.'

'We're going to need some time to adjust to this arrangement.' Gardner handed the court order back to King. 'And we're going to have to confirm the logistics with Danforth. I'm not doing *anything* until he specifically tells me.'

'He *has* told you.'

'I didn't hear it.' Gardner positioned himself to block King's access to the interior.

'You *know* this doesn't look good,' King said nonchalantly.

Gardner remained silent.

'You've been accused of obstructing the investigation, and you're still doing it. That's bad.' His lips made a 'tisk, tisk' sound.

Gardner pointed a finger in his face. 'If you think I've done something wrong, then charge me. In the meantime, get the hell out of my office.'

King knew he was outflanked. He shrugged and began moving towards the door. At the last minute, he turned around. 'About that last comment,' he said smugly. 'I'd like to make a little correction.'

He paused for effect. 'It's *my* office now.'

Doctor Alva Charles was becoming agitated. For the past two days he'd been trying to get Ruth's fingerprints for Brownie, but he'd failed. Ruth's body *had* been shipped out the day they'd talked on the phone, and the file had been misplaced. When he'd finally located the paperwork, there was no fingerprint card inside. But there was an unusual notation: 'HANDS RETAINED FOR FURTHER TESTING.' If Ruth's hands were still on ice, the fingers could be inked, and Brownie could get his prints.

The late shift at the morgue was over. The autopsy rooms were unlit and closed. And Doctor Charles was the only living soul in the building. He obtained an inkpad and blank print sheet from the supply closet. Then he set out to find the hands.

The storage chambers were spooky at night. Echoes were louder, the glare of the lights harsher. A notation in the file had documented bin 8-C as the repository of the hands. That was on the top row of a four-level tier.

Charles pulled a metal stepladder over to the C section, and climbed up to the highest rung. There was a ticket attached to the aluminium handle: 'MISC. SPECIMENS'. This was bodypart central.

The doctor pushed the latch and opened the door, releasing an explosion of icy air. His eyes teared, and he wiped them off. Then he peered into the vault.

It was stacked with plastic packages from its base to the top, chunks of flesh awaiting study. Charles groaned. He hadn't expected this much tissue. He'd have to sort through them all.

Fifteen minutes later, the doctor still hadn't located any part of Ruth. There were hearts, livers, brains, and feet, but no hands. Charles was getting tired and numb. He would not be able to go much longer before his own hands froze.

At the bottom of the second column of bags was a flat piece of plastic. The doctor yanked it out, and rubbed the ice off its label. 'RUTH, T., D/O/D 09/25' it said. Charles looked in the vault to see if anything had fallen out, but everything inside was packaged. He checked the fastening and found the seal broken. The bag was empty.

Charles closed the vault door and slowly climbed down the ladder. He'd have to tell Brownie that Ruth and his hands were gone, along with any hope of a fingerprint.

CHAPTER 11

'Let's get going,' Kent King said to the five people gathered in his law office. It was 6 p.m. on the evening of his appointment, and he was off and running with the case. He'd assembled a team from a list of ringers he'd encountered in practice. 'Handey' Randel, and 'Ace' Dixon were former Baltimore city police officers, now private detectives. They had a combined forty years of experience in homicide investigations, and were the best black-white team in the business. Handey covered the suburbs, and Ace handled the projects, and nothing escaped their net.

Dr Art Welk was a former forensic pathologist turned consultant. He was qualified as an expert witness in most scientific fields, including hair, fibre, and fingerprint examination. He was a master of details. Next to him was Harvey Morgan who owned an electronics business in Baltimore. He had helped King defend several electronic surveillance cases, and he would handle the wire work.

Rounding out the group was King's 'secret weapon'. Lin Song was a sexy Asian attorney with long black hair and tempting eyes. She had run the 'high impact' trial section of the Baltimore county prosecutor's office before entering private practice a year ago. She had the reputation of a defendant-killer in the courtroom and a man-killer on the street. And she was referred to by her detractors as the 'Samurai Slut', which was really a double insult since her ancestors were Mandarin Chinese.

'I want to set the agenda for the operation,' King said. 'I had some fun with Lawson this afternoon, but it's time to get down to business.' The hubbub over the files had been a ruse. King had *already* retrieved them from the police. 'You know the background, history and all that. I'm not going through it again. We're going to start the investigation from scratch, and *we're* going to do it right.'

The group was attentive. They had all worked with King before on other cases. He was precise and focused, and he paid well.

'First, let's get our centre of operations straight. We'll work everything out of *here*.'

'What about Lawson's office?' Handey asked. 'Thought you wanted to set up there?'

King laughed. 'That was just to rattle Lawson's cage. We'll take a slot in the State's Attorney's office, but we won't use it for anything important. I'm not letting Lawson near *our* files. He may try to sabotage the operation. We'll create a diversion down there to keep him guessing.'

'Nasty,' Lin Song said with a cat-like grin.

'OK,' King continued, 'I've already gotten phone trap orders signed by the court. Harv, I want you to set up the pen registers immediately. Here is the list.' He handed a paper to the pudgy fifty-year-old. This authorized the special prosecutor to learn what numbers were being called by certain phones. It wasn't a phone 'tap', but if there was a conspiracy afoot, this would help them prove it.

Morgan adjusted his glasses and read the page. 'All these?'

King nodded. 'Can you do it?'

'I can *do* it, but . . .' Almost everyone on the list was either a cop or a prosecutor.

'Let me remind you,' King said, 'that *we* are the good guys this time. *Those* people are all under suspicion.'

Morgan rubbed his double chin and walked to the door. 'I'll get on it right away.'

'Good. Now, Ace and Handey . . .'

The two private eyes looked up, like a dog-sled team ready to run.

'I want you to trace Thomas Ruth's final hours every step of the way. From the time he left the compound until he got fried. Every step. Where did he go? Who did he talk to? Who did he call? What happened to his car?'

The men nodded in tandem. 'Aye-aye, sir.'

'And I want Doc with you,' King added, motioning to Art Welk. 'He's to process any hard evidence you-all come up with, *after* he processes these.' King pulled a plastic bag out of his desk drawer and waved it in the air. Inside was the set of handcuffs that Ruth had died in. Another court order had required chief Gray to turn them over.

Welk took the bag. 'Fingerprints, I presume?'

'Yes,' King replied. 'Use an electron microscope if you have to, but get me a print.'

'I'm set up in the storeroom,' the doctor said.

'Then get going.'

Welk took the cuffs and left the room. The others stood up. 'On your way,' King said to Ace and Handey. 'I'll have another job for you later, so stand by the cellular. And be prepared for an all-nighter.'

The men gathered their things and walked out, leaving King and Lin Song alone. 'What about *me*?' she asked in a sultry voice.

King walked over and stroked her hair at waist level behind her back. 'We have to work late too,' he said teasingly.

She blinked her thick eyelashes. 'That sounds interesting. What are we working *on*?'

King stopped stroking and picked up a file from his desk. 'A search warrant.'

It was dusk, and Gardner and Jennifer were jogging in Rockfield Park. After the confrontation with King they'd tried to go back to work, but couldn't. Unbelievable as it was, King, the beast of the bar, was now a prosecutor. The enemy had changed sides.

The sun had long since disappeared behind Anderson Mountain, and darkening shadows lay across the path. It was starting to get cool. Flat layers of ground fog were rising from the meadow, and the air tingled their faces. The prosecutors were coming into the stretch, two and a half miles done, a half-mile to go.

'He's going to screw us,' Gardner puffed. They'd run most of the course in silence. 'We can't let him into our files.'

Jennifer kept up the pace. 'But Judge Danforth...' Gardner had called after King left and confirmed the dreaded truth. Danforth did order full co-operation on the part of Gardner and crew. And that included all the amenities. *And* an office.

'Danforth can stuff it. The law only authorizes appointment of a prosecutor.'

Jennifer lengthened her stride to keep up. Gardner was pushing harder than he normally did on this section. The last hundred yards was a gentle uphill rise to the finish, and he usually took it easy. But today Gardner was sprinting. 'Gard!' Jennifer called. She was falling behind.

Gardner didn't reply. He lowered his head and notched up the pace, opening a lead on his partner.

'Gard!' she called again. He shouldn't be doing this. He wasn't in good enough shape for such a strain.

Gardner maintained his speed until he passed between the boulders at the three-mile mark. Then he doubled over, hands on his knees, gasping for breath.

'Gard!' Jennifer yelled, racing to his side. 'Are you OK?'

He didn't answer. His breath was coming in convulsions and his face was beet red.

Gardner straightened up. 'I'm OK,' he said between gasps.

'You have to take care of yourself,' Jennifer admonished.

Gardner's breaths were slowing. 'God, you sound like my *mother*.'

Jennifer fell silent. She may have sounded like a mother, but she could tell he heard her as a *wife*.

They walked slowly back to the car, cooling down from the run. It was completely dark now, and a smudge of amber in the western sky was the only light.

'We've got to tell Brownie about King,' Gardner said.

'Didn't you call him?' Jennifer asked.

'Yeah, but he's not answering the phone.'

'Can't we go see him?'

Gardner stopped walking. 'King may be watching. He's into the conspiracy shit big time. He'd love to catch us together and draw a conclusion.'

'But we have a *right* to talk to our friend.'

Gardner mopped his forehead. 'Normally, yes. But we *have* pushed the ethics line.'

'So you think it's dangerous.'

'Possibly. We've *already* conspired to protect Brownie in a way, but it's not provable, at least I don't think it is. Brownie has to be warned about the situation before it goes any further.'

There was a pay phone at the rest area nearby. Gardner decided to play it safe and not use his cellular. 'Give me a quarter,' he said.

Jennifer tossed him a coin, and Gardner ran to the phone. A short time later he returned.

'What happened?'

Gardner looked worried. 'Still no answer.'

Paul Brown looked out of the window of his Southwest DC apartment. It was night, and drug dealers were cruising the crumbling street in plain view of the cops and the passers-by. That was life down here, the reality suburbanites didn't understand.

He watched a young boy walk to a dealer's car, make a trade, and run to the alley. He should be home, but in ten minutes he was going to be high, and in ten years, he was likely to be dead. Paulie looked away from the window. His people were dying. Slowly, painfully, tormenting themselves with poison.

Paulie switched on his stereo, trying to drown his thoughts in the rhythm of an African chant. He sat on his couch and lay his head on a pillow. The sounds began to soothe his torment. He closed his eyes.

The boys were in high school. Paulie was a sophomore, and Joseph was a senior. They were studying the Civil War, and the teacher put the students in groups: one North, the other, South. He asked each group to explain 'why' they were fighting. Paulie was assigned the South group, filled with farm-boys who smoked in the bathroom and hung Confederate flags in their primer-coated cars. The leader was a nasty teen named Rod Mullins. 'We're fighting to keep them on the plantation,' he said, pointing to Paulie. The others laughed, and Paulie hit Mullins in the back of the head. There was a free-for-all, and Paulie ended up on the bottom of the pile. The teacher restored order and sent them all to the principal. But Paulie was the only one suspended from school. And that was the way it was. Whenever he spoke up he got smacked down. The harder he yelled, the harder they hit. And brother Joe did nothing. He was too busy grinning and jiving, and slapping five with the white boys like nothing was wrong.

The phone startled Paulie and he grabbed it. 'Hello?'

'How are you?' It was Aunt Gladys.

Paulie turned down the music. 'I'm OK. What's wrong?' Gladys never called.

'Nothing. I want to know about *you*.'

'Me?'

'Joseph Junior was by here. Got me worried.'

'What did he want?'

'He was asking questions.'

Paulie pushed the phone closer to his ear. 'What kind of questions?'

'About you. What you did *that* night, what you were wearing, who you were with...'

'What did you tell him?'

'I said to leave you alone.'

'What else did you tell him?'

'Nothing. Just that I thought you went down to see the Reverend...'

Paulie rubbed his face. 'Anything *else*?'

'No.'

Silence on the line.

'What did you *do*, Paulie?'

'Keep out of it, Aunt Gladys.'

'*Please* talk to Joseph Junior. He can help you.'

Paulie laughed. 'Like he did last time?'

'He said he wasn't doing this for the police.'

Paulie moaned. 'And you *believe* that sh...uh, bull? He's *always* playing cop.'

'He'd never hurt you, I know it.'

Paulie laughed again. 'He already did! Don't you remember?'

'He loves you, Paulie. That other stuff is all in the past.'

Paulie didn't answer. The past was coming around again.

'*Please* call him,' Gladys said. '*Please*.'

'Leave it alone, Aunt. It's not gonna happen.'

They conversed for a minute longer and said goodbye.

Paulie paced the room after he hung up, trying to gather his thoughts. Then he picked up the phone and dialled a long-distance number. A man answered.

'Hello, Reverend Taylor?' Paulie said. 'We've got to talk.'

Fall festival was in progress at the Apple Valley elementary school, and despite the latest catastrophe the prosecutors were there. Gardner and Jennifer sat in the third row of the auditorium, waiting for the curtain to go up. Tonight was Granville Lawson's big debut. The sixth-grader had a speaking part in the programme.

The lights dimmed, and a woman walked onto the small stage. 'Thank you for coming,' she said into a microphone. 'On behalf of all the teachers and students, welcome. Tonight we pay tribute to this glorious season, in song, and dance, and verse.'

The curtain went up, and children dressed as autumn leaves and pumpkins began dancing and gyrating to recorded flute music.

'Adorable,' Jennifer whispered.

Gardner's preoccupations were fading. The melody was haunting, and the children were surprisingly rhythmic. 'Yeah,' he whispered back, 'not bad.'

There were several younger kid's acts before the fifth- and sixth-graders appeared: a song called 'bringing in the corn', a skit about protecting the environment, and another costumed dance number. Finally, it was Granville's turn.

Gardner tensed as his son walked to centre stage. His blond hair was combed neatly, and he wore a dark green sweater. He didn't seem nervous.

'Fall,' the boy said into the microphone. 'A poem by Granville Alcott Lawson.'

Jennifer glanced at Gardner. He was entranced.

'Fall begins with a drop of rain, and fills the fields with ripened grain...'

Gardner smiled.

'The wind turns cold and chills my nose, and frost creeps up between my toes. The school bell rings, and footballs fly, and the bluest blue is in the sky...'

Gardner's smile widened.

'Winter, Spring, Summer, Fall, I love this season best of all!' He stopped speaking and bowed his head. Then he strode into the wings.

The room broke into applause. Jennifer whistled, and Gardner clapped until his hands were red. The only thing that mattered at the moment was the poetry of a little boy.

Officer Bobbie Thompson was jittery. The heat was on at the department following the appointment of the special prosecutor. Every cop on the force was terrified that King was gunning for him. The attorney had been their bane as a defence lawyer, and now he commanded the power of the state. That made him dangerous as hell.

It was 8.15 p.m., and Bobbie had just come off day shift. He was still in uniform, driving his marked patrol car. He turned off Mountain Road and entered Blocktown from the north. That would make him less conspicuous.

Reverend Taylor's church was quiet and dark. There were no lights in the windows and no cars on the parking lot.

Bobbie pulled next to the building and shut off his engine. A shadow suddenly approached the car, and the officer rolled down his window.

'Evening Bobbie,' Reverend Taylor said.

'Reverend.' Word had been passed that Taylor wanted to see him. It had come through the Blocktown network, from the church, to the gas station, to Bobbie Thompson on his rounds. There were no phone calls or written messages. But the word got through.

'Need to talk to you,' the reverend said.

Bobbie looked around. No telling who King was watching. 'Where?' he asked.

'Inside,' Taylor whispered.

Bobbie locked his car and accompanied the reverend to the rear of the church. They entered the basement and walked to a table in the middle of the room. Bobbie looked around. He'd never been down here. It was cosy and opulent, filled with comfortable furniture. There was a modern entertainment centre and what looked like a wet bar. The windows, high against the ceiling, had been painted over like a World War Two blackout.

'My thinking room,' Taylor said.

'Uh huh,' Bobbie muttered. It looked like the man did more than think down here. 'What's up, Rev? I don't have a lot of time before I gotta report back.'

'What's the latest on the Ruth case? I heard an announcement today about a change of lawyers.'

'The cops and Gardner Lawson are out. Kent King is in,' Bobbie replied.

'What, exactly, does that *mean*?'

'King is running the investigation.'

'Tell me about King.' Taylor seemed concerned.

'He is one nasty sonofabitch, uh, sorry, Rev.'

Taylor smiled. 'Don't worry, Bobbie. You can speak freely here.'

'King is one bad dude in the courtroom. He'll work this thing till he gets blood.'

'Who's the target?'

'Uh, Brother Joseph Brown, they say.'

'Old man Joseph Brown's son?'

'That's him. Took Ruth out to avenge his daddy's death, so the rumour goes.'

'Have you heard any *other* rumours?' Taylor asked.

'About what?'

'Are they looking at anyone else?'

'As a suspect?'

Taylor nodded.

'Not as far as I know. Lawson and the chief were taking their time with the investigation. They were going to probably let it all slide, but . . .'

'But this new guy is gonna do things different.'

'Yeah. He's going to dig till he gets his man. He's a persistent sucker.'

'So Sergeant Brown is in trouble.'

'It looks like it, sad to say.'

Taylor stopped talking and pursued some inner thought. Then he stood up. 'Thanks for coming by, Bobbie,' he said. 'And thanks for the information.'

Thompson shook his hand, and Taylor walked him out the door. 'Keep me posted,' the reverend said at the car.

'Do what I can,' Bobbie replied. Then he drove away and left Taylor alone by the church.

* * *

Brownie had been out all day and most of the night, following leads in his secret investigation. After Dr Charles had called to say that Ruth's prints, hands, and body were missing, he couldn't stay put. He'd disobeyed Gardner's orders to lay low and returned to the woods. There was a fact he hadn't told Gardner about, a fact that still needed clarifying. And now, finally, at 4.05 a.m., he was in bed.

Brownie heard a 'thud' on his front door and leaped up. There was another 'thud', followed by voices.

Brownie grabbed his nine millimetre, scrambled down the stairs, and took a defensive position. 'Who is it?' he demanded.

'Prosecutor's office! We have a search warrant. Open up!'

Brownie cocked his automatic. This had to be a trick, a ploy by break-and-enter thugs. It sure as hell wasn't Gardner.

'Open the door, or we'll bust it in!'

Brownie prepared to fire.

'You'd better do it, Sarge.' *That* voice was familiar: Frank Davis.

'They have a warrant...'

Brownie released the hammer with his thumb and opened the door.

'Put down your weapon,' a voice boomed, as a light blinded his eyes.

Brownie placed his gun on the floor.

'Now step outside.'

Brownie walked forward until he saw Davis. The other men were still invisible behind their flashlights. 'What's going on, *Frank*?' he demanded.

Davis handed him a piece of paper. 'By authority of

special prosecutor Kent King,' he said. 'Sorry, Sergeant, I'm just their escort. These men are in charge.'

'Yeah, you're *sorry*,' Brownie snorted cynically.

'King was appointed special prosecutor in the Ruth case yesterday afternoon,' Davis continued. 'They work for him . . .'

Brownie finally got a look at Ace Dixon and Handey Randel.

'And this is an authorized search warrant,' Davis went on. 'I am here to observe, but I cannot interfere.'

Davis directed Brownie into the yard and forced him to watch as the two investigators entered his home. He was dazed; there had been no warning, no time to clean up.

'This wasn't *my* idea.' Davis said.

'Fuck you,' Brownie replied.

There were rummaging sounds within the house, drawers banging, books toppling. But Brownie said nothing. He'd served hundreds of warrants and knew the drill. The document authorized them to search, and that was exactly what they were doing. There was no way he could stop it.

An hour and a half later, Ace Dixon and Handey Randel came out of the door. They each had an armful of items: files, clothing, uniforms, handcuffs, and several plastic bags. They signalled to their escort.

'You can go in now,' Davis said. 'They're done.'

Brownie observed silently as the private eyes unloaded their merchandise.

'You can go in,' Davis repeated.

But Brownie didn't answer. He was too busy watching the men place Thomas Ruth's shoes into the trunk of their car.

CHAPTER 12

Brownie and Gardner met at the interstate rest area at 8.00 a.m. the morning after the raid. Brownie had called at first light and delivered the bad news. It was time to talk, but not on the phone.

The rest area lay in a grove of trees, away from the highway, just beyond the county line. Brownie arrived first and took a position at a picnic table overlooking the valley. The sun was elevated, and smoke lay in the lowlands. The air was calm, the sky clear.

Gardner parked next to Brownie's car, walked to the bench, and sat down. 'What happened last night?' he asked.

Brownie sadly engaged his eyes. He looked dreadful, unshaven and unusually sloppy. 'Frank Davis and two Baltimore city brownshoes rearranged my furniture.'

'I tried to warn you. King was appointed Ruth special prosecutor. Where were you yesterday?'

Brownie looked down. 'Out.'

'Where?'

'Out'

'You were supposed to stay *home*.'

Brownie raised his chin. 'Leave it alone. I had things to do.'

Gardner drummed his fingers on the table. 'You could have at least left your message machine on...'

'It's busted.'

'OK. Too late now anyway.'

The two men looked at each other. A crow squawked in a nearby tree, and an airhorn blared on the highway. 'What were they looking for, Brownie?' Gardner asked.

'Some stuff I had.'

'What *stuff*?'

'Evidence in the case.'

'*Evidence*? What the hell were you doing with evidence? I told you to keep clear!' He suddenly sensed where Brownie had been during the unanswered calls.

'You know me,' Brownie replied apologetically. 'Can't stay out of things...'

'Shit!' The handcuffs revelation had been bad enough, but this was worse. 'OK, OK,' he said, trying to regroup. 'What did they take?'

'Ruth's shoes.'

'Oh, God...' Ruth had been barefoot when he was found on the grid. His shoes were not accounted for. And Brownie had them. 'You had his shoes? How did that happen?'

'I went out to the power station, found them...'

'Shit,' Gardner cursed. 'King is going to go nuts with this...'

'That's *his* problem.'

'No. It's *our* problem.'

Brownie slowly shook his head. 'You're not involved.'

Gardner was taken aback. 'What do you mean?'

'It's not *your* concern. I can handle it.'

Gardner put his hands on the table and tried to calm down.

'I don't mean to disrespect you,' Brownie said. 'What I did *I* did, and *I'll* take responsibility for.'

'Don't push me away,' Gardner answered. 'We have to stick together.'

'No. *You've* got to stay clear.'

'But I'm not clear; I'm involved, no matter what the court order says.'

'I think we'd better go separate ways for now. I made some bad decisions. I do not want *you* hurt because of it. I know you tried to help me, and I appreciate it, I really do. But I'll be OK. I wanted to tell you that.'

What Brownie was saying made sense. Collusion, conspiracy, and cover-up were at the heart of King's mandate. The more Gardner tried to *help*, the worse it would look.

'I *told* you I didn't kill the man,' Brownie said.

'I know.'

'But that's all I can really say right now. I had my reasons for doing what I did. No sense talking about it.'

'We're screwed either way,' Gardner said. 'If we work together, we bolster King's conspiracy case. And if we don't, we split the team...'

Brownie smiled ironically. 'The man's a fucking genius.'

Gardner sighed.

'He's been waiting for this a long time, a chance to cut *both* our nuts off. Between you and me he's got a whole lot of scores to settle.'

'So you think this is personal.' Gardner and Brownie had kicked King's behind in court on a regular basis.

'Pay-backs are hell, man.'

'We can't let him do it,' Gardner said. The only problem was, how could they prevent it? King had the knife now.

'You play it *your way* and I'll play it mine.'

'We don't share game plans?'

Brownie shook his head. 'Don't see how we can. King's gonna watch every move we make and try to take *you* down too. You know that. Right now I'm the only dirty one. You're *clean*. Best leave it alone.'

Gardner rumpled his hair. There *had* to be another way.

Brownie stood up and extended his hand. Gardner looked at it as if to say, 'What's that for?' Then he gripped it.

'Take care of yourself,' Brownie said.

There was something frightening about this, a feeling that King had finally changed the rules forever. Gardner squeezed his friend's hand. 'You too,' he whispered.

Kent King was back on the job early. In less than a day he'd accomplished more than the cops had managed in weeks. But then, *he* was interested in solving the case. The special team was again assembled in King's office command centre, the players minus one. Lin Song had been dispatched to Lawson's to claim the space allocated under the appointment order. There was nothing like getting the morning started with a bang.

'What's the status on the car?' King asked the detectives. The cops had dropped the ball on this one. Ruth had left the compound in his vehicle and never returned. The car would be a logical place to search for clues, but it had not turned up yet, at least not according to the police reports. As with everything else, they had let it slip.

'At the state park,' Ace Dixon said.

'It was in the ranger's maintenance section,' Handey Randell added, 'so *allegedly* no one noticed.'

King looked up from his notes. 'I assume it was not logged in at the station.' All visitors to the park were supposed to sign in upon arrival, but the rule was seldom enforced.

'Correct,' Ace replied. 'There were a couple of abandoned cars next to it, and the area is unlit.'

King was incredulous. 'So no one saw a brand new Lincoln sitting there for a week?'

'Apparently not.'

'OK,' King decided to move on. 'What was its condition?' He looked at Handey.

'Clean.'

'Locked or unlocked?'

'Locked. Lights off. No accessories operating.'

'Uh huh.' King made a note. 'Keys?'

'Unaccounted for.'

'You checked the area?'

'Yes, sir.'

'What about the interior? Anything of interest *in* the car?'

Handey pulled a plastic bag out of a carry-all. 'This pad was attached to one of those windshield devices.' He passed the bag to King. 'Nothing on it.'

The special prosecutor examined the small note tablet through the clear plastic. Several pages had been ripped out, but there was no writing and no indentation of letters impressed in the paper. King handed the bag back. 'What else?'

'Nothing, really. The car was *clean*, real clean, right out of the showroom.'

Wing turned to Ace. 'A scrub job?' A clean car was as suspicious as one full of bloodstains.

'Don't think so,' Ace answered. 'It was *untouched*.' That ruled out a struggle.

King motioned to Doc Welk, his forensic man. 'Did you dust for prints?'

Welk opened a large folder. 'Yes.'

'How many did you lift?'

The doctor sorted through a stack of four-inch cards. On each one was a taped latent fingerprint. 'Thirty-five in all. I'll be running the classification and comparisons later this morning.' King had provided him with a computer and an optical scanner linked to the law enforcement network of fingerprint files. It would not take long to match a name to each print.

'Speaking of prints . . .' King digressed. 'What about the handcuffs?'

Doc smiled and pulled a single card from a pouch in his briefcase.

'Got one!'

'Good. Who does it belong to?'

Welk put the card on the table. 'Haven't run it through yet, but it's the first one on my list.'

'Good,' King repeated. 'Let me know as soon as you have a hit.' He turned back to the detectives. 'Great job at Brown's last night. The shoes are dynamite, and the files on his father's death case are going to fill the 'motive' blank. Great going!'

Ace and Handey smiled at the pat on the head.

King picked up a file. 'Brown had been specifically ordered off the investigation of his old man's demise. Can anyone here tell me *why?*'

'They didn't want him messing with Ruth,' Ace said.

King arched his eyebrows. 'Now *why* wouldn't they want that to happen?'

'They were afraid of what he might do.'

King smiled and picked up another file with the county seal on it. 'Precisely.' Inside was Brownie's disciplinary record. Over the years there had been fifteen charges of police brutality filed against him, all unsubstantiated. King raised the document in the air. 'Brown has a tendency to be a hothead. You put him with Ruth and *wham!*'

'The cops knew that, and tried to keep him away,' Ace said.

'Tried,' King replied.

'Yeah,' Handey echoed. 'But it obviously didn't work.'

After another hour of evaluating evidence, King pointed to Handey.

'Did you obtain the ranger station sign-in sheet?'

Handey dropped several photostats on the table. 'Right here.'

'Excellent. What about calls?'

'As soon as we get done here, Ace and I are on it.' Again, the police had been lax. The register listed every person who had come to the park on the evening Ruth died. It was a list of potential witnesses.

'Run down each name and get a statement,' King said.

'Will do.'

King surveyed his team. So far, the electronics man,

Morgan, had said very little. The special prosecutor nodded at him. 'So what are our chickens up to?'

'They're busy,' the wire expert said. 'Lawson keeps calling Brown.'

King smirked. Lawson and Brown, the 'righteous' brothers. It was to be expected that they'd increase communication about now. But it wasn't going to do them any good.

'OK, that about wraps it up for the moment,' King finally said. 'You-all get back to work.' He dismissed the troops, closed his door, and picked up the phone. Soon he had Betty Harrison of the clerk's office on the line. 'Betty, Kent King. How soon can you bring in the Grand Jury?'

'How soon do you need them?'

'Tomorrow, or the day after.'

'That can be arranged.'

'Good,' King replied. 'We're preparing the indictment now.'

Gardner had planned to go right to his office after meeting Brownie, but he was sidetracked by a call from Granville's school. The boy had been injured on the playground. They'd tried to call his mother, but she was out. Did Gardner want to come and pick him up? Despite the fact the child lived with his mom, Gardner, it seemed, always received the call. And he always answered.

Sixth-graders are rambunctious. They run with abandon, and sometimes they get hurt. Granville had chased a classmate around the building and bumped his head on a wooden swing-set frame.

'It's not serious,' the school nurse had said. 'Cold

compresses have brought the swelling down, and he won't need stitches.' Granville smiled guiltily and followed his dad out to the car. It hurt too much to stay in school.

'Better?' Gardner asked as they drove towards town. Granville had a pretty hard head. He'd taken quite a few bumps and survived.

'Yeah,' Granville replied.

'*Yes*,' Gardner gently corrected.

'Yes.'

'You want to go home?' They'd finally located his mother, and she was waiting for him at the house.

'Now?' Granville liked being with his dad. Any excuse was OK, even a knot on the head.

'Mom's waiting.'

'Can we stop by Chico's first?'

Gardner looked at his son. He'd lowered the compress from his temple. 'I thought you were hurt.' Chico's was a restaurant that featured a video gameroom. Granville's crowd loved it.

'I'm better,' the boy answered.

Gardner had a lot on his mind. How could he justify Chicos?

'Can we?' Granville asked.

Gardner thought about it again, then clicked his turn-signal. 'Why not?'

Granville had all but forgotten his head. He was ten dollars into the machines, and back for more.

'Sit down a minute,' Gardner said. 'Take a break.'

Granville flopped himself into a chair.

'Who's winning? You or the Martians?'

The boy crinkled his nose. 'They aren't Martians, Dad.'

'Venusians, then.'

Granville laughed. 'Not venoosians.'

'Jupiterians?'

'No!'

Gardner shook his head. 'Who are those little guys you're always blowing up?'

Granville looked into his father's eyes. 'They're Megatrons from the Tenth Dynasty of Zaar.'

'Oh,' Gardner said.

Granville laughed and leaned his head against Gardner's arm. The swelling was almost gone. Gardner touched the outline of the bump.

'Getting better.'

Granville hugged him, and Gardner felt a tiny pain in his heart. He pictured Jennifer, a baby, and himself, and Granville in trouble. And he suddenly realized that he might not be able to answer the call.

Handey Randell and Ace Dixon were on the final leg of their witness quest. They had followed King's advice and obtained the ranger log from the night Ruth died on the electrified rack. Seven people had signed the register in addition to the Allisons who had found the body. The detectives had tracked down six of them and taken statements. No one had seen anything, knew anything, or was particularly anxious to talk. They'd all hiked in the woods and come home. That was it, end of story.

Now, the former cops had one more name: Julie Beane. She'd signed into the park at 4.45 p.m., and out at 6.30 p.m., the time frame of the electrocution, according to the medical examiners. She was the final hope for obtaining an eyewitness.

Julie was a hard-bodied twenty-six-year-old with a blonde ponytail and perfect teeth. She had no problem talking about what she did that night.

'So you were *power-walking*,' Handey confirmed as they sat in the living-room area of her efficiency apartment. 'What exactly is that?'

'High-aerobic, low-impact exercise,' Julie replied.

'I see. And you were wearing your walkman.'

'Yes. My "Stormy Seas" tape.'

'OK. And what route did you take?' Ace laid out a map of the park on the coffee table.

'Let's see,' Julie mused, 'I started here, walked to here, cut across to here, and ended up back *here*.'

Ace looked at Handey. She had come very close to the crime scene.

'Now did you see anybody when you were out there?'

Julie touched her chin, then looked at the map. 'I *did* see someone in this area.' She pointed to a spot that was within several hundred yards of the power station.

'Can you describe the person?'

'It was a quick glimpse. I was on the trail, and he was off in the woods. I was startled and wanted to get out of there.'

'Can you describe him?' Ace repeated.

'He was big, I remember that much. Well-built.'

'How was he dressed?'

Julie closed her eyes for a second. 'Uh ... Can't say. He was behind some bushes, moving away.'

Handey turned up the volume on the recorder. 'What else can you tell us about him?'

'That's about it,' Julie said. 'He was big. He was a man. He was moving away from me . . .'

'What was his *race*?'

Julie hesitated.

'Was he white or black?'

Julie closed her eyes again.

'Try to remember, Miss Beane.'

Her eyes opened. 'There was no way to know.'

'Why not?'

'He had a hood over his head.'

The Grand Jury had been in session all day, and the jurors were tired. They had been listening to Kent King lay out his case in the death of Thomas Ruth. Fingerprint cards, handcuffs, documents, witness statements, photographs, clothing, and a pair of shoes lay on the table. King had summarized it all in a persuasive and effective argument. His prime suspect had motive, opportunity, and the means to carry out the crime. There was physical evidence against him, eyewitness testimony, and a propensity for violence. Now all the jurors had to do was vote. If they agreed that there was probable cause to hold the suspect for trial, they should cast their ballots to indict.

Kent King left the room, and the Grand Jury foreman took over. Legal precedent required secrecy. Whatever the jurors did behind closed doors was inviolate. But today there was no possible dissent, no argument. Their decision could only go one way.

'You've heard the presentation,' the foreman said. 'Is there any discussion on the facts?'

No one spoke a word.

'Is there any discussion on the law?'

Again, silence.

'Very well,' the foreman said, 'it's time to vote. All in *favour* of the indictment as drawn, please signify.'

Every hand went up.

'Very well. I certify this a true bill of indictment.' The foreman turned the page and signed it.

At the top was the caption: '*STATE OF MARYLAND V. JOSEPH BROWN, JR.*' And the charge: 'FIRST DEGREE MURDER'.

'Place your hands on the car, and don't move,' Ace Dixon said. He was pointing his sidearm at Brownie's head. 'I got nothing against you personally. The warrant says we got to arrest you, and that's what we're doing. You can make it easier on everybody if you just co-operate.'

Brownie put his hands against the unmarked vehicle, and leaned forward in the spread-em position. He'd been pulled over on his way home from the grocery store, and his bag of ice was beginning to melt.

Brownie felt Ace's hand slide along his leg. 'If you're packing, please tell me,' Ace said. 'I hate surprises.'

Brownie gritted his teeth as Ace's hand hit the bulge on his ankle. It was his backup gun, a Walther PPK strapped to his leg in a velcro holster. Ace raised his trouser and snatched out the weapon. 'That's one. What else you got?' Ace tossed the weapon to Handey Randell who was standing guard several feet away.

Brownie closed his eyes and didn't respond. His mind was beginning to play tricks. *He* was the arresting officer, and someone else was against the car. That was the history, the only past he knew. *He* was the one giving the orders, immobilizing his prey.

'One more,' Ace said, removing Brownie's nine millimetre from his waist holster.

'Cuff him, and let's get the hell out of here,' Handey said. King had suggested that they ride Brownie a little and try to provoke a reaction. Resisting arrest would be a nice charge to add to the list. It would verify his temper and imply guilt on the murder charge.

Handey glanced at the sky. Darkness was encroaching, and in a few more minutes it would be night. They were on a lonely road, and there were no backup cops upon the direction of King. Their authority derived from the court order; King could use his mercenaries to make the arrest. He didn't want the local police involved, not even Frank Davis. Too much could go wrong.

'Place your hands behind your back,' Ace ordered. 'You know the routine.'

Brownie took a breath and tried to stay calm. Then he slowly put his hands behind his back.

'That's good,' Ace said, tightening the cuffs down as far as they would go.

'Read his rights and let's get out of here,' Handey said. It was now so dark they could barely see each other.

'You got the right to remain silent, blah, blah, blah...' Ace said.

'The *proper* way. King said to go by the book.'

Ace pulled out a plastic card and read the Miranda warnings. When he finished, he looked at Brownie. 'Do you understand these rights as I have read them to you?'

Brownie didn't answer.

'That's a *yes*,' Handey said.

'Knowing your rights, do you, or do you not wish to make a statement?'

Brownie remained silent.

'That's a *no*.' Handey took Brownie by the arm and guided him towards the back seat.

'Watch his head.' Ace pushed the prisoner from behind.

Brownie wanted to break his chains and run away. This was demeaning, humiliating. With King as prosecutor, he'd expected an arrest. But he'd never imagined that it would feel like this.

The detectives locked the doors and began driving. 'How about a bedtime story?' Ace joked. 'In case he has trouble sleeping down at the jail.'

'Leave him alone,' Handey said.

'Better not sleep on your stomach,' Ace chuckled, '... if you know what I mean.'

'Can the shit,' Handey scolded. 'We picked him up, and our job is done. Cut the man some slack.'

'Guess he's gonna need it,' Ace replied.

'Yes he is, but it's not our concern any more. From now on Sergeant Brown is the exclusive property of Kent King.'

CHAPTER 13

Reverend Taylor had called an emergency meeting of the elders in the basement of his Blocktown church. The inner circle was there, and so was Officer Bobbie Thompson. It was late the same evening of Brownie's arrest. Taylor rose from his chair and spoke to the group.

'You-all know what's happened.'

There was an 'uh huh,' from the crowd.

'Brother Joseph Brown has been selected as the scapegoat for the CAIN man's killing. He's incarcerated at the county detention centre.'

Taylor looked at Bobbie. 'Can you elaborate, Brother Thompson?'

The officer stood and checked his epaulette radio to make sure it was off. He had completed day shift and was in uniform. The grapevine had caught up with him on the way back to headquarters. 'Brownie, uh, Sergeant Brown was taken into custody by two auxiliary cops assigned to special prosecutor Kent King. He was charged with the murder of Thomas Ruth, taken to the station, processed, and locked up on a "no bond" status.'

A murmur raced through the crowd.

221

Thompson looked at Taylor. 'That's all I know. King isn't letting anyone from the department near the case. He's using his hired goons to do the field work.'

Reverend Taylor unbuttoned his coat and swept it open with his elbows. 'We have to *do* something, friends. We cannot allow one of our lambs to be slaughtered.' He began to pace, then stopped suddenly and looked at Thompson again. 'Did Brother Brown really kill the man?'

'They got a ton of evidence that says he did.'

'What do *you* think?'

Bobbie looked down. 'He might have . . .'

A rumble swept the room.

'If he did, he did it for *us*,' the reverend said. 'Threw himself on the spear.'

'Yes, sir!' a man declared.

'Sacrificed himself.'

'Amen!'

'We've got to help him.'

'Uh huh!'

Taylor pointed to Bobbie. 'Does he have a lawyer?'

Bobbie stood up again. 'Don't think so. Not yet, anyway.'

'Then I say we get him one.' Taylor began pointing around the room. 'We got to help, brothers. *You* going to help?'

An elder said yes.

'What about *you*?'

Another yes.

'And *you*? And *you*?'

Yes. Yes.

Taylor pulled out his offering dish, and held it aloft. 'Pile

222

it high, friends, the brother needs help, a *lot* of help.' He produced a stack of hundred dollar bills and dropped them in. 'A lot of help,' he repeated.

The dish made the rounds, and at each stop, a handful of bills was added. Everyone in the room was eager to 'help'. Finally, it was returned to the reverend. He smiled and put it on a table at the front of the room. 'At this point I would like to nominate Brother William Stanton as Sergeant Brown's legal defender.' Stanton was the only black attorney in town.

Bobbie Thompson frowned. 'What's the problem, Brother?' Taylor asked.

Thompson looked around self-consciously. 'Do you think he's up to it?' Stanton had taken the bar exam six times before he'd passed and was often steamrollered by other lawyers.

Taylor squared his shoulders. '*I* believe he is. We can put it on the floor for discussion, and take a vote, if that's what you people want.' *You people* was meant for Bobbie Thompson. None of the congregation dared challenge Taylor's judgement, especially now. 'What about it? Shall we vote?'

The elders agreed.

'OK. *I* say we hire William Stanton to represent Brother Brown. Any discussion on the issue?'

Thompson looked down.

'Let's vote. All in favour so signify.'

Every hand but Thompson's went up. Then he slowly raised his.

'It's unanimous. William Stanton will defend Brother Brown.'

There was a murmur of approval.

'Anticipating this, I took the liberty *before* the meeting to ask Brother Stanton if he could do it, and he said "yes".'

There was another rumble of approval.

'Let's keep the faith, friends. We have to stand by Brother Brown at all costs. He's one of *us*.' There was a burst of applause, and Taylor adjourned the meeting.

Bobbie Thompson waved goodbye and walked to his car. Taylor seemed sincere in his desire to help Brownie. He'd raised a lot of money and contributed a bankroll of his own. But his choice of Stanton didn't make sense. Sure, he was black, part of the community. But he was a lightweight at trial. And his chances of beating Kent King were just about zero.

Brownie was in Warden Todd Frenkel's office at the detention centre. His handcuffs had been removed, and there were no guards present. This was a private meeting between two old friends.

'I'm so sorry about this, Brownie,' Frenkel said. He was a paunchy, acne-scarred civil servant, devastated that Brownie was his new resident. Brownie usually delivered the clients and went home.

'Not your fault,' Brownie replied. He was still visibly shaken, but trying to be strong.

'I've got to make some decisions about your ... "living arrangements".' As a charged felon on no-bond status, he was supposed to be kept under heavy security. 'I suggest first-off that we keep you in protective segregation.'

Brownie shook his head. 'No.'

Frenkel frowned. 'No? We got a hundred twenty-two inmates in here now, and by my count *you* turned the key on at least fifty of them. You're not good cellmate material.'

'I don't want segregation,' Brownie said. 'I can handle it.'

The warden sighed. 'A shiv could come from *any* direction, at *any* time.'

'I know.'

'And we can't protect you fully if you're in general population.'

'I understand.'

'So why don't you let us keep you safe?'

'No,' Brownie repeated. He had the right to decline secure lock-up. That was one of the few choices a prisoner could make.

'You're sure about this?' the warden asked.

'Absolutely.' If word got out that Brownie was in segregation, he'd be in even more danger. The animals would sense fear and attack for sure. No. Brownie had to go into the jungle and take a stand. And he had better access to information there. The thug network was plugged into a lot of county secrets. And Brownie still needed answers.

'All right, then,' Frenkel said reluctantly, 'you're going to have to sign a release that we offered you segregation and you declined it.'

'I'll do that.'

'Is there *anything* else I can do to help you get through this?'

Brownie leaned forward in his chair. 'There is one thing...'

'Say the word.'

'I might need a secure phone, computer, and fax machine from time to time. Think you can arrange it?'

'Done.'

'Thanks Todd,' Brownie said.

'If you need *anything*, Brownie, *anything* at all, let me know.'

'I will.'

'And for God's sake, watch your back.'

Gardner leaned across Tanya Peters' desk. 'I don't care if he *is* in conference, I want to talk to him *now*.'

Kent King's dark-haired secretary tried to smile. She had been with King for three years and was stronger than her one-hundred-pound body implied. 'He's not to be disturbed.'

'We'll see about that.' Gardner flanked her desk and banged on the inner office door. 'Get out here King!'

Tanya tried to block him, but Gardner's eyes stopped her. 'If you don't leave, I'll call the police,' she warned.

Gardner turned. 'Go ahead. They'll be *most* helpful after last night.'

Tanya suddenly realized that was a bad idea. The cops had no love for King as it was, and with a fellow officer under arrest, they'd probably be hostile. 'I'll talk to him,' she said, lifting her phone.

'It's Mr Lawson,' she whispered. Then she hung up. 'He'll be right with you.'

Gardner stood by the door with his arms crossed. In a

moment, King emerged. 'What's going on?' he asked nonchalantly.

'Step outside,' Gardner said.

King nodded and opened the front door.

Gardner followed, and they walked to the parking lot. It was morning, and Gardner's breath showed in the chilly air.

'Let me have it,' King said.

'You made a big mistake last night.'

King hitched up his collar. 'Pardon?'

'Brownie didn't kill anyone, and you know it. The case is *bullshit*.'

'You're wrong.'

'How can you go from appointment to indictment in *two days*? That's ridiculous. It takes time to put together a case...'

'You ought to know,' King retorted.

'What do you mean by that?'

'You were taking all the time in the world, now weren't you?'

Gardner didn't reply.

'That's why they appointed *me*. They wanted to get something done. You didn't have the guts to do it, but *I* did. Stop whining about it.'

Gardner gritted his teeth. This was playing like a thousand other King confrontations. Civility barely ruled. 'Brownie did *not* kill Ruth. It was someone else.'

King put his hands in his pockets. 'Have you *seen* the evidence?'

'Some of it.'

'Your *friend* is guilty. Two days or two years in the

investigation would not make a difference. I have motive, opportunity, means, eyewitnesses, fingerprints ... it's a dead lock.'

'There's an explanation for those things. He was working on the case, trying to solve it. *He* didn't do it. The real killer is still out there.'

King laughed. 'How does it feel?'

'What?'

'How often did *I* tell you "My client is innocent"? And how often did you spit the evidence in my face?'

'Is *that* what this is about? A revenge attack on me?' Maybe Brownie was right.

'Don't flatter yourself,' King said, 'I could *care less* about you and your pathetic little life. This is about *law*. As a defence attorney I defended. And now I'm a prosecutor, I'm gonna prosecute. It's as simple as that.'

Gardner fumed. King was yanking his chain, flaunting his role.

'You have anything *else* on your alleged mind this morning? I have the *state* business to attend to.'

Gardner looked him in the eye. 'You have to set bond.'

King feigned alarm. 'I do?'

'Goddamnit, Kent. You cannot keep Brownie in with the criminals he's locked up!'

'Brownie's a big boy. He can take care of himself.'

Gardner put his finger on King's chest. 'Set a bond, Kent.'

King squared his shoulders. 'Or what? You have no jurisdiction any more.'

The realization that he could do nothing was beginning to seep through, and Gardner dropped his hand.

'I suggest you back off until the case is over,' King said. 'I've got it under control.' He turned towards his office.

'Kent.' Gardner had finally regained his voice.

King stopped.

'If anything happens to Brownie in the lock-up, *anything*, I don't care who's on what side, or who's got what title. It's between you and me.'

King turned and smiled. 'That's not a nice thing for a fellow *prosecutor* to say.'

'I mean it,' Gardner continued. 'You want to get personal, I'll get personal.'

'You're deluded,' King said. 'Go home.' Then he trotted up the stairs and disappeared into the building.

Gardner considered running after King and pounding his head into the wall. He could cut Brownie loose in a minute by setting a bond. But he wasn't going to do it, not as long as he held the prosecutor's stick. Gardner gazed up at the sky. Clouds and contrails littered the blue like shattered glass. And he shivered at the sight.

'What did I tell you about the equation?' Paulie Brown asked as he handed a book to the youngster seated on his couch. The boy's name was Joey Sill, and he was Katanga's 'little brother' in the outreach project.

Joey ran a finger alongside of his shaved head. He was thirteen years old, groomed and dressed like a rap musician. 'Where it came from?' Joey asked.

'Yes. Look it up again.'

Joey opened his book. On the cover was a black-over-green outline of Africa. It was entitled: 'THE FOUNTAIN

OF KNOWLEDGE'. He turned to a section and read to himself.

'What does it say?'

Joey looked over the page. 'That we invented it.'

'Who is *we*?'

'The people who lived in Egypt a long time ago...'

'That's right. That formula came from *our* ancestors, so don't give me no BS 'bout not being able to remember it.'

Joey's face went blank. 'But I...'

'No but-buts!' Katanga replied. 'If you have to stay here all day, you *will* memorize it. You got that?'

Joey nodded. Katanga was a great guy. He helped him with his tests and kept him out of trouble. He was more than a big brother. He was a dad.

'Here it is again. The square of the length of the hypotenuse...' He pointed to a diagram in Joey's math book laid out on the table. 'That's this thing here. The square of *this* length is equal to the sum of the squares of the other two sides. You take the squares of *these* two...' He pointed again. 'Add them up, and it comes out the exact same as *this*.'

'The hippopotamus,' Joey said.

'No,' Katanga corrected, 'hy-pot-en-use.'

'Hippopotamus comes from Africa.'

'So does hy-pot-en-use '

'Hy-pot-en-use,' Joey repeated.

'That's it,' Katanga laughed.

Just then the phone rang. Katanga picked it up. 'Yeah?' It was his mother, and she was crying.

'Mama, what's wrong?' She sounded bad.

'Joseph Junior's been arrested. They say he killed the CAIN preacher. He's in jail!'

Katanga stopped breathing for a second.

'Paulie, are you there?'

'I'm here, Mama.'

'Gladys says you know something about this. That Joseph was asking questions about what happened.'

Katanga didn't answer.

'What's going on, son?' She was in anguish.

'Nothing, Mama.'

'If you *know* something, you have to speak up!'

Katanga put his lips against the mouthpiece. 'I do *not*! What's the matter with you all? Don't you remember anything? When *I* needed help, big brother sure as hell didn't help *me*!'

'He *couldn't*,' Althea sobbed. 'And you know why.'

''Cause he was a cop? Mama, I don't accept that. Could have done something!'

'Joseph had no control over that situation. He suffered as much as you did. I *know*.'

'Let him suffer some more.'

'Please, Paulie.' Althea was crying again.

'Sorry, Mama.'

'You're not going to help?'

'I *can't*.' The history was written, and the arrest couldn't change it. Katanga said goodbye and hung up the phone.

'What's the matter, man?' Joey asked.

His mentor slowly emerged from his trance. 'You got that equation yet?'

'Think so.'

Katanga put his arm around the boy. 'You better,' he

231

said, ''cause I'm gonna quiz you, and if you *don't* get it right, I'm gonna kick your little black ass.'

The judges were in a special meeting. The decree unleashing the special prosecutor had just been issued, but he had moved faster than anyone expected. The indictment had suddenly made the case a court matter. And the bench was not prepared to handle it.

Judge Danforth surveyed his colleagues. 'We have to reach a decision,' he said. 'Do we keep the case or assign it out? *I*, for one, am going to recuse.' Recusal was withdrawal.

The judges looked at each other. They all knew Brownie. He had testified in their courtrooms hundreds of times, and they'd seen him around town. No one wanted to preside at his trial.

'I won't do it,' Judge Simmons said.

'Me neither,' added Harrold.

'Count me out,' Hanks said.

Everyone looked at Judge Cramer. 'No way,' he replied.

'That's what I thought,' Danforth declared. 'We can each formally withdraw, citing our relationship with the accused. We have no choice as I see it. This thing started because insider corruption was alleged. And now we have to protect *ourselves*. If we ruled in Sergeant Brown's favour at trial, *we* could be accused of collusion. It's better if we *all* back off.'

There was agreement around the room. The case was poison. Anyone who touched it was bound to get hurt.

'All right,' Danforth said, 'let's check the roster to see who gets the honours.' He pulled a folder from his desk drawer. In it was a list of state judges on stand-by for just such a contingency. Their schedules permitted reassignment in conflict-of-interest situations.

'Let's see.' Danforth ran his finger down the October column. He finally stopped, and his face paled.

'Who is it?' Harrold prompted.

'Judge Rollie Ransome,' Danforth said.

A murmur of surprise ran around the table. Rollie Ransome was a judge from Baltimore city. He was fat, crude, and bull-headed. And he had once shared office space with a streetwise gunslinger named Kent King.

Brownie had manoeuvred Henry Jackson against the wall of the prison gym and was blocking the twenty-two-year-old inmate's exit. Recreation time was over, and the other prisoners had vacated the area. Brownie and Jackson were alone. It was thirty feet to the door, and another fifty to the guard on the other side.

'Let me go, man,' Jackson pleaded. He was a two-bit punk from the Blocktown fringe, a thief who specialized in luxury cars and electronic equipment. Brownie had busted him at least three times, but the little rat kept coming back.

Brownie put an arm on either side of Henry's head. 'I want to talk.'

'You ain't a cop no more,' Jackson responded nervously. 'Leave me alone.'

The arms stayed in place. 'Talk to me, Henry.'

Jackson considered his options. Brown was a hardass, now an accused murderer. No telling what he might do. 'What do you want to know?' he finally asked.

Brownie dropped one arm to his side. 'You were in Blocktown the night the man from CAIN got burned.'

'Yeah,' Henry said cautiously.

'And you were hangin' outside Reverend Taylor's church.'

'Maybe.' Henry was not sure how to answer. Was Brownie still trying to pin something on him?

'How long were you there?'

'Didn't say I *was* there.'

Brownie put his other arm up. 'You *were* there and you were casing cars, weren't you, Henry?'

Jackson puckered his lips. 'Fuck you.'

'Take it easy. I don't give a shit if you stole a whole goddamn fleet. I'm not concerned with that now. I want to know if you saw a particular car in the lot that night. That's all.'

Henry stared at him sceptically. Brownie still smelled like cop. 'What car?' he asked.

Suddenly, there was a noise at the end of the room. The metal door clanged open, and six inmates entered. They were brawny and white and out for blood.

'What the fuck's going on here?' Bobo Hynson twanged through his fight-flattened nose. 'You playin' button, button, which nigger's got the button?' Bobo was a cycle jerk who fancied himself the prison Godfather. He was ugly and mean-tempered. And Brownie had added at least two pages of arrests to his rap sheet.

Henry's face went stiff with fear. If he got pegged as a collaborator he was as good as dead. 'He's trying to hurt me!' Henry yelled suddenly.

Brownie's arms still encircled his neck.

'Let him go!' Bobo ordered.

Brownie lowered his arms and moved against the wall. Henry ran out, and Bobo grabbed him. 'Whut was he doin', tryin' to get a piece?'

'Yeah,' Henry gasped.

Bobo pinched his shoulder. 'Did you suck him?'

'No! I swear!'

'You *sure* about that?' Bobo was gripping hard.

'He refused my advances,' Brownie interjected.

'Yeah? Is that right boogie pig?' He released Henry and turned his attention to Brownie.

'That's right,' Brownie replied calmly. 'He said I wasn't his type. Said he was *your* girlfriend.'

The bad guys formed a V with Bobo at the point. There was no way out. 'That's real funny,' Bobo snarled, 'but I don't do black meat. It stinks too much.'

Brownie said nothing.

'We got to reprimand you anyway.' Bobo led the V forward. Brownie made two fists.

'What goes around, comes around.' The V took another step.

Brownie knew he had three seconds, no more. He had to act.

'Gonna fuck you up . . .' Bobo hissed, but the words were cut off by a savage pivot-punch to his nose. The leader gurgled and lurched as Brownie struck, swinging his own fist into nothing but air.

'Get him!' a sidekick screamed.

The V became a semicircle.

Brownie lowered his head like a fullback and raced for the door, slashing and flailing at the men in his way.

235

'Motherfucker!' Bobo bellowed. He'd recovered enough to get back in the chase. 'Grab the motherfucker!'

Brownie had almost reached the door when he was caught from behind and tackled. He fell against the hardwood with a 'thud', tried to crawl forward, but couldn't. He was trapped.

'Hold him!' Bobo wheezed. He wanted to administer the punishment himself.

Brownie struggled to get up as Bobo moved into place above him.

'You're mine, motherfucker!' Bobo stomped his foot on Brownie's neck and raised a sharpened nail. 'And you're fuckin' dead!'

Brownie twisted as the nail came down, and it hit the fleshy part of his upper arm. 'Aaaaaah!' he screamed.

Just then the alarm sounded, the door flew open, and guards flooded the room.

'Drop it, Bobo!' the captain hollered, brandishing a baton. The nail clanged to the floor, and the prisoners were subdued.

Bobo's nose was bloody and misshapen worse than before. He glared at Brownie as he was escorted to detention and mouthed 'KILL YOU' with his fattened lips.

'Any time,' Brownie snarled defiantly.

Brownie was taken to the infirmary, medicated, bandaged, and released. His arm ached, but he was otherwise all right.

On the way back to his cell, Brownie encountered Henry Jackson on the tier. 'You OK?' Henry whispered. He was grateful that Brownie had taken the heat off him. It had given him a chance to escape.

'Doin' fine,' Brownie said. 'Guess you rang the alarm.'

Henry glanced around. 'Yeah,' he replied.

'Thanks,' Brownie said.

Henry hesitated before walking on, as if he still had something on his mind. Brownie began to move, but Henry blocked his path. He pressed close to Brownie's ear. 'The car you were looking for,' he asked, 'what kind was it?'

Gardner was distraught. He'd returned to his office after the King confrontation and found a very different woman where Jennifer should have been. Lin Song had presented her credentials and an amended court order from Judge Danforth spelling out the awful truth: the State's Attorney's staff was at the mercy of the special prosecutor.

'Can't get a goddamned thing done around here,' he told Jennifer when he'd located her in the law library. So they fled the building and tried to regroup. Gardner suggested jogging to clear their minds. But even that failed to work. Gardner quit halfway through the course and sat on a rock. And that's where he stayed while he sorted things out.

'I've never felt this way,' he told Jennifer, 'so helpless.' They'd been swept out of the picture with two strokes of Danforth's pen. 'By statute and ethics there's *nothing* we can do. We're legal eunuchs. We can't work with King, and we can't work for Brownie.'

'Unless...'

'Unless what?'

'There's a change of status.'

The sun had seared a hole in the clouds, and orange fire dribbled onto the ridge.

'*Status*,' Gardner echoed. 'As in *prosecutor*?'

'Right.' Jennifer touched his neck. 'As prosecutors we're sidelined. There would have to be a drastic change.'

'Drastic,' Gardner said. 'You mean like *quit*?' Prosecution was his whole life. He'd been in the job since leaving law school, and he didn't know anything else, didn't *want* to know anything else.

'You'd never do it, of course. Your career would be over.'

Gardner put his head down. Things had happened so suddenly he hadn't had a chance to think. But now that the words were uttered, he realized Jennifer had a point. The only way to get back in the case would be to resign. And that was *not* something he was prepared to do.

'Am I right?' Jennifer asked. 'You won't do anything drastic?'

Gardner raised his head. The concept was overwhelming, and scary as hell. He could never become a defence attorney, never become a Kent King.

'Right?' Jennifer repeated.

'Right,' Gardner said. 'Nothing drastic.'

'We'll find another way. Maybe we can help get Brownie a lawyer.'

'That's a thought, but he'll have to be damn good to take on King.'

'There's one out there,' Jennifer said. 'We'll just have to find him. Or *her*.'

Gardner smiled and put his arms around her. 'Thanks, Jen,' he whispered. 'Thanks for being there.' They hugged silently.

'It'll work out,' Jennifer said.

But Gardner wasn't so sure. The winds of change were suddenly buffeting the door, and he was having trouble holding it shut.

CHAPTER 14

Judge Rollie Edgar Ransome pounded his gavel in courtroom one and called for order. It was 10.00 a.m., and a bond hearing had been scheduled for Brownie's case.

Gardner and Jennifer sat in the first row. The news had whipped through the courthouse like a brush fire, and they'd rushed over. The local judges were bailing out.

'He's even fatter than last time,' Gardner whispered. Rollie looked like he'd put on a few pounds since he'd handled a conflict case in the county two years ago. A court clerk's wife had been accused of stealing funds from her bowling league. And Rollie had ended up nailing her to the wall with a one-year jail sentence.

'Look at King,' Jennifer said. The special prosecutor was smiling broadly, pleased with the Ransome appointment. The tracks were being greased for Brownie's death train.

'Let's get moving,' Judge Ransome told Willie Stanton. 'I'll hear from the defendant first.'

Stanton stood up and adjusted his bow tie. He was a man of medium height, complexion, and build, reserved and polite. 'We ask, uh, we ask your honour to consider setting a bond in this, uh, this case,' the attorney mumbled. Brownie sat beside him in prison orange, his arm in a sling.

'Speak up!' Rollie retorted. 'I can barely hear you.'

Gardner's stomach burned. So it begins. Brownie had told him about Stanton yesterday at the jail, and Gardner had almost blown a gut. Stanton? He couldn't believe it. He was the *least* qualified candidate for the defence job. Gardner promised to get him an ace, but Brownie insisted on keeping Willie. And that didn't make any sense at all.

'Set a bond...' Willie repeated, 'want you to set a bond...'

'What is the amount now?' Rollie asked, opening the file.

'No bond,' King interjected.

The judge glared at Willie, his jowls quivering as he breathed. 'What do *you* suggest, Mr Stanton?'

Willie put his hand on Brownie's back, 'Your honour, my client is a man of reasonable means. A man who has never before been charged with *any* crime. He is a resident of the county and has family and friends here. He is not going anywhere. Please consider something less than one hundred thousand dollars.'

Rollie looked at King. 'That sound acceptable to you?'

King took his customary go-to-hell stance. 'No, it does *not*. This is a murder charge, and the defendant violated the public trust. He is trained in the use of weapons, and would pose a substantial risk of danger to the community...'

'Your Honour,' Willie tried to interject.

'Let him finish, Mr Stanton.'

'Yes, sir,' Willie replied.

Gardner covered his eyes. This was not only embarrassing, it was a preview of things to come. Rollie and Kent were going to swallow Willie whole. And Brownie along with him.

'No bond status is appropriate,' King continued, 'because of the nature of the charges, the dangerousness of the defendant, and the distinct possibility that he might leave the jurisdiction.'

'There's no evidence of that,' Gardner whispered to Jennifer.

Rollie looked at Stanton. 'This *is* a serious case, and your client's background in law enforcement makes him savvy to violence. Tell me why I should risk it.'

'He's a good man, Your Honour.'

'He may have been at one time,' Rollins replied, 'but *why* should I take a risk on him?'

Willie hesitated. 'He goes to church,' he finally said.

Gardner exhaled. Willie was floundering.

'So what?' Rollie replied.

'So he's not going to cause any trouble,' Willie answered.

'Can't you do better than that?' the judge asked.

'Sir?'

'Can't you give me a *reason* to take the risk. Tell me anything, but make it germane to the issue. I'm trying to help you here. *Why* should I change the bond?'

Willie put his hands on the back of his chair, and looked at the ceiling for a moment. The courtroom was hushed and waiting. 'Because I will vouch for him personally, your honour,' he said at last. 'You have my word.'

Rollie broke into a grin. 'Well, that's comforting to

know. *You'll* take responsibility for Sergeant Brown. We'll all be safe.'

King began to rise, but the judge waved him back down.

'Anything further, Mr Stanton?'

'No, sir.'

Rollie looked across the bench. 'Bond status remains the same,' he declared, banging his gavel. 'Remand the defendant to the custody of the sheriff!'

Then Brownie was led away through an inner door without being allowed contact with anyone.

Gardner turned to Jennifer. 'That's it, then,' he moaned. 'With Stanton in there, Brownie is *fucked.*'

'What are you going to *do*?' Jennifer asked. He had a wild-man look in his eye.

Gardner didn't respond.

'What are you going to do?' she asked again.

'He has a lawyer, and he wants to keep him.'

'So?'

Gardner dropped his head. 'So what *can* I do?'

Gardner and Jennifer encountered King in the hallway after the bond hearing.

King spoke first. 'Aren't you going to congratulate me?'

'Brownie's no danger to the community,' Gardner fumed. 'That's pure bullshit. *He's* the one in danger. He's already been stabbed...'

'He could have avoided it,' King replied. 'He declined segregation.'

'I warned you...' Gardner said.

King smirked. 'Don't threaten me.'

'It's not a threat; it's a *promise*.'

'You *know* Brownie's not going to run, and he's not going to hurt anyone,' Jennifer interrupted.

King turned. 'That's what Willie was trying to say. He's just a puppy dog in a blue suit. A puppy dog who *kills*.'

'Give him a break,' Jennifer urged.

King arched his back. '*I* don't give breaks. Brown is guilty, and you better start realizing it. You hooked your wagon to a falling star.'

'Show me your proof,' Gardner said suddenly. The evidence was still under wraps. Only the Grand Jury had seen it, and they were sworn to secrecy.

'What?'

'Show me *your* files. If it's as locked as you say, I won't bother you.'

King sensed a trick. 'No way.'

'What are you afraid of?' Gardner asked. 'You keep saying it's open and shut. Let me see for myself.'

King had waltzed himself into a trap, taunting Gardner about the strength of the case. Now his bluff was being called.

'Can't do it, can you?'

'I don't show my files to anyone outside the office,' King finally said.

'What are you hiding? Exculpatory evidence? Other suspects? What's the secret?'

King was suddenly at a loss for words. He turned and began to leave. Gardner followed him down the hall. 'You didn't think about it when you took the job, but now you're stuck. You've got evidence that goes the other way, that clears Brownie...'

245

King kept walking.

'That's *it*!' Gardner said. 'You have *exculpatory* evidence, and you don't know what to do with it!'

King turned around and raised his finger.

Gardner put his hands on his hips. 'So the case is not as much of a lock as you say.'

King started to reply, but stopped himself. Instead, he hustled off down the hall.

'What are you doing?' Jennifer asked. 'Trying to piss him off even more?'

'No,' Gardner answered. 'I'm testing his armour.'

Jennifer understood. 'He's got cracks in it,' she said.

'Definitely. Judging by the reaction.'

'So what now?'

Gardner looked at his watch. '*You* go to the office and try to work. Keep an eye on King's new girl ...'

'What are you going to do?'

Gardner had resolve in his eye. 'I'm going to see a man about a job.'

'But you have a job,' Jennifer said.

Gardner pecked her cheek. 'Got to run.'

Brownie was in the detention-centre library, poring over a stack of technical manuals. His arm ached and his neck throbbed, but he had work to do. The bond hearing this morning had gone as expected: Willie Stanton was ineffective. He knew that going in. But there was a reason for keeping the lawyer's services. He was a link to the Blocktown power élite. And Brownie needed to keep that communication line open.

Brownie picked up a book entitled *Cellular World*. He

turned to the section on phone operations and read the first line: 'Each unit transmits a unique ten-digit identification code to the receiving station on an eight millisecond cycle.' He knew that. Cell phones were constantly transmitting and receiving while the power was on, identifying themselves to the cellular net. When a call was placed, the phone's identification number ensured that it would be properly billed. Brownie read on: 'Current research and development on "secure phone" identification procedures lags behind the production curve. Over ninety per cent of cellular phones in use today do not incorporate security devices which protect against interception of the ID number. This makes them more susceptible to cloning.'

Brownie closed the book. He knew about cloning too. Someone steals an ID signal from the air using a scanner then programmes the number into an unregistered phone. The calls are then billed to the registered owner of the phone, and the person who made the calls can never be traced.

Brownie stood up and adjusted his sling. Then he made his way down the corridor towards the main cell block. The warden had told the guards to give him free rein in the place, and the guards complied. Brownie was waved through the 'air lock' that separated the housing area from the passageway to the dining hall and library. Soon he was outside of Henry Jackson's cell.

Jackson had been locked in for his 'protection'.

'Brown,' he said sullenly. 'Did you tell them to do this to me?'

'No' Brownie replied. 'Would you rather be down in the south wing with Bobo?'

'No.'

'Then don't complain.' Brownie put his face against the bars.

Henry eyed him cautiously. 'You still want to talk about the car?'

'No,' Brownie said.

'I told you I didn't see that one.'

'I believe you.'

'So why are you here?'

'What do you know about cellular phones?' Brownie asked.

Henry sat back on his bunk. 'Shiiiit.'

'I'm not after *you*, Henry. You've got to believe me.'

'You always have been.'

'I'm sorry about that, but I was doing my job.'

'Yeah, sure,' Henry said sarcastically.

'You fucked up, and I locked you up. That's all it was.'

'So now you know what it feels like,' Henry said.

'I sure do.'

'I'm not sorry for you.'

'No doubt,' Brownie replied. 'But maybe you can help me out. You help me, maybe I can help you.'

Henry recalled the set-to in the gym. Brownie *had* stood up for him.

'I don't know nuthin' about no cellular phones.'

'Yes you *do*, Henry,' Brownie said. 'Most of the cars you took were wired, and you disposed of the phones before you chopped them up.'

'Maybe a few.' Henry was softening.

'Ever clone any of them?'

Henry cocked his head. 'Clone?'

248

'You know what I'm talking about: stealing an identification number from one phone and keying it into one you took.'

Henry walked to the bars and checked the hallway. What Brownie was talking about was a federal offence.

'You *did* clone some phones, didn't you Henry?' Brownie prodded.

'Might have,' Jackson whispered.

'Now we're getting somewhere,' Brownie said. The last interrogation of Henry had produced nothing. But this one looked promising.

Gardner drove west through a light rain as autumn leaves floated down to the slickened road. The corn fields were stubble now, and rolls of hay lined the meadows. It was time to take stock of things.

The windshield wipers slashed across a sign pointing south from Mountain Road: 'The Heights'. Gardner turned onto a two-lane snaking up the steepest ridge in the county. He'd been here six months before when another crisis was afoot and he needed advice. So he'd come to the mountain, to the wise old man who lived at the top.

Gardner's car strained as it reached the tin mailbox inscribed with Gothic letters. He entered the short driveway and parked beside a jeep. A thin stream of smoke threaded the raindrops above the log cabin. The judge was home.

Gardner ran to the porch and knocked on the door. Soon a round face with laugh-lined eyes and a balding forehead appeared. 'Judge Thompkins,' Gardner said. 'Hope I'm not disturbing you.'

The retired judge smiled. 'Gardner! Come in, son.'

Gardner wiped his feet and entered the house. It was cosy and warm, decorated with antiques and a lifetime of collectables.

'Come, sit.' The judge motioned him into the den. A stack of hardwood crackled in the stone fireplace and the air smelled of pine needles and dried flowers.

They sat in matching leather chairs. An open book lay on the side table next to a pipe in a wire stand. Thompkins picked it up and lit it. 'I had a notion I might be seeing you,' he said.

Gardner smiled weakly. The judge was a widower with no children. He had taken a liking to Gardner long ago in court, and they'd kept in touch. 'You heard the news,' Gardner said.

'Hard not to,' the judge replied, puffing his pipe. He still kept up with the courthouse scuttlebut. 'The papers have given it a ride, that's for sure. Kent King, a prosecutor. Who could have imagined?'

Gardner inhaled the apple-flavoured smoke. 'He's got Brownie by the balls.'

The judge expelled a white ring through his pursed lips. 'You, of course, believe he's innocent.'

'I *do*.'

'So it's a question of allegiance.'

Gardner didn't answer.

'Allegiance to your career as a prosecutor or allegiance to your friend. You're feeling the strain.'

Gardner nodded.

'You're at a crossroads, and you have to decide which way to travel. On one side is Brownie, on the other side is the life you've carved out for yourself.'

'And there's no middle path.'

The judge blew another circle. 'There never is,' he said. 'Remember the Alvarez case?'

Gardner recalled a mean little Mexican accused of molesting his stepdaughter. 'Never forget it.'

'You fought me tooth and nail on that one. Tried to put in inadmissible evidence, ranted and raved like a lunatic. I even called you a *persecutor*, not a prosecutor.'

Gardner sighed. 'Don't remind me.'

'I'm not,' Thompkins said. 'You were doing your *job* as you perceived it, an all-out advocate for the State. You were trying to get a conviction and were focused on that and nothing else.'

'I thought that's what I was supposed to do,' Gardner replied. 'Put my head down and fight for my side.'

'You were fighting too hard. You lost sight of the truth.' Judge Thompkins had acquitted Alvarez on insufficient evidence. Then he'd reprimanded Gardner for his over-reaching. Later, the girl's own mother admitted to the abuse.

'You made your point then: I screwed up,' Gardner said. 'What's your point now?'

'There are *two* sides to every issue. You've spent your whole life arguing *one* side...' his voice trailed off.

'And?'

The pipe smoke formed a halo above the judge's head. 'Maybe it's time to look at things from the *other* perspective.'

Gardner sat in silence for a moment.

'You *understand* what I'm saying?'

Gardner nodded absently.

'Sometimes you just have to step out of the plane, free-fall for a while, let the wind hit you in the face. It can be exhilarating...'

'If you jump voluntarily,' Gardner replied. 'But what if you're pushed?'

'It's the same either way. Change is not *always* bad...'

Gardner fell silent again, and Thompkins puffed his pipe. 'What about logistics?' he finally asked. 'Jumping is one thing; *landing* is another.'

The judge crossed his legs. 'You want to know how to make the transition?'

'Brownie is currently represented.'

'So I hear.'

'I just can't walk in.'

'What's Brownie's attitude? Does he know what you're contemplating?'

'No.'

'Why not?'

'He wants to keep the lawyer he's got.'

The judge wrinkled his brow. 'Why?'

'I don't know why. The Blocktown community put up the cash. Maybe it's a race thing. Maybe he doesn't want to insult them.'

'So you have *two* logistical problems,' Thompkins said. '*One*: how to neutralize a retained lawyer, and *two*: how to substitute yourself.'

'That's it.'

'As to problem number one...' The judge leaned back in the chair and pulled on his pipe. 'The attorney in question is a gentleman of colour with an affinity for the bow tie and a lack of courtroom presence, correct?'

'Willie Stanton.'

'How many jury trials has he had?'

'Six, maybe.'

'How many felonies?'

'None.'

'What's his success rate?'

'Zippo.'

Thompkins put down his pipe. 'There *is* one avenue that could be pursued. It has little precedent, but it could resolve problem number one...' He then outlined the procedure.

Gardner took it all in, recording the 'hows' and 'wherefores' in his mind. 'And what about problem *two*?'

Thompkins smiled. 'That's easy. If step one is successful, step two is practically automatic. Here's how you do it...'

In a moment, the business was concluded. Gardner had his answers, and it was time to leave. He stood up. 'As always, Judge, thank you.'

Thompkins gave him a firm handshake. 'It's going to be very disorientating at first. I hope you realize that. You'll have to change your way of thinking, your whole approach to the law.'

'I understand.'

'I hope so. Good luck. And keep me posted.'

'I will.' Gardner waved and ran to his car. Soon he was skidding down the hill towards town. The rain had increased, and it beat on the roof like a drum-roll. A decision had finally been made. One segment of his life was now over. And another was about to begin.

PART THREE

DECISION

CHAPTER 15

An urgent meeting had been called in the chambers of Judge Danforth. It was late afternoon on the same rainy day as the bond hearing. Present were Gardner, Rollie Ransome, and Kent King. The judge sat at Danforth's cherry-wood desk. This was to be his office while the Brown case was pending, the least the local bench could do to accommodate him.

Gardner and King faced each other in silence. The subject of the conference had not yet been broached.

'OK, we're here,' Ransome said impatiently. 'What's going on?'

'We need to talk about the representation of Joe Brown,' Gardner said.

'We?' King asked.

'Kent,' Rollie looked at his former associate. 'I'll handle this. What do *we* need to discuss?'

'Brown's counsel is incompetent.'

King laughed, and Rollie scolded him with his eyes.

'This is not *my* concern, it's *yours*,' Gardner handed a stack of papers across the desk. 'Here is a list of recent rulings concerning incompetence of counsel. If an attorney handles a complex matter he has no

257

prior experience with, it's tantamount to malpractice...'

King began to speak, but Ransome silenced him with another look.

'You have seen Mr Stanton in action, and it doesn't take a genius to realize that he's in way over his head.'

The judge nodded. 'He's a bit slow on the uptake.'

'Slow is hardly the word,' Gardner continued, 'stopped, is more like it.'

King interrupted. 'Rollie, don't listen to this crap.'

The judge turned to Gardner. 'Where are you going with this, Lawson?'

Gardner stared at Ransome. 'If you proceed with trial, and *convict* Sergeant Brown, the case will be overturned on appeal. This is not supposition, it is fact. The man is incompetent and you *both* know it.'

The judge and special prosecutor fell silent. What Gardner was saying was true. A post-trial attack on Willie Stanton's competence would probably be successful.

Gardner looked at King. 'You want a conviction, one that will stand up on appeal, one that's locked in and can't be taken away. And you...' He went back to Ransome, 'you do not want to be subjected to criticism that you allowed a miscarriage of justice to occur. If you let Stanton proceed with this case, the court of appeals will chop off your head.'

'So what's *your* answer?' the judge finally asked.

'Dismiss Stanton and appoint new counsel in his place.'

Ransome frowned. 'Do I have the authority to do that?'

'Yes, you *do*.' Gardner handed another paper across the desk. 'Here are the citations permitting the ruling. It is within your discretion.'

'Ask him who you should appoint in Stanton's place,' King suggested.

Ransome turned to Gardner again. 'And who should that be?'

Gardner didn't hesitate. 'Me.'

'You can't defend a criminal case, you're still a prosecutor,' the judge said.

'Not anymore.' Gardner passed another paper across the desk, 'Here's my resignation, effective immediately.'

Ransome looked at King. 'What's your position?'

'I strongly object.'

Ransome studied the papers Gardner had handed him. 'It appears I *do* have the power to make the switch...'

'Don't do it,' King warned.

'And Stanton is definitely not up to the task...'

'Rollie!'

'And having you two in the case would make it a hell of a lot more interesting ... Motion is granted. Stanton is out, and Lawson is in.'

Gardner looked at King. 'I warned you...'

King remained cool. 'You haven't got a chance. Brown is *still* dead meat.'

'Not anymore.'

King stood up. 'Oh, I'm shaking now...' He laughed and made a trembling motion with his hands. 'Mr big bad defence attorney gonna hurt me...'

Gardner faced him. 'It isn't a joke, Kent. I *will* beat you.'

King's smile vanished. 'Not *this* time.' The lawyers were jaw to jaw.

'Gentlemen!' Ransome interjected. 'Thanks for the

preview, but the bell hasn't even rung yet. Save it for the courtroom!'

Brownie hurried to the warden's office to meet his visitor. The evening meal was over, and the other prisoners were back in lock-up. He entered the room and encountered his friend. 'Gard. What's going on?'

Gardner pushed out a chair by the warden's desk and directed Brownie to sit. He eased into the seat as Gardner slid a copy of Judge Ransome's order across the table. 'I'm your new lawyer,' he said.

Brownie picked up the paper and read it slowly. Gardner's resignation letter was attached to the flip side of the page. He put the documents down and looked across the table. 'What the hell is *this*?'

'Just what it says: an order dismissing Stanton and appointing me in his place. I'm not going to let King take a free shot at you.'

'You've got to withdraw it.'

'I can't. It's final.'

'But your career...'

'It was time for a change.'

Brownie slowly shook his head. 'You made a mistake, man...'

'Don't argue with me. The deed is done, and we've got work to do.'

Gardner was surprised at the negative response. He'd expected more enthusiasm, more support. Brownie almost seemed sorry it had happened.

Brownie glanced at the paper again. 'What about Stanton? He was paid to represent me.'

'He'll have to refund the money. He's not competent, and they were aware of that when they hired him.'

Brownie didn't reply. Stanton had been a key player in his secret plan. Now he was out of the game.

'You know Willie's no match for King. He proved that at the bond hearing. I couldn't sit by and watch.'

'You think you can do better?'

'I know I can.'

'You've never defended anyone in your life.'

'I'll learn on the job. Don't fight me, for Christ's sake.'

'I didn't ask for this.'

'I know. It was *my* decision.'

They sat quietly for a minute, reflecting on the situation. The fates had just dropped them in a bizarre world where all the roles were reversed. King now wore a white hat. And that left Gardner and Brownie in black.

'We have work to do,' Gardner finally said, 'and I need your help. You have to tell me the truth, from the beginning. Every nasty detail.'

Brownie clasped his hands and shifted position as a buzzer sounded in the corridor.

'You have to tell me everything, Brownie. *Everything.*'

'I told you I didn't do it.'

'I know that, but I think you might have an idea who *did*.'

Brownie laughed. 'If I knew, I wouldn't be here.'

'You've been working this case from day one. You had to have some leads the cops know nothing about.'

'I wish.'

Gardner fell silent. His client was being non-communicative, uncooperative. 'You were secretly collecting evidence. What were you looking for?'

'I'm a detective. Detecting is what I do.'

'You were ordered off the case. What were you after? And why all the secrecy? Why wouldn't you tell *me*?'

'Don't push it, Gard. I told you before. What I was doin' had a reason.'

'I can't protect you unless I know everything. You know how it works, damnit. Now cut the bullshit and tell me the truth. This is *serious*. That fight the other day was just the beginning. The animals in here are out to kill you. We've got to put a case together, and we've got to get you out of this place.'

Brownie closed his eyes. 'I can take care of myself.'

'Fine. We'll do it another way. Let's start over ... from the beginning. I'll ask questions; you give answers.'

Brownie opened his eyes and nodded.

'Good,' Gardner said. 'Let's go back, before the day of the crime ... Tell me what you had on Ruth, and his contact with your father.'

'I thought Ruth might have necklaced him with a snake. Already told you that.'

'Because of the unauthorized print test you ordered.'

'Right. Daddy was absolutely terrified of snakes. If one got on him I know it could cause a heart attack.'

'And Ruth was aware of this?'

Brownie closed his eyes again. 'I thought so.'

'*Thought*, as in past tense.'

'At the time.'

'So you decided to confront Ruth about your suspicions.'

'Yes. I told you that too.'

'I wasn't your lawyer before,' Gardner said. 'How many confrontations did you have with him?'

'One.'

'*One?*'

'Yes. The day he died.'

Gardner looked at his friend. There was still a secret lurking. 'How did you know where to find him?'

'I had Frank Davis' surveillance reports. Ruth took a drive out Mountain Road almost every afternoon. I tried to get him out there, but then got the info he'd gone to town. That's when I set up a trap on Dunlop.'

'What were you intending to do?'

Brownie stared into space. 'I don't know.'

'Did you want to kill him?'

'Yeah.'

'Did you *plan* to kill him?'

'No. I did not.'

'Well, what was your plan then?'

'Didn't have one.'

Gardner frowned. 'You always have a plan, Brownie.'

'Not this time. I was playing it by ear, improvising.'

'So why did you put your *spare* cuffs on him? Why didn't you use your regulation cuffs?'

'Why?' Brownie was stalling. If it was a spur of the moment thing, he would have used his current set of cuffs. He had to have planned to bring his spare set on that day.

'You did have a plan,' Gardner continued. 'You knew in advance you were going to roust him, so you brought your spares. What were you planning to do with him? Were you *planning* to take him out to the power station?'

'No!'

Gardner rubbed his eyes. This didn't make sense.

Brownie was the most meticulous person he knew. Behind every move there was a reason. Brownie had to be lying about his intentions with Ruth. And that was going to make his job as defence attorney even harder.

'What's the matter with you?' Lin Song asked. 'You had to anticipate that Lawson would enter the case in some fashion.'

Kent King moved a file to the side of his desk. 'Never thought he'd actually turn in his badge. He's always been a one-tune asshole.'

They were conferring over the latest developments and setting the strategy for the days ahead. There was a trial scheduling conference at the end of the week, and they needed to get their ducks in a row.

'So now you can have another macho duel at the OK Corral,' Lin said. 'You can gun him down at high noon.'

King opened the case file. 'Are you through?'

'No. I want you to tell me about Lawson. Why do you dislike him so much?'

King picked up a report from the file folder. 'We need to dispose of this.'

'You won't answer me?' Lin sounded irritated.

King looked over the paper. 'What?'

'What's with you and Lawson? The famous feud.'

'We don't get along.'

'Are you jealous of him?'

'Jealous?'

'His blue blood, his *girlfriend*...'

King's face reddened. He was a notorious loner, a one-night-stand champ.

'I heard you bonked his ex-wife. Is *that* the secret?'

King put down the report and glared at his colleague. Years ago he'd made a move on Carole Lawson while the divorce was pending. He'd done it to rankle Gardner, but there had been an unexpected twist. He'd actually fallen for her. She was cultured, elegant, the kind of untouchable woman he'd always craved. But his plan had backfired. After a brief fling, she rejected him. *She*, it turned out, had been using *him*. He'd let Lawson know the first part: that they'd been together. But the rejection was something he wanted to forget. 'Mind your own business.'

'This *is* my business.' Lin faced him across the desk. 'I need to understand the dynamics here. It's *my* case too, and I want to know if your war with Lawson is going to affect it.'

King's eyes narrowed. 'Lawson is not going to affect anything. He's irrelevant. We're going to nail Brown's hide to his living-room wall.'

'He really gets to you, doesn't he?'

'No psychology please. We have a case to prepare. You worry about the law, and I'll deal with Lawson. Now, are we ready to move on?'

Lin nodded.

'Good. Now tell me what we should do about the exculpatory shit.'

Gardner's prior accusations had been on target. King *did* have some proof leading away from Brownie.

Lin opened her file. 'I've reviewed all the items that could conceivably be classified as exculpatory. They fall into two categories: impeachment information and unfollowed leads.'

'The law only requires us to turn over information that specifically exculpates the defendant,' King said. 'We are not required to follow a lead that *might* incriminate someone else. Once we have our man, we can quit. Is that your reading?'

'Right. If we have evidence that the defendant did *not* commit the crime, we *must* give it to the defence, but we do not have to keep investigating after his arrest. If we had a lead on a suspect we didn't follow up, it's OK. We're under no obligation to keep going in that direction.'

'Good.' King reached across the table. 'What's on your impeachment list?'

Kim handed him a piece of paper. 'Five witness contradictions, three unconfirmed suspects, and a missing piece of physical evidence.'

King scanned to the last entry. 'Ruth's *hands*?'

'They were removed at autopsy and misplaced in the morgue.'

'Did they ever turn up?'

'No. The pathology people think a medical student might have pilfered them. An inventory revealed a string of missing parts, and there's a history of this sort of prank at the med school. The fact is, they're *gone*.'

King glanced at Lin's notes. 'So what? We have the autopsy report establishing the cause of death. How can missing hands impeach anything?'

'They could prove there was a struggle. The cuffs would have cut the wrists as he pulled away from the grid.'

King drummed his fingers on the table. 'Of course he struggled. He was being zapped like a bug!'

'The evidence doesn't show it,' Lin replied, withdrawing

the autopsy report. '"Hands removed for further testing" is all it says about the hand and wrist area.'

'So what? It's a minor detail.'

Lin disagreed. 'Minor now, maybe...'

'But?' King wasn't following.

'What if they decide to raise a particular defence?'

'Such as?'

Kim passed a photo of Ruth's blackened face across to her boss.

'Such as Ruth *didn't* struggle because he was the only one there.'

'What are you implying?'

'Maybe this wasn't a murder after all ... maybe he killed *himself.*'

'This is a *murder* case, Lin. Murder with a capital *M*.'

'But the evidence...'

'Don't say it again,' King warned. 'Ruth was *murdered*. And that's all there is to it.'

Indian summer had come to the valley. After weeks of heavy frost rising temperatures had killed the autumn chill. Gardner and Jennifer strolled arm-in-arm outside the courthouse. The air was alive with bees and the smell of burning leaves.

'I *am* being supportive,' Jennifer declared.

'That's what you say,' Gardner replied, 'but I know you're upset.'

They stopped by a park bench and sat down. Above, brown maple leaves jiggled in the soft wind.

'I'm not upset,' Jennifer said. 'It's just...'

Gardner rested his arms on his knees.

'You left me in limbo,' Jennifer continued.

Gardner kicked back against the bench. 'You starting on *that* again?'

'No. I'm not on *that*...' She stopped talking.

'What is it?'

'I don't understand you. Some things come really hard, and others seem so easy.'

'What do you *mean*?'

'When Brownie calls, you run. Snap! No hesitation, no agonizing, no second thoughts...'

'Brownie is my best friend, Jen. He saved my life. He needs me.'

'He's not the *only* one in your life who needs you.'

Gardner grimaced. 'Don't start, please.'

'Explain it to me.'

'Explain what?'

'How can you make such a decision so suddenly? You said you'd find another way to help...'

'It was the *only* thing I could do.'

'So you closed your eyes and jumped.'

Gardner nodded. 'Yes I did.'

'You ended a twenty-year career in a heartbeat.'

Gardner nodded again.

Jennifer looked down. 'I see ... You can jump for Brownie, but you can't jump for *me*.'

Gardner tried to raise her chin, but she resisted. 'It's not the same, Jen. This is different from our situation. There are a lot more considerations *we* have to deal with, a lot more complications...'

Jennifer's eyes slowly came up. '*Different?*'

'Yes. Apples and oranges . . .'

'It's not different. It's about commitment. You can make it for one friend, but not another. *That's* what I don't understand.'

'Let's discuss it later, Jen. *Please*. We have a case to prepare.'

'But not *now*,' Jennifer said under her breath.

'When this is over, we'll hash it all out. I swear. Just give me a break for now.'

'So what am *I* supposed to do in the meantime?' Jennifer finally asked. 'Stand by my man, or go my own way? Prosecution was *my* career too.'

'You do not have to quit, I told you that. We can do an Adam's rib routine, I'll play Tracy and you be Hepburn.'

A child suddenly raced past, laughing, revelling in his escape to the sun. Jennifer watched him turn the corner.

'You do not have to follow your man,' Gardner continued. 'I want you to do what *you* want, not what I want.'

Jennifer adjusted her glasses. The bright rays turned the auburn highlights in her hair a deep red. 'So you say.'

'What's the problem now?'

'You need me on the case. You haven't said it, but I know.'

Gardner hesitated. 'I can do this on my own. I'm capable.'

'But you still need me to help.'

Gardner did not reply. She was right, but he didn't want to admit it.

'You're pressuring me, and you don't even realize it.'

'I'm trying not to.' If Jennifer decided to stay with the prosecutor's office, Gardner would survive. Somehow.

'Let's examine the consequences,' Jennifer went on. 'If I did keep my job, what would happen?'

'They have to appoint an interim State's Attorney to complete my term. You could apply.'

'Me. State's Attorney. That sounds intriguing. Would the judges give it to me?'

'It depends on King. If *he* applies it's all over.'

'Do you think he wants a permanent position?'

'Not sure. Brownie's case is probably a one-shot deal.'

'But if King does apply, I'd be working for *him*.'

'Right.'

Jennifer rolled her head back and looked up. A lone cloud drifted in the cobalt sky.

'King cannot apply until this case is over,' Gardner said. 'Under the terms of the special prosecutor's order, he is a separate entity with no official affiliation to the elected office.'

'So there's time.' Jennifer was still gazing skyward.

'Yeah. You don't have to do anything immediately.'

'What about discussions?'

'What do you mean?'

'As Hepburn and Tracy we can't even discuss the case.'

Gardner inhaled. 'You're right. If I'm out and you're still in, ethically, we can't share information.'

They suddenly looked into each other's eyes, aware of the barrier imposed between them by order of law. 'So what now?' Jennifer asked.

Gardner touched his lips to her ear. The wind gusted, and a leaf drifted down to their feet. 'That's up to you.'

Jennifer reached into her purse and withdrew an envelope. 'What's that?'

Jennifer opened it and unfolded a letter. 'My decision.'

Gardner read it aloud. '"Resignation effective immediately." Jen, are you *sure* about this?'

Jennifer nodded sadly. 'Yes. Under the circumstances, I don't seem to have a choice.'

Gardner and Jennifer's resignations required them to vacate the State's Attorney's office immediately. There was no way they could conduct defence work from prosecution headquarters, so a hasty call to a colleague with space available across town solved the relocation problem. Now all they had to do was gather their personal belongings and leave.

Gardner was piling mementos in a box when his phone buzzed.

'Reverend Taylor to see you,' Miss Cass announced.

The door was yanked open, and the reverend rushed in followed by Willie Stanton. 'Sneaking out of town?' Taylor demanded.

Gardner placed a 'county service' plaque in the box, and tried to compose himself. He had been concerned this might happen.

'Reverend...'

'I thought you were different,' Taylor interrupted, 'but you're not. You're nothing but a patronizing hypocrite.'

Gardner glanced at Stanton behind the reverend. 'Hi, Willie,' he replied.

Stanton self-consciously raised his hand.

'Person of your stature should have shown more class,' Taylor blustered, 'had the courtesy to warn a man before sticking a dagger in his back.'

Gardner looked his accuser in the eye. 'I'm sorry I didn't contact you,' he said. 'I did only what I thought was best for Brownie.'

'His name is *Joseph* Brown, and you made a big mistake,' Taylor continued. 'You 'dissed *this* man here and the whole Blocktown community! We had Brother Brown taken care of. *We* did! Didn't ask for help from you or nobody else. Didn't want help from you or nobody else!'

'What's the trouble?' Jennifer asked. She'd heard the commotion from the next room.

'I seem to have stepped on some toes,' Gardner said.

'Mr Lawson has decided that the intellect in our part of town is inferior to his,' Taylor declared. 'He knows what's right for us better than we do ourselves.'

'No,' Jennifer protested. 'He's not like that...'

'He called this man a moron,' Taylor said.

Gardner looked at Stanton. 'Tell him, Willie,' he instructed. 'Tell him I didn't 'diss you, and tell him why.'

'Don't you order him to do nothin'.' Taylor snapped.

'I'm not ordering,' Gardner replied firmly. 'Please tell him why I had to do it, Willie. Tell him how much trial experience you've had. Tell him...'

Stanton was about to answer when the reverend cut in. 'You saying he *can't* do it? That he don't have the brains or the talent to do what Lawson can do?'

'No!' Gardner parried. 'Cut the race crap! I'm *not* questioning Mr Stanton's ability, just his experience. It's got nothing to do with who he is. It's a practical problem.'

'But you're saying he *can't* do it!' Taylor argued. 'And now you told it to the world. He's not up to the job! How's he gonna hold up his head in the neighbourhood? What are folks gonna say? Poor Brother William, he can sit up front on a small case, but when a big one comes, he's got to move to the back of the bus!'

Stanton lowered his eyes. People *would* say that.

'You see what you did?' Taylor charged. 'You stomped on his dignity.'

Gardner shook his head. 'I'm sorry. My only intention was to help Joseph Brown. I never meant to hurt Willie.'

'*William.*'

'William.'

'Why did you hire him in the first place?' Jennifer asked. 'You knew he was inexperienced and that it was a complicated case. You set this situation up yourself.'

'I don't have to justify my actions to you,' Taylor answered coolly.

'We tried to help, and Brother Brown accepted our offering. It was none of your concern. It was between *us*.'

'Brother Brown still needs your help,' Gardner said.

'That's out of our hands *now*,' the reverend replied. 'You just slammed the door.'

'You can still give him support,' Gardner continued.

'You want money? You want *us* to pay *you*?'

'No! He needs moral support, co-operation...'

'Co-operation?'

Gardner tensed. He had not wanted to raise the issue this way. Ruth's killer might still be in Blocktown, and the only way to save Brownie would be to find him.

'What do you mean by that?' Taylor seemed disturbed.

'As his lawyer, I'll want to question some folks in Blocktown as I put together my defence.'

Taylor eyed him suspiciously. 'About what?'

'What they saw or heard the night Ruth died...'

'We had that under control,' Taylor said.

'I understand. But if I'm going to help Joseph, I'll need to tap into your sources. Can you arrange it?'

Taylor did not respond.

'If we work together we can still accomplish the same goal,' Gardner continued.

Taylor took Stanton's arm and directed him towards the door.

'You *do* want to help Joseph Brown...'

But Taylor and Stanton left the room without saying another word.

Gardner looked at Jennifer. 'Can you believe that?'

'No,' Jennifer replied. 'They're upset you're in the case.'

'Do you think it's *racial*?'

'I'm not sure. Taylor talks that way, but...'

'There's something else going on.'

Jennifer nodded. 'What do you think it is?'

'I don't know,' Gardner replied, 'but we sure as hell better find out.'

'I don't like you, Frank,' Kent King said.

'That's gratitude...' Frank Davis pulled the bill of his cap down over his eyes. The sun backlit the attorney like a flare. They were in the parking lot behind King's office.

'I said I didn't like you, not that I didn't appreciate you.' Davis had volunteered his services after the special counsel appointment and filled in several crucial gaps in their proof.

'Why are you down on me? Without my help you never could have indicted Brown.'

'That's true, but I never requested your assistance.'

'So what's the problem?' King had summoned him to the late afternoon parley.

'I don't like traitors.'

'Traitors?' King was beginning to piss him off, the ungrateful bastard.

'A person who turns on his friends.'

Davis laughed. 'Brown is not my friend.'

'You know what I mean. He's a fellow cop.'

'What's going on, Mr King?'

'Gardner Lawson has just taken over as Brown's attorney, in case you hadn't heard.'

Davis nodded. Everyone in town was talking about it. 'So?'

'So he isn't going to be a walkover like Willie Stanton.'

'Yeah...' Davis still didn't get the connection.

'So your activities prior to Ruth's killing have a much better chance of coming to light.'

'I thought we resolved that.'

'We did, up to a point. But with Lawson in there I've got to take some precautions. I can't afford for my familiarity with that situation to compromise the prosecution.'

Davis squinted into the sun. 'What do you want me to do?'

'You have to take a polygraph examination. I need you absolved of any connection with Ruth's death.'

Davis didn't answer. He'd already told King he was clean.

'And then,' King went on, 'I want you to withdraw your application for promotion. You cannot step into Brown's shoes until he's permanently out of the way. You understand that?'

Davis nodded slowly. He understood. Even from his cell, Brownie was in control.

'You are more of a liability than an asset, Frank. Keep that in mind.'

'Fuck you too,' Davis said under his breath.

'What'd you say?'

Davis moved to the side so the sun didn't blind him any more. 'I said fuckin' Brown is through.'

'Oh.' King smiled. 'At least we agree on one thing. Do as I tell you, keep a low profile, and we'll get the job done. But don't fuck with me, Frank.'

'I wouldn't.'

'Funny,' King said. 'I just heard you say you would.'

The warden had done it again. He'd managed to get the computer in his office hooked up to the FBI fingerprint databank. And tonight, he'd turned it over to his number one prisoner.

Brownie adjusted the optical imager and placed the latent fingerprint card face-down over it. This was the print he'd lifted from Ruth's shoe and hidden in the lining of his wallet, the print *no one* could know about, not even Gardner.

The hardware was warmed up, and the software was on line. Brownie fed the electronic image into the fax machine linked to the network. He received a 'go-ahead' signal, and followed the on-screen directions that began the computer quest for a match.

Brownie's neck ached, and his heart pounded in his chest. This was going to be it. He'd wanted to run Ruth's print first, but the loss of his hands made that impossible. So now he had to switch to plan B. He had to run the print that he'd lifted from the shoe.

The monitor blurred with numbers and letters as the computer searched the fingerprint repository. The database contained eight million full sets, so it would be a while before the task was complete.

The numbers and letters finally stopped, and a notation appeared: 'ELEMENT ONE COMPLETE – NO MATCH.'

'OK.' Brownie whispered. So far, so good. In the first two million, nothing had come up.

'PROCEED TO ELEMENT TWO?' the screen prompted.

Brownie hit 'ENTER'.

'ELEMENT TWO SEARCHING,' the screen replied.

Soon the numbers and letters stopped again. 'NO MATCH.'

Brownie went on to the next element, and the next, finally completing six million comparisons without a positive response. There were only two million to go.

'READY FOR FINAL ELEMENT SEARCH.'

Brownie entered and sat back.

'ELEMENT FOUR COMPLETE,' the screen announced.

Brownie swallowed and looked at the words following the notation:

'ONE MATCH LOCATED.'

'ACCESS INFORMATION?' the machine queried.

Brownie hesitated and held his breath. If he hit a key, a name would appear on the screen, the name of the person who removed Ruth's shoes at the power station.

Brownie touched 'enter', and a name came up. 'Oh, God,' he sighed, fumbling with the keyboard. He quickly hit the 'DELETE DATA', 'EXIT PROGRAMME', and 'CLEAR SCREEN' commands.

Brownie punched the power button and shut off the machine. Then he balled up the fingerprint and set it on fire in an ashtray. It flared momentarily then crumbled to black ash. Brownie stirred it in with the cigarette butts. And when the smoke dissipated, he closed his eyes and banged his head against the warden's desk.

CHAPTER 16

Gardner's first order of business was to get Brownie out of jail. The vermin were massing for attack, and Brownie was vulnerable. He might not survive the next fight. So Gardner rushed himself through a crash course on bond law, filed an emergency petition with Judge Ransome, and called his accountant. And now, one day after his resignation, he was in court.

'Identify yourselves for the record,' Judge Ransome said.

'Kent King and Lin Song for the State,' King announced.

'Gardner Lawson for the defence.'

'I'll hear from you, counsel.' Ransome was ready to roll.

Gardner glanced at Brownie beside him. He was still in prison orange, sullen and withdrawn. He'd barely reacted this morning when Gardner told him they were trying again for bond. Something was eating him, and although Gardner tried, he couldn't draw it out. 'Let the record show the defendant is present in court,' he began.

The courtroom was crowded with spectators, but Reverend Taylor and his entourage were absent. At Gardner's request, Jennifer was off doing legal research. They were on their own.

'Proceed, counsel,' Ransome prompted.

'I've filed a motion to reopen the issue of bond,' Gardner said. 'Here is a memorandum of law and fact to support my position.' He handed a ten-page document he'd spent all night writing to the clerk. 'The citations and factual assertions stand for the proposition that bond in this case is warranted. The defendant has lived in the county all his life. He has no prior criminal record of any kind. He has been an officer of the court his entire career, and knows full well the responsibility to appear for trial. He . . .'

'Objection.' King stood up. 'We went through this last time.'

The judge looked at King. 'I'm willing to give Mr Lawson a chance to speak, counsel.'

King frowned and sat down.

'You can set a bond, Judge, based upon the facts as presented here. You're under no mandate to deny it, such as you would be if he were on parole or probation at the time of the commission of the offence. The issue does not revolve around the power to set bond, rather it revolves around . . .'

'How much bond to set,' Judge Ransome interjected.

'Exactly,' Gardner replied. The judge saw where he was heading.

'How much bond would you suggest, Mr Lawson?'

'Seven hundred fifty thousand dollars.'

There was a loud gasp in the courtroom. No one had expected such a staggering figure.

'Seven hundred fifty thousand, full amount,' Gardner continued. There was another gasp. 'Full amount' meant that a bondsman could not put up the cash. Brownie had to lay the entire sum on the table.

'That's a hefty number,' Ransome stated. 'It might be appropriate.' King started to rise but held back.

'*If* you set bond in that amount,' Gardner went on, 'I am prepared to post it today.'

The crowd stirred again.

Gardner pulled some papers out of his briefcase. 'I have taken the liberty of having this agreement drawn up, your honour. It has been certified by two accountants, and endorsed by the clerk of the court.' He held the papers up.

'What is it?' Judge Ransome asked.

'A pledge of my assets,' Gardner replied: 'real estate, bank deposits, stocks, bonds, life insurance.'

Brownie suddenly looked up. 'Awww...' he grumbled under his breath.

'So you're posting your *own* money to get him out?' Ransome asked.

'Yes, sir, I *am*.'

'What do you think about that, Mr King?' the judge asked.

King rose swiftly. 'Objection. The issue isn't the *amount* of the bond, it's public safety and the likelihood of flight. Besides, the *defendant* has no stake in the bond. That makes him even more likely to flee.'

Ransome thought for a moment, then spoke. 'I believe the amount is sufficient to guarantee Sergeant Brown's presence at trial. If he fails to appear, Mr Lawson will be financially wiped out, and I don't think the defendant wants that to happen. Bond is hereby set: seven hundred fifty thousand dollars, full amount!'

King threw his pen down on the table with disgust. Lawson had just pulled the same stunt as Willie Stanton: personally vouching for Brown. But this time it had worked.

'I *understand* the payment is due,' Nicholas Fairborne said. He was on the telephone to the Valley National Bank; they were enquiring about the unpaid mortgage.

'We will make every effort to have the payment to you soon!' He slammed down the phone. Damn Thomas Ruth! Accounts were due, and the money was gone, vanished without a trace like the man's mysterious soul.

Fairborne walked to the window and looked out. The camp was almost deserted now. Their spirit was broken, the food supply dwindling. CAIN was dying.

He went back to his desk and looked at the inventory. If he sold the cars and the computers he could hold on for another month or two, long enough to attract new blood. That was the only way he could keep the operation going. He'd called a meeting after Ruth's death and tried to rally the crowd, but the spark wasn't there anymore. Ruth was the glue that held it all together. And now the people were leaving, and the snakes were rotting in their barrel.

Fairborne rummaged through the desk again, scouring places he'd looked before, searching for traces of Ruth's secret stash. The money could not have just vanished. If he had time, he could find it. But time was running out.

He rifled a pile of papers in the bottom drawer. All cash receipts. Even the mortgage payments were in cash. He threw the documents into a trash bag and cleaned the drawer down to the wood. They were useless to him now. The money was gone.

Fairborne was about to close the drawer when he noticed a small piece of yellow paper stuck against the rear wall. He pulled it off and studied it. 'PRESCRIPTION, T. RUTH', the typed letters said. Underneath was an illegible scribble. He crumpled it and threw it into the bag. Ruth's pills couldn't help the bastard now. Whatever the hell they were.

The paperwork had finally been completed for Brownie's release, a package of financial pledges that laid all of Gardner's worldly possessions on the line. They'd talked briefly in the warden's office as the procedure was finalized. Brownie had squawked about Gardner's decision to pledge his assets; he didn't ask for it, didn't want it. Again, Gardner had stood firm. This is the way it's going to be, he'd said. At the end of the conversation they'd forged a reluctant truce. Brownie had agreed to co-operate. But Gardner still sensed a problem.

Brownie and Gardner approached the power station in silence. It was late in the day, and the forest obscured a dim sunset in the western sky. They hiked in the shadows as twisted limbs menaced them from all sides and crows croaked in the distance. Ahead, in the twilight, lay the squared-off enclosure of the electric killer.

Gardner switched on his flashlight and gave Brownie a hand over the last rocky step. At last they arrived on the plateau overlooking the crime scene.

Gardner directed the light through the fence and lit up the grid. It was still discoloured and charred despite the repairs. 'You've seen this before,' he said.

'Yeah.'

'Tell me again *why*.'

Brownie leaned against a tree. 'Wanted to see for myself.'

'See what?'

'Where it happened.'

Gardner put his hand on the tree. 'What do *you* think happened? Surely you have a theory.'

'I didn't get that far. I was still gathering evidence.'

'What about the shoes?' Gardner asked. The shoes were crucial to both the prosecution *and* the defence. How Brownie got them was key to conviction or acquittal.

'Huh?' Brownie's mind had wandered.

'How did you happen to find Ruth's shoes?'

Brownie snapped out of his reverie. 'I was doing a sweep like I always do. Came across them ... that's it.'

'You didn't just come across the shoes. This place was canvassed by the entire police team. They didn't find them.'

'They're not *me*.'

'OK, you get a medal. Now *where* did you find them?'

Brownie scanned the darkness, then approached the grid. 'Over in that area,' he said, pointing to some brush nearby.

'Over *there*?' From all the information available, it appeared that Ruth died *without* his shoes on.

'Yeah,' Brownie replied. 'They were under a sticker bush.'

Gardner shone his light towards the spot. 'I don't believe it. That's right next to the fence. The cops should have found them.' Gardner examined the bush. Its branches were spread down to the ground, and it was covered with vines. The shoes *could* have escaped the eyes of the police, but it wasn't likely. 'Why, Brownie?' he finally asked.

'Why what?'

'Why were the shoes off in the first place?'

Brownie sighed. 'Rained the day before the, uh, incident, guess he had to make sure he was grounded when the juice went through. Soles were rubber.'

'That's what I thought,' Gardner agreed. 'His bare feet were in a puddle, and there was no protection.'

'Like a lightning bolt. Through his arms and out his toes...'

Gardner saw Brownie visualizing the scene as he spoke. 'Right through the heart,' he added.

Brownie didn't respond. He was gazing at the grid.

Gardner considered making a follow-up comment but held back. An electrocution was an induced heart attack. The shock caused cardiac arrest. In an eye-for-eye situation, it would have been the ideal retribution for Joseph Brown's untimely death. 'You know what I'm thinking,' Gardner said.

'Yeah. It's a perfect weapon for revenge.'

'Right. Whoever *did* kill him must have known that...'

Brownie didn't reply.

'I don't think it was a coincidence that electrocution was used. I think it was planned...'

Brownie stood quietly in the dusk.

Gardner decided to go onto something else. 'I'm still having trouble with the shoes, Brownie.'

'What?'

'I'm trying to understand why they were hidden. Why not leave them in the open or cart them off? Why *hide* them in such an obvious spot? They were sure to be found.'

Brownie shrugged.

'You've considered that,' Gardner said. 'I know you. I know how you analyse things.'

'Could be a lot of reasons.'

'Such as?'

'Maybe he wasn't thinking straight...'

'Who?'

'Whoever did it.'

Gardner tried to look into his face, but Brownie was turned away.

'Who did it, Brownie?'

'Told you I didn't get that far.'

'You must have an inkling...'

'*No.*'

Brownie walked away from the tree, towards the trail.

'Where are you going?' Gardner asked.

'This is a waste of time. You're going in circles, and you're taking me with you.'

Gardner grabbed his arm. 'Then help me get out of it, Brownie! Whose print did you find on the shoes?'

'Huh?'

'I *know* you processed the shoes for fingerprints.'

'Says who?'

The two men faced each other. 'I know. Don't bullshit me! Whose print did you find on the shoes?'

'Nobody's ... Yes, I *did* process them. But they were clean.'

Gardner felt like punching him. 'Clean? I don't believe it!'

'Yeah,' Brownie replied, '*clean*. Nothin' on them. Not a damn thing.'

Then he turned back to the trail and wandered off in the darkness.

Kent King and Judge Rollie Ransome were conferring in

Judge Danforth's chambers. It was an off-the-record conversation, the courthouse was closed, and they were alone. Two glasses of whiskey lay on the desk.

'So how's the old Baltimore beat?' King began.

Rollie leaned back in Danforth's chair and put his stubby foot up.

'Still a jungle.'

'So you miss me?'

'Like a toothache.'

King laughed, then changed his tone. 'I need to discuss some things with you,' he said.

'Fire away.'

'First of all, thanks for fucking me at the bond hearing. How could you let Brown out?'

Rollie wheezed. 'It's Lawson's money. If Brown runs, your pal loses everything. Thought you'd like that.'

'He's *not* going to run,' King replied. 'He's got the damn loyalty disease.'

'No big deal,' the judge said. 'Let him have a few free days before you bury him.'

'That's so thoughtful of you.'

'I've mellowed.'

'I can tell.'

Rollie took a sip of liquor. 'What else is on your mind tonight?'

'We need to talk about trial scheduling. How much time have they given you?'

Rollie's stomach quivered. 'No time limit, I'm in for the duration.'

'So you're not going to rush the case through?'

'Hadn't planned on it.'

King pulled a day-timer out of his pocket. 'How are you fixed for January eighth through the thirtieth?'

Rollie smiled. 'Fine with me.'

'Can you set it then?'

'If it's OK with Lawson.'

'And if it's not?'

'We'll have to find another date.'

King dropped his calendar book on the desk. 'You're really playing this straight, aren't you? Right down the line.'

Rollie rolled his giant body forward, and plunked his feet on the ground. 'What do you mean by that?'

'I mean you've gotten damn independent in your old age. You sound like a real judge.'

'Told you I'd mellowed,' Rollie said.

'I seem to remember a day when Kent King suggested a trial date and Rollie Ransome approved it without hesitation, a day when Ransome asked King for a favour or two...'

'Stop right there,' Rollie interjected. 'They weren't *favours*.'

'Really? What would *you* call them?'

The judge hesitated. 'Accommodations to the court.'

'*Accommodations?*' King laughed. 'Setting you up with my secretary was a hell of an accommodation.'

'That was personal.'

'While I was tryin' a murder case before you? Get real, Rollie.'

Ransome began to respond, but restrained himself. King was hitting some sensitive spots in his judicial past. 'So what do you want, Kent? You want to make a stink over a friggin' trial date?'

288

'I wouldn't mind getting January,' King answered.

'And that's *it*?'

King fell silent. The real reason he came by was to check out the second item on his list, the exculpatory materials in his file he didn't want Lawson to see. Would Rollie side with his position or not? Judging by the responses so far, it didn't look good.

'What else did you want to discuss?'

King stood up. 'Nothing,' he said.

'Don't get bent out of shape, Kent. We're in a fishbowl here. Everyone is watching. I've gotta play it straight.'

'I understand,' King replied. In point of fact, he *did* understand. Rollie would give the case law a fair reading, and ignore the old boy protocol. That meant that Gardner might get a look at his file. And that could never be.

Jennifer sat in the end booth at Russel's Deli, sipping a milkshake. It was early evening, and she felt like she had just wandered into a cyclone. Gardner had assigned her the task of outlining defence options, so she'd been buried in the law library stacks all day. It was foreign territory, and they were lost. She and Gardner were prosecution experts who knew the ins and outs of building a case against someone. But they didn't know beans about how to tear one apart.

Jennifer sipped a mouthful of chocolate. It numbed her lips, and sent a chill into her brain. The legal research had helped her escape the funk she'd been in since Gardner announced his resignation. Logically, she'd accepted the change. His friend was in trouble and needed help. Jennifer could go along with that. But emotionally, she was irritated.

Gardner had risked everything for Brownie on a moment's notice. And that left *her* future on hold.

Jennifer swallowed more shake, opened her notebook and reviewed her outline. The defence options were listed in order. The client either *did it* or he *didn't*. If he *did it*, there were a slew of mitigating defences at his disposal: accident, mistake, self-preservation, duress, insanity, diminished mental capacity. But these were all premised on the fact that the client was guilty of the act. It was much more difficult to allege the client *didn't* do it. The defence menu was more limited: alibi, physical incapacity, or scientific impossibility. And the only sure way to prove the client *didn't* do it was to prove that someone else *did*.

Jennifer closed her eyes and remembered how Gardner helped her set strategy in her first murder case. She was going to fly solo, and Gardner was getting her 'up' for the trial.

'I won't be there,' he had said, 'so you have to rely on yourself. And the best way to do that is to plan *now* for any eventuality. Psych out the opposition. Think like they would. Play devil's advocate, and come up with objections to your own evidence. Then prepare counter-arguments. In other words, pre-try the case. That way you'll always have an answer. And if they throw in something you didn't anticipate, just wing it.'

Jennifer opened her eyes. This situation was unprecedented. They could anticipate King's moves because they'd been there. But they lacked any moves of their own. Unless they solved the case and caught the killer, they'd have to wing it. Brownie would have to choose a defence. And his choices were inadequate, to say the least.

* * *

Katanga picked up the phone in his apartment and dialled his mother's number. He'd been working the streets all day, and he'd just opened his mail. One of his letters contained a surprise.

'Mama?'

'Paulie?'

'Yeah. Sorry to call so late. You OK?'

'I was just gettin' ready for bed.'

'Why'd you do it, Mama?' Paulie asked. 'What's going on?'

'What?'

Paulie removed a cheque from the letter his mother had just sent. It was written to 'Paul Brown' in the amount of ten thousand dollars.

'The money came today. What's this about?' He'd been on his own for years and never asked for a hand-out.

'Thought you might need some cash,' Althea replied. 'I know how hard it must be down there.'

'I'm gettin' by. You shouldn't have done it.' Katanga paused.

'Where'd you get it anyway?' His mother had always been frugal.

'The railroad cashed Daddy's pension and mailed me a great big cheque. I thought you could use some of it.'

'I'm sending it back,' Katanga said.

'No.'

'Yes, Mama. I don't want it. The money belongs to you...'

'I've got all I need. Please keep it, son.'

'Can't do that.' Katanga slid the cheque into the envelope.

291

'Please, Paulie...'

'Can't Mama, and that's it.' The conversation was over, but Katanga hesitated. 'Uh, how's...'

'Joseph?'

'Uh huh.'

'He's out of jail. Mr Lawson put up every cent he had to bail him out...'

'Heard he got hurt,' Katanga said.

'He was in a fight, but he's going to be all right. I wish you'd talk to him...'

Katanga didn't respond.

'He needs you.'

'Sounds like he's got some high-priced help now,' Katanga replied. 'Fancy white bread on his table.'

'Don't speak that way, son. Gardner Lawson is a fine man...'

'Yeah. Heard he kicked one of our people in the teeth. Blocktown's finest lawyer.'

'It was for the best. Mr Lawson knows how to deal with the prosecutor better than Willie Stanton.'

'Yeah, yeah.'

'But Joseph still needs you. *Anything* you can do. Call him, talk to him...'

Katanga moved the phone away from his ear. Big brother cop was against the wall. He'd spent his life shoving other people there. But this time *he* was facing the firing squad. And that was something he had to do alone.

Gardner, Jennifer, and Granville sat around the kitchen table at the townhouse. Files and books were stacked everywhere, and they were all hard at work. Gardner and

Jennifer were planning trial strategy, and Granville was studying for a vocabulary test. His mom was out for the evening, so Gardner agreed to babysit.

'What's *merge*?' the boy asked.

Gardner glanced up. Granville was eyeing the back of a flash card.

'What do you think it is?'

Granville crinkled his nose. 'Dunno.'

'Think,' Gardner said. 'When a car goes onto the interstate it...'

'Crashes?'

Gardner tapped him playfully. 'Gran! A car *merges* with the traffic. That's what the highway sign says. What does it mean?'

'Goes *in*?'

'Close. Try again.'

'Goes *together*?'

'Closer.'

Granville did not reply.

'How about joins or blends together?'

Granville flipped the card. 'You're right!' Dad was brilliant.

'Now do the next one on your own.' Gardner turned back to a file labelled 'DEFENCES'.

'That's the whole lot,' Jennifer said. She'd just briefed him on their range of choices. 'We either go the *did do it* with an explanation route, or the *did not do it* route. That's it, end of list.'

Gardner turned to page two. 'Brownie says he didn't do it.'

'So why is he acting this way?'

293

'Maybe he's protecting someone.'

'Who?'

'The killer.'

Jennifer glanced at Granville's head behind a card. 'So he *knows* who did it.'

'It's a possibility.'

'*Revise*,' Granville said suddenly.

'Use your cards,' Gardner told him.

'Re-*vise*,' Granville repeated.

'*Cards*.'

'He's not going to tell us what he knows?' Jennifer asked.

'Apparently not.'

'Revise means *change*,' Jennifer whispered to Granville. He smiled and wrote it down. 'So we're in trouble right from the start.'

'We can't defend him in the blind,' Gardner said. 'We need his support, his full co-operation.'

'So what's the next step?'

Gardner stroked his son's back. 'Try again tomorrow. We sit him down and go through it again. Maybe he'll soften.'

'And the defence? What are we going to do about that?'

Gardner exhaled loudly. '*That* depends on Brownie.'

CHAPTER 17

Kent King and Lin Song stood by the power station fence. It was a damp and dreary autumn day punctuated by showers and patches of fog. He wore a trenchcoat, and she was buttoned up in a poncho. They shared an umbrella and huddled together against the chill as raindrops pattered the silent trees. They too were preparing for trial, putting a face on the words in their investigative reports. King had done it many times as a defence lawyer, but never as a prosecutor.

'So that's where he died,' Lin said, looking through the wire at the grey high voltage cabinet. This was their first actual encounter with the execution device.

'Old Sparky,' King joked.

Lin looked at the heavy padlock on the metal gate. 'How'd he get in?'

King fingered the lock and let it drop back against the fence. 'This wasn't here. Power company put it on "after the fact".'

'What *was* here?'

King shrugged. 'Don't know. It wasn't in any of the original police reports. No one noticed at the time.'

Lin seemed disturbed by that. She frowned deeply.

'It doesn't matter. Brown removed whatever lock there was...'

'So where is it now?'

King looked into the forest. The trees extended to the horizon. 'Out there,' he said.

'So he removed the lock, or whatever it was, put it in his pocket, and later discarded it.'

'Probably,' King said. Who gave a damn about the lock? The rest of the evidence made that little detail irrelevant.

'He threw it away in the woods,' Lin continued.

'Yeah. So what?'

'And he took it off while holding his prisoner under guard, preparing to hitch him to the grid.'

King looked his assistant in the eye. 'We're here to assess the proof we *have*. Why are you nitpicking?'

Lin gazed back steadily. 'I've been thinking about it.'

'What?'

'How, exactly, Brown was able to pull it off. By himself. At night. With a locked gate and an uncooperative prisoner.'

'That may *never* be answered,' King argued. 'We have motive, opportunity, fingerprints, the victim's shoes, witnesses...' He was back on the party line. With proof like that, why sweat the details?

'You're still thinking like a defence attorney,' Lin replied.

'You're used to feeding the jury contradictions and hoping they will raise reasonable doubt. Now, you have to come at it from another direction. You have to be specific.

296

The jury's going to want to know exactly *how* it happened. And you have to be prepared to tell them.'

King realized that she was right. His usual approach wouldn't work here. It was a damn good thing he'd brought her on board. 'OK,' he said, 'I understand. We have to give the jury a schematic to go with the circumstantial proof.' As good as their evidence was, it was *all* circumstantial. No one had actually seen Brownie attach Ruth to the grid.

'We have to walk it through and be comfortable with how it all went down. Then we can lay it out for the jury.'

'OK.' King smiled. This *was* a new experience. As a defence attorney he'd always denigrated proof and scoffed at theories, not *wanting* the jury to piece together what happened. He had been a destroyer of logic, not a builder of it. 'Why don't we start again. How do you think he pulled it off?'

'That's the *problem*,' Lin replied. 'I've been going over and over it, and it doesn't piece together.'

'Try this on,' King suggested. 'Brown stops the car, interrogates Ruth about his father's death, takes him into custody, puts the cuffs on him, holds him at gunpoint, drives to the park, walks him up the trail, *busts* off the lock, and shoves him into the sparkler machine. How's that?'

Lin shook her head. 'No.'

'No?' That was a theory, and it was logical.

'What about his car?'

'Car?'

'How did Ruth's car get over here?'

297

King wiped mud from his shoe onto a rock. 'Brown drove it. He made the stop, but took *Ruth*'s car instead of the police vehicle. And the rest of the story plays out the same. We found Brown's fingerprint on the car, remember?'

'On the passenger side,' Lin replied. 'On the *outside* of the passenger side.'

'So?'

'So who drove the car?'

King blinked. 'Ruth drove while Brown held him at gunpoint, directed him to the park, et cetera, et cetera...'

'So he left the police van on the road, drove ten miles in the victim's car, parked and locked it, leaving his fingerprints on it, walked another mile, electrocuted Ruth, and somehow made it back to his van, all in one night.'

King drew a lungful of air. 'He was under stress, duress, whatever you want to call it. He was grief-stricken about his old man, and obsessed with Ruth. People in that condition do amazing things.'

'I'll buy the grief, stress, and obsession part,' Lin said. 'That fills your "motive" blank...' Her voice faded.

'*But?*'

'I just don't think it's physically possible. Not for *one man*. With the distances and logistics, I just don't see it.'

The rain was falling faster now, and the clouds seemed to hang over them. It was getting nastier by the minute. King moved closer to Lin to stay out of the splash. '*One man*,' he said, repeating her words.

'We only have *one man* charged.'

'True, but the jury's going to wonder the same thing: how did he accomplish it alone?'

King tried to laugh. 'That's a non-issue. No one's going to think of it. Not even Lawson.'

Kim looked at him sternly. 'The jurors will come up with it on their own. They won't need Lawson or anyone else to tell them. You know how juries think.'

King knew she was right. 'So they're going to assume there was more than one person involved, that Brown had help.'

'Yup.'

'Or ... that *someone* else did it, and Brown wasn't involved. The logistics were too complicated.'

'It occurred to *me*,' Lin said. 'And it *will* occur to the jury.'

'So the evidence we have won't make a difference. It will all go up in smoke.' King had won countless locked-in cases the same way, by raising an anomaly the state couldn't explain. 'So what do we do about that, Miss Prosecutor?'

Lin smiled smugly. 'We re-work the theory until we *can* explain it.'

'Oh, shit,' King said suddenly.

'What is it?'

'The file. The other suspects we considered might play into the two-man theory.'

'Let *me* handle that,' she said confidently. 'What Lawson doesn't know will never hurt *us*.'

King smiled and moved closer. 'That sounds good. Now what say we get out of this mess and grab a cup of coffee, or *something*.'

'This is it, Brownie,' Gardner said, 'decision day. We have

to select a defence.' They were gathered in their makeshift office, a cubby-hole in a commercial building complex. Rain lashed the window, and the overhead fluorescent light pulsed as Gardner, Jennifer, and Brownie faced each other across a card table.

Brownie picked up Jennifer's notes. 'So these are my choices, huh?'

'That's it,' Jennifer said. Every conceivable defence was listed.

Brownie slowly lowered the page. 'You missed one.'

Jennifer looked at Gardner. Brownie *was* being recalcitrant, not to mention antagonistic.

'We don't have time to play games,' Gardner warned.

'I'm serious, there's one defence you haven't written down, one I've been considering since you dragged me back to the power station.'

Gardner gripped his pen. 'Which one is that?'

Brownie looked him in the eye. 'Suicide.'

'Suicide?' Gardner's jaw almost hit his knees. They'd never even discussed that. From day one it had always been murder.

'Yes,' Brownie replied. 'I think Ruth killed him*self*.'

'But *you* don't really believe that,' Gardner said.

'Who is the defendant and who is the lawyer?' Brownie asked.

Gardner glanced at Jennifer. She was stunned, wide-eyed with disbelief.

'Does the *defendant* get to choose his defence? Or is it up to the lawyer?'

'It's usually a joint effort,' Gardner answered. 'They arrive at the decision together.'

'I want you to go with suicide,' Brownie said firmly.

'Just like that?'

'Just like that.'

'But *we* know it wasn't suicide,' Jennifer interjected. '*We* know that someone *did* kill Ruth. He did not take his own life.'

'How do you know that?' Brownie countered. 'Were you there? Was *anyone* there at the time he died?'

Jennifer turned to Gardner, and he shook his head 'no'. If one thing was certain, it was that there were *no eyewitnesses* to the crime. All the proof was circumstantial. 'Why are you doing this, Brownie?' she asked.

'Because it's my right.'

'You're making a mistake,' Gardner said. 'Ruth was murdered. He had a lot of enemies, not just you. If we could locate the killer, we could get you off. I've told you that a thousand times.'

Brownie did not answer.

'I could do the job if you'd let me. I could do a lot of things if I had your co-operation. But you've made it impossible.'

'I told you everything,' Brownie protested.

'So you say.'

'I have, damn it.'

'So that's the way it is,' Gardner continued. 'You're sticking with that line...'

'It's not a line.' Brownie rubbed his forehead.

'Shit,' Gardner sighed. This was getting tedious. A defence had to be planned, with or without Brownie's co-operation.

Brownie dropped his hand. 'I have the right to select a

defence. You said that yourself. I select suicide. If you don't agree, I guess I'll have to get another lawyer.'

'You *can't* get another lawyer. I was *appointed*.'

'I can un-appoint you.'

Gardner grimaced. Brownie was technically right. As a client *he* could set the agenda. The lawyer had to either go along with it or quit. The lawyer worked for the client, not the other way around.

'Don't *do* this, Brownie,' Jennifer pleaded. 'Please let us help you.'

'Sorry, Jennifer. I've made up my mind. This is the way I want to go. The *only* way.'

Brownie had them in a bind. If they couldn't agree on a strategy, they had to get out of the case. And Brownie would be convicted for sure.

'Do you know what you're doing?' Gardner asked.

'I *know*. I take full responsibility.'

'And you realize the consequences? You could get life in the penitentiary.'

'I know.'

'Suicide,' Gardner said sarcastically. 'It's not *my* choice, but under the circumstances...' He looked at Jennifer. There was deep concern in her eyes. 'Jen?'

'Whatever you say.' Her voice was weak.

'Go with it,' Brownie urged.

Gardner picked up his pen. A co-operative Brownie was better than an uncooperative Brownie. 'Maybe we can put something together. What's the basis for your hypothesis?'

'Ruth was strung out when I saw him,' Brownie declared.

'Strung out? On drugs?'

Brownie shook his head. 'No. His pupils were normal, not dilated. But he went off when I made my accusation about Daddy.'

'Get specific,' Gardner instructed. 'I want you to recount in minute detail everything you and he said after you stopped him.'

Brownie nodded.

'Your first words?'

'Out of the car, asshole.'

Gardner shook his head. The ugly truth, at last.

'I was upset.'

'All right. Let's keep going. What did he say?'

'"*Again*,"' Brownie answered.

'"*Again?*"'

'That was it. The first thing he said when I pulled him out of the car was "*Again?*"'

Gardner wrote the word on his pad. 'Thought you only stopped him once.'

'I did.'

'Then what did he mean by that?'

Brownie shrugged. 'I didn't give him a chance to explain. I frisked him and ordered him into the van.'

'What did he say?'

'"Leave me alone. I didn't do anything." Stuff like that.'

Gardner made more notes. 'And what did you say?'

'Nothing then. I put the cuffs on and shoved him into the van.'

'His comments at that point?'

'"Don't. Stop this. Leave me alone…"'

'Did he struggle?'

'No.'

'Did you strike him or injure him in any way?'

'No.'

'What happened next?'

'I told him what I thought he did.'

'Your exact words.'

'You put a fuckin' snake on my daddy and killed him.' Brownie stopped suddenly.

Gardner looked up from his notes. 'Go on.'

'You motherfucker this, you motherfucker that. I was cursin' him good.'

'Any physical contact?'

'No. Just words.'

'What did he say when you gave him a chance to respond?'

'Said he was sorry.'

Gardner wrote 'sorry' and underlined it. 'Did you take that to mean that he *had* done something to Joseph?'

'No.'

'How did you take it?'

Brownie changed position in his chair. 'I don't know.'

'You can't know?'

'I sort of skipped over it. I started yelling again. Telling him what I wanted to do to him . . .'

'Were these threats?'

'Sort of.'

Gardner wrote 'threat'. 'What, exactly did you tell him?'

'I said he should pay for his crime. That he should die like Daddy did . . .'

'And what did he say?'

'He went quiet. Sounded like he was mumbling prayers or something.'

'So what did you do then?'

'I stopped talking.'

'Describe him at that moment.'

Brownie didn't answer. That image of Ruth had haunted his nightmares for weeks. 'Never seen anything like it. He had some kind of fit or seizure. His eyes rolled back, he was chanting something, uh, like speaking in tongues, acting weird, crazy, talking about death, and bodies, and God...'

'Then what happened?'

'Then he stopped, and told me he was sorry again, and that he'd never hurt anyone.'

Gardner put down his pen. 'What was going through *your* mind at the time? You had no plan, you said. You were just rousting him. But after seeing his reaction, what effect did it have on *you*?'

Brownie took a breath. 'It was strange...'

Gardner watched him relive the moment.

'I began to believe him.'

'What?' That was unexpected.

'Gard, I must'a locked up ten thousand guys, heard a million excuses. I *know* when a guy is lying to me, but this time it was different. I had a feeling that he was telling the truth. After all that, after I had decided he was the one...'

'So you let him go.'

Brownie nodded silently.

'You were convinced at that point that he had not harmed Joseph.'

'No.'

'No? You just said you believed him.'

'The guy was fucked up, really fucked up. I decided to give him the benefit of the doubt. I wasn't quitting the investigation, just giving him a reprieve till I got myself together.'

'So you released him in handcuffs to make your point. He wasn't off the hook yet.'

'You keep bugging me about the cuffs.'

'I have to. It doesn't make sense to me, why for God's sake you'd let a man walk away in a set of your handcuffs...'

'Told you I wasn't a hundred per cent myself.'

Gardner looked him in the eye. 'That's obvious. It's the stupidist thing you ever did.'

'Well I did it, and that's that. Can't we move on to something else?'

Gardner picked up his pen again. 'You said he was fucked up. Would you say he was suicidal?'

'Yes. That's the point. When I let him go, his fuse was *lit*.'

Gardner glanced at Jennifer. For a start, this wasn't too bad. They might be able to make a case for suicide after all. He shot her a 'what do you think?' look with his eyes. But Jennifer stared back in silence. It was clear she was unhappy. And that she wasn't buying a single word of the suicide theory.

The scheduling conference for Brownie's case was set for 2.00 p.m. in Judge Danforth's chambers. Rollie Ransome presided, and Kent King and Lin Song were there for the state. Gardner was late. The meeting with Brownie had gone into overtime.

Gardner finally arrived at 2.20 p.m., wet, out of breath, and alone. He'd sent Jennifer off on another mission.

'Good afternoon,' Judge Ransome said, 'so glad you could make it.'

'Sorry,' Gardner apologized, shaking out of his overcoat. 'I got held up...'

'Let's get started.' Ransome was tired of waiting. He looked at Gardner. 'Kent has asked that we begin trial the first week of January. How's that for you, Lawson?'

Gardner scrutinized the fat man as he sat down. So it was 'Kent' and 'Lawson'. 'Let me check my calendar,' he replied, pulling out his book. The pages were filled with State's Attorney's business, but that no longer applied. January was free. 'Got a conflict,' he finally said. If King wanted *that* time slot, he didn't.

'When can you do it?'

'Not then.'

'How about we slip it back a month, say into December?' King suggested.

Rollie looked at Gardner. 'The second week of December. How's that?'

Gardner sensed a 'fix'. 'Christmas holidays,' he replied. 'It'll conflict.' Court was always suspended the last two weeks of December.

The judge smiled. 'I'm Jewish, Lawson.'

Gardner reddened. He didn't want to insult the man who controlled Brownie's fate. 'Uh, your honour,' he stuttered, 'I meant the court, uh, our court is usually shut down during that time.'

'You forget,' Rollie grinned, 'I'm specially assigned. I

307

don't have to follow the rules. *I* can work through Christmas. How about you, Kent?'

'Sure,' King said. He had no family.

'December, then?' the judge asked.

Gardner didn't respond. December was special. It was the one time of year when he and Granville spent a lot of time together. A trial then would interfere.

'Well?' Rollie said. 'Whenever you're ready, Lawson.'

'On second thought, the first suggestion might be OK after all.' Gardner *was* clear then, and it would give them a greater opportunity to prepare. He'd only balked in the first place to screw up King.

Rollie wrote a date in his book. 'We begin trial in State v. Brown on January eighth. Agreed?'

The lawyers said 'yes'.

'Now let's discuss motions, discovery, and other house-keeping issues.'

The judge checked an entry on his pad. 'OK, then, what about discovery?' He looked at King.

'Complete,' the special prosecutor said.

Gardner did a double-take. 'I haven't received anything yet.' The state was required to send the defence an outline of the witnesses and evidence it intended to use at trial.

'Mailed out this morning,' Lin Song added.

'Obviously not received,' Gardner answered. 'But that's all right. I'm filing a supplemental discovery request today.' He handed a sheaf of papers to the judge and a copy to King. 'I want all exculpatory information in Mr King's files under the *Brady* case, and I want the additional items outlined in this petition.' He and Jennifer had pounded out the pleading earlier, after the Brownie meeting.

Lin Song glanced at King.

'I suggest you read this carefully,' Gardner said. 'It's quite specific.'

The room went quiet while the documents were perused. Suddenly King dropped the papers onto his lap. 'What is this, a *joke*?'

'No joke,' Gardner replied.

Rollie was still reading. Finally he put the papers down too. 'Your request goes beyond statutory requirements,' he told Gardner. 'The state is under no obligation to give you any of its internal reports. You, of all people should know that. And this paragraph about medical records, what's that about?'

'I want every witness statement, investigative report, background check, medical, and psychiatric record that the state has pertaining to Thomas Ruth,' Gardner answered. '*Every* one.'

Rollie looked at King.

'Don't look at me,' King said.

'You have such reports?' the judge asked.

'No.'

'He has them, and what he doesn't have, he can get,' Gardner said.

Rollie turned back to King. 'Can you?'

King shrugged. 'Maybe and maybe not. I really don't care. None of that information is relevant to the case. We're going to try a *live* defendant, not a dead one. *Brown* is on trial, not *Ruth*. What possible relevance does his background have? We know he was alive, and we know that he's dead. End of discussion.'

'Under normal circumstances that might be true,' Gardner

replied, 'but we're raising a defence that makes it relevant.'

'What defence?' Rollie asked.

Gardner stared at King. '*Suicide.*'

King looked like he had been hit by a stray bullet. 'What?'

'Suicide,' Gardner repeated. 'Ruth's records become relevant under that defence. They can be used to establish his state of mind.'

King looked to Lin Song for help. She had tried to warn him about this. 'We do not have any such records,' she said.

'But if you *did*,' Rollie interjected, 'you understand that you might have to turn them over to the defence.'

'The law says that it's their obligation to release what they have and to *obtain* what they lack,' Gardner declared, 'because they have exclusive access to the victim's personal files.'

'What about that?' Rollie asked.

King and Lin had their heads together. They had just been ambushed.

'Are you going to secure Ruth's records for Mr Lawson or not?'

King glanced up. 'I'll have to get back to you on that one.'

'You have three days to reply,' Rollie said firmly.

'Yeah. I understand.' King jerked to his feet. 'Three days to help Lawson with his defence. Can't do it himself, so *we* have to do it for him. Pathetic...'

Gardner smiled. 'I'm going to beat you, Kent.'

King started to answer, but bit his lip. A few days ago he was certain they had Brown in the bag. But now he wasn't so sure. Being a prosecutor was a lot tougher than he'd imagined.

Jennifer placed her name on the sign-in sheet of the courthouse vault and told the clerk she was there to review exhibits from a post-conviction proceeding. But she was acting under false pretences. The vault contained evidence from criminal cases, stacked in folders, awaiting appellate action. And it also stored evidence from current cases assigned to special prosecutors.

The attendant released the bolts, drew back the metal door, and switched on the light. Jennifer entered the elongated chamber and walked to the shelves at the far end. Soon the attendant left, and there was no one else in the iron room.

Jennifer scanned the top shelf and found two new cardboard boxes labelled: 'BROWN'. She checked the door and took a box down. The top was covered with masking tape. Jennifer peeled it back and opened the flap.

There was a plastic bag inside the box; inside that, a pair of men's shoes. The tag read: 'THOMAS RUTH'. Jennifer examined them through the transparent covering. Traces of black fingerprinting powder clung to the plastic. She put them down.

Jennifer lifted another bag from the cardboard box. It was a set of police files, marked 'SUSPICIOUS DEATH INVESTIGATION – JOSEPH BROWN, SENIOR'. She flattened the plastic and read the name 'DAVIS' at the bottom of a report. The report itself was a surveillance log of Ruth sightings. 'DAILY ADHERENCE TO SCHEDULE', the officer had noted.

Jennifer moved on to the next exhibit, the autopsy file of 'JOSEPH BROWN, SR'. She caught a glimpse of Joseph on the slab, and covered it with her hand. Below that was a supplemental report by Davis. She speed-read to the bottom line: 'AFTER THOROUGH INVESTIGATION IT HAS BEEN CONCLUDED THAT THERE IS INSUFICIENT EVIDENCE OF FOUL PLAY TO WARRANT FURTHER ACTION. PURSUANT TO THE MEDICAL EXAMINER'S FINDING AND THE LACK OF FORENSIC PROOF TO THE CONTRARY, THE DEATH OF JOSEPH BROWN, SR. IS HEREBY RULED TO BE: BY NATURAL CAUSE.' There was a notation stamped below the conclusion: 'CASE CLOSED'. And under that, Brownie had written in red ink: 'BULLSHIT'.

Jennifer shut the file. This didn't look good. The police closed the case on his father's death, but Brownie didn't accept it. That was sure to be brought out in court.

Jennifer removed another plastic bag from the box. It was inscribed: 'PERSONAL PAPERS AND PHOTO-GRAPHS'. She scoped the door again for intruders. It was still quiet, but she had to hurry. She peeled off the tape and dumped out the contents: letters, notes, lists, and old photos.

Jennifer picked up one of the notes. 'TO DO LIST' was written at the top. Typical Brownie, so organized, Jennifer mused. She then dropped her eyes to the single entry below. 'EXECUTE', was all it said. Jennifer shuddered, and let the note slip from her fingers.

She moved on to the photos. They were high school shots of a younger and thinner Brownie. At the bottom of the pile was a picture of a teenaged Brownie and a lookalike, arm-in-arm. She turned to the back of the picture. 'P. & J.' was inscribed at the top.

Jennifer returned to the box and lifted the single remaining plastic bag. It contained a rap sheet: a certified criminal record. The requesting authority was: 'BROWN, SGT. JOE', and the record was listed as: 'BROWN, PAUL'.

Jennifer began to remove the rap sheet from the plastic when the sound of voices entered the vault. She slipped the bag into the box and piled the other exhibits on top of it. In a second, everything was back in its proper position. Jennifer moved away from the shelf.

The security man poked his head into the door. 'Find what you were looking for?' he asked. He was signing someone else in.

'*Yes*,' Jennifer replied on the way out.

She ran down the corridor, and out into the squall. The wind was driving the chilly rain against the granite building. Raising her collar, she sprinted for the car.

Brownie's insistence on suicide had been a tip-off. He was refusing to call it murder anymore, and he was even willing to be convicted. For Brownie, that had to mean one thing: he was covering for someone. Jennifer leaped into her car and shut the door.

Brownie knew who killed Thomas Ruth and was protecting him. And now Jennifer had a clue as to who it was.

CHAPTER 18

Jennifer looked at the clock. It was 8.00 p.m., and Gardner had not returned to the townhouse. The autumn squall had settled in the valley, and the wind was rattling the windows and whining in the vestibule. Jennifer hoped that he was all right.

She tightened the cord on her bathrobe and adjusted the thermostat. Then she sat at the kitchen table to wait.

At nine o'clock, Gardner dragged himself through the back door. He looked haggard, exhausted. His eyes were as red as his wind-burned cheeks.

'Gard,' Jennifer exclaimed. 'I was worried.'

He dropped an armful of files on the table. 'Sorry, Jen. I tried to call, but the storm must have knocked down a line.'

Jennifer checked the wall phone. There was no dial tone. 'It's out,' she said, putting her arms around him.

He tried to give her the customary peck, but she clutched him tightly and prolonged the kiss. Gardner relaxed and opened his mouth against hers. The warmth was intense. Finally he broke it off and leaned back so he could focus on her face. 'What was *that* all about?'

She held him around the waist. 'Told you I was worried.'

Gardner smiled. 'I'm OK.' He removed his overcoat and hung it on the peg.

'So how did the meeting go?'

Gardner sat down. 'I dropped the bomb.'

Jennifer sat next to him. 'What was King's reaction?'

'He played it cool, but I could tell it stung him.'

'What did you do later?'

'Research and phone calls, trying to line up an expert witness to help out with the defence.'

'Any luck?'

Gardner shivered. He was still cold and wet. 'Got some leads on a guy we might want to use. His name is Dr Julius Sand.'

'So you're firm on the suicide defence?' Jennifer asked.

'Yeah.'

'*I* think it's a mistake.'

Gardner shivered again. 'I got that impression this morning.'

Jennifer retrieved a quilt from the hall couch and put it across his shoulders. 'We *know* it wasn't suicide. How can we present a defence we don't believe in?'

'I don't think we have a choice. You heard Brownie. We either accept it or get out of the case. There's no wriggle room.'

'We have to get a complete profile on Ruth to make it work,' Jennifer said. 'What did King say about the files?'

'Claims he doesn't have them.'

'Then we have to make a good faith effort to obtain them on our own, before the court will order him to comply.' She had researched the law on that point prior to typing the discovery request.

'That's going to be the hard part.'

'What do you mean?'

'*Nobody* at CAIN wants to talk. I called the new honcho, Fairborne, several times this afternoon. He won't take my calls, and he won't call me back. We need his co-operation...'

They lapsed into silence. Jennifer wanted to tell Gardner what she'd learned in the vault, but held back. It was only supposition, and she needed more proof before she broke the news. No sense confusing the issues at this point. 'How *firm* is the suicide defence?' she finally asked.

'Firm?' Gardner didn't follow.

'Do we have a back-up position to go to?'

'At the present, no. Brownie has made *that* impossible.'

Jennifer touched his arm. 'So what would happen if a new defence presented itself? Would you be amenable?'

Gardner sensed her drift. 'What are you up to, Jen?' He'd sent her out earlier to gather suicide evidence, not work a new case angle.

'Nothing.'

'Don't BS me. You're scheming. What are you working on?'

'Nothing,' Jennifer repeated. 'Really.'

'This is dangerous territory, Jen. We can't play both sides. We made a commitment to go with suicide and we have to stick with it. We can't jump and switch every five minutes. That's what being a defence attorney is all about.'

'How do *you* know?'

Gardner adjusted the quilt around his neck. 'I'm *learning*. As prosecutors we were trained to go for the *truth*, always the truth. But we don't have to do that anymore. We have to please our client. And he wants us to go the other way.'

'*Away* from the truth.'

Gardner did not reply.

'Do you think you can do it?'

'What?'

'Ignore the real truth?'

Gardner closed his eyes for a second, then opened them. 'I'm gonna *try*, and so are *you*.'

'Is that an order?'

'Yes.'

Jennifer stood up and moved behind him. There was a lot left to say, but this wasn't the time. Technically Gardner was right. As defence attorneys they had to dance to Brownie's tune. But that went against their legal grain.

Jennifer kissed the top of Gardner's head. 'Do you think it might be possible for a couple of defence lawyers to make love?'

'That might be arranged,' Gardner replied.

'Sure you're not too tired?'

Gardner rose and held her in a loose embrace. Then they climbed the stairs.

Kent King and Lin Song were barricaded in King's law office library. It was a legal fortress lined with books and computer terminals. The nor'easter finally had moved out, and early morning sunlight filled the room with the promise of a clear day. The lawyers had their heads down, hard at work.

'I warned you about this,' Lin said. 'It makes sense. They blast holes in our case and drive the suicide theory through.'

King turned from his monitor. 'There are no *holes* in our case, Lin. Get that through your head.' The evidence was overwhelming. No jury would ever buy the self-electrocution theory. 'This is a disclosure problem. Lawson is on a fishing expedition, hoping to find a smoking gun. It's up to us to see that he doesn't. It's that simple. What have you come up with on the medical records issue?'

Lin pushed a book aside and laid out her pad. 'Rollie was right. If we have such records in our possession and the suicide defence is raised, we are obligated to turn them over.'

King put the clicker of his pen against his eyebrow. 'What if we have them and *don't* comply?'

Lin checked her citations. 'That would be a violation of the discovery rules.'

'For which there are *no* sanctions.'

Lin pulled a photocopy out of her file. 'Most of the time, no. But in this situation, there could be a problem. *Fanner* here says that dismissal of the case would be appropriate if the state knowingly refuses to turn over relevant psychological evidence.'

King grabbed the copy. 'Was that a suicide defence?'

'No. It was an insanity plea on a felony, but the principle is the same.'

King tossed the paper back. 'It doesn't matter. We don't have the records anyway.'

'That brings us to the next point. What is the state's obligation to obtain information not in their possession?'

'I say *none*,' King replied.

'Again, you're right ... up to a point.'

'None is none. That's *it*.'

'The question turns on access,' Lin continued.

'Access?'

'Lawson claims that only *we* have access to the records in question, that he is not in a position to obtain them himself.'

'So?'

'So the law says that if access is denied to one party, and the information sought is necessary and relevant to the defence, there may be an obligation to produce it.'

'*May*,' King said. In legal terms that was an escape valve.

'The defence has to make a good faith effort to obtain the information themselves, and then, if they fail, they can apply to the court for an order requiring the state to get it for them.'

King smiled. 'So we don't have to do anything out of the gate.'

'Not now, no. We can submit a memorandum to Rollie spelling it out, but ...'

King waited. There was obviously more.

'But by doing so we acknowledge that it's our responsibility. We can't say no if Lawson comes back empty-handed. Then we have to make an attempt to get them.'

King frowned. He hated to concede anything to Lawson. 'Any other options?' he asked.

Lin shook her head. 'No.'

'OK. The bottom line is that *we* determine whether or not the records exist. If we find that they *do*, we have to turn them over, but if we find that they *don't*, then the issue

is moot. Lawson is out of luck, and we're back on track.'
King picked up his telephone.

'Who are you calling?'

King dialled a number. 'Frank Davis. He's the resident
CAIN expert. He should know if Ruth had a medical file.'

'And if Ruth did?'

King cupped the phone. 'Frank will just have to lose it.'

'Please,' Gardner asked. 'Let me talk to someone.' He was
at the gate to the quarry where a new sign and a reinforced
fence had been erected. 'KEEP OUT', the painted letters
warned as an armed guard patrolled to be sure that visitors
understood.

'Sorry,' the guard said through the wire. 'Mr Fairborne
does not wish to talk with you.'

Gardner looked past the guard, towards the buildings
that lay at the far end of the road. There was smoke drifting
skyward from a chimney, and a couple of vehicles. 'I don't
have to speak to Fairborne. Anyone else who saw Thomas
Ruth the day he died would be fine.'

The guard was in his early twenties, short-haired and
blue-eyed.

'Can't do it. No one can discuss the case unless they get
summoned to court.'

'Says who?'

The sentry shifted his hunting rifle to the other shoulder.
'That's the order.'

'So no one can talk to me.'

'Right.'

'Do you know if they received my letter? I requested a
release of Ruth's medical records.'

The guard looked towards the quarry. 'You're Mr Lawson, lawyer for the guy who killed Thomas Ruth?'

'*Alleged* to have killed Ruth,' Gardner corrected. 'Yes, I'm Lawson.'

'They got a letter. I heard talk about it.'

Gardner touched the fence with his fingers. 'Then you know what I'm claiming ... Thomas Ruth took his own life.'

'I heard that.' The man smiled.

'You think it's funny?' Gardner gripped the wire.

'Some of *them* do. You didn't know Thomas Ruth. No way he killed himself. They say it's a lawyer trick to get his killer off.'

'Were *you* here then?' Gardner asked. Maybe he could get something out of CAIN after all.

'Yeah, I was here.'

'You knew Thomas Ruth?'

The guard swept the gun barrel past Gardner's knees. 'Yeah. I knew him pretty good.'

'And you don't think he could have killed himself?'

He shook his head. 'No way.'

'Ever see him angry or upset?'

'Yeah. A few times.' The guard leaned against the fence.

'Ever see him go into a trance, anything like that?'

The guard stopped pacing. 'When he was preaching. But he never preached nothin' about suicide. We're into *life* here, not death. This ain't no Jonestown or Waco.'

'I understand that,' Gardner said. 'Do you remember what he got angry about?'

The guard swung the gun again. 'You people.'

322

'Us?'

'He was bein' harassed. *That* upset him.'

'Do you know who was harassing him?'

The guard laughed. 'You're asking *me*?'

'Yes.' Gardner tried to look sincere.

'The cop.'

'Sergeant Brown?'

The guard nodded. 'Thomas Ruth got stopped every time he left the quarry. By a cop. He even went to a lawyer about it. But ... it was too late.'

Gardner suddenly felt burning in his chest. Brownie had stated that he'd only stopped Ruth one time. 'Are you sure it was Sergeant Brown who did this?'

'I know it was a *cop*,' the guard replied.

'But did Ruth ever specify who it was?'

The gun came up. '*I* never heard a name, just that it was a cop.'

Gardner drew a breath. 'Did you ever hear *anyone* say who it was?'

The guard shook his head.

Gardner breathed out. Thank God. Maybe Brownie *wasn't* the one. Maybe it was someone *else* in the department. Maybe...

Brownie stopped his car at the gas station on Blocktown road. It was a secluded spot, away from the major traffic patterns. He'd spent most of yesterday with Gardner, going over endless questions about the case. The suicide option was a possible way out, but he still felt like a shit. Gardner was trying so hard. Too bad he couldn't tell him the truth.

Brownie checked the perimeter. The run-down station was empty of vehicles, and the single set of pumps was unoccupied. Old man Jakes was snoozing in his warm office. It was a typical fall morning in the Blocktown shallows.

Brownie walked to the pay phone at the rear of the building. He'd concluded a while back that he couldn't use his own equipment. King was probably still monitoring his calls.

He picked up the receiver and dialled.

'Mid-State Cellular,' a feminine voice answered.

'This is, uh, county police,' Brownie said. 'Need to talk to your security chief.' He'd been so tied up with his own case, he'd not had a chance to follow up the cellular phone lead he'd pried from Henry Jackson at the jail. Now he finally had a window of opportunity to check it out.

'One moment, sir.'

There was a click-over, and a man came on the line. 'Travis.'

'This is Officer Brown from the county police,' Brownie said, 'how're you today?'

'OK. What can I do for you?'

'I'm workin' a cellular theft ring and got a lead on some stolen phones. Do you have an updated printout of clone complaints in the past year or two?'

'Believe we do, yes.'

'How about I run some numbers by you, and you tell me if they're on the list?'

There was a pause. 'Who did you say you were again?'

'Brown, county police.'

'We don't usually do this over the phone.'

Brownie ground his teeth. He'd expected resistance. 'Listen,' his voice went low. 'I'm in the field right now. Got a suspect in the squad car, and he's spilling his guts. I don't have enough to lock him up yet, but if you can confirm some of the numbers he gave me, I'll bust him on the spot. What do you say?'

There was another hesitation.

'Come on, man. The dude is getting restless.'

'OK,' Travis agreed, 'since it's an emergency.'

'That it is.'

'Read me the numbers.'

Brownie pulled a list from his pocket, and ticked off the digits Henry Jackson had given him in the jail.

'Slow down, man,' Travis said. He was entering each one into the computer. 'File searching now.'

'Let me know when you have something.'

'OK,' Travis finally replied. 'Two hits.'

Brownie readied his pen. 'Give 'em to me.'

Travis read the two cellular phone numbers that had been scanned and cloned.

'Great,' Brownie said. 'That'll fix this bozo's wagon. Now I'm gonna need some call information on the clones, what numbers were called in September. Can you hook me up on that too?'

'You're going to need a subpoena,' Travis responded.

Brownie blinked. 'Can I send it to you?'

'Yeah. That's OK.'

'Great. Uh, thanks a lot, *Officer* Travis.'

'It's just Travis.'

Brownie grinned. 'But you *were* Officer Travis at one time.'

'You got me. Badge 2464, DC police, fourteen years.'

Brownie thanked him again and hung up. While Gardner worked his murder case, he was working another. He looked at the numbers in his hand. The net was closing in. Now all he had to do was draft a bogus subpoena, send it to Travis, and pick up the printout. If the 911 call was listed, he'd be halfway there.

Jennifer had slept fitfully the night before, despite her love session with Gardner. She was still restless and irritated about the sudden change in their lives, and not even a prolonged 'O' could make it go away. While she tossed and turned, she thought about the case. The suicide defence was just that: suicide. She didn't like it at all, but *she* wasn't leading the defence team. Today she'd agreed to do some field work, to interview a witness who *would* talk to them: Officer Billy Hill, first cop on the scene the night Ruth died.

The police dispatcher told Hill to wait for a contact by the off-ramp of the interstate highway. When Jennifer arrived, the rookie was standing by his car.

'Hello, Ms Munday,' he said.

'How are you, Billy?' Jennifer had met him a few times as prosecutor and heard his debriefing the morning after the electrocution.

'You want to talk to me?' Billy seemed nervous. King had tried to intimidate him, ordering all witnesses to remain silent until trial.

'Yes,' Jennifer replied. 'Do you want to sit in my car?' The wind had picked up, and it was getting quite brisk.

Billy declined. 'Can we do it here?'

'Whatever you say.' Jennifer didn't need to press. Gardner had asked her to get the facts, nothing more. 'I need you to tell me about Ruth's body position against the grid.'

Billy fluffed the hair out of his eyes. He was a freckle-faced redhead with long bangs. 'He was just hangin' there.'

'I need you to be more specific than that. I know you told Mr Lawson about this before, but it's more important now, especially for Brownie. Think back. Exactly what did you see?'

The wind blew Billy's bangs down again, and he fluffed one more time. 'The handcuffs were hooked into one of the levers.'

'What do you mean "hooked into"?'

'Dunno exactly. The lever was *here* and his hands were *here*.' Billy demonstrated.

'Were the cuffs *attached* in any way?'

'Attached?'

'You said they were "hooked into" the lever. Were they attached to it, or were they just draped over it?'

'Dunno.'

Jennifer rubbed her hands together. 'Think, Billy. This is important. You had the power shut down, and you removed him from the grid before anyone else got there. Did you have any trouble unhooking the cuffs, or did they come right off the lever?'

'He was hung up on the lever.'

'I understand that, but did you have any difficulty lifting him off?'

Billy fluffed his hair again. 'No. Not really.'

'Then, if you're asked in court, you could say that the

cuffs were simply *draped* over the lever, they weren't *attached to it.*'

Billy hesitated.

'That's what you just told me in so many words.'

'Yeah,' Billy replied. 'Guess I could say that.'

Jennifer smiled. At last some direct proof supporting suicide. Ruth was not 'chained' to the grid. Gardner should be pleased.

'But . . .' Billy had a second thought.

Jennifer stopped smiling. 'What?'

'That's not what I told Mr King.'

Jennifer frowned. King had already locked in his testimony. 'You gave a statement?' she asked.

'Yeah.'

'In writing?'

'Yes, ma'am.'

'And he got you to say "attached", that the cuffs were "attached" to the grid . . .' Jennifer knew King's blitzkrieg routine: get there first, and get a statement that supports your theory, factually correct or not.

'Yeah.'

'But that's not altogether true, is it?'

Billy looked upset. 'No, I guess not.'

'OK,' Jennifer said. 'At least *we* know how it really was. The cuffs were merely resting on top of the lever. They weren't *hooked* to it.'

'Right.'

'If we ask you about it in court, you know what to say?'

'I guess so: that he wasn't attached . . . but what about my statement? Mr King's gonna have a shitfit if I change my testimony.'

Jennifer pushed back her glasses. 'Don't worry about that. You just tell the truth, what you *really* saw. Let us worry about King.'

She said goodbye, entered her car, and drove away. Brownie and Gardner had set the suicide agenda, and she was *trying* to do her part. At the very least, Hill's testimony wouldn't hurt them. But it wouldn't do them a lot of good either.

Brownie was dreaming. It was 3 a.m., and his mind was spinning a whirlpool of bizarre images. He had been out all day, working his covert investigation, trying not to think about the tragic truth he'd dug up after Ruth had followed his father into eternity. He'd kept it from his thoughts, lost himself in his tasks. But tonight, in his sleep, he couldn't escape. The memories were rising from the grave.

'Breaking and entering in progress at the high school,' the dispatcher said on the radio in Brownie's squad car. The trees were pink, the sky was black, and there were office buildings in the meadow.

Brownie flicked on his siren and sped towards the scene. He arrived at the hill leading to the school and stopped his car. There was a pond where the athletic field should have been and a waterfall pouring down over the road.

Brownie gunned the engine and splashed into the lake. The squad car became a boat, and he ran it up on the shore on the far side.

'Armed and dangerous,' the dispatcher said. Brownie drew his service weapon and kicked in the front door of the school. Twisted corridors ran off in all directions, and the scene was lit with an eerie blue light.

Brownie raised his gun and started down a dim hallway. He heard voices in a room, so he entered. Gardner was instructing a class. He looked at Brownie, then went back to teaching.

The passageway suddenly got dark. Brownie could hear more voices. He entered a room, and people scurried for cover. There were books and papers strewn on the floor, and the walls were spray-painted with graffiti. Brownie dropped behind a desk.

There was movement in the darkness.

Brownie pointed his weapon. 'Come out, motherfucker!' he screamed.

It went quiet.

'Come out!' Brownie repeated.

The light suddenly returned. The sun had come up, and the classroom glowed gold. A head appeared from a pile of overturned chairs.

'Hands up,' Brownie ordered.

The person stood but didn't comply.

'Hands up!' Brownie shrieked.

The person didn't move.

Brownie squeezed the trigger to the last possible stop-point. 'Do it!'

The person changed into a child just as Brownie fired, just as he realized who the person was.

'Aahhh!' Brownie sat up in bed. The dream had awoken him. He rubbed his eyes, and mopped the sweat from his forehead. That was too real.

Brownie turned on the light, and plumped his pillow. His heart was racing, and the sweat was dripping. He switched on the TV to a minister giving the benediction. For a few minutes he sat there, trying to calm down. Then he opened the drawer to his nightstand and withdrew a phone book.

Brownie lifted the phone and dialled a telephone number in Washington DC.

It rang eight times before a groggy voice said 'hello?'

Brownie froze.

'Hello?'

Brownie couldn't do it. He hung up the phone, and sat in silence as the TV sputtered snow across the room. He had a lot to say to Paulie. But when he tried, nothing came out.

CHAPTER 19

Gardner held the telephone to his ear as he stood behind his desk. He was back at work early, pursuing a comment the guard had made at the quarry. *Someone* in the police department had been harassing Ruth before he died. Gardner was committed to the suicide defence, but this was a lead he couldn't ignore. Maybe they could get out of Brownie's straitjacket after all.

'Don't do this to me, Larry,' Gardner told the police chief. 'The information I'm looking for isn't privileged. I'm entitled to it.'

'Take it easy, Gard,' the chief replied. 'I'm giving it to you straight. I was unaware of any sting operation against Ruth.'

'He was being hassled,' Gardner countered, 'by a cop. And I'm certain it *wasn't* Brownie.'

'Well, whoever it was didn't have official authorization.' Larry Gray hated this, being on opposite ends of the court with a former teammate. 'I haven't heard anything about it. You've got to believe me.' His tone was sincere.

Gardner went silent.

'Gard?'

'Still here, Larry.'

'Please listen to me. I've got nothing to gain from saying otherwise.'

'I believe you, Larry.'

'Sorry.'

Gardner thought about his options. 'Can you give me Frank Davis' patrol schedule the week preceding Ruth's death?'

'Davis?'

'Maybe *Frank* knows something. He was assigned to that beat, remember?'

'You never give up, do you?'

'What do you mean?'

'You're always after Davis. Why don't you leave him alone?'

Gardner pressed his knee against the desk. 'The guy's a loose cannon.'

'That may be, but we told you before he was not involved in the killing. We confirmed that right after the fact; he has an alibi. He's been cleared of involvement.'

'By whom?'

'By *us*.'

Gardner sat down. 'By you, maybe, but not by *me*. I want his schedule.'

'You can have it, but it won't do you any good. His time has been accounted for.'

'Please fax it to me.' Gardner said.

'Sure,' Larry answered. 'Right away. Gard...'

'What?'

'I really *do* want to help. Really.'

'I appreciate it, Larry.'

'Give Brownie my best. We're all pulling for him.'

'OK,' Gardner said. Then he hung up and stared at the wall. They had been close, he and Larry. But now that he'd changed sides, it wasn't the same.

Gardner picked up the phone again and dialled the clerk's office. He had one more chance to find the harasser, and it was a long shot. The CAIN guard said Ruth had seen a lawyer, and the logical thing for a lawyer to do was file a civil injunction. Maybe Judy Field had heard something about it. She was the gatekeeper for all injunctive pleadings.

'File desk,' Judy said.

'Gardner Lawson here.'

'Hi Mr Lawson. How are you doing?'

'Getting by. Judy, I have a request, and it may sound strange...'

'What?'

'Before Thomas Ruth was killed, I believe that a police officer was harassing him. Did you ever hear anything about that?'

'There *was* something, as I recall,' she said hesitantly.

'What?'

'A petition involving Ruth...'

'Injunctive relief for harassment?'

'I think so.'

'Who filed it?'

'Who?'

'What *lawyer* filed the petition?'

'Uh...' She was trying to remember.

Gardner's pulse began to rise.

'*King*,' Judy exclaimed. 'Kent King. But...'

'Damn!'

'But Mr Lawson,' Judy cut in. 'It was withdrawn *prior* to filing. I pulled it out myself.'

'On whose orders?'

'Mr King. Had me pull it *before* it was logged.'

'Judy, think hard,' Gardner said. 'Was that before, or after Ruth died?'

'After, I'm pretty sure. Mr King made a joke about the guy being dead.'

Gardner smacked his lips. That was King: represent a guy today, dance on his grave tomorrow. 'Judy, this is *very important*. Do you remember the name of the police officer?'

'Uhhh...' Judy had only scanned the petition for a moment, and that was a long time ago. 'His name?'

'It was ... officer ... *Davis*!'

'*Frank Davis*?'

'That's who I remember.'

Gardner wrote the name in huge black letters on his pad. 'Judy, you're beautiful. I owe you big time.' He thanked her and hung up. So it *was* Davis after all, just as he'd suspected. Brownie was *not* the cop after Ruth. And 'Special Prosecutor' King had known it all along!

Jennifer walked up the front steps of Valley High School. She had decided to follow up her visit to the evidence vault with some additional investigation. Without revealing her plan, she'd drawn Gardner out on the relationship between Brownie and his brother. She'd seen them at their father's funeral and verified the chill. There was something going on between the two men, a deep secret that neither wanted to reveal. And Jennifer theorized it might explain Brownie's decision to throw in the towel.

Jennifer checked at the front desk and confirmed that 'Miss Bertie' was in the principal's office. She had never met the legendary teacher, the person whose lessons had shaped a generation.

'Go right in,' the receptionist said.

Jennifer entered and found a grey-haired woman grading papers. 'Miss Bertie,' she said tentatively, 'I'm Jennifer Munday. We spoke earlier.'

The teacher eyed her as if she were late to class. 'Sit down please.'

'Thanks. I hope I'm not disturbing you.'

Miss Bertie laid her marking pencil aside. 'No, dear. I'm just getting caught up on exam papers ... what did you say your name was again?'

'It's Munday, but I'm not from around here. I went to school in Baltimore.'

'That's nice, dear.'

'I'd like to talk to you about a couple of your former students.'

Bertie adjusted a cable-knit sweater draped around her thin shoulders. 'You are a lawyer?'

'Yes, ma'am.'

'Good for you, dear.'

'Thank you. I want to know about the Brown brothers, Joseph and Paul. They were students here almost twenty years ago. They lived in Blocktown.'

'Blocktown,' Bertie repeated. That was synonymous with 'black'.

Jennifer nodded. 'Paul and Joseph Brown. One has been on the police force for some time as a sergeant...'

'And he's in trouble.'

'Right. I'm one of his attorneys. Do you remember him as a student?'

The teacher nodded. 'Nice boy. Smart. Polite. Friendly.'

'That's him.'

'His brother was not as nice or as smart.'

'Do you remember them being together?' Jennifer asked. 'Do you know how they got along?'

'Fine, as I remember. The smaller one followed the big one around like a puppy.'

'Tell me about Paul. What was he like?'

'He was a scallywag, not like Joseph. He was always getting into scrapes.'

'Scrapes?'

'Fights. He'd fight at the drop of a hat, didn't matter how big the boys were or how many. He didn't care.'

'Did Joseph ever fight?'

'No.' Bertie moved her sharp chin to the side. 'Not that I remember. He got along with everyone, had a lot of friends, white and black.'

'But how did the two brothers relate to each other?'

'As well as brothers can, I suppose.'

'So they were friendly?'

'Yes, as I recall. Until the incident...'

'Incident?'

'The vandalism case.' Bertie frowned deeply. 'They almost destroyed the school, those nasty little thugs ... I haven't thought about that for a long time...'

'What happened?'

'They tore the history room up, spray-painted the walls, ripped up books ... such destruction!'

'Was Paul Brown involved?'

'Yes, my Lord. He was the main one.'

'So he was a student at the time?'

'Yes, a senior. The older one had already graduated and joined the police ...'

Jennifer made a note on the back of an envelope.

'That was such a shame,' Bertie said suddenly.

'What?' Jennifer looked up.

'What they made him do.'

Jennifer put the envelope in her purse. 'Who?'

'The older one, the nice one,' Bertie said wistfully. 'I could never understand *why* they did that ... Why the police made that boy arrest his own brother.'

Gardner was pumped up. He stopped by the courthouse to obtain a copy of the log where King's injunction motion had been noted. Then he raced to King's office to confront him with the facts.

'You can go in now,' the secretary said.

Gardner entered the inner room. King was wearing reading glasses, poring over a file. 'This better be good,' he said, 'I'm *very* busy.'

Gardner tried to compose himself. He'd been imagining King's reaction when he heard the news. 'Take a look at this,' he said, passing the log across the desk. The entry regarding King had been circled in red marker.

The special prosecutor picked up the paper, read it slowly, and put it down on the desk. 'So?'

'You knew that Ruth was being harassed by a police

officer *before* he was killed,' Gardner charged. 'You knew it was *Davis*, not Brownie, and you kept it quiet.'

King's expression was calm, almost bored. It began to unnerve Gardner. 'You suppressed exculpatory evidence and indicted a man you knew was innocent. As a prosecutor, you fucked up.'

King laughed. 'How long have we known each other?'

'Too long.'

'Really,' King continued. 'How long? Seven, eight years?'

'Yes. So what?'

'Do you have *that* low an opinion of my intelligence? Do you really think I would expose myself to that kind of allegation?'

Gardner didn't reply. The normal answer would have been: no, King wasn't that stupid. But with the change of sides and the new perspective, maybe he'd slipped.

'First of all,' King removed his glasses. 'I am, and have been fully aware of what you're saying from the beginning. I *did* see Ruth, I knew that Davis was bothering him, and I did prepare the injunction. But after Ruth died, I cancelled the pleading, and I interrogated Davis at length about the allegations...' King reached into his desk, and took out a piece of white paper. 'Davis was polygraphed, and he passed with flying colours. I concluded with absolute certainty that Davis was clean and eliminated him as a suspect.'

'But you obstructed Justice,' Gardner blustered. 'You had a duty to disclose your relationship with Ruth before accepting the appointment as special counsel!'

'Not so. I took the job with a commitment to find and

prosecute Ruth's killer. Davis, in fact, was my *first* suspect, and had he not been cleared, he'd be standing trial now. My actions were proper in every respect.'

Gardner swallowed. King was a master at covering his ass. 'So why was Davis jacking up Ruth in the first place?'

'Bird-dogging a promotion. *You* set the agenda for the CAIN surveillance, remember? Ruth was implicated in old man Brown's death, all that shit? Davis got caught up in the hunt, figured if he made Ruth confess, he'd be a hero and get the recognition he deserved.'

Gardner frowned. This was definitely *not* what he'd expected to hear.

'At the very least this is exculpatory information. You had an absolute obligation to turn it over to me. Remember the *Brady* case? The Supreme Court wasn't kidding. You *have* to reveal evidence that clears the defendant!'

'*Brady* doesn't apply here,' King replied coolly. 'I confirmed that the information did *not* exculpate Brown. I followed the lead, and satisfied myself that Davis did *not* commit the crime. There was nothing exculpatory to report.'

'I still should have been told,' Gardner argued. 'I could use it at trial...'

'Not *now*,' King interrupted. 'I was planning to inform you about it until you came up with the suicide defence. Now I don't have to give you anything.'

Gardner stopped talking. The someone-else-did-it defence and the suicide defence were mutually exclusive. By choosing suicide, he had abandoned the legal argument that a third party killed Ruth. In that situation, proof of someone else's involvement became irrelevant. He couldn't have it both ways. He had to choose one or the other.

'Have you changed your mind about suicide?' King asked.

'No.'

'Then you get no discovery under *Brady*. I don't think you intend to tell the jury: "Ruth killed himself, and oh, by the way, if you don't believe that, someone *else* did it."'

Legally, King was dead right. Brownie's choice of defences had boxed them in.

'You see your dilemma?' King asked.

'Yes,' Gardner said bitterly. 'I see it.'

'*You* decided to go this way, and *I* didn't force you. Now what were you saying before about *beating* me?' King smiled nastily.

Gardner stood up suddenly and started for the door.

'See you in court,' King chuckled.

Gardner turned. 'I still want those medical records. The affidavit to Ransome certifies a good faith effort to obtain them without success. The ball is in your court, and you'd better turn them over.'

King crossed his arms. 'For the fiftieth time, I don't have the fuckin' records.'

Gardner pointed his finger. 'Then you'd better get them.'

King saluted as Gardner slammed the door. The Davis lead had been a total disaster. It wasted time, went nowhere, and allowed King to humiliate him. How could he have screwed up so badly? As a prosecutor, this never would have happened. But he was *not* a prosecutor anymore. And that fact was painfully obvious.

* * *

Brownie entered the driveway of his mother's house and braked suddenly to avoid a vehicle parked behind Althea's sedan. The car was a shiny full-sized job, polished and waxed, fitted with every bell and whistle in stock. The sky was a cold grey; there were snowflakes in the wind, and Brownie's visit was unannounced.

Brownie opened the kitchen door and entered quietly. 'God's will be done,' Reverend Taylor's voice echoed from the parlour. Brownie moved into sight of the sofa.

'Joseph Junior,' Althea exclaimed.

Reverend Taylor stood up and almost spilled his coffee.

'Mama, *Reverend*,' Brownie replied, moving closer.

'Brother Brown,' Taylor said.

Brownie kissed his mother on the cheek. 'How're you doin', Mama?'

'Reverend Taylor was just paying me a visit,' Althea responded guiltily. She had always been a member of Reverend Boyd's congregation.

'During these hard times,' the reverend began, 'I try to comfort ... as I can.'

'I'm sure you do,' Brownie answered.

'So how goes it with you, Brother Brown, since you saw fit to abandon the efforts that *we* were attempting on your behalf?'

Brownie looked him in the eye. 'I didn't abandon you.'

Taylor lifted his cup towards his lips. 'You got yourself a new lawyer.'

'That was done *for* me, not *by* me.'

'Reverend Taylor says that everyone in Blocktown is praying for you, son,' Althea interjected.

'I appreciate the help,' Brownie said to Taylor. 'I know what you-all tried to do. Just didn't work out, that's all.'

Taylor smiled. 'We were trying to hold it together for you, brother, trying to come up with our own solutions to our own problems.'

'But it's *my* problem,' Brownie replied.

Taylor put down his cup and stood up. 'I can see that you two need time together,' he said. 'I'll be on my way, got more folks to visit today.'

'Thank you for coming,' Althea said.

'Keep the faith,' Taylor replied. 'And remember what I said.' He then turned to Brownie. 'God be with you, Brother.'

In a moment, Taylor was out the door, and mother and son were alone.

'When did that start, Mama?' Brownie asked.

'What, son?' She looked disappointed that her visitor had departed.

'How long has he been comin' over here?'

'Uh ... For a while now. I ... I've been lonely, depressed. He's been helping...'

Brownie felt discomfort. He'd been scarce around here, almost nonexistent. Being in jail was one thing. Mama visited him there a lot. But after his release, he'd avoided her.

'You haven't paid me much mind,' Althea continued.

Brownie put his arms around her, squeezing tightly. 'Sorry, Mama,' he said against her head. 'Really sorry.'

'I'm tryin' to understand, Joseph,' she said.

'I'll do better, Mama, I really will.' They embraced for a minute without talking. Finally, Brownie let go.

'Mama, I need to ask you something.'

Althea gave him an attentive look.

'Have you heard *anything* from Paulie?'

Althea frowned. 'Why, son? Is this about the killing?'

'No, Mama. Not at all. I'm just wondering how he's doing.'

Althea shook her head sadly. The tragedies in her life were never-ending.

'Has he been in touch with you lately?' Despite the rift with Brownie, Paulie was close to his mother.

Althea shook her head again.

'Has he called?'

'Just one time.'

'And what did he say?'

Althea's eyes teared. 'That he didn't want Daddy's money.'

Brownie raised an eyebrow. 'You sent him the pension?'

'Yes, a piece of it. But he sent it back. He's such a proud boy.'

Brownie suddenly wasn't listening. His eyes were locked on Taylor's coffee cup. 'Uh, Mama, do you think I could get something to drink?'

'Sure, son.' Althea stood and walked towards the kitchen. 'Coffee?'

'That's fine.'

Althea disappeared, and Brownie took out his pen, poked it through the handle of Taylor's cup, and raised it.

'Cream and sugar?' Althea called.

'Black,' Brownie replied, carefully covering the cup with a napkin and placing it in his coat pocket. He'd noticed

Taylor touch the side of the ceramic when he'd laid it down. And that surface was ideal for fingerprints.

Gardner and Jennifer navigated the twisting road to the Watson Road house where Carole and Granville lived. It was Sunday afternoon. Snow was falling, and Christmas was two weeks away. Gardner and Jennifer had been so preoccupied with Brownie's case they hadn't prepared for the holiday. So now they were off on a tree-cutting expedition.

'I'm worried,' Jennifer said.

Gardner glanced at her out of the corner of his eye. 'About what?'

'About whether we're doing the right thing. We shouldn't be so *rigid* with Brownie's defence. We have to keep our options open.'

'Jeez, Jen,' Gardner complained. 'There aren't any options. You know that.' They'd discussed the situation endlessly. Selecting suicide *precluded* all other defences.

'But it isn't ... right.'

'It may not be *right*, but it's all we have, and we have to make the best of it. Stick with me on this and I'll make it up to you, Jen. When it's over. I promise...'

She waited for an explanation, but it didn't come. 'How?' she finally asked.

Gardner didn't answer, and concentrated on his driving. A thin layer of snow had coated the road, and the lines were obscured. The forecast warned of accumulation up to three inches. 'I'll make it up,' he said at last. The magic words still wouldn't come.

Gardner braked and fishtailed in the slush. The entrance

was coming up on the right. There was no use haggling about it now, especially in front of Granville. 'Let's talk about it later. Please?'

Jennifer assented silently. Everything important was always 'later'.

They pulled up to the mansion and tooted the horn. Soon Granville appeared, bundled in outerwear. 'Four-thirty,' Carole hollered from the door. 'Have him back then!'

'Fine,' Gardner yelled as his son leaped into the car.

'Hi Dad, hi Jennifer.' Granville said excitedly. They were all going to cut a tree on the Hempstead farm.

Jennifer kissed him on the cheek.

'Hey,' Granville protested. At his age a kiss was considered icky.

'Sorry.' Jennifer pulled away.

'It's OK.'

Gardner touched his son's head. 'Let's have fun. How about it?' They started out of the driveway, and the car spun wheels several times.

'Hang on,' Gardner warned, 'and put your seatbelt on, Gran.'

The wind picked up, and snow-flakes plastered the windshield. Gardner tuned the radio to 'White Christmas'.

'Let's sing along,' he suggested.

'Like the ones we used to knowwww...' their voices rang.

After twenty minutes, they reached Hempstead's. Gardner paid thirty dollars to a man in a booth and was directed onto a gravel road.

'Best ones are up there.' The man pointed to a rise a

hundred yards away. Gardner drove in as close as he could and parked. 'Let's go get her,' he said.

Granville carried the pruning saw and held onto his dad's hand while Jennifer followed close behind. The conditions were worsening, and the icy gusts burned their faces. Granville spotted a tree he liked and ran to it. 'This one, Dad!' he exclaimed.

'You're sure?' Gardner said against the wind.

'Uh huh!' The boy was certain.

They took turns sawing, and soon the six-foot perfectly-shaped evergreen toppled. 'Merry Christmas!' Gardner said, patting Granville's back and looking into Jennifer's eyes.

'Whoopie!' Granville hooted.

Jennifer said nothing. Her face was wet with droplets, her expression suddenly sad. And any sign of joy was lost in the blowing snow.

CHAPTER 20

Gardner answered the knock on the law office door. With no secretary or support staff, he and Jennifer had managed everything alone since their resignations. And now, on January 2nd, a week before trial, their ten o'clock appointment was here.

Christmas had been forgettable. They'd tried to play-act for Granville, but the black cloud over their heads had spoiled the mood. Dread predominated through New Year's Day. And the tree was buried in the county dump.

'Doctor Sand?'

An elderly man in a blue topcoat extended his hand. 'Julius Sand.' He was wearing glasses and an obvious toupee.

'Thank you for coming,' Gardner drew him inside. 'I'm Gardner Lawson, and this is Jennifer Munday.'

'Nice meeting you both.' Sand removed his coat. He was a psychiatrist and forensic pathologist by profession, an expert witness for hire. He'd been contacted long ago about helping Brownie, but other cases had tied him up until now. His speciality was suicide. And that put him in heavy demand across the state.

349

'Coffee?' Jennifer asked.

'Might stunt my growth,' Sand joked through a row of yellow teeth.

'OK then,' Gardner began, 'mind if we get to work?'

'That's why I'm here.' Sand sat at the card table, opened his battered briefcase, and withdrew an envelope.

Gardner glanced at his papers. 'You have our letter with the case summary and court documents?'

'Yes, and I've reviewed them.' The doctor looked fragile, but his voice was strong.

'What do you think?'

Sand laid out the papers in front of him. 'Not much, I'm afraid. It's too thin.'

'Too thin?'

Sand peered over his glasses. 'When a person dies under suspicious circumstances and suicide is alleged, there must be evidence showing a propensity for self-destruction in the final hours. I don't see it here, not in the facts you've asserted. There was no note. The deceased was chained to the power station...'

'I explained that,' Gardner interrupted. 'He wasn't attached.'

'No matter. He was in handcuffs, which implies third-party involvement. I've seen *one* hand cuffed in a suicide, but never *two*.'

'I explained that also,' Gardner argued. 'He was wearing the cuffs when he drove away.'

'All right. We might be able to discount it then. And the trancelike behaviour of the decedent observed by Officer Brown is a favourable point. But other than that we have nothing to go on, nothing on which to *base* the defence.'

'What about the magazine article?' Jennifer pointed to a photocopy of Sallie Allen's exposé on CAIN. 'Doesn't playing with snakes show mental imbalance?'

The doctor perused the page, then looked at Jennifer. 'To some degree, perhaps, but it doesn't get us where we want to go. Do you remember the Winters case down in Baltimore?'

Gardner and Jennifer both nodded. *Winters* was a blockbuster defeat for the Baltimore City State's Attorney's office about four years ago. The media had deified Dr Sand and crucified the prosecutor. Every lawyer in the state knew about that one.

'We had little to go on there either. No eyewitnesses, little physical proof. But we were able to conduct a *psychological autopsy* on the victim. The deceased, Betty Layton, had been severely depressed before she died. She talked about death and seeing God. She acted confused and complained of hearing voices. That laid the groundwork for the argument that *she* used the gun. That, and the psychiatric history ... The police charged Mrs Layton's brother, Henry Winters, with the crime because he was in the house when the gun was fired, and there was no note. He also stood to inherit a substantial estate. There were no fingerprints on the gun, and the gunpowder tests were botched by police so they couldn't tell *who* had actually pulled the trigger. But my psychological autopsy showed that she had a pathology of suicidal tendencies and a history of mental hospitalizations. That's what got the brother off. That's what won the case.'

'Can't you do the same thing here?' Gardner asked.

'That's the problem. Other than Officer Brown we have *no* witnesses who will say he was suicidal, and we have *no* mental or physical records on the man. If he had *any* mental history at all, *any*, we could make a case. But without it, there's not much I can do.'

Gardner looked at Jennifer. Sand was right. There were no witnesses at CAIN willing to come forward, and the personal records were still unaccounted for. Rollie Ransome had accepted King's oath that the records did not exist and overruled Gardner's insistence that they did. That put the ball back in the defence court.

'Your problem is the victim,' Sand declared suddenly.

Gardner glanced up.

'He's a complete cipher. There's no way *to possibly do* a psychological autopsy on someone you know nothing about. According to the case summary, you don't have a clue as to who the victim really is, and until you find out, my hands are tied.' Sand realized he'd made a macabre pun. 'Sorry.'

'I get the picture,' Gardner said. 'We're out of luck.'

'As far as the suicide defence is concerned, yes.'

'Would you be willing to give it a shot anyway, without the records? Base the defence on Brownie's testimony, the public information on Ruth's personality, and anything else we can come up with?'

'If you asked me to, I'd be willing to give it a try, but...'

'Don't count on success,' Jennifer interjected.

'We'd have a lot *better* chance if we could dissect Ruth,' Sand said.

'No question about that,' Gardner added. 'But how?'

Ruth was gone body and soul. And neither was ever coming back.

After Dr Sand left the office Gardner and Jennifer sat in silence, contemplating what they'd just heard. Gardner fiddled with the file, then raised the telephone.

'Who are you calling?' Jennifer asked.

'The only *other* person who might help us.'

The connection went through, and a woman answered. '*Interview Magazine*.'

'Sallie Allen, please,' Gardner said.

Jennifer moved closer to the phone.

'Sorry, she's unavailable at the moment. Who's calling?'

'Gardner Lawson, attorney from Maryland. It's urgent that I speak with her. Can you tell her I'm calling about the Joseph Brown murder case?'

'She's on assignment.'

'Can you get a message to her? This is *very, very* important.'

Gardner repeated his name and added the phone number.

'We'll let her know.'

'Thank you.' Gardner hung up and turned to Jennifer. She had a sceptical expression on her face. 'It's worth a try,' he explained. What else did they have?

Several minutes later the phone rang. Jennifer answered, and her eyes widened. She handed the receiver to Gardner. 'It's *her*.'

Gardner grabbed the phone. 'Miss Allen?'

'Yes. That's correct.'

'Thank you for returning my call so promptly.'

'No problem. They beeped me. What's happening with the Brown case?'

'Joseph Brown is in trouble, and I'm his attorney.' Thanks to *you*, he wanted to say. 'We need background information on Thomas Ruth. We're alleging he killed himself, and we need to show that he was mentally imbalanced. What do you know about his true identity?'

There was a muffled sound as Sallie covered the phone. 'What do *I* know about who he was?' she finally asked.

'Yes.'

'Zero. Our research people couldn't come up with anything concrete. I tried to pump him, but I was pulled out before I could get him to talk.'

'So you have *no idea* who he really was.' Gardner looked at Jennifer, and she nodded knowingly. The article was bare bones on the man. Sallie had obviously struck out in the ID department.

'Not really.'

Gardner took a breath and tried to change direction. 'In your *personal* contact with Ruth would you say he acted strangely?'

'That's an understatement.'

'So he *was* wacked out.'

'In a controlled way.'

'What does that mean?'

'He was crazy, but like a fox. Calculating, intense, but . . .'

Don't say it, Gardner thought.

'Definitely *not* suicidal in my opinion. He was a lot more likely to kill someone *else*. Not himself.'

'So *you* don't believe he committed suicide.'

'Me? No.'

'But would you be willing to testify about his mental condition anyway?'

'Testify...' Sallie hesitated. 'Maybe. If our lawyers okayed it. But I have to be honest with you, Mr Lawson, I don't buy the suicide bit at all.'

'So *you* think Sergeant Brown is guilty of murder.'

'From the information that's been reported so far, yes *I* do.'

'Thanks for your time,' Gardner said. Then he smacked down the phone.

'No help, huh?'

'Help? She'd be a great fucking help ... To *King*.'

Jennifer stood up.

'Where are you going?'

'I've got something to do.'

'What?' Gardner asked.

'I have to *think*.'

Jennifer left the office, and Gardner sat at the table staring at the case file. Then he muttered 'Shit!' and knocked the folder across the room with his fist.

Reverend Taylor handed the teller a cheque at the Forest National Bank. She was very familiar with his account, and she smiled through the iron grate. Her name tag read Mary Burt.

'Where's the deposit slip?' she asked.

'It's not a deposit,' Taylor replied. 'Like you to cash it out.'

Mary glanced at the cheque. 'The whole thing?'

'Yes, please.'

'I'm going to have to get authorization on a cheque this large.'

'But you *know* me.'

'That doesn't matter. The cheque's not drawn on our bank, and it's over the limit. I've got to get authorization.'

Taylor glanced behind him. A queue was building.

'Sorry,' Mary said. 'I'll be right back.' She left her alcove and entered the manager's office. They spoke for a moment, and the manager peeked over her shoulder. Soon Mary returned. 'You're *sure* you want to cash this?'

Taylor smiled and tried to stay calm. 'Yes, I would.' It had taken him long enough to get the damn thing. Of course he wanted it cashed.

'Put your social security number below the endorsement.'

Taylor stopped smiling. *That* wasn't normal procedure. 'Do what?'

'Put your social security number below the signature.'

Taylor glanced around. The people in line were getting restless.

'The cheque is okayed. We just need your social security number...'

Taylor folded the cheque and put it in his pocket. 'Never mind,' he said. Then he stepped away from the counter and left the bank.

Brownie arrived at Gardner's office after Dr Sand and Jennifer had left.

'Where were you?' Gardner demanded.

Brownie unbuttoned his coat. Snow flurries had been sweeping the valley all morning, and his hair was wet. 'Got held up,' he said. 'Sorry.'

'You missed Sand.'

'Sorry. How did it go?'

Gardner glanced at his notes. 'Not good. He can't work his magic without explicit background information on Ruth. We're in a bind, here, Brownie. If we keep going in this direction, you're going to get *convicted*. Do you understand that?'

Brownie said nothing.

'We've got absolutely nothing on Ruth and it doesn't look like we're going to get anything, not at this rate. Sand says his personal history is *crucial* for the psychological autopsy. Without it, we're in serious trouble.'

Brownie crossed his arms. 'Is he willing to proceed without it?'

Gardner nodded. 'He will...'

'OK, then.'

'If we do, *you're* committing suicide. It won't fly. We've got to change tactics.'

Brownie cocked his head.

'Trial begins in a few days, and we have *no* defence. Do you realize that?'

'Take it easy.'

'Take it easy? Jennifer and I quit our jobs to defend you on a murder charge, and you give us *no* support in return.'

'I do,' Brownie argued.

'Really? That's bullshit. You've eliminated every viable defence and forced us into a dead end. I thought we could get through this before, but now I'm not so sure. You won't let us pursue other suspects, and we're stuck with a defence that won't work. We're fucked, Brownie.'

Brownie remained calm. 'Exactly what did the doctor say?'

Gardner gave his client an exasperated look. 'That we need records to confirm Ruth was a nutcase.'

'And he could make a go of it if he had them?'

'Yes. If they establish any history of psychotic behaviour, Sand says he can pull it off.'

'Do you believe him?'

Gardner nodded. 'Yes. He can do it, no question. But there's another problem here. We're not sure that Ruth ever *had* any records to begin with . . .'

'He had 'em.'

'How do you know?'

'He *was* a nutcase. Somewhere along the line he either committed himself or someone committed him . . .'

'How can you *say* that?'

'I've been around enough flakes in my life, Gard. This guy was definitely a flake. Sometime *somebody* had to treat him. I'm certain. He was way out over the edge.'

'But if he was treated, it was not under the name of Thomas Ruth.'

'Right. He had another identity.'

'Which we don't know, and don't have any hope of knowing. Without fingerprints, a body, or witnesses, we're shit out of luck.'

Brownie leaned back in his chair. 'All the conventional routes to get the skinny on Ruth have been tried, right? Records checks, teletype inquiries, all that stuff.'

'You know that.'

Brownie's expression darkened. 'Maybe it's time we went unconventional.'

Gardner listened. At this point *any* suggestion was better than what they had.

'A friend of mine produces the *Fugitives At Large* TV programme out of DC. He could air a blurb on the show, display Ruth's picture, and ask if anyone in the audience knows who he was. They get some heavy-duty ratings. A viewer might be able to give us a lead.'

Gardner wrote 'Fugitives' on his pad. What a great idea. The show was seen by millions and helped capture a lot of dangerous criminals. Someone had to know the real Ruth, and maybe his psychiatric history as well. 'I like it,' Gardner said, 'but...'

'What?'

'It'll probably smoke out a lot of kooks. We may waste time following false trails.'

'What *else* we got?'

'*Nothing*.'

'Right. So we go straight to the people and pray someone recognizes Ruth.'

'At this point it's our only hope. If we don't get him identified before it's our turn to put on a defence, we're sunk.'

Brownie picked up the telephone. 'I'll call my buddy right now. The show airs tomorrow night.'

'Tell them it's an emergency,' Gardner advised.

Brownie hit the buttons. 'Emergency,' he repeated. That it was.

Jennifer moved cautiously through the file storage room at police headquarters. It was dark, musty, and smelled of mildew. She covered her nose and skirted the shadows of the metal cabinets. After the Dr Sand meeting and Sallie Allen call, the futility of their position had become grimly apparent. They were racing towards disaster, and Gardner wouldn't change course. Jennifer had to do something to resolve the situation. And her first order of business was a long-forgotten internal affairs report.

Jennifer checked the reference number the administrative officer had given her. There had been several notations for Brownie in the report index. Over the years the police had secretly investigated his activities on a number of occasions. This was normal. Cops were always spying on their own; it was a part of the programme.

'Twenty-eight, thirty-nine, zero, zero, B,' Jennifer read from the note in her hand, flipping the dividers until she reached her letter. Then she sorted through the folders, and finally, there it was: 'BROWN, JOSEPH – SUSPICION OF ILLEGAL ACTIVITY.'

Jennifer set the file on top of the cabinet. The overhead light was weak, and she had to squint to see.

This case was related to the Paul Brown break-in at Valley High School. She had procured the vandalism report after her meeting with Miss Bertie and confirmed that Brownie had indeed arrested Paul Brown for the crime. But there had been a strange notation in the file: a reference to an internal investigation of Brownie himself.

Jennifer read the specification of charges: 'COLLUSION, INSUBORDINATION, CONDUCT UNBECOMING AN OFFICER.' She swept through the preamble. On the night of the break-in a silent alarm had been triggered at the school. Two officers were dispatched to the scene:

Maas and Pringle. They investigated and found no one on the premises, but fingerprints were lifted and a suspect was identified: Paul Brown. Jennifer skipped down the page. Several of the spray-painted epithets on the walls were racial, and the Civil War sections of the history books had been ripped out. The cops decided to bring young Brown in. At that point Brownie *volunteered* to make the arrest. Miss Bertie had assumed that Brownie was forced to do it, but that wasn't true. Brownie had *asked* for the job.

Jennifer turned to the overleaf. After the arrest and processing, Paul Brown was released on his own recognizance upon the recommendation of Brownie. That wasn't surprising. First-time offenders usually got personal recog. But the problem arose later. As the case was being prepared for trial, the fingerprint cards vanished from the evidence room. It was then that Brownie came under investigation. Internal affairs formulated the theory that Brownie had entered the case so he could obstruct it. They interviewed him and made the accusation. Brownie denied the allegations and took a polygraph examination which he passed. The investigators couldn't find any other proof to confirm their suspicions, so the case was terminated. And the prosecution of Paul Brown had to be dropped.

Jennifer closed the file. There it was, the missing page in the Brownie-Paulie story. This had happened before Gardner had come to the prosecutor's office and befriended Brownie. Surely Gardner knew nothing about it. But there it was anyway: a long time ago, Brownie had risked everything to protect his brother. And now, it appeared, he just might be doing it again.

* * *

It was midnight, and Gardner rolled and tossed in the bed covers. He was exhausted, but his mind was still sorting out the ups and downs of the day.

'It'll be OK,' Jennifer whispered beside him.

Gardner switched on the light. His eyes were disaster areas. 'Don't patronize me, Jen. I know I'm in trouble.'

Jennifer suddenly felt guilty. She should have tried harder to give him support. 'Gard...' she started to say.

'Let it go, Jen,' Gardner interrupted. '*I* made the decision...'

'We,' Jennifer corrected. 'It's still *we*.'

'We.'

Jennifer touched his neck. The muscles were knotted like a rope. 'I think I may be able to get us out of it,' she said. 'I have a theory...'

'No!' Gardner barked. 'Don't start with that second suspect crap again. It's useless. It wastes time, energy, and confuses the issues. I tried that road with King and it didn't work. We have to wait for the *Fugitives* show to air. Maybe we'll get lucky.'

Jennifer tried to massage his muscles, but Gardner pulled away. 'I may have figured it out,' she said.

'What?'

'Why Brownie's acting the way he is, who he's protecting...'

'Don't...' Gardner warned. 'We've dropped that ball.'

'Maybe you have, but *I* haven't.'

'Damn it! We *cannot* keep doing this. We have to stick to *one* plan. Don't you understand that? Legally and logically, suicide and a second suspect do *not* go together! For the millionth time! Whatever you're up to, stop it! I mean it, Jen. You'll mess up my mind even worse than it is now. Do you hear me?'

Jennifer recoiled. 'Don't talk to me that way. I *know* something, and it's time you heard it. Brownie is ...'

'Stop it!'

Jennifer leaped out of bed. 'You're impossible!' she cried, grabbing her clothes.

'Where are you going?'

'Out.'

'Why?'

'Because of *you*! You won't look at the truth.'

'Not *won't*,' Gardner protested, '*can't*. We're killing ourselves running up blind alleys.'

'This one isn't blind. It has an ending.'

'Does it end with suicide?'

Jennifer looked him in the eye. 'No.'

'Then *don't* say it.'

Jennifer continued dressing. 'Fine. If that's how you want it. This was all a mistake anyway.'

'What?'

'Trying to play your stupid game. I can't sleep here tonight.'

'Jesus, Jen!'

'I'm leaving.' Jennifer rummaged in the closet for her suitcase.

'Please!' Gardner begged.

'I have to.'

Gardner stood up. 'Jen, please ...' He tried to hold her, but she shrugged out of his embrace. 'Is this about marriage?'

CHAPTER 21

Gardner was up the rest of the night, looking for Jennifer. After phoning several friends, he started on the staff list of the State's Attorney's office. Finally, as the morning sun sparkled the snow outside his window, he reached the right number.

'Charlotte, I need to talk to Jennifer,' Gardner said to a likeable junior assistant prosecutor he'd hired two years ago.

'Why, Jen?' Gardner asked when she came to the phone.

'It's the situation, Gardner ... I don't agree with what you're doing. It's *wrong*. I want to help Brownie as much as you do, but you cannot allow him to control...'

'For God's sake, Jennifer!'

'See how you react?'

'Sorry. I'm getting tired of trying to explain this to you. I *know* Brownie. He's not bluffing. If we don't go his way, he *will* jump ship.'

'Maybe you should let him go.'

'What?'

'This obviously isn't working.'

'What isn't? The case or *us*?'

365

'Both.'

'So what are we going to do?' Gardner finally asked.

'I need time.'

'There isn't any time. Trial starts in a few days and we, rather, *I* have to be ready.'

Jennifer sighed. 'Does that mean I'm fired as co-counsel?'

'No. Of course not. But we have to agree on strategy.'

'So you're the boss, and I have to do what you say?'

'I wouldn't put it that way.'

'Are you going to let me tell you what's going on?'

Gardner hesitated. 'Just give me the general subject, no specifics.'

'I think I know who Brownie's covering for, why he's being so tight-lipped.'

'Jesus,' Gardner moaned. 'Do you have any *proof*?'

'Proof that this person committed the crime? No. But I have proof of the relationship and the cover-up.'

'What good does *that* do? We already figured out he's hiding something...'

'It's his *brother*,' Jennifer said.

'Shit!'

'Sorry, Gardner, but I had to tell you.'

'So what am I supposed to do *now*? Jack up my own client? Force him to turn over a member of his own family? He's not going to give in. He's as stubborn as ... stubborn as...'

'*You*.'

'Yes, *me*. But even if what you say is true, there's nothing we can do about it, not without Brownie's co-operation. That leaves us back at square one.'

'With the suicide defence?'

'It's all we have.'

366

'I can't go along with that,' Jennifer countered. 'I'm sorry, but I just *can't*.'

'Jen ...'

'It's best if I stay out of your way until I sort it out. Then we won't argue.'

'We're not arguing.'

'What do you call it? I don't like being yelled at in my own bed.'

'I'm really sorry.'

'I'll think it through, and get back to you,' Jennifer said at last.

'Are you coming home?'

'Not right now.'

'I do love you,' Gardner avowed.

'I'll talk to you later.' Jennifer hung up.

Gardner put down the phone and looked out of the window. The sun was higher in its southeastern arc, coldly illuminating the frozen day. He was tired and upset. And Jennifer was gone. But that wasn't the biggest problem. If he confronted Brownie with the current situation, he would go ballistic. He'd apparently gone this far to protect his brother. There was no way he'd turn on him now, so Jennifer's revelation meant nothing. They were still committed to suicide, and that was that.

Kent King reached for the TV remote control as Lin Song slumbered in the after-glow beside him. They were coasting now. Trial preparation was complete, and the close quarters had finally triggered some spontaneous sexual combustion.

King switched on the television and looked at Lin. Her long black hair was draped over her face, and her breasts were exposed. King felt another tingle of desire. The rumours had been right: she was one hot babe, in and out of court. Asking her to join the prosecution had been brilliant. She knew tactics, strategy, and some incredible bed manoeuvres. Together, they made a hell of a team.

King propped his pillow and channel-surfed with the remote. Sitcoms, news shows, and sports events all raced by on the screen. He speeded up the search. TV really wasn't his game. He preferred to *do* rather than watch. Suddenly he saw a familiar face. He overran and back-tracked several clicks.

There was a picture of Thomas Ruth on the monitor. Above was the logo: 'FUGITIVES AT LARGE'. King whacked Lin on the butt. 'Wake up,' he ordered.

Lin stirred, and sat up.

'Do you know this man?' a voice demanded. 'His name was Thomas Ruth and he died in October of last year...'

'What is this?' Lin asked groggily.

'Shhhh!'

'... but his true identity remains a mystery. As the leader of the notorious CAIN church, he received national notoriety, and ultimately death by electrocution. A police officer has been charged with his murder, but he maintains that Ruth, or whatever the man's real name was, committed suicide...'

'Shit!' King exclaimed.

'The police officer needs *your* help in preparing his defence.' A toll-free telephone number appeared under Ruth's picture.

Lin was fully awake now, and she looked at King. He was seething.

'If you know *anything* at all about this man: who he really was, where he came from, any psychiatric history he might have had, *please* call our Fugitives Hotline. Operators are standing by twenty-four hours a day. An officer is in trouble, a man with a long record of devoted service to the community. Please, if you can help, call our hotline. There is no charge for the call and callers may remain anonymous if they wish. Please. An officer needs your help.'

The show switched to a commercial, and King shut off the TV.

'Sonofabitch!'

'I told you . . .' Lin said.

King turned. 'Not about *this*.'

'You might have expected it. With nothing else available, where were they going to go?'

King begun to pace the floor, muttering. Suddenly he stopped. 'Get my book.'

'Where is it?'

'Downstairs. In my briefcase. Hurry!'

'Yes *sir*,' she responded sarcastically as she wrapped a shirt around herself and followed his directions.

King had resumed pacing when she returned a moment later. He snatched the phone book from her hand and thumbed the pages. Then he sat on the bed and picked up the phone.

'Davis, this is Kent King. Were you just watching TV? You saw the programme? Meet me at my office in twenty minutes . . . This isn't a *request*, Frank. It's an *order*. We have work to do.'

He hung up and began to get dressed.

'You want me too?' Lin asked.

'I'll take care of it.'

'This is no big deal,' Lin said. 'I hope you realize that.'

'How so?'

'If anyone identifies him, there's still the problem of proof. No one can *prove* who Ruth really was, not now. Not without a body or fingerprints.'

King listened as he buttoned his shirt. 'So what do we do, ignore it?'

'No. But there's nothing to worry about. The whole thing is a red herring. His true identity *cannot* be proven. Lawson has to establish that anyone the *Fugitive* people come up with is the genuine article before he can get it to the jury. And that's impossible.'

King walked to the door. 'You're *sure* about that?'

'Positive.'

King shook his head and ran down the stairs. Lin was a great lawyer, but she didn't know Gardner Lawson. If there *was* a way to resurrect Ruth, Lawson would find it.

Jennifer removed her glasses and rubbed her eyes as the television set ran the credits to *Fugitives At Large*. She was staying at Charlotte's apartment. Her friend was at a movie, and she was alone.

Jennifer lay back on the sleep sofa and surveyed the room. It was decorated in college dorm decor: an assortment of mismatched tables, chairs, and bookshelves. There were some decent paintings on the walls, and a plant or two, but the overall effect was depressing. Jennifer remembered the tiny warren she'd occupied in the pre-Gardner days. Her taste was different, but the ambiance was the same. For her there was a loneliness to the woman-on-her-own way of life.

She thought of Gardner and their situation. 'Is this about marriage?' he'd asked. No, she'd replied. But now, on reflection, she realized it might be about their relationship after all. Gardner had become a bully. *He* set the agenda. *He* decided when they could talk. *He* made the monumental decisions. She loved him, yes. But she couldn't continue to live this way. Something had to give.

Get back to the case, she told herself. If she couldn't work *with* Gardner and Brownie, maybe she could work *for* them. On the outside, maybe she could come up with something that could help the two hard-heads in spite of themselves.

Frank Davis was angry. King had no right to treat him this way, ordering him around, berating him, then asking for favours. Davis had just left King's office to return to the trailer park. The night was clear, but bitterly cold. He turned up the heat in the squad car to full blast and kicked the accelerator, spitting out blackened snow behind the wheels.

Davis drove down Valley Road, then turned onto Mountain. There was no other traffic as he shot through a narrow chute of wind-swept drifts. Davis slowed as he passed his secret hiding spot, a rock formation near the runaway truck exit. This is where he had set up to trap Ruth.

'I have nothing else to say, Officer,' Ruth declared. 'I told you everything at the quarry.'

'Get out of the car,' Davis ordered.

'What?'

'Out of the fuckin' car!'

Ruth's eyes went wide. 'Why? What did I do?'

'Get out of the car, or I'll drag you out!'

Ruth complied.

'Lean forward, and spread your legs!'

'Why?'

Davis grabbed his arm and spun him. 'Against the door!'

'But...'

'Shut the fuck up and do what I say, shithead!'

Ruth unsteadily assumed the position. 'What have I done?'

Davis frisked him. 'You know what you did, you stupid fuck!'

'No, I don't!' Davis patted him down hard, then went through his pockets.

'What the fuck is this?'

Ruth tried to turn his head.

'Stay put!' Davis was examining something in his hand.

'Transporting an illegal substance? That's a crime.'

'No,' Ruth protested. 'It's not illegal.'

Davis laughed and tossed the contraband into his squad car.

'I need that,' Ruth complained.

'Shut up!'

'But you don't understand...'

Davis yanked Ruth's shoulder, turned him around, and jammed his finger in his face. 'No. You don't understand. I run this part of the county. That's my quarry, and this is my road. I make the rules!'

'But, but...'

Davis suddenly walked away and opened the cruiser door. Too shaken to speak, Ruth stood by his car.

The officer started up and pulled alongside. Ruth's face was a pasty white. 'Have a nice day, sir,' Davis said. Then he drove away.

* * *

That was the *first* time. There were many more. Davis was on the access road to the mobile home park now. A few rusty mailboxes and silver trailers to pass, and he'd be home.

Davis roared around the corner and slid to a stop in front of his snow-piled unit. He got out holding a book King had given him and walked to a small storage shed in the rear yard. The snow had drifted against it, and Davis kicked and shovelled his way to the locked door. In a minute, he was inside, rummaging through piles of debris. Soon he emerged with a small cardboard box.

Davis entered his trailer and went straight to his desk, where he turned on the light and dumped out the contents of the box. A tiny cellular phone and three plastic bottles rattled onto the 'December' calendar mat. This was his 'take'. He'd confiscated these unreported and unrecorded objects from Ruth during his private sting. The phone was a clone job that he'd tried to connect to the 911 call the night of Joseph Brown's death, but records showed that this phone was *not* involved. And the pills were prescription, so they were legal, and, at the time, insignificant.

He opened the *USFDA OFFICIAL REGISTRY OF PHARMACOLOGY* and selected a pill bottle. He raised the small canister, scanned the label, and turned to the index.

Davis flipped to the correct page and located the entry.

'Sonofabitch!' he cursed.

'PHENOTHIOZENE', the heading read. 'ANTI-DEPRESSANT AND ANTI-PSYCHOTIC NARCOTIC. RECOMMENDED FOR USAGE WITH SEVERE MANIC DEPRESSION AND SCHIZOPHRENIA PATIENTS.'

373

'Goddamn motherfucker,' Davis cursed. King was right. Ruth was one fucked-up mess. But even they didn't know how bad off he really was.

Brownie locked the door of the police lab from the inside. He had entered the service bay with his pass key and made his way down the hall without being seen. He'd been barred from the premises since the indictment. But it was after 11.00 p.m., and the cop crew was at minimum strength. No one would know he was there.

Brownie walked to the teletype machine and switched it on. He was in the dark, but there was enough light coming through the frosted glass door to make out the keyboard. He sat down and switched the instrument into 'quiet mode'. Then he pulled a piece of paper out of his pocket and input the five names on his list.

The *Fugitives* show had run earlier that night, and the producer had called to say they were already receiving tips. By the next day they should have a run-down on the leads. But in the meantime, Brownie had some follow-up work of his own to do.

The teletype allowed retrieval of criminal records from around the United States. If the correct name, reference number, date of birth, and social security number were entered, a list of prior crimes and convictions could be obtained. But the problem was aliases. Criminals usually gave false names, birthdates, and other misleading information. In some smaller jurisdictions, the cops didn't bother submitting all of their cases to the FBI master file. That meant that a crime committed under a false identity might not show up on the person's official 'rap' sheet.

Brownie selected 'SEARCH' and 'ALL CRIMINAL JUSTICE REGIONS'. This ensured that the names submitted would be run against every record database there was. If a crime was committed under *any* of the aliases, it should show up.

Brownie completed his entries and sat back. It should take about an hour to complete the electronic circuit.

The teletype purred as a sheet of paper emerged. Brownie tore it off. 'NORTHEAST', the printout said. 'NO KNOWN RECORD'. Brownie crumpled it and put it in his pocket as the machine sent its inquiry to another geographic area.

The official book on his father's death had been closed long ago. The autopsy report had finally clinched it. The fibres imbedded in his wrists had been identified as cotton similar to the shirt he was wearing, and the 'natural cause' verdict was unassailable. The fingerprint test on his skin was not even attached, so the scale markings weren't considered. And after Ruth was killed it was all but forgotten. For everyone but Brownie the cause of Joseph Brown's death was no longer an issue.

There was another sound in the machine. Brownie tore off the next sheet. 'SOUTHWEST', the report said, 'NO KNOWN RECORD...'

Brownie crumpled that one too.

The Thomas Ruth case was settled also, as far as Brownie was concerned. He knew what *really* happened to the man, and that truth would never see daylight, regardless of how the jury ruled. But his father's case was different. Someone had murdered him. And Brownie was determined to find out who it was, no matter what the fates had arranged for his own future. He might end up in a prison. But he *would* solve the case. And he *would* exact his revenge.

Gardner was on his third martini at Paul's Place, the hangout he'd frequented in the gap between Carole and Jennifer. Country music still whined on the jukebox, and the singles still swarmed, but he was disorientated. He didn't recognize a single tune *or* face. It had been a long time.

'One more?' Big Paul asked.

Gardner looked at his favourite bartender. He was even bigger in the girth, at least three hundred pounds. But his dark beard and baby face hadn't changed. 'No,' Gardner said. 'Better not.' He was feeling the effects, and he had a long day tomorrow, preparing for trial.

'Want to talk about it?' Paul asked. Until Jennifer came on the scene, he'd been Gardner's surrogate therapist.

'Why don't you give me a beer,' Gardner requested.

Paul pulled a long-necker out of the cooler and placed it on the bar. Gardner took a sip and put it down. 'Am I a fuckhead, Paul?' he asked suddenly.

The barman smiled. 'Sometimes.'

Gardner took another swallow. 'I try, and try, and *try* to do the right thing, but it seems I'm fighting everyone all the time.'

'It's not easy to please people.'

Gardner pushed his stool closer to the bar. 'I'm trying to hold it together, to learn this new job, to protect Brownie, to love Jennifer the way she wants...'

Paul shrugged. 'Maybe you're trying too hard.'

'We were so close,' Gardner rambled on. 'All of us. We took hits, but we kept it together. Now we're falling apart...' Gardner chugged the bottle and plunked it down. 'Another.'

Big Paul raised an eyebrow.

'*Another*, Paul.'

A new bottle came up.

'Why should I fight?' Gardner asked. 'Why?' He took a long swig.

'Because that's *you*. You like to fight.'

'I really don't. These things just happen.'

'You know what your problem is?' Paul remarked.

Gardner looked over his beer.

'You're one of those control ... control...'

'Freaks?'

'Yeah. You always have to have things *your* way. When you can't get it exactly right, you blow up.'

'Bullshit!'

Paul put his hands on his hips. 'See? You're doing it now.'

Gardner finished his beer. 'Doing what?'

'Being a fuckhead. *You* have the answer. *You* know the solution. Everybody has to listen to *you*. Why don't you let someone else have an opinion once in a while, try to understand where they're coming from...'

'Even if they're *wrong*?'

'Even if,' Paul replied. 'People got to be *allowed* to make mistakes. You can't carry responsibility for the whole damn planet.'

Gardner stood up.

'Want me to get you a ride?'

'I'm OK.'

'Sure?'

'Sure.' Gardner started for the door.

'Take care,' Paul said.

Gardner waved behind his head and left the building. The air was frigid, and mountains of ploughed snow in the parking lot glinted in the floodlights. Gardner suddenly felt isolated. He walked to his car and began to unlock it when a wave of dizziness struck. He hesitated with the key, then put it in his pocket. His place was only two miles away. He trudged out to the street and began jogging west. The hard-packed snow crunched under his feet. Gardner speeded up, and soon the jog was a full run. Breath streamed white from his nostrils, and his arms swung frantically. Gardner ran hard, and he didn't stop until he reached the door of his empty house.

PART FOUR

TRIAL

CHAPTER 22

Brownie's trial began promptly on the morning of January eighth, a day of freezing temperatures, cloudy skies, and bitter winds. But there was heat in the ornate amphitheatre of courtroom one. The custodian had cranked up the furnace overnight, and by 9 a.m. the walnut-panelled room was toasty warm.

Gardner, Jennifer, and Brownie had each spent the previous day pursuing private agendas, working on solutions to their secret puzzles. The *Fugitives* producer had faxed some leads on Ruth's identity, but Gardner was too busy with last-minute legal details to check them out. Because the state led off, there was still time to prepare the defence. That was a reprieve, a last chance to find support for the self-destruction theory.

By noon, the first stage of trial was almost complete. Jury selection had proceeded quickly as the lawyers culled and weeded the human pool. Now the jury box was full, and they were ready to move to the next event.

'Are you satisfied with the jury, Mr King?' Judge

Ransome asked. He sat Buddha-like behind the bench, his robe a tent.

'We are, sir,' King replied. He was dressed in navy twill. Lin Song, impeccably groomed beside him, wore a dark green suit.

'What about you, Mr Lawson?'

'A moment please, Judge,' Gardner asked, turning to Brownie. Lawyer and client were both wearing charcoal outfits and muted silk ties. Jennifer watched from the gallery, surrounded by off-duty police officers, reporters, and townies. Her outfit mirrored the defencemen: black on black. 'We only have two strikes left,' Gardner whispered.

Brownie looked at the twelve white faces in the box. 'Whatever you say,' he replied.

'The next two on the list are even worse,' Gardner said. 'This is the best we're gonna get.'

Brownie nodded. 'Go with *them*.'

'Well, Mr Lawson?' Ransome was getting antsy.

Gardner stood. 'I am not going to exercise my remaining strikes, but I find the jury as constituted unacceptable. I renew my objection to the exclusion of African-Americans from the array.' There had been three blacks in the entire selection pool, and King had removed every one with a peremptory challenge.

King started to reply, but the judge waved him down. 'I'll handle this, Mr King,' he said. 'Your objection is noted, Mr Lawson, but if you do not choose to exercise your remaining strikes you accept the jury as constituted. There has been no showing of impropriety. The section of the county this group was drawn from has a low minority population, that is true, but the process itself was fair. Objection overruled.'

'Mr King conspired to exclude the residents of Blocktown from the jury pool,' Gardner argued.

'What evidence do you have of that?' Ransome asked.

'The jury commissioner just confirmed that Blocktown is out of the geographic area for jury selection one week in the entire year: *this* week. King specifically asked to begin the trial today so he could keep African-Americans off the jury. The motivation is obvious.'

King stood up. '*He* agreed to the date in chambers, your honour. I was willing to accommodate his schedule, but *he* agreed to set the case today. I cannot be held responsible.'

Gardner felt his ears tingle. King had set him up; he had been planning to get this date all along.

'You did say that the date was acceptable,' Judge Ransome recalled. 'Sorry, Mr Lawson, your contention has no merit.'

Gardner sat down. Brownie was stuck with an all-white jury because King had pulled a bait-and-switch at the scheduling conference, and he'd been suckered into it. So much for thinking like a defence attorney. Brownie suddenly poked his arm. 'It's OK, Gard.'

But Gardner knew that it wasn't. Twelve back-country whites were going to identify more with Thomas Ruth than with a black cop. And that was a problem.

'Call your first witness, State,' Judge Ransome said. The lunch break was over, the opening statements had been given, and now, at 2 p.m., it was time to get evidence on the table. King had laid out the facts in his address to the jury: motive, handcuffs, shoes, the sighting of Brownie with Ruth on the day of the crime. Everything sounded so reasonable, logical, correct. But when Gardner gave his opening statement, he'd been met with a wall of sceptical faces, calloused hands clasped on denim laps, inattentive eyes. After King's presentation, 'suicide' didn't sound plausible at all.

'The State calls Officer Frank Davis to the stand,' King announced.

Gardner looked up suddenly. Davis was a prosecution liability. Why would they call *him*?

Brownie placed his hands on the table as the officer took the stand.

'State your name and address for the record, please,' the clerk said.

'Frank Davis, officer, county police, headquarters building, Travis Road.' He was in a crisp blue uniform, his hair wetly swept back.

'You may inquire, Counsel.'

King moved toward the witness stand. 'What was your duty assignment in September of this past year?'

'Patrol, day shift.' Davis looked straight ahead, avoiding Brownie and the jury.

'What did that entail exactly? What duties did you perform?'

'Sector patrol, complaint response, routine police work.'

'Any other duties?'

'Investigations.'

'Did there come a time when you were asked to undertake a special investigation?'

'Yes, sir. I was instructed to look into a suspicious death.'

King glanced at Gardner then turned to the witness. 'Whose death, Officer?'

'Joseph Brown, senior. Father of Sergeant Brown.'

'Who requested the investigation?'

'I believe Sergeant Brown did originally, then Lieutenant Harvis assigned it to me.'

King turned towards Gardner and his client. 'Can you point out the person you've referred to as Sergeant Brown?'

Davis aimed his finger at Brownie. 'That man in the black suit.'

'Let the record reflect that the witness has identified the defendant,' King said.

'So noted.'

'Now, Officer Davis, can you inform the jury what, if anything, the defendant told you during the course of the investigation?'

'Yes, sir. He said he believed his father was murdered.'

Gardner glanced at Brownie. He'd never heard about *this* conversation.

Brownie made two fists and glowered at the witness.

'Did he say anything else?' King continued.

'Yes.'

'What?'

'He said he knew who did it, who killed his father.'

King leaned on the hardwood rail. 'Who was it, according to Sergeant Brown?'

Davis turned. 'Thomas Ruth.'

'Objection!' Gardner sprung to his feet.

'Grounds, Counsel?'

'Hearsay...' Gardner was still reeling from the comment.

385

Brownie maintained he'd never discussed his suspicions about Ruth with *anyone*.

'It's not hearsay,' King interjected. 'Statements of the defendant are admissible.'

'A moment please, Your Honour,' Gardner decided to play for some time. He bent close to Brownie's ear. 'Did you ever say that?'

Brownie's head turned slowly. '*No*. He's lying.'

'Anything more, Mr Lawson?' Ransome asked impatiently.

Gardner straightened up. 'The defendant did *not* make that comment, Your Honour. I object!'

'It's a dispute of fact, Mr Lawson,' Ransome replied. 'You can cross-examine or present contradictory evidence in your case if you wish, but the statement itself is *admissible*. Objection overruled. Next question, Mr King.'

Gardner sat down hard. The trial was barely underway, and King had already drawn blood. He eyed the jury, four women and eight men. They were eased back in their chairs, relaxed. Davis was one of them, one more farmer on the hayride.

'Relax,' Brownie whispered.

Gardner stretched his collar. The room was getting hotter. And the prospects for relief didn't look good.

Jennifer left the courthouse and drove towards the Heights. She had watched helplessly as King revved up the prosecution machine and aimed it at the defence. They were in trouble, that was obvious. Between the jury, the judge, and the prosecutors, Gardner and Brownie were overmatched. And the trial had just begun.

The sun was trying to break through the dense clouds as Jennifer chugged up the slope and parked by the log retreat.

Judge Thompkins opened his door. 'Jennifer. Please come in.'

She was bundled in a down overcoat, and her nose was red. 'Thanks. Hope I'm not disturbing you.'

'Of course not.'

Soon they were sitting by the fire. 'Gardner's got a problem,' she said.

Thompkins nodded. 'I've been following the case in the news.'

'King is about to chop him to bits.'

'Why do you say that?'

Jennifer put her hands over the hearth. 'He can't win with the suicide defence...'

Thompkins puffed his pipe. 'You have another idea?'

'Yes. I know, or, rather, I have a strong suspicion as to who may have committed the murder.'

'Do you have actual *proof* to that effect?'

Jennifer shook her head no.

'Is the prosecution *suppressing* proof to that effect?'

'No. They didn't pursue the suspect from the beginning. They singled out Brownie and dropped other leads. But this person is a real possibility...'

The judge lowered his pipe. 'You have no concrete evidence?'

'Correct, but I have a very good theory. It explains Brownie's behaviour, the murder, everything. It is even consistent with King's case. I think Brownie's younger *brother* did it.'

'Brother?'

'Paul Brown. He was in the county the night Ruth died. He had motive and opportunity. The brothers had a falling out a long time ago, but even then, Brownie protected him from prosecution in a vandalism case.'

'That mess at the high school in the late seventies?'

Jennifer nodded.

'That was a bad situation, a racial thing as I recall...' Thompkins touched his chin. 'Does Gardner know about this?'

'I told him, but he won't pursue it.'

'I can understand his reluctance.' The judge leaned back in his chair. 'Brownie wouldn't approve.'

'Right.'

'So they compromised. Suicide was a defence they could both live with.' Thompkins re-lit his pipe.

'Do you think they stand a chance proving Ruth killed himself?'

'Maybe, if they use Dr Sand. He's an effective witness, has an excellent track record.'

'But he had more to go on in his other cases. Gardner has nothing. He doesn't even know who Ruth really was, and he needs background information to show mental instability.'

'I saw the *Fugitives* piece on TV the other night. That should shake out something Gardner can get his teeth into. He's very resourceful, you know.'

'But *I've* got to help.'

Thompkins raised a finger. 'I don't think you *can*, Jennifer, not the way you want. You must accept the facts as they are. You cannot bend reality to suit your own purposes. You have to play by the rules. Defending a case is a different process than prosecuting one, quite different.'

'What are you saying?'

'The truth is absolute, and so are the rules. You chose to switch sides. You can't play defence attorney by prosecution rules. That's what you're trying to do, and that's what is causing you aggravation.'

'So what am I supposed to do? *Ignore* the fact that Brownie's brother might be the real killer?'

'If pursuing him is incompatible with the defence, yes. You *must* ignore it.'

'That's exactly what Gardner said.'

'He is right. Not in an absolute sense, but within the rules of the game. Prosecutors are practitioners of the absolute. Defence attorneys pursue the relative. That's what makes the system work, believe it or not.'

Jennifer stood up. This wasn't what she'd expected to hear, especially from a judge.

'What are you planning?' Thompkins asked.

'Don't know yet.' She buttoned her coat.

'Let it go, Jennifer. Accept the suicide theory, and give it all you've got. Forget the brother.' Thompkins put his arm around her.

'Gardner needs you on the team. You're good people, both of you. You belong together...'

Jennifer eyed him with surprise.

'Give it a try,' Thompkins said with a fatherly squeeze. 'You-all make a powerful combination. You can beat King at his own game if you stick to the plan. Remember the rules...'

'Right,' Jennifer whispered. Then she stepped out the door, into the biting wind.

King drew out the direct examination of Frank Davis for another twenty minutes, reinforcing a morose and moody image of Brownie in the days following his father's death. The spectators were riveted, but the jurors seemed bored, as if their minds had been made up during opening statements. Finally, King was finished. 'Your witness, Counsel,' he said to Gardner as he sat down.

Gardner approached the witness stand with a look of contempt in his eye. 'Officer Davis, did you in fact investigate the death of Joseph Brown?'

'To a certain extent.'

'Is that a yes?'

'I did conduct an inquiry.'

Gardner began pacing beside the witness stand. 'What role, specifically, did you play in the investigation?'

'I went to the scene.'

'What did you find?'

'There was no evidence of a struggle, or anything like that. Mr Brown apparently fell in the road after he had the coronary.'

'Did you explain this to Sergeant Brown?'

'I put it in my report.'

'Did you discuss that report with Sergeant Brown?'

Davis tried to catch King's eye, but Gardner blocked his view. 'I may have.'

'You testified that you discussed the investigation with the defendant. You remember that?'

'Yes.'

Gardner faced the jury. 'When was that conversation?'

'Don't remember, exactly.'

Gardner lifted a copy of the report and turned around. 'Do you pride yourself on being thorough, Officer Davis?'

'I try to be.'

'So you document *everything* that's important during the course of an investigation.'

Davis shifted in his seat, still trying to see King. 'Yes...'

Gardner handed him the report. 'Show me where you noted in this report that Sergeant Brown told you he knew who killed his father.'

'Objection!' King was on his feet.

'Overruled.'

'Show me, Officer Davis!' Gardner flicked the report with his thumb.

'It's not in there,' Davis said softly.

'It's not in there because the conversation never took place!'

'Objection!' King was up again. 'Argumentative.'

'This is cross-examination. Overruled.'

'He did tell me that,' Davis protested.

Gardner stood by the rail. 'Really? Where?'

'In the station.'

'*Where* in the station?' Gardner pressed closer.

'The hall, outside the lab.'

'Who was present?'

'Just us.'

'Just *you*.' Gardner grabbed the report and turned to the jury. 'There were no witnesses to the conversation, you don't remember *when* it occurred, and you didn't note it in your report...'

'We've been over this,' King objected again.

'Move on, Mr Lawson,' Rollie advised. 'We get the point.'

Gardner raised his eyes to the ceiling, then returned to the witness. 'You were personally familiar with Thomas Ruth, the deceased. What contact did you have with him in the days prior to his death?'

'Objection!' King was up like a shot.

'Approach the bench.'

The parties moved forward.

'What's the problem, Kent?'

'Mr Lawson is about to inject an inconsistent line of inquiry into the proceeding. He informed the jury that Ruth killed himself, but he's about to suggest that this witness may have done it. That's not relevant under his defence theory.'

Ransome looked at Gardner. 'What's he talking about?'

'I can prove that Davis harassed Ruth before he died.'

'He's been cleared of any wrongdoing,' King interjected. 'Lawson knows that. The man has been exonerated.'

Ransome turned to Gardner. 'Is that true?'

'Technically, yes.'

'Then how is this inquiry relevant? You say that Ruth killed himself. You know you can't go both ways.'

Gardner gripped the bench. 'We intend to prove that Ruth was a mentally unstable individual who became more and more paranoid as Officer Davis hounded him. That is *not* inconsistent with our defence, in fact, it's supportive.'

'So you're saying that *Davis* here may have driven Ruth to kill himself?'

'Contributed to it, yes,' Gardner said.

'Objection,' King groaned.

Ransome leaned back in his chair for a moment, then lurched forward.

'Overruled. The line of questioning seems fair under the circumstances. Let's get back to work.'

The attorneys returned to their places, and Gardner approached the stand. 'How many times did you stop Thomas Ruth's car, Officer Davis?'

Davis twitched nervously. 'Uh, what?'

'Did you make a number of traffic stops on Thomas Ruth's car?'

Davis looked down. 'Yes.'

'How many?'

'A few.'

'Seven, eight, nine?' Gardner's tone was sharp.

'I never counted.'

'Object again on the same grounds,' King declared.

'Overruled.'

'Why did you stop Thomas Ruth?'

'We had a surveillance going. I was trying to keep track of his movements.'

'Did that necessitate a stop? Couldn't you have observed him from a distance just as well?'

'I guess so.'

'Then *why* did you pull him over so many times? Wasn't it to annoy him? To harass him?'

'To keep track of his movements.'

Gardner looked at the jury. Every eye was locked on the witness.

'So you *admit* you harassed him?' Gardner said.

'Object.'

'Overruled.'

Davis remained silent.

'You *did* harass the man, didn't you?'

'Not exactly,' Davis answered. 'I was just doing my job.'

Gardner looked at the foreman of the jury, a heavyset trucker with bushy black hair. '*Overdoing* it is more like it.' He went to the counsel table and withdrew a document from his file. 'In fact, Mr Ruth obtained a restraining order to make you stop, didn't he?' Gardner started to hand a copy of the civil log to Davis.

'Object! Object! Object!' King interrupted.

'Approach!'

'This witness isn't qualified to admit this evidence,' King fumed at the bench. 'It is a copy of a pleading *I* filed on behalf of Mr Ruth, and which was withdrawn prior to filing. The witness knows nothing about it. It is irrelevant to the proceedings in any event. As I said, the officer has been cleared.'

Rollie looked at Gardner. 'Your position?'

'It supports the contention that Davis' actions had an *effect* on Ruth. He went to a lawyer to try to stop it.'

'But *this* witness is not qualified to admit the document,' King argued.

'I agree,' Ransome said.

Gardner looked at the judge. 'Then I request that the witness step down for a moment, while I call someone to the stand who *can* admit it.'

'That's improper,' King snapped. 'This is the State's case.'

394

'You can vary the order of proof,' Gardner declared. 'In order to complete my cross-examination of this witness, it is necessary for me to place that document into evidence. It lays the foundation for my assertion that *Davis*' conduct had a negative psychological effect on the deceased.'

'No,' King dissented. 'It's improper procedure...'

Rollie looked at Gardner. 'Who do you wish to call?'

Gardner faced his adversary. 'The prosecutor, Kent King.'

Jennifer entered the warden's office at the detention centre and extended her hand. 'Thanks for waiting, Mr Frenkel,' she said. It was 3.30 p.m., and he was late for an appointment outside the facility.

'That's OK,' the warden replied. He motioned his visitor into a chair. 'What can I do for you?'

Jennifer checked to be sure the door was closed. 'I want to talk about Brownie and his activities here after the arrest.'

Frenkel's expression turned quizzical. 'Activities?'

Jennifer nodded. 'I know he had some special privileges...'

'What did you expect me to do?'

'Don't get defensive. This isn't a complaint. I just want to know where he spent his time.' Jennifer had pondered the situation and come to a sudden realization. It wasn't *what* Brownie had done, but *where* he had done it that was the key. The time frame of his covert Ruth investigation had been extremely narrow. He'd barely had time to find the shoes and fingerprint them *before* he got arrested. Maybe he finished the job in jail.

'He used this office some,' Frenkel said.

'To meet visitors?'

'Yes, and...'

'There was another reason he came here?'

'To use the phone, the fax...'

'The computer?' Jennifer glanced at the equipment across the room.

'If he wanted to.'

Jennifer stood and approached the console. 'Did you keep track of the times he used it?'

'Yes, in my day book.'

'Can you get it for me please?' Jennifer switched on the monitor.

The warden retrieved the book and handed it to her. The machine was warming now, giving input signals. 'What's your password to the criminal justice net?' Frenkel peered over her shoulder. 'CROSSBAR', he replied. 'What are you looking for?'

Jennifer booted up the menu and struck a key accessing the FBI fingerprint classification files. Then she checked the notebook and pressed a few more keys. 'Were you present when Brownie used the computer?'

'No. He requested privacy.'

Jennifer entered the fingerprint database. 'So you don't know if he ran any prints for comparison, do you?'

'No.'

Jennifer selected the automatic backup file directory of the database. She keyed in a date, the access code, and the utilization authority account number she had found in her State's Attorney's manual.

'What are you *after*?'

The screen flashed a 'WAIT' signal as the mainframe in Washington tried to answer her request.

'What did Brownie *do*?' Frenkel repeated.

There was a beep, and a line of print appeared on the screen.

'What is *that*?'

'The response to a request Brownie made,' Jennifer said gravely. 'He submitted a fingerprint for comparison in the FBI master files.'

'And that's it?'

'That's it,' Jennifer sighed.

Apparently Brownie *had* lifted a fingerprint from Ruth's shoe and traced its identity through the computer. He had erased the actual inquiry, but the failsafe backup tape had preserved it. And there it was in bold print. The name of the person whose fingerprint had been matched: 'PAUL JEFFERSON BROWN'.

CHAPTER 23

'This is outrageous!' Kent King wailed. After a lengthy argument at the bench, Judge Ransome had agreed to let Gardner call him as a witness.

'You may call Mr King for a limited purpose,' Rollie cautioned the defence attorney. 'You may identify the document and lay the foundation for questioning Officer Davis about his actions, but that is all.'

'No, no, no!' King was still struggling against the ruling. 'He cannot offer evidence now. It's my case.'

'Take the stand, Mr King.'

King whispered to Lin Song and walked to the witness chair like a condemned man. His expression told Rollie there would be retribution later. In the gallery, anticipation rippled through the spectators, culminating in an audible buzz.

'Quiet, please,' Ransome said.

Gardner took a copy of the civil log up to the stand and handed it to King. 'Recognize this?' he asked.

'Yes,' King replied hostilely.

'What is it?'

'You know what it is.'

Gardner looked at the judge.

'The jury doesn't know, Mr King. Tell them what the paper is.'

King gave Rollie another hateful stare. 'The log of a civil pleading I filed and then withdrew.'

'What was the nature of the pleading?'

King crossed his arms. 'An injunction petition.'

'And on whose behalf was it filed?'

King took a breath. 'Thomas Ruth.'

'Thomas Ruth?' Gardner repeated loudly, as if that was a big surprise. There was another buzz in the crowd.

'Yes.'

'And what did Mr Ruth ask you to enjoin for him?'

'Objection!' Lin Song cried. 'Hearsay.'

'Not offered for truth of the matters contained therein, Your Honour,' Gardner countered.

'Overruled.'

'What conduct were you trying to stop?' Gardner went on.

'Questioning by police.'

'Is that how you phrased the pleading?' Gardner raised the document.

'Not exactly.'

'In fact, you termed the conduct that Mr Ruth wanted stopped as harassment. Isn't that true?'

'Yes.'

'The police officer who was doing the harassing, what was his name?'

'Objection!' Lin was back on her feet. 'Counsel declared that he is not trying to prove the truth of the matters alleged. He cannot therefore say the named officer was, in fact, the harasser.'

Rollie nodded. 'I agree. Rephrase, Mr Lawson.'

'Whose name did you put on the petition as the alleged harasser?'

'Objection!'

'He can answer that.'

King shifted in his seat but didn't reply.

'What police officer's name was on the petition?'

'Answer the question, Mr King.' Rollie advised.

'Frank Davis.'

'Frank Davis!' Gardner repeated.

'And can you tell the jury the mental state of Mr Ruth when he came to your office and asked you to help him stop Officer Davis from harassing him?'

'Objection!' Lin yelled. 'That's beyond the scope of the questioning parameters you outlined for the witness.'

'Yes, it is,' Ransome replied. 'Sustained ...'

'I'd like to answer,' King spoke suddenly.

'Do you withdraw the objection?'

King gave his co-counsel the OK signal. 'Withdraw,' Lin declared.

'Very well. Answer.'

King addressed the jury. 'Mr Ruth was in excellent mental condition when I saw him. He was calm, well-orientated, and alert, in a very good frame of mind.'

Gardner rolled his eyes. 'Really?'

'Really.'

'So the fact that he was being hounded by a police officer had no effect on him. He was in such a good frame of mind that he hired a lawyer ...'

'Object!' King replied.

'You withdrew the objection,' Ransome pointed out.

'Object!' Lin echoed.

'If Mr Ruth was in such a great frame of mind he wouldn't have needed a lawyer!' Gardner exclaimed. 'He had a problem, a big problem! And he went for help...'

'Object!' Lin tried again.

'What's the question, Mr Lawson?' Ransome asked.

Gardner looked at the jury. They were all wide-eyed, engaged. His point had been made, and then some. 'No further questions,' he said, sitting down. King had just dropped his right hand. And Gardner had nailed him good.

Gardner and Jennifer had agreed to meet after court for a 'talk'. They sat by candlelight at the Mountain Lodge restaurant, trying to converse over dinner.

'You look good,' Gardner said. They had only been apart a few days, but it seemed longer. Jennifer was particularly beautiful tonight, her hair pulled back, her peach lipstick shimmering in the glow of the flame.

'You look tired,' Jennifer replied. His eyes were baggier than usual, his skin sallow.

There were so many issues, and so little time. Talk about the day had filled the void to this point. The trial had forged ahead after King testified, and he was able to dig himself out of his hole. The points Gardner had scored were overcome by the mass of circumstantial evidence the other witnesses piled up. There was little cause for celebration.

The two lawyers ate their appetizers in silence, then looked at each other. 'I...' they both began.

'Sorry.' Gardner laughed self-consciously.

'I need to say something,' Jennifer announced, 'and I would appreciate it if you would remain calm. Can you do that?'

'I'll try.'

'Brownie matched a fingerprint to his brother's while he was at the detention centre. He used the computer and accessed the FBI files.'

'What?' Gardner's face flushed.

'Remain calm. Please.'

Gardner took a moment to get it together.

'I now have *proof* of Paul Brown's involvement in the Ruth case, and when you combine the fingerprint with *this*...' Jennifer pulled a copy of the internal affairs report on Brownie from her handbag and passed it to Gardner. 'It all comes into focus. Brownie has a history of covering up for his brother. He shielded Paul from a burglary and vandalism charge when he was a teenager.'

Gardner read the paper by the candle. 'Jesus Christ,' he whispered.

'You never knew about this?'

Gardner checked the date on the report. 'I didn't even know *Brownie* back then. I was in college.'

Jennifer had guessed right. Brownie had hidden his past from Gardner. 'I *tried* to explain the situation, but you wouldn't let me.'

Gardner put down the report. 'I told you why: the defences conflict and we had nothing specific to go on.'

'We do *now*.'

Gardner took a sip of his martini and gave her a

frustrated look. 'It doesn't make any difference. We still have Brownie to deal with.'

'Can't you go around him?'

'Not ethically . . .'

'Isn't there *something* we can do?'

Gardner finished his drink. 'Was the fingerprint image saved in the computer?'

'No. Brownie erased it, but he forgot about the backup log. It retained an entry confirming that Paul Brown's print had been matched.'

'So you couldn't retrieve the actual print?'

'No.'

Gardner put his elbow on the table. 'If we got our hands on the print itself, we might be able to do something . . .'

'But Brownie has it . . .'

'Or *had* it . . .' Gardner stared across the table, his dark eyes mirroring the flickering light. 'Without Brownie to say where the print *came from* there's nothing to incriminate Paul.'

'And Brownie won't talk.'

Gardner did not reply. That was the crux of it. The only way out would be to turn brother against brother. But Brownie was a man of honour. He'd die in silence before ever doing that.

By the time Gardner and Jennifer had finished their meal some of the ice between them had melted. Gardner ordered an after-dinner drink, and Jennifer asked for tea. They had stuck to business all evening. Gardner suddenly grasped Jennifer's hand and squeezed. 'I've missed you.'

Jennifer did not respond.

'Are you coming home tonight?'

Jennifer avoided his eyes. She'd been doing a lot of thinking the past few days.

'Jen, please,' Gardner said. 'You've made your point.'

Jennifer looked up. 'What point have I made?'

Gardner's lip twitched.

'What point have I made?' she repeated.

'I need to be more ... more *understanding*.'

Jennifer gently removed her hand. 'That's not what all this is about.'

'Please, Jen,' Gardner begged. 'The trial; Brownie. I listened to you. I let you have your say ... I'm *trying*, for God's sake...'

Jennifer stood up. 'We can talk about it tomorrow. I'll be at the trial, and maybe we can have dinner again, after court.'

'OK,' Gardner replied. 'Whatever you say. I'll walk you out.'

Jennifer pecked his cheek and turned to leave. 'No need,' she said. 'I can make it on my own.'

Gardner drove to Brownie's house after his dinner with Jennifer, his mind in turmoil. So that was it: Paul Brown *was* the second suspect. As Jennifer said, it explained everything. No wonder Brownie's attitude had been so strange. He'd done a brilliant detecting job. He'd uncovered his own brother. And then he'd covered him up again.

Gardner slowed for the turn onto Brownie's road. Snow ploughs had cleared a path through, but wind had blown white drifts across the surface again. It was desolate out here, a lonely stretch of rocks and bare-boned trees, a perfect place for a man to take refuge from his friends.

Gardner parked and made his way to the house. There was ice on the walk, and the footing was treacherous. He knocked, and Brownie opened the door. 'Gard. What's going on?'

'Sorry to disturb you,' Gardner apologized, 'but something's come up...'

Brownie let him in, and they moved to the living room. Gardner's expression made it clear that the 'something' was monumental.

'Spit it out, man,' Brownie said.

Gardner sat on the couch, and motioned Brownie to sit beside him. For the past hour he'd been plotting his move. Brownie's motivation was noble. He was sacrificing himself for family. Gardner couldn't attack him for that. He had to take a more subtle approach. 'I want you to tell me about Paul,' he began.

Brownie's eyes narrowed.

'You said at the funeral it was a long story about you and him. I want to hear it.'

'At this hour? In the middle of the trial?'

'Here,' Gardner said. 'Now.'

Brownie crossed his arms. 'We went different directions in our lives. That's all.'

'He became a racist, and you didn't?'

Brownie stared at the wall. 'I wouldn't say that.'

'What *would* you say?'

'Nothing. He had his ideas about the way life should be, and I had my own. That's it. End of story.'

'Was *killing* one of his ideas?'

Brownie jerked his head around.

'What are you talking about?'

'You know *exactly* what I'm talking about.'

Brownie stared in silence.

'I know the whole story, Brownie.'

'You don't know anything.'

'Jennifer retrieved the backup log of the fingerprint comparison you ran at the detention centre. We know whose print you matched.'

Brownie remained still. '*Where* did the fingerprint come from?'

'From Thomas Ruth's shoes, where you lifted them.'

'Is that right? How do you know?'

'Don't bullshit me, Brownie. Your brother is directly implicated in Thomas Ruth's death. We both know that.'

'Knowing and *proving* are two different things.'

'You destroyed the print, didn't you?'

'You said it. *I* didn't.'

Gardner took a breath. Brownie had out-flanked him. 'You *knew* nothing could be proven without the fingerprint, so you disposed of it.'

'*What* print? I told you I got nothing off the shoes.'

'Then where did you get the print you submitted for comparison? Paul Brown's...'

Brownie picked up a glass from the table. 'Here, maybe. Or the doorknob, or...'

Gardner gripped his knees. This wasn't going to work. If Brownie produced the fingerprint, he could clear himself instantly, but he'd already made sure the print never saw the light of day. 'Goddamn it, Brownie!'

'Take it easy.'

'No. You cannot *do* this!'

'I hear where you're coming from, Gard.' Brownie touched Gardner's arm. 'I *know* what you're trying to do, and I am grateful for it. I value your friendship and your help more than I can ever say. But you got to cut *me* some slack here. I got my mind set. I'm a grown man. I *can* make decisions. I have a right to decide how to defend my own case. I know what I want to put in. And I know what I want to keep out...'

Gardner wanted to grab Brownie and beat some sense into him, but as a defence lawyer he could only advise, not force. He had finally learned that part.

'It's suicide or nothing,' Brownie continued. 'We have leads to follow from the *Fugitives* show, and you're scoring points with the witnesses. You even got King himself on a pin. Let's stick with the plan. OK?'

Gardner didn't know what to say. His client was innocent, and his client could *prove* his innocence. But he was not going to do it.

'Can we please get back to suicide?' Brownie asked. 'Leave that other shit alone?'

Gardner remained passive. Further discussion was pointless, and argument was out of the question. The brothers' blood was thick, despite the rift. And Brownie had limited the options to one.

'Suicide,' Gardner finally conceded.

'We'll make it fly,' Brownie said hopefully.

'Yeah,' Gardner grumbled. But he knew otherwise. Without a miracle, Brownie was as good as dead.

'The State calls Dr Raphael Aguilar to the stand,' Kent

King announced. It was day two of the trial and, at 11.45 a.m., this was the third witness of the morning. Again, the gallery was full, and there was an overflow in the hall. Jennifer was up front, behind the defence table. And the temperature was rising.

The witnesses so far had been mildly damaging. The first established that Ruth was with Brownie on the day he died. 'That's the one,' Eunie Land had said without hesitation, pointing to Brownie. Gardner had left her alone on cross-examination; they were conceding that Brownie stopped Ruth. The next witness, Randy Allison, established that Ruth was lifeless on the grille when they encountered his body. Gardner brought out on cross-examination that the man and his sons had not seen him die, and they had no idea what actually happened. Again, there was no conflict with the defence. Now the autopsy technician was about to testify, and Gardner prayed that his testimony would be as superficial as the others.

'Identify yourself for the record,' King requested.

'Raphael Aguilar, MD,' the witness said, 'certified state pathologist, currently assigned to the Medical Examiner's Office, University Hospital, Baltimore.' He was a small Filipino man with thick grey hair and glasses.

'How long have you been a medical examiner?'

'Twenty-two years.'

Gardner stood. 'We'll concede qualifications, Your Honour. I acknowledge him as an expert in his field.'

'Thank you, Mr Lawson,' Judge Ransome said. 'The witness is qualified and will be permitted to render an expert opinion. Let's continue.'

King retrieved a set of photographs from Lin Song. He

ran them by Gardner, had them marked for identification, and showed them to the witness. 'Take a look at these pictures, Doctor. Can you identify them?'

Aguilar adjusted his glasses and sorted through the stack. 'Yes I can.'

'What do they depict?'

'The body of Thomas Ruth, a man sent to our facility in September.'

'Did you perform an autopsy on that man?'

'Yes I did.'

'And did you prepare a report as a result of that autopsy?' Lin Song handed her co-counsel a stapled set of documents, which he showed to Gardner, had marked, and handed to the witness.

'Yes. This is my report.'

'Was the autopsy performed in a routine manner?'

'Yes, sir.'

'And did you reach a conclusion as to the cause of death?'

The witness checked the report and looked up. 'Yes I did.'

King turned to the jury. 'And what was it? What caused Mr Thomas Ruth to die?'

'Heart failure due to electrocution.'

'And what did you conclude the *manner* of death to be?'

Gardner jumped to his feet. 'Objection.'

Judge Ransome looked surprised. 'On what grounds, Counsel?'

'The conclusion is speculative.'

King moved toward the bench. 'He conceded expertise, Judge.'

'I know, Mr King.' Ransome said. 'What about that, Counsellor? You agreed that he is an expert.'

'That is correct,' Gardner replied, 'but I don't have to accept everything he says as gospel. Attributing a *manner* of death in this case is pure speculation. The evidence is totally circumstantial. It is impossible to pinpoint the exact *manner* of death.'

Ransome thought for a moment. 'This is really an issue you can explore on cross-examination, isn't it? The witness is qualified to give his opinion as to *how* the man died, and you can attack the premise all you want. I'm going to let him respond.'

King smiled and moved back towards the stand. 'What was the *manner* of death in this case, Doctor?'

Aguilar faced the jury. 'Homicide.'

'In his opinion,' Gardner interrupted.

'Your Honour . . .' King said.

'You'll get your chance to establish that, Mr Lawson,' Ransome declared, 'but right now keep the sidebar comments to yourself.'

Gardner sat down. There was a minor stir in the crowd, and Jennifer whispered 'Hàng in there,' behind his back.

'On what do you base your *opinion*, Doctor?' King asked, glancing at Gardner. 'You said homicide. How did you come to that conclusion?'

'The fact he was in handcuffs and the way in which the body was subjected to the electrical current. That was a forcible act.'

King looked at the jury. 'So you don't believe that the man might have done it to himself.'

411

Aguilar shook his head. 'No. *I* don't believe so. Someone else did it to him.'

King kept questioning the medical examiner until the noon lunch break, pounding home the homicide theme. They had finally ended the morning session with King completing direct examination. Now, at 1.30 p.m., court was back in session, and it was Gardner's turn.

'Doctor Aguilar,' he began, 'you said earlier today that "someone else" killed Mr Ruth. Do you recall that testimony?'

'Yes, sir.'

'Who was it?'

'Sir?' That was a strange inquiry.

'Who killed Mr Ruth?'

Aguilar stirred. 'Who? I...'

'You don't *know* who killed the man. You're only guessing, in fact, that someone did it. Isn't that right? You don't have a clue as to what really happened?'

'Objection.' King's voice rang out. 'He's arguing with the witness.'

'It's fair cross,' Ransome ruled. 'Answer the question, Doctor.'

Aguilar looked confused. 'What was it?'

'Rephrase, Mr Lawson.'

'You do not have any idea as to who, in fact, killed Ruth. Isn't that right?'

'Who did it? No. *How*...'

Gardner held up his hand. 'We'll get to *how* in a minute. We're on *who* now. Tell the jury *who* killed Thomas Ruth.'

'I don't know,' the doctor replied.

'You don't know?'

'That's what I said.'

'So, in point of fact you don't know if someone *else* did it, or he did it to him*self* . . .'

Aguilar put his hand on his glasses. 'That's different.'

'Really?' Gardner had approached the stand and was now in the witness's face. 'Tell us the difference.'

'A man wouldn't cuff himself to commit suicide.'

'So you're basing your opinion on the fact he was handcuffed?'

Aguilar nodded. 'Yes, in part.'

'Not just in part,' Gardner replied. 'Your homicide theory is based *entirely* upon the fact that he was hand-cuffed. Isn't that right?'

The doctor didn't reply.

'Isn't that right?' Gardner repeated.

'He's already given the basis of his opinion,' King interjected.

'He can give it again,' Ransome replied. 'Answer the question, Doctor.'

'People don't usually handcuff *themselves*,' the witness ventured.

'Right,' Gardner said. 'So you've equated handcuffing with murdering. Haven't you?'

Aguilar frowned. 'I guess so.'

'What if he was handcuffed by an innocent party and then released? What if he was upset, distraught, and suicidal, and took it upon *himself* to go to the grid and end his life? How would that affect your opinion?'

'That's not likely . . .' the witness answered.

413

'Not likely, but it *could have happened.*'

King stood up. 'Anything *can* happen, Judge. That's not a proper question.'

'Overruled,' Ransome said.

'If Ruth was already handcuffed, he could have gone to the grid and killed himself. Isn't that right?'

'Possibly.'

Gardner turned to the jury. 'So your conclusion that someone *else* killed Ruth is not altogether firm. If he were handcuffed, released, and suicidal, he could have taken his own life.'

'Yes,' the doctor said nervously. 'It *could* have happened that way.'

'In that case, do you want to retract your previous assertion that the manner of death was homicide?' Gardner asked.

'Object!' King hollered. 'He cannot change what is already written in the report.' He waved the autopsy documents over his head.

'Approach the bench.'

'Let me see that,' Rollie said as they neared him.

King handed over the report, and they all paused while the judge read.

'The witness can re-state his conclusion,' Gardner declared when Rollie looked up.

'He cannot,' King retorted. 'He's already submitted his official finding. It's on the death certificate.'

'Gentlemen,' Ransome said, 'please. I think we're arguing semantics here...' He put the report down on the bench. 'The witness is not, as I understand it, contradicting his finding. He's merely responding to Mr Lawson's

414

hypothetical question. He can answer affirmatively and still not change his ultimate conclusion.'

King smiled.

'But...' Gardner said.

'The conclusion of homicide stands,' the judge declared. 'I will *not* allow the report to be modified.'

'But, Judge...' Gardner sputtered.

'Enough, Mr Lawson. Let's proceed!'

Gardner slowly returned to the trial table. So there it was in writing, and it could not be changed. Thomas Ruth had been *killed*. And that fact was beyond dispute.

Katanga lifted a broken wine bottle from the pavement and put it in his trash bag. They were cleaning up the neighbourhood. The church group, the Watch Programme, and the Brotherhood Forum had finally combined forces to attack the garbage-strewn Southside Alley. It was time to take back the streets. Katanga shivered as his hands touched the cold glass. The snow had melted into a grey mush, but the people were still out there.

'Don't touch that!' a volunteer called.

Katanga looked down at a pile of hypodermic needles he was about to pick up.

'AIDS,' the man warned. 'You get stuck with one of them, you got some trouble.'

Katanga ignored him. He grabbed a handful of syringes and threw them in the bag.

'You're crazy.'

'I'm not leaving them out here for the kids,' Katanga replied. He scooped up the rest of the pile and deposited them with the others. Then he moved down the alley in search of more contraband.

As Katanga worked, an image of the past entered his mind. He was eleven years old, and a fellow student had slipped him some smokes. He'd hidden them in his shorts and waited until he got home. Then he'd gone behind the shed to light up. He'd just taken his first puff when he heard a voice.

'What are you doin', Paul?' *It was Joe, home from high school early.*

Paul held his ground and took a drag. 'What does it look like?' *The cigarette was still clenched between his lips.*

'It looks like you're bein' a fool.'

Paul took another drag and tried not to cough. The smoke burned.

'Give it here!'

Paul puffed again.

'Give it here!'

'No.' *Paul was his own man. He could do what he wanted.*

Joe stepped close and snatched the weed out of his brother's mouth. Then he crumpled it in his hand.

Paul produced another from his pocket, and started to light up.

'Don't,' *Joe commanded.*

'Fuck you. You ain't my Daddy.'

Joe grabbed his brother and forced him to drop the cigarette. Then he rifled his pants and confiscated the others, grinding them up with his fingers.

'Get off of me!' Paul protested. But his brother was too strong, his grip overpowering.

'I'm gonna let you go,' Joe said. He released and stepped back. 'You mess with cigarettes, they'll eat you alive. Stay away from them.'

'Who put you in charge?' Paul demanded.

'Nobody. But I catch you smokin' again, I'll bust you up.'

Paul stared up at his brother in silence. Up to that time in their lives the two boys had never had a real fight. Joe was too big and too strong.

'You understand me?' Joe asked.

Paul nodded. He did understand. And he did not want to test the sincerity of his brother's threat.

'Gun-shells over here!' a neighbour yelled.

Katanga came out of his reverie. The street was littered with horrors: cartridges, liquor bottles, drug paraphernalia... He knelt down for another shard of glass and felt the rolled newspaper in his back pocket ride up. He put the glass in the bag and pulled out the paper. There was a small headline in a box: 'COP TRIAL IN CULT MURDER UNDERWAY, SUICIDE ALLEGED'.

Katanga stared at the article for a moment. Then he balled it up and threw it in with the rest of the trash.

Reverend Taylor placed his stereo in a box and sealed the lid with tape. It was almost midnight, and his basement hideaway had finally been stripped bare. This was the last box. The rest of the stuff was already in storage, and preparations were almost complete. There were a few loose ends to wrap up. And then he'd be off.

Taylor moved the box towards the door and set it beside the others. Just then, his cordless phone rang.

'Reverend Taylor here,' he answered.

'What's going on?' a voice asked.

Taylor turned his head so the signal strengthened. 'Status quo.'

'Have you been over to the trial?'

'Twice.'

'What's happening?'

The reverend sat on a box. 'A bunch of nonsense. Lawson is pushing suicide hard.'

'You think they *know*?'

'Know?'

'You think they figured it out?'

Taylor picked his teeth with the corner of an envelope. 'They don't know a thing. They're just guessing. Keep your cool...'

'Can't stop thinking about it,' the voice said.

'God works in wondrous ways,' Taylor replied. 'Your life was spared so you could enrich other lives...'

'And the wicked shall be punished for their transgressions?'

'Praise the Lord.'

'I'm tryin' to keep it together,' the voice continued. 'It's just hard, that's all.'

'I understand, my brother, but you gotta stay strong. Ain't nothin' you want to do. Ain't nothin' you *can* do.'

'Thanks, Rev.'

'Bless you, Brother.'

The caller hung up, and Taylor reflected for a moment. Then he picked up another box and carried it out to his car.

CHAPTER 24

Gardner and Brownie made it to the courtroom just in time. They had met early to go over the *Fugitives* leads and had run late. Now the judge was on the bench, the jury was in the box, and the trial was about to resume. They took their places at the defence table and signalled they were ready.

'Proceed, State,' Ransome ordered impatiently.

King prodded Lin Song's arm. He'd been handling the questioning chores so far, but today his co-counsel would do the honours. That was a message to the defence: conviction was in the bag. The second string was coming in.

'Ms Dorothy Eden to the stand, please,' Lin said. She was dressed in a form-fitting white suit, her hair pinned up and twisted.

Gardner glanced around, looking for Jennifer. She was several rows back, and she waved. He nodded and scanned the crowd around her. It was the same mix as usual, but there were fewer black faces. Maybe Blocktown had thrown in the towel.

'Swear the witness,' Judge Ransome directed.

Dorothy was sworn in and identified for the record.

'Ms Eden,' Lin began, 'did there come a time when you became acquainted with a man named Thomas Ruth?'

'Yes.' The witness, clad in a Laura Ashley print outfit, looked like she had never set foot in a cult.

'And when was that?'

'Approximately seven months ago.'

'And how did you happen to meet him?'

'I heard about his congregation, Church of the Ark, from a friend.'

'Is that church referred to as CAIN?'

'Yes.'

'And you decided to join?'

'After speaking with Thomas Ruth, yes.'

'You knew Thomas Ruth well during your tenure at the quarry?'

'Objection,' Gardner said. 'Leading.'

'Sustained.'

Kim remained cool. 'Can you describe your relationship with Mr Ruth?'

'I was CAIN's cook, so we were close.'

'He had a healthy appetite?'

A nervous laugh sounded in the gallery.

'No levity intended, Your Honour,' Lin said. 'Let me rephrase that.'

'Please do.'

'As cook, did you have occasion to be with Mr Ruth?'

'Yes.'

'How much time did you spend in his presence?'

'An hour or so a day, I'd say.'

Lin walked to the trial table and opened a cardboard

box. 'Would it be fair to say that you were familiar with Mr Ruth's wearing apparel?' She removed a plastic bag from the box.

'Yes.'

Lin lifted the bag. Inside were a pair of shoes. 'Mark this item, please, as State's Exhibit number...'

'Hold it,' Gardner interrupted.

Judge Ransome looked up from his notes. 'What's wrong, Mr Lawson?'

'Let me see that.' Gardner pointed at the bag.

'Approach. And bring the bag with you.'

The parties gathered at the rail, and Gardner scrutinized the plastic. 'Can you open it?' he requested.

Lin peeled off the tape and handed it back. Gardner removed one of the shoes and huddled with Brownie beside the bench.

'What is your *problem*?' Ransome asked.

Gardner put the shoe on the bench. '*Someone* has tampered with this exhibit.' He looked accusingly at King.

'That's bull,' King replied.

'Gentlemen,' Ransome cautioned. 'I'll decide what's bull and what's not. The basis of your complaint, Lawson?'

'When I viewed the shoes in the property room before trial, they were not in this condition. They were covered with fingerprint powder...' Gardner placed a shoe on the rail. 'But now they're clean.'

Ransome picked up the shoe, put it down, and examined the tips of his fingers. 'Are these the *same* shoes you looked at before?'

Gardner checked the evidence tag. 'The same.'

'Judge . . .' King began to speak.

'Hold on,' Ransome said to the prosecutor. 'I still don't get it. If they're the same shoes, what's your objection?'

Gardner pressed against the bench. 'The shoes were found in my client's possession. They are alleged to have belonged to the victim, alleged to have been worn by him on the day he died. They were fingerprinted by my client in an effort to find out what really happened. If *he* killed Ruth, why would he process the man's shoes? The presence of fingerprint dust corroborates his innocent intent. But the dust has been mysteriously removed. *Someone* wants to deny my client the exculpatory inference.'

Ransome looked at King. 'What's your response, Kent?'

King handed a piece of paper to the judge. 'This is the chain of custody log for the shoes. It lists everyone who had access to the evidence. You'll note the name "Lawson" is the last name there.'

'Is Mr King suggesting that *I* removed the dust?'

'No,' King replied, 'I'm not. I don't know who did it, or even *if* it was done . . .'

'You *know* they had powder on them.'

'I do not!' King countered.

Ransome interceded. 'Stop bickering! What am *I* supposed to do about this?'

'Object to the admission of the shoes!' Gardner huffed. 'They do not have the same appearance they had when confiscated, and their admission in a clean condition is extremely prejudicial to my client.'

'OK,' Ransome answered firmly. 'Everyone agrees that the shoes are the very same ones that were seized. They may be clean now, but there is no dispute that they were picked up pursuant to the search warrant. That, in my opinion, makes them admissible. As to their condition? That is a matter of conjecture. Each party can explore the issue with the witness who took the shoes into custody. If they were covered with powder at that time, the defendant will not be denied his innocent intent argument. Let's get back to work.'

'But Judge...' Gardner argued, 'saying and seeing are not equal.' The impact of *seeing* the powder would be lost on the jury. And that was obviously intended by whoever wiped them off.

'I've ruled, Mr Lawson.'

Gardner glared at King. So that was it: victory at any cost.

King smirked and walked with Lin back to their table.

'Proceed, please,' Ransome said.

Gardner and Brownie returned to their seats. They'd just been served another off-line ace. King was determined to convict, and there was no limit to how far he'd go to ensure it. Evidence the defence needed was either missing or altered. And that forced them even deeper into a corner. With no way out.

Brownie put down the telephone and crossed out the last name on his list. It was noon court recess, and he was trying to finish his share of the *Fugitives* leads that he and Gardner had split earlier. With time running short, they had to take advantage of every spare moment, so there would be no lunch today. He was in the conference room and Gardner was in his office, and all the lines were busy.

423

Brownie looked at the page of crossed-out names and notes in the margin. Of eight calls, only two had anything meaningful to say. That was to be expected. *Fugitives* really lured in the kooks.

A Werner Rosen said Ruth was his father, a rabbi obsessed with the biblical Cain who had disappeared three years before. 'How old are you?' Brownie asked. 'Fifty-five,' Rosen answered.

Five other calls were more or less the same. Ruth was a long-lost brother, former classmate, teacher, boyfriend, and itinerant musician. But when Brownie pressed for details, each came up short. The confirming information they gave was suspiciously inadequate. Brownie wrote them off as wishful thinkers or intentional deceivers.

That left two leads with promise: a disabled veteran named Adrian Anders, and a woman from California, Rosemary Blank. Both of them had identified Ruth as 'Barton Graves'. That caught Brownie's attention. It was unlikely that either person knew the other, yet their identifications intersected. That warranted a follow-up.

Brownie dialled a California exchange. Years ago he'd met a Highway Patrol officer at a crime conference. They'd kept in touch, and occasionally conferred on cases. He had no idea of Brownie's current predicament.

'Benny Jason,' a voice answered.

'This is Joe Brown.'

'Brownie! Long time, buddy. How's it going?'

'Oh, pretty good.'

'What's up?'

'I need a favour.'

'Anything, man. Just say the word.'

'I need you to run a records check on the California MVA list. Twenty years ago, a man named Barton Graves was living in LA, and to the best of my knowledge he had a state driver's licence. He may have been in the military at the time. Are you computerized that far back?'

'Yes. All I need is his date of birth.'

'Don't have it.'

'Social security number?'

'Negative. Can you do it just on the name?'

'I'll try. Give it to me again.'

'B-A-R-T-O-N G-R-A-V-E-S.'

'Got it,' Bennie said. 'Do you want to hold while I run it through, or do you want me to call you back?'

'I'll hold.'

'OK. Don't know how long this will take.'

'I'll be here.'

The line clicked, and Brownie waited. Fifteen minutes later, Benny returned. 'Brownie,' he said. 'Are you *sure* that was the right name? Barton Graves?'

'Pretty sure,' Brownie answered.

'And you're *sure* he had a California licence?'

'Think so.' Rosemary Blank had confirmed that.

'Well, there's no listing,' Benny said. 'None whatsoever under that name.'

'Can you try something else?'

'Absolutely.'

'Run the name through criminal records, vital statistics, hospital admissions, parking tickets, the whole tamale.'

'That's going to take some time. What's this guy done?'

Brownie hesitated. 'Tell you later. Do you think you could get back to me today?'

'I'll do my best.'

'Thank you, Bennie. Thanks a lot.'

Brownie hung up, and looked at the name: BARTON GRAVES, a man with no driver's record and no apparent identity. He probably used an alias to get his licence and other cards. 'GRAVES' might even be an alias, like 'RUTH'. And if it was, they were headed down another dead end.

'Chief Gray,' Kent King said, 'please take a look at State's Exhibit number five, and identify it for the jury.' Trial had reconvened, and Larry Gray was on the stand as a prosecution witness. The afternoon sun through the west-wall windows spotlit the defence table, and the gallery was packed. They were in for another sweltering session.

'What *is* State's Exhibit five?' King repeated.

'Handcuffs.' Gray's voice was low. He was a reluctant witness, unhappy about testifying.

'Can you tell us where they came from?'

'The department.'

King eyed the jury. 'You mean the county *police* department?'

'Yes.' Gray avoided looking at Brownie.

'When were they issued?'

'Some time in the 1970s.'

King held up the bag containing the cuffs. 'For what purpose?'

'Police work.'

'What exactly does police work entail?'

'Objection.'

'Grounds, Counsel?'

426

'He's drawing an illicit inference,' Gardner asserted, 'inferring guilt from a use of the cuffs that does not conform to police standards.'

'I'm entitled to do that,' King replied.

'I agree,' Rollie said. 'Overruled.'

'What is police work, Chief Gray?'

Gray kept his eyes down. 'Investigation, detention, arrest, and processing of persons involved in criminal behaviour.'

'So the handcuffing of a person *not* involved in criminal behaviour would fall *outside* of that definition?'

'Objection!'

'Overruled. Please answer.'

'Yes,' the chief responded softly.

'Say again?'

'Yes.'

King hefted the evidence bag. 'Were handcuffs of this nature issued to the defendant, Joseph Brown?'

'Objection.' Gardner rose. 'We do not dispute that the handcuffs belonged to the defendant. His fingerprint was on them and he *admits* they were his. Sergeant Brown *did* possess the cuffs on the day in question, and he *did* put them on Thomas Ruth, but that was as far as it went. This line of inquiry is moot.'

The judge looked at King. 'Where are you going with this, Counsel?'

'Bear with me, please, Your Honour.'

'Don't beat a dead horse.'

'I won't.'

'Proceed.'

'Was Sergeant Brown on the force at a time when

427

this type of handcuff was standard equipment?' King continued.

'Yes.'

King went back to the counsel table and took two pieces of paper from Lin Song. He gave one to Gardner and handed the other to the clerk. 'Please mark as State's Exhibit thirty-three.'

Gardner scanned the page. It was an outdated police review board complaint form.

'Take a look at this document,' King said.

'Object!' Gardner bounded to his feet.

'What's wrong *now*?' Ransome asked wearily.

'This is an atrocity!'

'Approach the bench!'

Gardner was pumped up when he reached the rail. 'Mr King is attempting to introduce a brutality complaint from twenty years ago. It's totally irrelevant!'

'Let me see,' Rollie reached for the paper.

King handed it up, and the judge skimmed the contents. 'What is this, Kent?'

'What it purports to be. A few years back, a citizen made a complaint against the defendant regarding the use, or *misuse*, I should say, of a set of handcuffs identical to the ones at issue here. It seems Sergeant Brown left a man chained to a fence for over three hours...'

'You contend this is relevant?' Ransome inquired.

'Yes I do. It establishes a pattern of unprofessional behaviour with respect to handcuffs. The defendant employed them once before to punish and intimidate someone. This prior bad act has a bearing on his motivation here.'

The judge turned to Gardner. 'What's your position?'

'That is absurd!' Gardner pointed to the complaint. 'The act of a rookie officer in a difficult situation had nothing to do with punishment or intimidation. There was no disciplinary action taken against the defendant at the time, so the allegation must be regarded as unproven. It's *not* relevant in any event.'

The judge looked at King.

'The allegation was confirmed,' King countered. 'The department chose not to sanction him, but what is alleged to have happened *did* happen. And that is the important part. The facts are true. He used handcuffs as a weapon.'

'No!' Gardner's cheeks reddened. 'That's *not* what happened.'

Ransome read the complaint form again, then looked down. 'It *is* an old incident, but...'

Gardner's heart sank.

'I think it *does* have a bearing on the defendant's state of mind towards the victim. Objection overruled.'

'But,' Gardner protested, 'handcuffing does not equate to *killing*. It's an illogical inference!'

'Enough!' Ransome said sternly. 'You've heard my ruling. The document will be allowed into evidence.'

Gardner and Brownie slowly returned to the defence table. Again, King had hit below the belt. The brutality complaint was garbage. It had *nothing* to do with this case, but it did portray Brownie as a wild man with a set of cuffs. And that was a hard image to overcome.

King called four more witnesses after Larry Gray and finished filling in the cement. To date he'd established that Brownie's father had died under mysterious circumstances;

Brownie was grief-stricken; Brownie had threatened Ruth; Brownie was with Ruth within hours of the electrocution; he had diagrammed the power station *before* the crime; a man Brownie's size was near the scene at the exact moment of death; Brownie's handcuffs were on Ruth's wrists; Brownie had Ruth's shoes in his possession; Brownie had a temper; Brownie was reckless with handcuffs, and Brownie had no credible alibi. The jurors had been up-and-down with Gardner's cross-examination, but now certainty was setting in again. Their arms were crossed, and that was a bad sign for the defence. They were going to convict.

It was four-thirty in the afternoon, and the pace was slowing. 'Call your next witness, Mr King,' Rollie advised.

'The State rests,' King said.

Gardner looked at Brownie with shock. What the hell was this? There were still twelve witnesses on King's discovery list, enough to keep them busy for another week. The defence was not ready to proceed. Not today.

'Something wrong, Mr Lawson?' Ransome could see Gardner's concern.

'We were under the impression that the state had more witnesses.'

'I guess they don't. Are you ready to go forward with your case?'

Gardner glanced at King. He was well aware of the havoc he'd just caused. 'No,' Gardner said. 'Not at *this* time.'

'When *will* you be ready?'

Gardner gripped the back of his chair. 'Day after tomorrow.' They still had the Ruth leads to run down, and they needed at least that much time.

'That's impossible,' Rollie snapped. 'The jury's in the box. I'm not going to make them wait. We'll reconvene tomorrow morning, no later!'

'Your Honour . . .' Gardner protested.

'Court's adjourned until 9.00 a.m.!' The gavel sounded, and Rollie left the bench.

Gardner sat silently as the court emptied.

'King did it again, huh?' Brownie said.

'Yeah. And I know why.' Gardner pointed to the prosecution witness list. The next name was 'Fairborne', and the rest were other members of CAIN. 'He didn't want me to ask them about Ruth's mental condition. He knows he's got enough to convict, so why risk it? He just destroyed our chance to establish a suicide case from the inside.'

'So why can't we call the same witnesses?'

'I considered that, but it won't work. If we call them as our witnesses they'll insist Ruth was sane the day he died and every day before that. I've got no leverage on direct examination, not like I'd have on cross, even if Rollie let me have leeway. I could have gained some ground by attacking them on cross. King knew it, so he pulled the plug.'

'So now we hustle,' Brownie said. He was eerily calm, resigned to the inevitable.

'Now we hustle,' Gardner echoed. 'I'm going down to the VA Hospital tonight. You have your assignment from this morning. We'll meet up at my office later.'

'Good luck.'

Gardner thanked him and broke for the door. He had a lot of territory to cover by tomorrow morning. And a little luck would certainly help.

431

* * *

Gardner and Jennifer sat in the rear booth at Russel's. 'I can't believe that fat bastard,' Gardner complained, 'allowing the brutality complaint into evidence, then not giving us more time!' He squeezed the mayonnaise out of his BLT.

'He's screwing you,' Jennifer said.

'No kidding. We are A-number-one screwed.'

'You make it sound hopeless.'

'It *is*.' Gardner dropped his sandwich on the plate. 'We've lost the jury. There's no doubt about it.'

'What about your *new* evidence, the background leads?'

'They're a long shot at best. We still haven't come up with anything firm.'

Jennifer took a sip of her soup. 'But you do have a track on Ruth's identity. That should get you something...'

'What? What can it get me?'

'Psychiatric records. If you get them you'll win.'

'*If*.' Gardner shook his head. 'They are no doubt destroyed along with every other document relating to his true self. We're never going to find any records...'

'Then why are you wasting time with it?'

Gardner gave her an exasperated look. 'What *else* can I do?'

'You *could* go after Paul.'

'Jeez, Jen, that's out of the question.'

'So you refuse?'

Gardner pushed his plate. 'Of course. I already confronted Brownie about it, and he stonewalled, as you'd expect. I *cannot* look in that direction.'

'Then maybe you need to look within yourself.'

'Huh?'

'You're not a defence attorney.'

'Thanks for the vote of confidence, Jennifer.'

'I'm not putting you down. I've been thinking about this for weeks... Why are you so tormented by what you're doing? Why is it so hard?'

'It would be a hell of a lot easier if you were back in our bed.'

'I don't want to talk about *that*. This is about the law. Defence attorneys don't care about the truth. You do. You always have. You are *not* a defence attorney, not at heart.'

'At least I'm *trying*. It's driving me nuts attempting to raise reasonable doubt, generating smoke. But Goddamn it, at least I'm trying!'

'Maybe you should consider changing directions.'

'You mean go against my own client?'

'I mean go for the *truth*. That's what you really know how to do. That's what you've done all your life. That's the real *you*.'

'I can't, Jennifer. I made a commitment to Brownie to see this through to the end, and that's what I am going to do. We've got one more promising lead on the Ruth ID. I'm checking it out tonight.'

'At the Veteran's Hospital?'

'Yes.'

'Do you want me to come with you?'

Gardner shook his head. 'No. I've got to do this alone. But it *would* be nice if you were at the house when I got back.'

Jennifer didn't reply.

'No deal, huh?'

'Let's get through *this* crisis first.'

433

'Then work on *us*?'

Jennifer nodded.

'But what if we don't get through? What if it all blows up?'

Jennifer touched his hand. 'You can't let that happen.'

CHAPTER 25

Gardner flicked his turn signal and moved into the exit lane of the Virginia Interstate highway. 'SOUTHEAST VETERANS HOSPITAL' the sign said. This was it, the last viable lead, a name that had surfaced *three* times in the *Fugitives* call-backs. Two people on Brownie's list and one on Gardner's identified Ruth as 'Barton Graves'. That had to be more than coincidence. It had to be a match. And of the three, only one had had more than a fleeting contact with the mystery man: Lieutenant Avery Anders, a Vietnam vet who said he'd known Graves during the war.

Gardner parked beside a red brick building and walked to the door. It was evening, and perimeter lights illuminated the four corners, casting knife-edged shadows across patches of hardened snow. The place looked more like a prisoner compound than a hospital.

Gardner entered the reception area and encountered an elderly nurse at the desk. 'Here to see Lieutenant Anders,' he said.

She checked the roster. 'Room 625. Take the elevator to the top floor, turn left, and go to the end of the hall. It's right there.'

Gardner thanked her and went to the elevator. Soon he was in a drab foul-smelling corridor lined with the rooms of forgotten heroes. He found 625 and knocked.

'Come in,' a voice called.

Gardner entered cautiously. The light was off, and it was dark as a well inside. 'Lieutenant Anders? It's Gardner Lawson. I'm here about Barton Graves.'

'Come in Mr Lawson. I've been expecting you.'

Gardner fumbled in the murk. 'Mind if I turn on the light?'

'Sorry. My eyes are hypersensitive. Prop open the door with a chair. That will let light in from the hall.'

Gardner located a chair and propped the door. In a moment his vision had adjusted, and he could make out the image of a man in an adjustable bed. He was under the covers, and by the lay of the sheets, body parts were missing.

'Sit over here,' he said, 'by me.' Anders retrieved a pair of thick glasses. 'I took a hit of white phosphorus in the face. I can see, but the brighter the light, the more painful.'

Gardner focused on the man's face. An ugly scar roped across his chin and cheek. 'You knew Barton Graves,' he began.

'Yes,' Anders said, 'I did, but ...' He was struggling with a pillow. 'Uh, can you help me?'

'Certainly.' Gardner adjusted his pillow. Up close, his face was more grotesque, the odour of medication strong.

'Thank you. I can talk easier now.'

Gardner took out a note pad and moved into the shaft of light from the hall. 'Tell me about Graves. What makes you think he was Thomas Ruth?'

'I saw the *Interview Magazine* article, the one about the snake church and the preacher. I *can* read, you know... At first I didn't make the association. Another offbeat cult, I thought, but then I began thinking. Something about Ruth was familiar. The picture was wrong. His face was different when I knew him. But then, when I saw the *Fugitives* show ... I can watch TV, too... Anyway, they were asking to identify him, and I began to think that maybe I *did* know who he was.'

Gardner leaned closer to the bed.

'It was in Quang Tri, 1969, the rainy season, when I met him the first time. We were dug in against the NVA, North Vietnamese regulars, who were making assaults against our outpost almost every night. We were fighting two storms, the rain, and the attacks. It was a real mess. Graves was a medic, non-combatant. Told me he'd been a CO, conscientious objector, for a while, but then decided to sign up to find out what it was all about...'

Anders started coughing. He took several breaths, apologized, and went on. 'They sent him to the hottest spot of the war. Our zone was drawing more casualties than anywhere else at the time. They called the road into Quang Tri "the highway of no return". Most who went up it never came back... Anyway, we got to know each other up at "kill central" the northern perimeter where the NVAs came calling after dark. He and I got posted there for different reasons. I was supposed to fight, and he was supposed to clean up the guys who got hurt. We used to talk before the shit started, in the rain, when everything was calm and quiet. He'd go on and on about God, and the Bible, and the glories of paradise...'

Gardner looked up. That sounded like Ruth.

'He knew his scripture and a lot of other things like books, literature. He was well educated, very smart. Knew about snakes, too. I think he was raised in a fundamentalist family where they used snakes in their services. He mentioned that once, but never again. I don't know why... Anyway, we got nailed one night. Hardest ever. That was the night I took the "willie pete", the white phosphorus grenade. He put me in a chopper, and then went back for another wounded grunt. The gooks were firing rockets, shells, rifle-launched grenades, blowing up everything and everybody... I was airborne, in the medevac unit, but he was still on the ground...' Anders' voice dropped off.

'What happened?'

'Massacre. Worst of the war. The camp was overrun, two platoons wiped out...'

'What about Graves?'

'Went through hell, but he made it. Him and another guy. Spent five days in the bush, running, hiding, escaping, evading... Finally rejoined our unit down south. But it messed him up bad... He wasn't wounded, but the whole scene screwed his bean something awful. The CO referred him to the mental ward, then section-eighted him and shipped him home. I recommended him for a silver star, but he turned it down. I never understood that, why he wouldn't accept the medal.'

'So you think Barton Graves and Thomas Ruth are the same person?'

'I do.'

'Why?'

Anders rolled his head to the side. 'I knew the man, what he was like inside. I knew his mind. That's him. No question about it.'

Gardner opened a file he'd brought and withdrew a photograph. It was an autopsy photo of Ruth, showing a view of his back. 'You spent a lot of time with Graves?'

'A lot.'

'In intimate circumstances?'

'In a foxhole.'

Gardner concealed the photo from Anders. 'Can you tell me if he had any unusual marks on his body?'

'Marks?'

'Yes. Birthmarks, for example?'

Anders closed his eyes, trying to recall. 'There was something . . .' His eyes opened. 'You just reminded me . . .'

'What?'

'He had one of those Gorbachev blotches on his back, below the shoulder.'

Gardner looked at an ugly purplish outline in the picture. 'Graves *was* Ruth!'

Anders tried to smile.

Gardner leaned over the bed again. 'I want you to tell me about the mental problem,' he said. 'Detail by detail, if you can.'

'OK.'

He was about to speak when the door swung open and the light came on. Anders shielded his eyes as a doctor and two nurses came in.

'Sorry,' the doctor said, 'visiting time is over.'

'I made an appointment,' Gardner protested.

'Let him stay,' Anders argued.

'Sorry. For Mr Anders' welfare, I have to ask you to leave.' The nurses moved by the bed.

Gardner put his hands on his hips. 'I need to talk to him.'

'You can come back tomorrow.'

Gardner suddenly noticed a photograph on Anders' wall. He stepped closer and took a look. It depicted a grimy-faced platoon in the bush.

'May I ask a couple more questions?'

The doctor nodded reluctantly. 'Hurry up.'

'Was this your unit?'

Anders still had his eyes covered to block the overhead light. He spread his fingers and peeked through. 'That was *us.*'

'Is Ruth, uh, Graves in the picture?'

'Yes.'

Gardner reached for the frame. 'Mind if I take it down?'

'Go ahead.'

Gardner removed the picture and approached the bed.

'Make it fast,' the doctor urged.

Gardner gave the photo to Anders. 'Which one is Graves?'

Anders squinted and ran his finger across the men under the glass. At the end of the first row he stopped. 'Him.'

Gardner bent down and studied the face. It was grainy and shadowed, but the bone structure looked right. 'May I *borrow* this?'

'If you return it.'

'Of course. I just need it for a little while.'

Anders handed him the picture.

'Time's up,' The doctor said. 'You can come back tomorrow if you like, but this visit is through.'

440

Gardner thanked Anders and backed out of the room. Ruth *was* Graves. And Graves had a history of mental illness. Gardner began walking down the hall, then broke into a jog, then a run. The defence *finally* had something concrete to support the suicide theory. Now all they needed was documentation.

Jennifer rang the bell at Kent King's Tudor residence in the upscale 'Hunt Meadows' development. It was almost 9.00 p.m., and the lights were on. She rang again, and suddenly, the door opened.

'Miss Munday...' Lin Song was dressed in a bathrobe, her eyes dreamy with afterglow.

'I have to see King,' Jennifer said brusquely.

Lin kept her standing outside on the frigid marble step. 'He's indisposed.'

'Well un-indispose him.' It was bad enough being here in the first place, behind Gardner's back. But the clock was ticking on all their lives, and she had to try to stop it.

'Wait.' Lin partially closed the door.

A moment later, King appeared. 'Well, well, *well*.' He wore a silk smoking jacket and the same sated smile as his co-counsel.

'Don't patronize me, King,' Jennifer cautioned. 'I'm here on business.' She shivered as cold air knifed down her neck. 'I'd appreciate being asked in.'

King widened the door and gave an exaggerated 'entrez' signal with his hand. He ushered her to a spacious den and offered her a seat. Lin walked to a mahogany wet bar in the corner. 'Would you care for a refreshment?'

'No thank you.'

King settled into a green leather chair. 'I'm listening,' he said.

Jennifer cleared her throat. 'I have proof that someone other than Brownie killed Thomas Ruth.'

King looked at Lin who had taken up a flanking position on the couch. 'I thought it was *suicide*.'

'That's the official defence position, but I'm not here about that.'

'Why are you here?'

'To offer my services to the prosecution.'

King glanced at Lin. 'I already have an expert.'

'She's not doing a very good job.'

Lin frowned and started to say something, but King waved her off. He was enjoying this. He had Gardner on the ropes, and Jennifer's visit confirmed it.

'Despite the bad blood, the longtime feud, and all the water over the dam between you and Gardner, you have to take a look at what you're doing here. You *know* that Brownie was investigating the killing. If he had killed Ruth why would he bother to investigate?'

'As a cover,' Kim suggested.

Jennifer dismissed her with a look and turned back to King. 'You've known Brownie a long time, almost as long as we have. You *know* he doesn't behave that way. He investigated the killing, and he turned up a suspect.'

King stifled a smirk. This was getting better by the minute. 'So your boyfriend can raise that as a defence.'

Jennifer took a breath. 'You *know* that isn't going to happen, and you know *why*. Brownie is protecting the person he identified.'

King looked at Lin, then at Jennifer. 'What does this have

442

to do with me? The defence can assert any issue they want. If they choose not to, *it ain't my problem.*'

'Yes it *is*.' Jennifer clasped her hands. 'You have a duty to seek the truth and a responsibility to prosecute the *right* man.'

King smiled. 'Thanks for the lecture, but I am prosecuting the right man.'

'You're not. There's another person out there who's implicated more than Brownie.'

King arched his eyebrow. 'Who?'

'Brownie's brother, Paul.' She handed a computer print-out to King. 'Brownie matched his print to the print he lifted from Ruth's shoes. Remember the fingerprint dust? This is the result.'

'Really?' Lin moved behind King and read the note over his shoulder. 'What *else* do you have?'

'He was in the county when Ruth died. He had the same reason to kill: to avenge his father's death. And *he* matches the description that the jogger gave of the man in the woods.'

'Anything else?' King was still feigning concern.

'No, but there's enough right there for you to reopen the investigation. I'm sure he doesn't have an alibi. You have to check it out.'

'*I* don't have to do a thing. That avenue can be pursued by the defence if they wish. I, for one, decline.'

Jennifer faced Lin. 'Tell him he's making a mistake. As a prosecutor you *know* it's your duty to follow this up.'

'Not necessarily,' Lin replied. 'What you said does not *preclude* the guilt of Joe Brown. It may actually reinforce it. Maybe they were accomplices. Maybe they committed the crime *together*.'

Jennifer stood. 'If Paul Brown did it, he acted *alone*.'

King stood also, and Lin moved close beside him. 'Then let the defence *prove* it in court.'

'*You're* not going to do anything?'

King shook his head. 'Not my job.'

'You're an asshole, King,' Jennifer said under her breath.

'Is that so?'

Jennifer turned and walked to the front hall. 'And you're a disgrace to the profession. No prosecutor would do what you're doing. No *real* prosecutor.'

'Thanks for stopping by,' King replied. 'Have a nice evening.'

As Jennifer walked out, a sharp wind off the mountaintop watered her eyes. She had done the right thing making an overture to the enemy, calling on the voice of reason. But tonight, reason had left town.

'The war messed him up?' Brownie asked. It was late, almost 11 p.m., and Gardner had just returned from his visit with Anders. Brownie was waiting at the office.

'I think he was messed up *before* the war,' Gardner replied. 'He was talking scripture and snakes before his unit got wiped out.'

Brownie was awash in papers at a card table. His laptop was hooked into a modem attached to Gardner's telephone line.

'How did *you* do?' Gardner asked.

'Not good. I couldn't find a single reference to Barton Graves in *any* public record.'

'Did you use your contacts?'

444

'Every one.'

Gardner eyed the scrawl of notes and the balled-up pages. 'Criminal record?'

'None.'

'Employment? Social Security? Income Tax?'

'None.'

'Vital Statistics? Credit references? Motor vehicle registration?'

'None.' Brownie looked at his lawyer. 'There's nothing there.'

Gardner wrote RUTH and GRAVES on his pad. 'Have you ever seen anything like this before, Brownie?'

'Like what?'

Gardner underlined the names. RUTH. GRAVES. 'Like a person's entire identity being missing?'

'It's happened,' Brownie replied. 'A guy piles alias on alias, creates a maze of paperwork that never leads to the right place.'

'But there should be *something* on Graves. He was going by that name. He had to have *something* in writing.' Gardner put his briefcase on the desk and opened it. 'Anders confirmed that he knew Graves, and that Graves *was* Ruth.' He removed the picture.

Brownie looked at the photo.

'That's Graves.' Gardner pointed.

Brownie studied the battle-worn face.

'Can you computer-enhance it?'

Brownie nodded. 'Got the equipment at home.'

'Good. I'm going to DC in the morning to run down Graves' military service record. There has to be a reference to his mental condition as the cause for discharge. You enhance the photo and be ready to collate whatever I come up with.'

Brownie frowned. 'Tomorrow morning? I thought we had to be in court.'

'Rollie will have to continue the trial.'

'What if he won't?'

Gardner made a fist. 'He *has* to. The defence isn't ready. And if I don't come up with *something* tomorrow, it never will be.'

Rollie Ransome was furious. He was in chambers, robed and ready to go, and Gardner had just asked for another continuance. 'I gave you yesterday afternoon, and *that* was a gift.'

Gardner tried to remain calm. 'I *told* you there's been a new development, new evidence we just discovered last night...'

Rollie looked at King. He and Lin Song had objected to any further delay. 'What new evidence?'

'I have confirmed that Thomas Ruth had a history of mental disorders,' Gardner answered. 'I need time to obtain documentation and witnesses to that effect...'

'He's bluffing,' King cut in. 'It's a ruse to disrupt the jury. There are no such records.'

Gardner glared at King. 'Kent *knows* they exist and that Ruth was a bona fide lunatic. Isn't that right?'

King shrugged casually. 'The man seemed OK to me.'

Gardner took a step in his direction. 'You're a *liar*!'

'Gentlemen!' Rollie intervened. 'And I use that term loosely. You will display none of that macho crap in here!'

Gardner turned to the judge. 'This is not a bluff. It's a

genuine plea based on fact. I can *prove* Ruth was a mental case. You have to allow me a chance to do it!'

'I do not have to allow anything,' Rollie replied, 'I only have to conduct a trial.'

'A *fair* trial,' Gardner added.

'I've tried to be fair.' Rollie fluffed his robe. 'I've given you every imaginable break so far, but I've got a jury in the box ready to go.'

'Give me another day,' Gardner begged. '*Please!* One more day!'

Rollie hesitated.

'Don't do it,' King warned.

'What is the *nature* of the new proof?'

'I have a line on Ruth, like I said. I now know his true identity, and by tomorrow I'll be able to substantiate his psychiatric history.'

'Can you be more specific?' Rollie pressed.

'Ask Kent. He can tell you all about it. I don't have time to go into the details now. Please accept my word as an officer of the court.'

King tried to look nonchalant. 'This is pure bull . . .'

'All right,' Rollie interrupted. 'Against my better judgement, I'll permit it.'

'Shit,' King muttered.

'But this is *it*!' Rollie warned. 'We resume trial tomorrow morning regardless of what you have accomplished. You got that?'

Gardner thanked the judge and quickly left his chambers.

'You fool,' King sneered. 'You pig-brained fool.'

Rollie gave his former associate a threatening look. 'Watch it, Kent!'

'You've been had,' King continued. 'Lawson just jammed that "fairness" bullshit up your ass.'

Rollie looked at Lin as if to say 'my next words are private', and she diplomatically left the room.

'Don't you *ever* talk to me that way in front of another person, you arrogant bastard!'

'Lin is family.'

'I don't give a shit if she's your Siamese twin. You show me some fucking respect!'

King stood toe-to-toe with the big man. 'Then you better damn well earn it! You're letting Lawson skate; don't you realize that? What the hell's happened to you?'

Rollie's jowls tightened. 'I *told* you we're under a microscope here...'

'You could have denied the continuance, and no one would have complained.'

'Lawson would have.'

'*Fuck* Lawson!'

Rollie pulled off his robe. 'What's he got on Ruth?'

King shrugged.

'He said you knew what it was.'

King shrugged again. 'I have no idea. It's all a bluff, I told you.'

'For your sake that better be true.'

King didn't answer. Even if Lawson was on the right track, there was no way he could succeed. Frank Davis had assured him that Ruth's records were forever buried. And for *all* their sakes, that had better be true.

CHAPTER 26

Gardner sat in the waiting area of Colonel Samuel Higgins' office at the Pentagon. It was 11.30 a.m., and he'd driven non-stop from the county. The strategy was to go straight to the top, to confront the chief military records custodian with the situation and ask for help. There wasn't time to process the request through channels.

'He'll see you now,' the receptionist said.

Gardner entered the inner chamber and was met by Higgins, a tall white-haired soldier. 'Good morning,' he said politely. The silver eagles on his shoulders gleamed in the fluorescent light.

Gardner shook his hand. 'Thanks for seeing me.'

'My pleasure.' The colonel revealed a set of capped teeth.

He ushered Gardner into a black leather chair. 'What can I do for you today?'

Gardner cleared his throat and handed the officer his business card. 'I need your help. I represent a police sergeant in Maryland accused of murder. The victim was a person named Thomas Ruth, but Ruth's real name was Barton Graves, a former army medic. We contend Ruth, or Graves, rather, committed suicide. His military service records can help us prove it.'

Higgins leaned back in his chair. 'Tell me more about Graves.'

Gardner opened his briefcase and removed his notes. 'He served in Vietnam in the late sixties and was discharged after the battle of Quang Tri.'

Higgins activated the computer console on his desk. 'Spell his full name, please.'

Gardner complied.

'Date of birth?'

'Unknown.'

'Social security number?'

'Unknown.'

'Race?'

'Caucasian.'

'Any other pertinent data you can give me?' Higgins peered around the monitor.

'He was a medic in the 215th. Force Recon company, 1969.'

'That's good...' Higgins keyed in the information. 'The retrieval programme cross-references names, units, statistical fragments. If there was anyone named Graves in that unit at that time, we should know soon.' After several minutes the colonel smiled. 'Hello.'

'You have it?' Gardner leaned forward.

'Yes, sir. "BARTON GRAVES, PFC, MEDICAL CORPS. RECOMMENDED FOR THE SILVER STAR AND BRONZE STAR. MEMBER OF THE 215TH..."'

Gardner thumped his knee. 'When was he discharged?'

'January, 1970.'

'What was the reason for discharge?'

Higgins returned to the screen. 'He completed his term of service and was separated in normal course.'

'Does it say anything about his mental condition at that time?'

'There's no reference to it here, but...'

'How about *any* psychiatric treatment he was given after Vietnam?'

'Those records are confidential under 28 US Code section 1453. All military personnel medical and psychological treatment is kept under seal.'

Gardner cursed inwardly. 'Can you tell me *if* he had treatment? I am not asking for his diagnosis, just whether or not he was treated.'

Higgins shook his head. 'Sorry. The fact of receiving treatment is confidential as well.'

'What would it take to get the records?'

'A subpoena from the federal court, but...'

'But what?'

'I've *never* seen one issued. They're strict about this confidentiality business.'

'*Please*, Colonel. I'm in a jam here. I've got a man on trial I know is innocent and a victim I *know* was a mental case. *Please*, just tell me whether or not he had treatment.'

'I'm not supposed to.'

'I understand that, but a man's life is at stake. I don't want to waste time getting a summons if there are no records in the first place. If there are records, I'll go the summons route. Please help me.'

Higgins thought for a moment, then played his keyboard.

Gardner tapped his fingers restlessly on his knee.

Finally, Higgins shut off the machine. 'There are no

references to psychiatric treatment, none at all. Not by any *military* facility.'

'Shit,' Gardner whispered.

'But that *doesn't* mean he wasn't treated.'

Gardner looked up.

'During the late sixties, early seventies, we contracted out most psychiatric referrals. There were a lot of mental problems associated with jungle combat, and our system was overloaded...'

'You're saying that Graves could have been treated by a civilian shrink?'

'Possibly.'

'Do you have access to *those* records?'

'No. There was a blanket agreement for treatment referrals and no individual patient billing. The civilian doctors were required to keep the records in their own files. We retained nothing.'

'Is there any way to determine if he was in that programme?'

'No.'

'So how could I find out whether Graves was referred?'

'You'd need the name of the treating doctor and a release or court order. But even if he *was* referred, I doubt his files still exist. Civilian physicians have a twenty-year disposal rule on prior-patient medical files. After two decades, they're usually incinerated.'

Gardner stood up slowly. 'Thanks anyway,' he said.

'Sorry,' Higgins replied. 'Good luck with your case.'

Gardner opened the colonel's door. So that was it; plan 'A' was dead. He'd have to move to plan 'B'. But the only problem was, plan 'B' didn't exist.

* * *

Brownie was in the lab at his house. It was late morning, and he was upset. He'd hit a wall in the secret investigation of his father's death, and it was similar to the one they'd hit in the case. There were too many aliases floating around out there. People were never who they purported to be.

Brownie removed the Anders photo from its frame and slipped it into the imaging receptor networked with his computer. He had installed a a photo-enhancement programme and a 'morphing' protocol into the software that allowed him to pull images out, clean them up, enlarge them, and age them. It made the computer an electronic time machine that could transform a twenty-year-old into a forty-five-year-old at the touch of a button.

Brownie activated the programme and brought the photo up on his view screen. He ran the cross-hairs along the first row and centred them on Graves. He was wearing a jungle hat, and it cast a sharp shadow across his nose like a streak of greasepaint.

Brownie selected 'ENLARGE'. The image grew until it filled the screen.

Brownie then clicked 'ENHANCE'. The graininess disappeared, and the image clarified.

Brownie took his 'mouse' and erased the shadow. Then he selected 'RECONFIGURE'. The darkness was replaced by light; the right eye and cheekbone came into focus.

'AGE PROGRAMME' blinked in the upper corner of the monitor. Brownie moved the cursor there and clicked.

'YEARS?' the menu asked.

Brownie selected 'TEN'.

Graves' face changed; his skin began to sag.

Brownie advanced the years: 'FIFTEEN', 'TWENTY', 'TWENTY-FIVE'.

Wrinkles spread, eyelids drooped, and the image morphed into middle age. 'Yeah!' Brownie exclaimed, selecting 'PRINT'.

In a moment the computer-modified picture dropped into a tray. Brownie studied it under the light. Here was Barton Graves twenty-five years later. There was no question about it. Here was Thomas Ruth.

Brownie exited the enhancement programme, and the image on the screen returned to normal. He was about to shut off the unit when another soldier caught his eye. He moved the cross-hairs over and reactivated the enhance programme. There was something about the man next to Graves that seemed familiar.

Soon the other face was enhanced, clarified, and aged twenty-five years. When the process was complete, Brownie's mouth gaped in shock. 'Sonofabitch! I don't fuckin' believe it!' He'd been searching high and low for months, but it had been in front of him all the time. He threw a glass against the wall, and it shattered with a loud 'crack'. 'Sonofabitch!'

Brownie grabbed the photo from the enhancer. Anders had written each soldier's name on the back. Brownie circled the next-to-last one. 'Sonofabitch!' he hollered again. He'd been searching for months, and finally, *there* it was. Brownie had found his man.

* * *

Gardner was woozy. What the hell was he doing? He'd anticipated that things might turn out this way, and sure enough, they did. Now he was in Washington, miles from home, with no defence and a case that wouldn't wait another day. That called for a drink.

Gardner manoeuvred his car off Constitution Avenue. Chinatown was just up the street. He could take a breather there and gather his thoughts.

Traffic was light, and soon the ornate Dragon gateway passed over his head. On either side of the street, Chinese letters touted food and goods. He parked at a meter and entered the 'Orchid Inn', a small restaurant on the corner. 'Best Peking Duck in town,' the sign said.

Gardner entered a dim hallway and was ushered into an even dimmer dining room. He took a seat in a booth.

'Cocktail, sir?' the waitress asked.

'Martini. A double.'

The waitress slipped behind the bar and returned with a heavy glass. Gardner took a sip. The chill made his eyeballs ache, but the alcohol warmed his throat.

'Order food now?'

'In a minute.' Gardner took another sip, and then another. Soon the drink began to kill the pain.

The waitress returned again. Gardner ordered spareribs and asked for the telephone.

'In the back.' She pointed.

Gardner found the phone near the men's room. He dialled a number, and Lieutenant Anders' doctor came on the line. 'We met last night,' he said.

'I remember.'

'I want to summons the Lieutenant to court tomorrow. I need his testimony.'

The doctor didn't reply.

'This is an emergency, Doc. Life or death.'

'It is for Anders.'

'He's that bad off?'

'He has a bacterial infection that isn't responding to antibiotics. He may not last the week.'

Gardner closed his eyes. 'How is he doing right now?' Maybe they could get a videotape deposition.

'He's on life support.'

'Since yesterday?'

'He had a relapse after you left.'

'He seemed OK when we talked.'

'He was acting. The man is *very* sick. Too sick to help you with your case, I'm afraid. Sorry.'

Gardner gritted his teeth. Everyone was 'sorry' today.

He hung up and dialled another number.

'Judge Thompkins?'

'Gardner!' There was surprise in his voice.

'I'm in deep trouble.'

'Tell me about it.'

'I think I made the *wrong* decision switching sides. I can't take a chance on reasonable doubt. I know that now. Jennifer said it best: I'm no defence attorney.'

'Jennifer is here as we speak. Do you want to talk to her?'

Gardner didn't know how to respond. 'In a minute.'

'OK, then,' Thompkins said. 'Take a deep breath, and tell me what's going on.'

'It's this damned suicide defence. I'm trying like hell to prove a man killed himself when I know it's not true. I'm only playing games, going after Ruth's alter ego. And just now, the thought hit me: so I come up with the psychiatric records and witnesses, and I prove Ruth was a lunatic, *then* what do I get?'

'You get your client off.'

'*Maybe*,' Gardner replied. '*Maybe* I get him off *if* the jury buys it, but...'

'But the killer walks free.'

'Correct.'

'And the prosecutor in you is uncomfortable with that.'

'Correct again. *You* told me to check out another perspective before I quit my job.'

'Don't blame me, Gardner. *You* made the choice. I didn't push you ... you know what your problem is? You're a perfectionist. That's the number one obstacle in your life. It's got you turning circles.'

Gardner sighed. *Everyone* seemed to know Gardner's problem but Gardner.

'Defence attorneys are eternal pragmatists. They go where the wind blows; they ride the waves; they take whatever they can get. If they can raise a doubt, they've done their job. That's satisfaction enough for them, and it's all any client has a right to expect.'

'But you said *I* could do that,' Gardner argued. 'You encouraged me.'

'You *can* do it if you *choose* to. I just told Jennifer that there comes a time in every attorney's career when he has to let things work out the way they will. That time has come for you.'

Gardner sighed again. The truth about himself was finally emerging.

'Do what you *can* to raise doubt, then let it go. That's the secret to defending a case. You have no duty or obligation to seek a greater justice than that...'

'Let me speak to Jen.'

'Here she is.'

'Gard? Where *are* you.'

'Frankly, where *you* are is more interesting...'

'Judge Thompkins is trying to help.'

'With what?'

'Things.'

Her voice buoyed him up. 'Where were you last night? I called the apartment after I got back from the VA hospital, but there was no answer.'

'I didn't feel like talking.'

'We got a major lead on Ruth. He was messed up in 'Nam.'

'Are you going with it?'

Gardner hesitated. 'Not sure. That's why I called the Judge.'

'And what did you two decide?'

'Maybe I've been approaching this thing from the wrong direction. Maybe it's time I took a different route.'

Jennifer pressed him, but Gardner wouldn't explain. 'Will I see you later?'

'Maybe.'

Gardner said goodbye and returned to his table. He finished his drink, ate two ribs, paid his cheque, and went out to the street.

There was a Seven-Eleven in the next block. Gardner walked quickly to it. 'Is your fax working?' he asked the counter man.

'Yes, sir.'

Gardner went to the pay phone and dialled the county clerk's office. Soon Judy Field was on the line. 'Judy, this Gardner Lawson. I have an emergency request.'

'What?'

'I need a criminal summons in Brownie's case, and I need it now.'

'There's no time to get service.'

'Don't worry about that. Just draw it up and fax it to me at...' He covered the phone. 'What's the fax number here?'

'202 455-7888.'

'202 455-7888,' Gardner repeated.

'But...' She was about to say it wasn't valid if done that way.

'Don't worry about formalities, Judy. I'll take full responsibility. Just prepare it and fax it. OK?'

Judy agreed. 'What name goes on the summons?'

'Paul Jefferson Brown.'

Brownie was in the county jail. It was late afternoon, and the investigation of his father's death was *almost* complete. He just needed one more detail.

Brownie tried to relax as he waited. The final solution was at hand. Suddenly the door opened.

'Here he is,' Warden Frenkel said. 'I had to pull him out of the chow line, but he's here.' He directed Henry Jackson into the office. Henry had a dazed look on his face. He had no idea what was going on.

'Guess you want privacy,' the warden said.

'If you don't mind.'

'Take all the time you want. When you're ready to leave, give me a buzz.'

Frenkel left the room, and the two men were alone. Henry stirred restlessly in his chair. Brownie didn't look happy.

For another moment neither spoke. Brownie stared at him in silence. 'What's wrong with *you*, man?' Henry finally asked.

Brownie stood and put his hand on Jackson's shoulder. 'You lied to me.'

'What?'

Brownie started to squeeze. 'The last time we spoke, you gave me information on some cloned cellular phones. I wanted to know who you fenced them to, and you gave me some names. You remember that?'

'Yeah.' Brownie's grip was painful.

'But you lied. I said was that all, and you said yes. But that wasn't all, was it, Henry? There was one particular name you didn't give. Another person you supplied with a phone...'

Henry didn't answer.

'Give it up, Henry.' Brownie said. 'In case you didn't know, my time is running out. I'm liable to be your cellmate in a couple of days, and you don't want me mad at you.'

Henry dropped his head, and Brownie released his shoulder.

'I know *why* you held back, and I don't care about that now. I just need for you to say it. Tell me who you gave that last phone to.'

Henry's face came up, apology in his eyes.

'Tell me,' Brownie repeated.

'I can't,' Henry moaned.

'You can, and you *will*.'

Henry shook his head, and Brownie drew back his fist. '*Don't* make me do it, Henry. You got no protection in here, and I can hit a hell of a lot harder than *he* can!'

Henry covered his eyes.

'Tell me!' Brownie screamed.

'OK,' Henry blubbered. 'OK...' And he whispered a name.

Gardner hesitated outside of Paul Brown's apartment door. It was 6.30 p.m., and he was in foreign territory. Earlier today, he'd been met by suspicious looks on the street and distrustful stares in the building, sullen faces peering from unlit halls. This was Paul's world, a place defined by pigment.

Gardner knocked.

'Yeah?'

'It's Gardner Lawson. Joseph's attorney.'

'Go away!'

'I have to talk to you.'

'I said go away.'

Gardner drew a breath. He could leave the summons, and Paulie would be served. But that wouldn't do. 'In the name of God,' Gardner shouted, 'open the door!'

A lock clicked, and the door cracked. 'In *whose* name, motherfucker?' A pair of dark eyes burned through the opening.

'Almighty God,' Gardner answered. 'We have to talk, Mr Brown.'

The door opened slowly, and Gardner entered a small candle-lit room. A man was seated on the couch and another stood beside Paulie, both muscled and strong.

Gardner looked at Paulie. 'I'd like to talk with you privately.' One of the men laughed. 'Didn't know you had a white-meat boyfriend, K. Want us to leave?'

'No,' Paulie looked at Gardner. 'What did you come here for?'

Gardner straightened his back. 'Your brother is in trouble. He needs your help.'

Paulie moved closer. He was wearing a tribal hat, and his skin looked burnished in the dancing light. 'Did *he* send you?'

'No he didn't. I came on my own to ask you to help him.'

'Yeah?'

'Paul...'

'That's my slave name.'

'He's called Katanga,' a man interjected.

'Katanga. Your brother has been accused of a crime he didn't commit, and it doesn't look like he's going to beat the charge.'

'That's *his* motherfucking problem.'

'But he's your *brother*.'

Katanga squared off aggressively. 'I don't have a brother. I got a shufflin' uncle Tom who shares a mother and daddy. That's all *I* got.'

'He loves you.'

'Bull-motherfucking shit!'

Gardner swallowed. It was time to fire the big gun. '*You* were at the power station the night Thomas Ruth died.'

Katanga froze.

462

'*You* were there. *Not* Joseph.'

Katanga took a step forward.

'Sounds like he's making an accusation against you, Brother K.' The man on the couch stood up.

Gardner looked Katanga in the eye. 'I *am*.'

The other man approached. 'Be careful now...'

'*You* were at the power station!'

Katanga's jaw tightened, and the two men moved on either side of him.

Gardner stood firm. 'Your brother is going to prison to protect *you*.'

Katanga scowled. 'White-assed mother...'

'He's shielding you again. Like he did *last time*!' Gardner aimed a finger at Katanga's chest.

The men started to react, but Katanga stopped them.

'I *know*,' Gardner said. 'I know *all* about it. *You*, a police officer's brother, vandalized your school, defaced your history classroom, and destroyed the books. You've always blamed Joseph for arresting you. You thought he was doing it for whitey, but he wasn't. He was doing it for *you*.'

'What the fuck are you talking about?'

'What was the verdict in your case?'

'What?'

'Kick his butt out.'

'Not yet,' Katanga replied. 'What about my case?'

'Did you ever wonder why it was dismissed, why you weren't prosecuted?'

Katanga didn't answer.

'Your *brother* destroyed the evidence. He put his career and his life on the line for you...'

463

Katanga's eyes widened.

'They investigated him at the police department; accused him of misconduct; had him up on charges. And he went through it all in silence. He never told a *soul* what he'd done.'

'That's bullshit.'

Gardner pulled a copy of the internal affairs report out of his pocket and thrust it forward. 'It's all here. Joseph *asked* for the case so he could get you off the hook. That's why *he* made the arrest. He didn't want anyone else messing with you. And he wanted to make sure the case never went to trial.'

Katanga read the report.

'And now history repeats itself. Joseph lifted *your* fingerprint from Thomas Ruth's shoes . . .'

Katanga looked up.

'But he destroyed it, and there's no other evidence to incriminate you. You are his ticket to freedom, but he will *not* turn on you! No matter how much you hate him. No matter what you do!'

Katanga crumpled the paper and threw it on the floor.

'Time to go now?' a man asked.

'Yeah,' Katanga replied. 'Time to go.'

'You can help him by testifying,' Gardner said. 'You have to.' He shoved the summons into Katanga's hand.

'What the fuck is this?'

'A subpoena for court tomorrow.'

Katanga crumpled that too.

Gardner glared at him. 'You talk brotherhood, but look how you act towards your own brother. Joseph is a *man*, one of the finest *men* on earth, black or white. He's sacrificing himself to save *you*. What a fuckin' waste. You're not worth saving!'

The henchmen sprang forward, and Gardner braced for the attack.

'Get out *now*!' Katanga warned.

Gardner took a step backward and felt for the door. 'Why don't you be a *man* for a change and take responsibility for your actions? Stop letting your brother cover for you!'

'Kick his ass!'

'Leave now!'

'See you in court, Katanga.' Gardner leaped down the stairs and ran all the way to his car. He was shaking so hard he could barely unlock the door. And he was still trembling when he roared up the street toward the interstate. The seed of truth had been planted. And tomorrow it would either germinate or lie dead in the ground.

PART FIVE

WITNESS

CHAPTER 27

Trial resumed promptly the following morning. Gardner dragged himself in after a couple of hours' sleep, a shower, shave, and quick-change into a pin-striped suit. He'd arrived in the county close to midnight, then spent time with the case file. If Paul Brown didn't post, he'd still have to make a go of the suicide defence. Judy Field had been right. The summons he'd served was *not* valid because it wasn't delivered seven days prior to trial. If Paulie read the fine print he'd know that. So Gardner was in limbo.

Doctor Sand was waiting in the hallway when Gardner arrived at court. He'd been briefed on the records situation, and he'd repeated that unless they had firm documentation of Barton Graves' mental problem, they couldn't mount a strong case. Gardner then tried to phone the CAIN compound from the public booth, but the service had been disconnected. A nearby deputy sheriff told him the quarry had been vacant for days; Fairborne and the others had apparently skipped town. That meant Gardner couldn't call them as witnesses as a last resort.

There was only one avenue remaining. The defence

would rest entirely on Doctor Sand's assessment of Ruth's mental condition from the public record and *Brownie's* testimony of what happened. That would be it, their *only* hope. Unless, of course, Paulie showed up. But Gardner kept that part to himself.

Rollie hit the gavel and called for order. The jury was in the box, the lawyers were in place, and the gallery was full. Jennifer watched nervously from the front row.

The judge looked at the defence attorney. 'Counsel?'

Gardner stood. 'Motion for judgement of acquittal,' he said.

'Excuse the jury,' Ransome ordered.

A moment later the jury was gone, and Gardner delivered his legal argument as to why the case should end at that point. The prosecution had not made out a 'prima facie' case, he said. All of the evidence, taken in a light most favourable to the State, failed to present a level of proof sufficient to convict. It was a canned, pro forma presentation, offered at every criminal trial. And it was almost always overruled.

'Overruled,' Ransome said. 'The State has met its burden at this point. Proceed with the defence, Mr Lawson.'

Gardner looked at the clock. Ten-fifteen and Paulie hadn't arrived.

The jury returned to the box, and the courtroom quieted.

'Proceed, Counsel,' the judge repeated.

Gardner checked the door of the courtroom and then Dr Sand in the back row. This was the end of the line. His gamble had failed. Paulie's summons said 9.30 a.m. If he was coming he'd be here by now. They'd have to argue suicide.

'Any day, sir,' Ransome said sarcastically.

Gardner was still playing for time. 'We call Doctor Julius Sand,' he finally announced.

Sand rose and walked down the aisle. He then took the stand and the oath.

'You may examine, Counsel.'

'Please give your name and address for the record,' Gardner began softly. After yesterday, his heart was barely in it. He was played out.

'Julius Sand, MD, 105 South...' he stopped talking.

'South what?' Gardner asked.

But Sand didn't respond. He was staring past Gardner, at the door.

Gardner spun around, and the people in the audience followed, craning their necks towards the rear.

'Counsel?' Ransome asked.

But Gardner ignored him. 'Yes!' he whispered. Standing at the back of the room was a man in a business suit. There was no African hat, no fierce expression. Paulie Brown had come home to help his brother.

When Brownie saw Paul, he grabbed Gardner by the arm. 'What is this?'

'My witness.' Gardner said.

'Like hell!'

'Gentlemen!' Judge Ransome interrupted, 'are we proceeding or not?'

'A moment please, Your Honour.'

'Hurry it up!'

'Yes, sir.' Gardner put his hand over Brownie's. 'Let me do this!'

Brownie's eyes turned ice cold. 'No!'

'What's happening?' King whispered to Lin Song.

'I don't know,' she answered.

'Whenever you're ready...' Ransome prompted.

Suddenly Brownie stood and addressed the court. 'I want to dismiss my attorney, Your Honour.'

'Stop it!' Gardner pulled on his sleeve.

'Time out!' Ransome banged his gavel. 'Approach the bench!'

The parties rushed forward. 'What the hell is going on?'

'He...' Brownie began.

Ransome stopped him. 'Do *you* wish to address the court?'

'I can handle this,' Gardner broke in.

'Your Honour...' Brownie was livid.

'Stop it now!' The judge pointed his finger at Gardner. '*You* be quiet and let *him* speak.'

'But...' Gardner protested.

'Quiet!'

'I want to fire my attorney,' Brownie said. 'I want to represent myself.'

'Judge...' Gardner could not keep silent.

'One more word, and I'll have you in contempt,' Ransome warned. 'Now *why* do you want to release your attorney?'

'We don't agree on the defence. I'm the client. I have the right to say how I want to defend my case.'

The judge turned to Gardner. 'You may speak *now*.'

'I propose to call a witness who I proffer will exculpate

472

my client and offer relevant testimony on the death of
Thomas Ruth...'

King smelled double-cross, a last-minute trick. Lin
jabbed his ribs.

'But *I* don't want the witness,' Brownie interjected. 'I
don't agree.'

'Who's the witness?'

'Paul Brown,' Gardner said, 'brother of the defendant.'

'Is that him?' Ransome pointed.

'Yes. I served a summons on him last night.'

'Without my permission!' Brownie whispered.

'OK, OK!' Ransome composed his thoughts. '*You*,' he
pointed at Gardner, 'want to call the witness, and *you*,' he
pointed at Brownie, 'do not. Is that correct?'

Both men nodded.

'And *you* want to fire your lawyer if the witness is called,
and *you* insist that the witness has information crucial to the
defence.'

Again, both men nodded.

'So we have an impasse here...' He leaned back in his
chair and cogitated, then lurched forward. 'To resolve this,
I'll call him. In the interest of justice, I'll designate him a
court's witness. That way, there is no conflict between
lawyer and counsel.'

Gardner smiled. That was a brilliant solution, one he
wouldn't have thought Rollie capable of. Brownie could
not interfere with the calling of a court's witness.

'Judge...' Brownie blustered angrily.

'Sorry, Sergeant Brown. *I'm* in charge here. And I want to
hear what the man has to say. Step down please, Dr Sand...'

'Not so fast!' King interjected. 'Don't *I* get a turn?'

Ransome faced the prosecutor. 'Why? This is between the defendant, his counsel, and me. You have no standing to object.'

'Yes I do!' King snapped. 'The witness you're calling is the defendant's *brother*, arriving at the eleventh hour to bail him out.'

'So?'

'So the whole thing is suspect! He's going to ... going to incriminate someone *else* so his brother can get off a murder rap? It's a set-up for perjury.'

Ransome stared at King. 'I don't see it that way. I'd say the reliability is enhanced by the fact that the defendant doesn't *want* the testimony.'

'Get real!' King scoffed.

'What?'

'It's an act. He's pretending he doesn't want it for that very reason! They're setting you up.'

'I don't agree,' Ransome said firmly. 'I'm calling the witness, and that's that. Return to your seats. Paul Brown, please step forward!'

Paulie walked down the aisle, and the hushed crowd watched him approach the witness stand. No one understood what was going on, but they could tell something extraordinary was about to happen.

'Are you Paul Brown?' Ransome asked.

Paulie nodded yes.

'Step up please and be sworn in.'

King was quaking with anger. In his wildest fantasies, he'd never envisioned this. Not even after Jennifer's visit the other night. He'd thought he'd covered everything, blocked every counter-move that Lawson could make. But, from the looks of it, the defence had pulled a rabbit out of the hat. 'Got to do something,' he whispered to Lin Song.

'Rights,' she replied.

'Huh?'

'He has to be given his rights before he says anything.'

King leaped to his feet. 'Wait a minute, Judge!'

Paulie had already taken the oath and sat down.

'What is it *now*, Mr King?' Ransome was irritated.

'He may incriminate *himself* in the course of his testimony.'

'So what?'

King put his hands on his hips. 'So that's tantamount to a judicial confession. He needs to be aware of the consequences before he testifies.'

'You want me to read him his rights?'

'That's correct.' Maybe Paul would get frightened off when he realized that *he* could end up on the hook for the crime if he said the wrong thing. He could take the Fifth Amendment and decline to testify. And if he *did*, the case against Brownie would still be intact.

The judge turned to the witness. 'Do you understand you have a right to remain silent if anything you say may incriminate you?'

Paulie listened calmly. This was a different person from the one Gardner had encountered last night. That man was burning with hatred. But this man was serene. 'Yes, I do,' Paulie replied.

Gardner glanced at Brownie. He was trying to get his brother's attention, to call him off, to tell him no. 'Let it go,' Gardner whispered. But Brownie kept trying.

'If you *do* say something incriminating, you could be prosecuted for the crime. Do you understand that?'

'Yes.'

'And, knowing that, you're still willing to go forward, to testify in this matter?'

Paulie looked down at Brownie. 'Yes.' The answer was firm. Brownie bit his lip.

'Very well,' Ransome declared. 'He knows the consequences, Mr King. I'd say we're ready to move on.'

King groaned. So much for discouraging the witness. 'Object to anything this witness has to say.'

'On what grounds?'

'Bias, prejudice, manufactured testimony, whatever you want to call it. It's obvious what's happening here.'

'Overruled. You can explore those issues on cross-examination if you like. But the witness *will* have his say.'

'Shit!' King whispered to Lin Song.

'You'll bury him on cross,' Lin encouraged.

King snapped a pencil between his fingers. 'I'll have to!'

Judge Ransome looked at the witness. 'I understand you know something about the death of Thomas Ruth. Is that correct?'

'Yes, sir.'

'What can you tell us about it?'

'Don't!' Brownie suddenly jumped to his feet. 'Don't do it!'

'Sergeant Brown!' Judge Ransome cautioned, 'please sit down and be quiet.'

Gardner was pulling on him, whispering in his ear, telling him the same thing.

'He doesn't know anything!' Brownie insisted.

The judge squinted his eyes. 'Don't make me bind and gag you, sir. Be quiet and let the man talk.'

Brownie set his jaw. It was clear there was nothing he could do now to stop it. He glared at Gardner. His so-called friend had betrayed him.

'I *had* to,' Gardner said.

Brownie dropped into the chair and clasped his hands in front of him. His body was trembling with pent-up anger, but he was controlling it.

'That's better,' Ransome said. Then he turned to the witness. 'Sorry about the interruption. Now, what do you know about the demise of Mr Ruth?'

Paulie cleared his throat and faced the judge. 'As you heard, I'm that man's brother.' He pointed at Brownie. 'I grew up out here in the county and later moved to DC. It was no secret that me and my brother didn't get along. He ... he became a policeman, and ... and I had other ideas...' He looked at Brownie, 'about a lot of things...'

King stood up. 'This is a nice history lesson, Judge, but I don't hear anything substantive.'

'Sit down, Mr King,' Ransome answered. 'I'm sure he'll get to the point sooner or later. Proceed, sir.'

Paulie nodded. 'Just wanted to give you some background...'

'No problem. Please go on.'

'Anyhow,' Paulie continued, 'my mother and father lived out in Blocktown. They were pretty normal folks, reasonably happy and all that...'

King rolled his eyes with disgust, but the judge ignored it.

'Then, in the fall, my daddy died suddenly...' Paulie's chin dropped. 'Had a heart attack, they said. I came back for the funeral. We buried him at All Saints' Cemetery...'

Gardner peeked at Brownie. He was calmer now, but his face was stiff with pain.

'Then I heard rumours. People were talking about Ruth and his church at the quarry, and then an article came out in a magazine, and...'

Paulie kept his head down as he spoke. 'I heard that he might'a done something to Daddy on the night he died: tortured him, caused the heart attack...'

King turned to Lin. 'This isn't good,' he whispered.

'So I decided to check the man out. I shadowed him when he left the quarry, and I worked up a plan...'

King clenched his fist.

'I convinced myself that Ruth killed my daddy, after the article, and the rumours, and the talk in the community. I got more and more angry. Nobody was doing anything about it. Not the family, not even the *police*. Seemed like nobody really cared, like this crazy white preacher was running loose, and they were gonna let him... So I decided to do something about it myself...'

King stood up. 'Re-read him his rights, Judge.'

'What?' Ransome asked.

'He's about to incriminate *himself*.' Maybe he would still balk if he realized his predicament.

Ransome turned to the witness. 'You *do* understand that if you tell us you committed a crime, you could go to prison?'

Paulie didn't flinch. 'Yes.'

'And you're *still* willing to go on?'

'Yes I am.'

Ransome looked at King. 'Satisfied?'

King sat down without replying, the word 'shit' on his lips.

'Continue.'

'I decided that the man had to be taken out...'

'Taken out?' Ransome interrupted. 'You mean *killed*?'

'Yes, sir.'

King shook his head.

'He's been *warned*, Mr King,' the judge said. 'Go on, Mr Brown.'

'So there was a meeting one night at the Blocktown community centre, and everyone went up there. Everyone but me.'

Gardner glanced at Brownie again. Tears brimmed in his eyes. He put his hand on Brownie's arm, but Brownie shook it off.

'I was on the trail of Thomas Ruth, the cracker who killed my father. I stalked him, and followed him up to the state park. He was acting strange, talking nonsense, singing to himself. And he had a pair of handcuffs on his wrists, but that didn't seem to slow him up a bit. He just kept movin' on through the woods, singing and chanting. And all the time I was getting ready to do the job...'

The courtroom was silent. Every person there, from spectator to juror, was riding on each word.

'So it was getting dark, and it was just me and him up in the park, and he was stumbling on through the woods like he knew what he was doing, or where he was going, and I was following behind, waiting for my chance...' Paulie stopped talking.

He sat there for a minute, catching his breath.

'Want some water?' Judge Ransome asked.

'No, sir. I'm OK... Anyway, we were in the woods, alone, and it was getting darker and darker, and he was going deeper and deeper on the trail. And then...' His voice changed octaves. 'I saw it. This weird outline in the dusk.'

'Power station,' King whispered.

'And then I knew...' He went silent again.

'What?'

'What was going to happen... There were signs all over it about danger and high voltage, and a fence, and a gate that was open, and he was next to it and...'

Gardner gripped Brownie's arm, and this time Brownie let him. The jurors and spectators held their breaths, and King closed his eyes.

'And then...'

Ransome looked down expectantly.

'And then the dude walked through the gate, kicked off his shoes, and threw himself on the grid!'

CHAPTER 28

'Objection!' King yelled. The courtroom was in turmoil. Spectators, jurors, and lawyers all buzzed with confusion while Gardner and Brownie stared at each other, speechless. No one had expected anything like this.

'Order!' Judge Ransome hollered. 'Please come to order!'

King was beside himself. He'd been set up by Gardner, set up by the oldest trick there was, the *deus ex machina*, the lying witness. 'Move to strike this ridiculous testimony,' he argued.

Ransome finally restored a semblance of order. 'On what grounds, Mr King?'

'Falsified testimony.'

Ransome frowned. He'd never heard of that ground. 'What?'

King pointed at Paulie. 'This is a joke! The defendant's brother comes in at the last minute with a fabricated story that just happens to support the defence theory! Come on! It's obvious what's happening here!'

'I told *you* before that you can bring out those points on cross-examination. The witness is duly qualified, and I will not strike his testimony.'

481

'Bullshit!' King fumed under his breath.

'What did you say?' Ransome's ire was rising rapidly.

'He's lying!' King went on.

'I'm not,' Paulie responded. 'I can *prove* it.' He reached into his pocket and pulled out a piece of paper.

King stiffened. What was happening now?

'The man left a note.'

'Awwwr...' A note! Now they were manufacturing evidence!

'Let me see that,' Ransome reached out his hand.

'Objection!' King roared. 'There's no authentication! *They* wrote it!'

'Approach the bench.'

The prosecution and defence came forward. 'I'm gonna look at this, Mr King, whether you like it or not.' Gardner and Brownie pressed close, trying to get a look. They were still in a state of shock.

'A TIME TO LIVE AND A TIME TO DIE ... CAN'T ENDURE THE PAIN ... MY TORMENT ... MY SINS ... PRAISE GOD,' Ransome read from the paper.

'For Christ's sake!' King exclaimed, 'there's been no fingerprinting, no analysis, it's been in *their* possession all this time. It was not turned over to the authorities as evidence. They withheld it. No way it's authentic!'

The judge was still scrutinizing the note, and Gardner was looking at it from the other side. 'The evidence,' Gardner suddenly exclaimed, turning to King. 'Do you have the rest of the evidence you collected in the investigation? The exhibits you *didn't* offer at trial?'

King looked at Lin Song, and she nodded.

'Bring them out,' Gardner demanded.

Rollie glanced up from the note. 'What's going on?'

'I need something from King's evidence box.'

King crossed his arms. 'Get it yourself.'

'What's it for?' Ransome asked. 'Why do you want the evidence?'

Gardner looked at the judge. 'Authentication.'

'Get it *for* him,' the judge told King.

Grudgingly, King complied, sending out for the exhibits. Soon a large box was brought forward and laid by the bench.

Gardner rummaged through the contents and lifted out a plastic bag. Inside were items he'd viewed several weeks ago, miscellaneous bits of proof. Gardner removed the note pad holder from Ruth's car and put it on the bench. 'May I have the note, Your Honour?'

'This is bull...' King protested.

Ransome handed Gardner the note, and he placed it above the pad.

'Look,' Gardner instructed.

All eyes focused on the jagged edges of the paper as they were compared with the edges of the last note to be ripped from Thomas Ruth's pad.

'It fits,' Gardner said. 'Exactly.'

And sure enough, when the jagged edges joined, the paper again was one.

King's face was white. He took a step back from the bench. This was a disaster. The note *was* genuine. It had to have come from Ruth, and only from Ruth. The handwriting was unmistakeable, just like the scrawl on the retainer agreement in King's office. An expert would have no problem matching them up. Ruth *was* crazy. Crazy enough to take his own life.

'Return to your tables,' Judge Ransome said. 'In the light of this revelation, I have a few more questions to ask the witness.'

King and Lin Song staggered away. Brownie and Gardner did the same. For different reasons, no one could speak.

Ransome turned to Paulie, waiting patiently on the stand. 'Mind if I ask you something?'

'No, sir.'

'You've known about this all along?'

'Yes, sir. Since it happened.'

The judge raised his eyebrows. '*Why* didn't you come forward before? Why allow your brother to go through a trial?'

Paulie looked at the judge, then lowered his eyes. 'When it first happened, I, uh, I had no idea that, Jo..., uh, my brother would get in trouble. *I* went there to kill the man. *I* went there for revenge, but *I* got cheated. The man killed my daddy...'

Gardner glanced at Brownie. He was calm now. The nightmare was over.

'I *wanted* folks to think that he was murdered. I wanted the CAIN church and everyone else to take warning: this is what happens if you mess with our people! We're not gonna be tortured and enslaved anymore! We're gonna protect ourselves. We're gonna fight back! That's what I was thinking at the time.'

'But then your brother got charged,' Ransome said. 'You could have done something *then*.'

'Yeah,' Paulie replied. 'I thought about it, thought about it a *lot*.' He looked at Brownie apologetically. 'But as I said, I, we didn't get along. For a long time, most of my life, I felt like he was a traitor...'

'Traitor?'

'Something between *us*, Judge, the way we were brought up, the way we lived, the way we believed ... I thought he went against our race, his own kind. I sort of hated him for it. But I thought about telling the truth, I agonized over it. Should I come forward? Should I tell what happened? I even asked advice, told someone about the situation. And I was *advised* to keep my mouth shut. If I said anything, the cops would hang *me*. My brother could take care of himself...' He looked at Brownie again.

'You were actually *advised* to keep silent?'

'Yes, sir.'

'By whom?'

Paulie lowered his eyes. 'I'd rather not say, sir.'

'OK, then,' Rollie continued, 'why *did* you come forward?'

Paulie looked at Gardner. 'I was probably gonna do it anyway, but...'

Gardner stared back.

'Someone suggested that what I was doin'...' He straightened his shoulders. 'Maybe I wasn't bein' a *man* about things. You see, Judge, down where I live I try to teach the kids to take care of themselves: to work, to study, to stay off drugs, to have pride in their heritage ... to be responsible...' He looked at Gardner again. 'Maybe it was time for me to be responsible *myself*.'

Judge Ransome nodded.

'What about the shoes?' King had finally found his voice. 'How did they end up in the possession of the defendant?'

'I hid them,' Paulie explained, 'in a hole off the trail. After I realized what Ruth had done, I figured people would know he'd killed himself if they saw the note and the shoes. Like I said, I was real upset at the time. I wanted folks to think he was executed for his crime. So I put the note in my pocket and stuck the shoes in a hole so no one would find them. They were too big to lug around. I hid them good. Never thought they'd be found. I also threw away his car keys and a pill bottle...'

King looked at Lin. So much for the missing keys.

'My client *did* recover the shoes when he went to the crime scene to investigate,' Gardner added. 'The keys and pills are probably still out there. What kind of pills were they? Does he remember?'

'Some long word,' Paulie said. 'Some kind of "ZENE".'

Gardner smiled. An antidepressant, no doubt. That settled it. That brought everything full circle. Point, set, match.

Judge Ransome looked at Gardner. 'Do I hear a motion, Counsel?'

Gardner took the hint. 'Renew my motion for judgement of acquittal.'

'Wait!' King interjected. 'That's out of order. There's already been evidence presented on the defence case. He *can't* renew his motion.'

'Who's in charge here, Mr King?' Rollie asked.

King dropped into his seat without replying. It was over.

'Motion for judgement of acquittal as to all charges

against Sergeant Brown granted,' Ransome said, slamming down his gavel. 'The jury is dismissed!'

Paulie left the stand and approached Brownie. They eyed each other cautiously, unsure of how to proceed. It had been a long, long time.

'What's up, bro?' Brownie finally asked.

Paulie put out his hand. 'Not much. How 'bout you?'

Brownie ignored the hand and grabbed his brother in a bearhug.

'Thank you,' he mumbled.

'Sorry, man,' Paulie whispered. 'I'm so sorry...'

'What for?'

'Everything. Mr Lawson told me what you did.'

'What do you mean?'

'The school case. My arrest. Getting it thrown out. I didn't know...'

'I never did anything like that.' Brownie released the hug.

Paulie smiled. His brother was straight to the end. 'OK. We don't have to talk about it.'

'Nothing to talk about.'

Paulie nodded. Brownie had been his guardian angel his whole life and never admitted it. That was the *brotherhood* Paulie had somehow missed. *He'd* been fighting the war all these years, but Brownie hadn't. They were on the same side all along. And now it was time to start over.

Bedlam filled the courtroom. Spectators ran forward to congratulate the defendant and his lawyer, among them,

Jennifer and a string of police officers. The news had swept the courthouse, and the hallway was packed with well-wishers. King and Lin Song escaped through chambers. They had nothing to celebrate.

'Unbelievable,' Jennifer said. 'I never expected *this*.' She stood awkwardly next to Gardner, as shocked about the last-minute revelation as everyone else.

'Neither did I,' Gardner mumbled. He was still dazed.

'*You* did it,' she continued. 'You went for the truth after all.'

Gardner didn't reply. He was thinking how gorgeous Jennifer looked in her red suit and how much he'd missed her. He felt like ravishing her on the spot. It had been a long time. 'I only did what *you* told me.'

'Well, you did *good*.'

He looked into her green eyes. 'I've been pretty stupid these past few months...'

She didn't answer.

'And I think I've finally figured it out. I *do* tend to overreact, to be overbearing. I know that now...'

'It's OK,' Jennifer said.

'It's *not* OK. *I* drove you away. I never want to do that again. I'm ready to talk.'

'Talk?'

Gardner put his arm around her waist and his lips to her ear. 'Talk. You know...'

Jennifer relaxed a little. 'You mean it?'

'I mean it.' The ordeal was over. As Judge Thompkins said: you do what you can and let nature take its course.

Gardner suddenly held up his hand. 'Excuse me everyone

I have an announcement to make! May I have your attention please?'

Someone whistled; the pandemonium died, and every eye in the courtroom focused on Gardner. 'I want to thank you all for your support during this very tough time, and I want to acknowledge one individual in particular...' He looked at Jennifer.

She blinked nervously.

'To her I wish to say, first of all, I'm sorry for being such a blockhead...'

Someone clapped.

'And second of all...' He paused and took a deep breath. 'Will you marry me?'

Jennifer crossed her arms and stared at him.

'Well?' She wasn't responding.

'I'll have to think about it,' she finally answered.

Gardner's face fell.

Jennifer suddenly smiled and embraced his neck. 'I've thought,' she said.

Gardner kissed her hard. And a mighty cheer went up from the crowd.

They slowly disentangled, and Gardner gathered his files. 'Let's get out of here,' he told Jennifer. 'I'm sick of courtrooms.'

They were still being praised and patted on the back.

'Gard...' The brothers had finally made their way through the throng. 'Sorry about...' Brownie began.

'*Nothing*!' Gardner interrupted. 'We've never apologized to each other before, and we're not going to do it now. The case is closed.'

Brownie gave him a hug. 'I respect you for what you did.'

Gardner squeezed his friend's shoulders. 'You'd have done it for me.'

'Hey, congratulations on your proposal,' Brownie added.

'Thanks.'

'Mind if I kiss the bride-to-be?' He gave Jennifer a peck on the cheek. 'Way to go, girl. You chased him till he caught you.'

'Thank you, Brownie.' Jennifer was glowing.

They all smiled and chatted for a moment. The pressure was off, and they could be themselves again. Like old times.

Just then, Brownie's expression changed. 'Am I reinstated with the department?'

Gardner signalled to Larry Gray, struggling through the crowd.

'Better ask *him*.'

The police chief finally got past the human wall. 'Congratulations!' he yelled.

'Am I still on the force?' Brownie asked.

'Of course!' Gray was surprised by the question.

'With full powers?'

'Of course.'

'What's going on?' Gardner asked. Brownie was behaving strangely. He should be ecstatic, but he suddenly had a detective look in his eye. Something was up.

'Unfinished business,' Brownie said.

'What?'

'Another case.'

'What case?'

'I'll explain later. First, me and Paul got to go somewhere.' He pulled his brother aside, out of earshot.

'Brownie!' Gardner yelled.

But Brownie was talking to Paul. And a moment later they both bolted from the courtroom.

CHAPTER 29

Althea Brown looked up from her Bible. There was a noise at the front door. She had been reading and praying all morning, as she'd done for the past two weeks. She could not bring herself to attend her son's trial. Her time could be better spent here, asking the Lord for guidance.

Suddenly a man entered the living room. 'Joseph,' she cried with surprise.

Brownie smiled. 'Hello, Mama.' There was a shadow behind him in the hallway.

'Who's that?'

The shadow emerged.

'Oh my God, Paulie!'

The brothers embraced their mom. 'Son, son,' she cried. Her prayers had been answered.

'It's all over, Mama,' Brownie said when he finally broke away.

'The trial?'

'I'm free. Paulie, uh, *Katanga* saved my life. He came to court and testified, and he proved that Ruth killed him*self*. The judge dismissed the case.'

493

Althea looked at her other son. 'Praise God,' she said.

Paulie tried to speak, but his mother grabbed him, hugged, and sobbed against his shoulder. 'I've waited so long,' she whispered. 'So long...'

Paulie finally found his voice. 'I did wrong, Mama...'

'Don't...'

'I hurt you, I hurt Joe. It took me a long time to realize that I was hurting *me* too. I'm sorry...'

'That's not important now,' his mother said. 'What *is* important is that we're together.'

They sat down, and visited, and caught up, and talked about the strange twists and turns that had brought them to this point.

'Well, it's all over now,' Althea sighed.

'Not quite.' Brownie pulled a slip of paper out of his pocket and handed it to his mother. 'We got *one* more thing to do. One more piece of business.'

'What's this?' she asked.

Brownie looked her in the eye, his expression sombre. 'A phone number. I need you to make a call.'

Althea didn't understand. 'What for?'

'For Daddy.'

The police van was parked in the trees behind Althea's house. It could not be seen from the road. Night had fallen, and a light powdery snow sprinkled from the black sky: a dusting, the weather report said. Inside the van, Gardner, Jennifer, Brownie, and Katanga waited.

'I want to know the full story, and I want to know it now,' Gardner demanded. Brownie had been tight-lipped about why they had to set up a surveillance at his mom's. He only

494

promised that a lot of questions would be answered before the night was through. They had been waiting for two hours, and so far nothing had happened. Gardner and Jennifer were bundled together in the back of the van, and Paulie and Brownie sat up front.

'You'll see,' Brownie replied.

'See *what*?'

'When it goes down, you'll see.'

'Come on, Brownie,' Jennifer said. 'Don't keep us in suspense. What's this all about?'

'Yeah. How 'bout it?' Katanga added.

'OK, OK,' Brownie conceded. 'I wanted to *show* you, and then explain...'

'Just tell us!' Gardner urged.

'All right.'

Gardner and Jennifer leaned forward, and Katanga turned. Brownie shifted around so he could see their faces in the shadows. 'I never gave up on the investigation of Daddy's death,' he began.

The listeners didn't react. They'd expected as much.

Brownie continued. 'And from the beginning, something bothered me. I knew that a snake had been wrapped around Daddy's neck. The tests showed scale marks, and it didn't matter what the examiner concluded. I knew what I saw. I *knew* what happened. Then the article came out about Ruth and the snakes, and I got sidetracked. I thought "Ruth" and "snakes" and "Daddy" and got all balled up in the idea that he did it...' Brownie's voice drifted off. 'But I had overlooked something. Something important. There was no way that Ruth could have known about Daddy's fear of snakes. That was a secret that only a few of *us* knew. Daddy didn't talk about it to anyone. He was ashamed and kept it to himself...'

'So whoever put the snake on your father had to *know* about his fear,' Gardner said.

'Exactly. And that person could *not* have been Ruth. No way he could have gotten that information...'

A headlight against the side of Althea's house interrupted his words. 'Showtime!' Brownie exclaimed.

'What?' Gardner asked.

'Follow me, and see for yourself.' Brownie opened the van door and jumped out.

They ran to the rear of the house, Brownie leading, Gardner, Jennifer, and Katanga following behind. Then they entered the kitchen and tiptoed to the doorway beside the den. Voices could be heard on the other side.

Brownie drew his nine millimetre and raised it in a vertical position. Then he sprang through the door.

'You're under arrest! Get down on the floor!'

Reverend Taylor dropped the cheque that Althea had just given him.

'Get down on the floor now!'

Althea stepped back, and the others rushed in.

'What's the matter with you, Brother?' Taylor asked defiantly. He was still on his feet.

Brownie cocked the hammer on his Beretta. 'If you don't hit the floor now, I'll put a hole in your head.'

'You're making a mistake,' Taylor protested, going to one knee.

'All the way down!' Brownie shoved the barrel against the reverend's skull.

Taylor lay flat, and Brownie cuffed him behind his back.

'Mama,' Brownie said, 'this is the man who killed Daddy.'

Althea put her hands to her face, and Katanga leaped forward. 'Him?'

'Lie!' Taylor hollered 'It's a lie!'

Brownie frisked him and rolled him on his back. 'Tell them your real name.'

'Taylor!'

'Try Jenkins!' Brownie snapped. 'Corey *Jenkins*, a con man who cleaned out a small town in Oregon five years ago. Took life savings, conned old folks out of their cash, preachin' and pretending to give a damn about them and their lives. Slipped out of town with the loot, but got caught and served time in jail...'

'That's not true!' Taylor struggled to get up, but Brownie pushed him down with his foot.

Althea was crying softly. Gardner and Jennifer were speechless. And Katanga had a strange look on his face.

'It took me a long time to get a line on him. I had my troubles to worry about, so it took longer than it should have. He used a lot of aliases, moved around to a lot of places, but I finally tracked him down. He makes his living cheating people...'

'This is an outrage,' Taylor blustered. 'God has forgiven my sins. I have done nothing wrong here!'

'Try again,' Brownie said sarcastically. 'You set this whole thing up. You came into *this* little town and began laying your trap. You talked to folks about their lives, gained their confidence, learned private things about them. *Who* had the money, *who* was vulnerable, what people's fears were...'

'*He* used the snake,' Gardner said suddenly.

497

'Yes *he* did.'

'No!' Taylor began struggling again.

'He found out about Daddy's phobia. And he also found out about the railroad pension. If he got rid of Daddy, and got close to Mama, he could also get close to the money...'

'No!'

Katanga picked up the cheque that Taylor had dropped. It was written to Taylor in the amount of $80,000.00

'He *was* after the money,' Althea said. 'For the church... He said he was going to set up a fund in Daddy's name...'

Katanga's eyes glazed as he stared at the cheque.

'I knew he'd come back for it,' Brownie declared.

'You can't prove anything!' Taylor sputtered.

'That's where you're wrong. I've got a witness who puts you in possession of the cellular phone that made the 911 call the night Daddy died. And I've got you in possession of the pension money...' He took the cheque out of Katanga's hand. 'But here's the best part. He had help on the outside.'

'No,' Taylor sputtered.

Brownie took a copy of Ander's picture from his pocket. 'I have evidence. Mr Jenkins here had help from an old friend, a man known as Thomas Ruth...'

'What?' Gardner, Jennifer, and Katanga looked at each other with shock.

'That's *right*! Taylor, a.k.a. Jenkins, and Ruth, a.k.a. Graves, were in the same unit in Vietnam.' He handed Gardner the photo. 'They went on after the war to run cons together, and this was the best con of all, a double-edged hustle. Taylor worked the dark side of the street, and Ruth worked the light. And they split the proceeds. It was a symbiotic relationship from hell.'

'Shut up!' Taylor hissed.

Brownie placed his foot on the reverend's neck. '*You* shut up!' He then turned to his amazed audience. 'Ruth was a psycho, and Taylor supplied him with pills. But Taylor got greedy. As I read it, no one was supposed to get hurt because Ruth had this aversion to violence. Taylor, on the other hand, could care less. He "snaked" Daddy and killed him for the pension. Ruth got blamed and hounded, and went off the edge. And when I got in trouble, Taylor hired Willie Stanton. He must'a figured that would eliminate *me* too...'

Up to now, Katanga had remained silent. Without warning, he grabbed Brownie's gun.

'Hey!' Brownie yelled. Althea's eyes went wide, and Gardner and Jennifer jumped back.

'*You!*' Katanga shrieked. He pointed the gun at Taylor. 'You suckered me! Told me to let my brother go down! Told me to shut my mouth...'

'Give me the gun,' Brownie said. 'Come on, bro...'

'*You* killed my daddy!' He clicked the hammer.

Taylor's face went slack with terror. 'Brother,' he begged.

'Don't Brother *me*!' Katanga leaned close. 'You're no brother!' His hand was trembling as much as his voice.

'Give me the gun,' Brownie urged.

Gardner and Jennifer had moved beside Althea. Her body was shaking with horror.

'You're gonna die,' Katanga said, pressing the gun to Taylor's face.

'Please,' Taylor pleaded. Tears rolled down his cheeks. 'Please...'

The reverend closed his eyes.

'Look at him,' Brownie said. 'Look at his skin.'

Katanga hesitated.

'What *colour* is it?'

'Black,' Katanga muttered.

'And what colour was Ruth's?'

'White.'

'So what colour is *greed*?' Brownie was standing over Taylor now.

'No colour,' Katanga quavered.

'Right,' Brownie replied. '*Colour*'s got nothin' to do with it.'

Katanga's hand dropped, and Brownie took the gun. 'He'll be punished, don't worry about that. No reason for *you* to mess yourself up doin' it. We *all* know what happens when you use self-help.'

Taylor lay back on the floor and sobbed while the others collected themselves.

Brownie addressed them. 'You had to *see* what caused the trouble. I couldn't just tell you.'

'I'll call the police station,' Jennifer said, 'and ask them to pick up the prisoner.'

Gardner shook Brownie's hand. 'God, Brownie. That was incredible. Ruth and Taylor, working a scam together. I'd never have guessed.'

'No one would have. That's what made the damn thing work. Between the two of them they sure screwed things up around here.'

'But *you* smoked them out. You never gave up...'

'Neither did *you*.'

They looked at Katanga and Althea comforting each

other in the corner. 'There's nothing like family,' Gardner said. 'Real *family*.'

Brownie turned. 'You are right about that.' He smiled and punched Gardner's arm. 'My *brother*.'

EPILOGUE

'Tired?' Gardner asked.

Jennifer looked over her shoulder from the bench of the make-up table. 'A little.' Her hair glinted auburn highlights in the glow of the lamp.

Gardner picked up her silver brush. 'May I?'

'Of course.'

Gardner stroked her hair with the tines until it bristled with static electricity. 'It's happy tonight,' he said.

Down the hall, Granville slept. He was in his old room, in the mansion on the hill. Carole had finally moved out and acquired a place in town. Gardner had returned to his ancestral home.

Many months had passed since the Ruth case, and the world had changed. Brownie was now a lieutenant, chief of detectives. His wounds healed, he was back chasing felons and visiting his brother's outreach programme in DC. Reverend Taylor was convicted of the murder of Joseph Brown, and sentenced to life in prison. Frank Davis, terminated from the police force, was now a security guard.

Kent King quietly folded his practice, moved to Baltimore,

and entered partnership with Lin Song. He was tired of the county, he said. The city was more exciting.

'Ready for bed, Mrs State's Attorney?' Gardner inquired. With King out of the way, Jennifer had taken the prosecutor's job.

'Ready, Professor.'

Gardner now taught a legal tactics course at Western Maryland Law School, instructing future lawyers on the nuances of trial. He also dabbled in criminal defence on the side, easing his way into that frame of reference. He still had a lot of prosecutor left in him, and the transition wasn't easy.

Gardner gave Jennifer's hair another sensuous stroke and put down the brush. 'You know it's all-or-nothing with me, Jen. I can't go half way.'

She eyed him in the mirror. 'I know.'

'Are you *sure* you can handle it?'

'I'm going to try.'

'Do you think we'll make it?'

Jennifer turned and hugged his waist. 'We'll *make* it,' she whispered. Then she reached over and turned off the light.